THE KING'S CHAMPION

To Suzanne

Thank you so much for
helping me with this tome.
Hope you enjoy it properly
now it's in print!!

Jacqui xxx

THE KING'S CHAMPION

JACQUELINE ARMITAGE

First paperback edition 2024

Book design by Publishing Push

978-1-80541-592-3 (paperback)
978-1-80541-650-0 (hardcover)
978-1-80541-591-6 (eBook)

www.jacqueline-armitage.co.uk

Table of Contents

Dedication

I had intended to write a sequel to Devonmere, but whilst I was attempting to think of a plot, this prequel just literally popped into my head; the whole thing, just like that, so I thought it better to write it, than struggle for a story for the sequel.

I sent my friend of long standing the first three pages of 'The King's Champion', to see what she thought, as I knew she would be brutally honest! The words, "I'm gripped!" came back, and gave me all the encouragement I needed to continue this prequel to Devonmere. Thank you, Wendy.

Once again, I dedicate this book to my dear friend, Edward, who would have made a fantastic Duke Morgan Bodine. He was never allowed to reach his full potential on screen, having been taken far too soon from us all. He is sorely missed and thought about every single day.

I offer my thanks to Wendy for checking the manuscript and pointing out the glaring errors before I submitted it, and also to Suzanne for checking it when the final formatted version arrived.

Finally, for Dave, Pam, Melanie, and especially the 'Edward Gang' (Sara, Marie, Penelope and Edward's daughter, Tai), for supporting my first book and wanting to read this one as well.

From the speed that the entire plot for this story came into my head, it was obvious that Morgan Bodine's back story could not be left untold, so...here it is. The King's Champion is book one in the Devonmere series.

But now I am faced with a dilemma. There is a four-year gap between the end of this novel and Devonmere...do I write a sequel to the prequel or crack on with the actual sequel to Devonmere?! Decisions, decisions! Perhaps I will leave it up to you to decide...

Actually, I've decided, but you'll see...

Enjoy!

Foreword

God created the Kadeau in his own image, and they were one with the earth, the sea, and the air; and they flourished, although life was hard.

Then a faction grew, that did not want the hard life, and they turned to stealing and taking what they wanted and because of this, they lost their affinity with the elements. Over time, two separate races developed, the Kadeau and the non-Kadeau Humans.

The Kadeau stayed with the elements and were despised by the Humans, for they had magic. Every year their crops and animals flourished because they watched and listened to nature. Feeling they had suffered enough persecution from the Humans, a few Kadeau rose up and, using their magic did some terrible things, but the Humans retaliated and almost wiped them out.

Eventually, an uneasy truce arose; the Kadeau hid their powers, fearful of further persecution. The church tried to have any they found burned at the stake, but the rise of the Cantrell royal family stopped those atrocious actions, and they started to employ Kadeau as royal protectors for the princes and kings.

Now finding favour, the Kadeau started to secretly infiltrate the church and began to grow in strength again, with some having titles bestowed upon them.

Our story is based several generations down the line. King Rhisart is searching for a Kadeau protector for his son and heir, Prince Stuart. The Kadeau wife of the Duke of Rossmere has given birth to a son—

Morgan—initially a healthy, strong baby, that gradually seemed to weaken and fade, as did his mother.

The Duke is killed in battle shortly after, leaving both mother and baby fighting to survive. Rhisart receives a worrying communication from the Rossmere steward, that results in him travelling quickly to Belvoir, the ducal capital of Rossmere, with his battle surgeon and his own Kadeau protector and champion, Sir Trahaearn, who confirms his worst fears, using his Kadeau powers. Both mother and baby are slowly being poisoned and everything points to the newly appointed wet nurse.

Rhisart is furious and immediately orders her to be executed, and for his battle surgeon and Trahaearn to do what they can to save young Morgan and Eirian, his mother. They use all their skills and manage to save the baby, but lose the battle to save Eirian, and thus the youngster is orphaned and in need of someone to look after him and begin to educate him in his future role until the boy is ready to join Rhisart's court.

The Duke of Invermere, Richard Coltrane, rules the neighbouring Duchy and is one of Rhisart's most trusted supporters. The King is loath to send the baby far to the north to his nearest relatives, because of the plans he has for the child, and thus asks the Duke if he will take Morgan into his care and look after him until he reaches the age of seven, when he will be delivered to the King's castle in Ellesmere to start his new role as a page boy, and gradually work his way up to knighthood and the position of Prince Stuart's protector.

The Coltranes immediately agree and prepare to receive the new Duke of Rossmere into their care.

The child finally arrives at Inver Castle, a few months later, when he is deemed well enough to travel, which is where our story starts...

Chapter One

———◆———

"Well?" Richard Coltrane, Duke of Invermere, asked of his wife. Bronwyn Coltrane studied the letter from the King, glanced at her husband and then at the King's Champion and protector, Sir Trahaearn, who looked somewhat awkward, holding the nine-month-old Duke of Rossmere in his arms. Armour and surcoat dusty from his ride from Rossmere, it was an odd sight to see him holding the baby boy.

Her expression softened as she looked at the blond, blue-eyed child, whose countenance was profoundly serious as he frowned back at her, but his eyes were wide with apprehension.

"Of course, we will take him. Poor child; to have lost both his father and mother so close together. He has not had a good start to life; and I understand the King's logic of asking us, rather than sending him so far north to his uncle." She looked at Trahaearn again. "Is he Kadeau?"

"Yes, Your Grace. I have confirmed it myself."

"Well, it doesn't matter one way or another," Bronwyn replied, holding out her arms, indicating for the knight to hand him to her. "Is he talking or making any sounds?" she asked.

"No, Your Grace. He has said nothing."

"I see...and his name is Morgan?"

"Morgan Rhys Geraint Bodine."

"A fine name for a most handsome young man," the Duchess said, taking him in her arms, noting with some concern that he appeared to

1

be thin and underweight; but that was to be expected after what he had been through. *How could anyone poison an innocent child*, she wondered sadly. "I think you could do with feeding up, don't you?"

She smiled fondly at him, and gave him a squeeze, but the boy said nothing, and his expression remained most serious.

"Morgan, know that you are loved, and we will do our very best to make you happy whilst you are with us. Now, you may address me as Bronwyn or Mama if you like; and this will be Richard or Papa."

His pale blue eyes bored into her hazel ones, as he lifted his right hand and placed it on the side of her face.

Bronwyn watched his expression change slightly, and his eyes widened a little further.

"See Morgan, you have nothing to fear," she said softly.

"Bwon," he managed to babble.

"Yes, my darling!" she exclaimed happily. "That's right!" She gave him another hug and kissed his cheek.

Richard observed the two of them, realising his wife would make a wonderful mother, once they were blessed with their own child. They had been married two years now, but so far, no heir had been produced. She was young, still only sixteen, there was plenty of time yet; so there was no need to panic.

It had been an arranged marriage, which Richard had initially been against, but when he had finally set eyes on his intended bride, all doubt had been swept from his mind, for Bronwyn was pretty, but like a delicate flower, with a refined, heart-shaped face that possessed hazel eyes, a lovely slightly turned-up nose and full lips. The whole picture was framed by long mahogany coloured hair.

The Duke looked at the child. Even at this tender age, Richard could see he had the looks of the previous Duke of Rossmere, but his colouring was that of his mother, Eirian.

As if knowing that Richard was staring at him, Morgan turned his gaze to him. "Chad," he said, and the Duke nodded, smiling.

"Has he been fed and changed?" Bronwyn asked of Trahaearn.

"Yes, Your Grace. The temporary wet nurse carried out the deed."

Bronwyn smiled to herself at the way the knight had spoken those words. Babies and knights did not mix as far as Trahaearn was concerned!

"Well, in that case, my young man, I think you should have a little sleep, don't you?" Bronwyn said, interrupting the knight's thoughts.

"Your Grace, His Majesty has asked that I be involved in the selection of his replacement nurse, as he does not want another... mishap to occur."

Bronwyn frowned before speaking. "Yes, of course. I will arrange for suitable candidates. In the meantime, Sir Trahaearn, you must be hungry and tired from your journey," she said, studying the knight's appearance. He was tall, well over six feet, with rugged good looks, dark brown eyes and a square-jawed face. Underneath the helm she knew he possessed shoulder-length brown hair, but he looked as if he could do with either a good wash or bath.

"I will arrange that my love," Richard said. "I have duties to perform and am heading in that general direction." He smiled at her and turned to the knight. "Trahaearn, please accompany me."

The knight inclined his head at Bronwyn and took his leave, following the Duke from the main hall, leaving Bronwyn alone with Morgan, but not for long, as Dilys, Bronwyn's personal maid appeared in the doorway.

"Your Grace, I have the crib ready and prepared."

"Thank you, Dilys. I'll put him down."

"May I be of further service?"

"No, that will do for now, thank you."

Dilys curtseyed and left the hall.

Bronwyn smiled down at Morgan, who was staring intently at her. "I'll sit with you until you are settled, my sweet," she said to him as she left the hall and made her way to Morgan's chambers. "You, my young man, are going to break many a young girl's heart when you're older."

They arrived at his rooms after a few minutes. Going through the day room to the bed chamber, the Duchess placed him down in his cot and drew the blankets around his small form, to keep out the chill of the November day. There was a hearty, warming fire burning in the room, but the air was still not comfortably warm enough for a baby.

Morgan grabbed a couple of her fingers and held them tightly.

"Looks like I'm not going anywhere, for a little while; bless him," she said softly to herself, looking down fondly at him, and watched as his eyes slowly closed; but somehow his grip remained tight. Bronwyn sat down and waited patiently, her mind wondering what—if anything—he understood of his circumstances.

Morgan Bodine was a Kadeau, whose people possessed magical powers. However, they had many enemies. They had once thrived in the land, but there had been war, long in the past and they had been persecuted by the now non-Kadeau humans. This had led to the few Kadeau who were left, rising up and inflicting their own form of revenge, using dark magic and spells against their oppressors, and terrible deeds were done by both sides during what was known as the Reign of Terror.

In the end, the sheer numbers of humans had driven them into hiding, but the ascension to the throne of the Cantrell royal family, had brought an end to the violence and persecution, for they employed the Kadeau as royal protectors, and even bestowed titles on the favoured, trusted few, but the hate was still there, bubbling under the surface and still struck, as it had against Morgan and his mother.

People had long memories, they would never forget the atrocities that had befallen their ancestors and some still sought revenge. Morgan had been fortunate. Justin, the head steward of Rossmere, had been suspicious and sought help from the King. It had been too late to save Morgan's mother, but fortunately had saved him, which was just as well, for the child was destined to be a royal protector.

The fact that Morgan was destined to become Duke of Rossmere, giving him substantial power in the kingdom made him a tempting target. One attempt had already been made to deprive the child of his life, so it was imperative he be kept safe until he was ready to be delivered to Ellesmere at the age of seven, to begin his training.

The Duchess assumed his earlier action of touching her face, was an inborn, instinctive Kadeau practice of some kind, to ascertain the truth of what was in her mind. In that moment, she decided she would see if his aunt would pay a visit, once her own child was old enough to travel. Mereli McLeod was known to be Kadeau, but her husband was human, and the Duchess wasn't sure whether her young son, Colin, had taken after his mother or father. There seemed to be no half measures; you either were or you weren't, if only one parent was. It would be good for Morgan to have some company of a similar age and heritage. Hopefully, that would bring him out of his shell; for he was such a serious and quiet, young child. Obviously, his cousin would not be able to stay indefinitely, so Bronwyn would need to find some other children belonging to her own ladies she could trust, to teach him the beginnings of the social skills he would need in his adult life, but it would be difficult for him.

Bronwyn sighed as she looked down at the child. The mother instinct in her longed to see him smile and laugh, like any infant of his age should. He was far too quiet for her liking. *He should be babbling away*, she mused, and was convinced he was actually very bright, but he needed to communicate more and—most importantly—play.

Finally, Morgan's grip on her fingers relaxed, but she was loath to leave him; scared that he might think he was being abandoned. The letter from the King had been quite detailed and had stated the child was currently being weaned and starting to eat solid food, hence why the need to look for a new wet nurse; but Bronwyn was determined she would be present as often as she could to stabilise the relationship.

His life was going to be unsettled again when he reached the age of seven, when he would go to the Devonmere capital of Ellesmere, to start duties as a page and eventually a squire and knighthood. At some point, once he was old enough and trained in the use of weaponry, he would become young Prince Stuart's protector.

It was far too early to know how skilled Morgan was likely to be with a sword and lance; but if he were good enough, he could become the King's Champion; perhaps more.

Once he reached ten, he would be officially recognised as the Duke of Rossmere, although the title was already his, he was currently far too young to have the responsibility of a duchy.

Bronwyn gazed upon his features, now relaxed in sleep. She was sure he was going to be an exceedingly handsome man when he grew up, especially if he kept his blond hair, and it did not darken too much; but she also realised his life was going to be challenging—more so for him—with his Kadeau heritage. Female Kadeau were tolerated more than males. Somehow, she had to educate him not to be filled with resentment and hate. Hopefully Mereli would help him too and teach him how to defend himself with magic when required.

Many still saw the Kadeau as a threat, and the fact that the current royal household held them in such high regard, and used them as protectors, meant that they had many enemies. Depriving the Cantrells' of their magical defenders was seen as a conceivable way to usurp them from their ruling position, and it was not unheard of, for male Kadeau to meet untimely deaths before they reached adulthood.

One attempt had already been made on Morgan's life. A huge responsibility now rested on the Duke and Duchess of Invermere to ensure the child remained safe until he reached the court of Ellesmere, where responsibility for his life would be transferred to the King.

A couple of hours passed, and Morgan began to fidget. Bronwyn knew she should not, but she succumbed and picked him up, making sure the blanket was securely wrapped around him. Immediately, he settled down again.

She stood up and began to walk around the room that was now his, humming a soft lullaby.

Finding him becoming rather heavy, she sat down on an armchair which helped to relieve the strain and stayed there, until she was interrupted by the arrival of Dilys.

"Your Grace, let me take him," she said curtsying and then stepping forward.

Bronwyn reluctantly handed him over; realising she was feeling exceedingly 'broody'; longing for her own child. *Well*, she thought, *until I am blessed with my own, Morgan shall be treated as if he is my son; and even after I have my own child, he will still be treated as one of my children.*

The Duchess watched as Dilys placed the child back in his crib and tucked him in, then turned her attention to the layout of the room, whilst Bronwyn left and headed for the library. To be able to do her duty for the King and guide Morgan towards adulthood, she needed more knowledge about the Kadeau, having had little interaction with them. She scoured the rows and rows of books and parchments looking for the right ones that would provide her with the information she so desperately needed.

The castle library was impressive, with rows upon rows of bookcases holding precious tomes and manuscripts that dated back hundreds of years. There were a number of small reading areas, and at the back of the huge room was a section that was cordoned off with floor-to-ceiling decorated iron work with an ornate gate, that was unlocked only when the head of the library was present. High windows along the long wall allowed a fair amount of light in, but candles were available to provide additional illumination when required.

William Aulean, Bishop of Inver also happened to be in the library and approached her.

"Your Grace, may I be of assistance?" he asked. He had been at Inver a number of years but had recently been appointed Bishop and was eager to show his worthiness of the position, for he was rather young; a mere thirty-two years of age. Most of the other bishops of Devonmere were in their late forties or fifties. His aura was surprisingly calm for one so young, and brown eyes seemed to hold the wisdom of someone much older. He couldn't be called handsome, but he was passable to look at.

"Bishop," she responded. "I am looking for any books or manuscripts about the Kadeau. If I am to carry out my duty to the King, I must have some knowledge."

"Is this in some way related to the arrival of Sir Trahaearn and his young charge?" the bishop asked. "I am deducing the child is the Duke of Rossmere?"

"Bishop, you are indeed perceptive. I ask that you tell no one of your knowledge of the child's arrival."

"I give you my word, Your Grace, but I must ask, why is he here, and not with his mother? Where is his mother?"

"Duchess Eirian is dead. Poisoned. An attempt was also made on Morgan's life, but he was saved, and the King has decreed that the Duke and I look after the child until he reaches the age of seven."

"The King has given you and the Duke a most difficult task. Come, you are in the wrong section. You will not find anything on the Kadeau here in the main library; they are sectioned off in a separate room, for safety."

He guided her to what she had thought to be just a cupboard, but beyond the heavy door, hidden away was a couple of rows of books and manuscripts.

"Thank you for your assistance, bishop."

"Your Grace." He bowed and left her to browse at her leisure.

⁂

The Duke and Duchess gave Morgan a few days to settle into his new home, visiting him every day and spending time with him. He said very little, and he still wore a serious expression; although Bronwyn had started to notice a slight softening whenever she approached him.

She also brought several toys with her, and they spent time playing together. She soon realised he was a very bright little boy, and thus set about giving him challenges to overcome. In between this, and her other duties, Trahaearn had helped her select a new wet nurse for Morgan, and Bronwyn also began to read about the history of the Kadeau; learnt of the war, and the atrocities that had taken place. Having grasped that, she began to read about the magic and other skills they possessed. It was said they could read minds, make people bend to their will, and even influence the action of animals, but Bronwyn was slightly sceptical about some of this, as this particular book had been written by a non-Kadeau and she suspected it was slightly biased against these remarkable people.

Richard also did some reading, and began Morgan's education in practical matters and, making sure the child was wrapped up warmly for the harsh winter weather, took him riding, with him sitting carefully between his arms, on the saddle, to get used to being around horses and to start work on his balance.

In addition, he decided that he should appoint a protector for the child and approached his new Master-at-Arms, Sir John MacKenzie. The knight had been in service to Invermere for a few years, and Richard trusted him without question. Thus, he introduced him to the child.

Sir John felt honoured at being given the responsibility and swore on his sword that he would protect the young Morgan with his life. He knew it was important to build a bond of trust with the child, and so ensured he spent some time with him every day, to build that relationship.

Sir John was a loyal and faithful knight and took his duties very seriously. He appeared to be relatively easy going, with a cheerfulness that could lull people into a false sense of security. Of average height, with straight brown hair that he kept short, brown eyes that possessed laughter lines around them, and of stocky build, he could move surprisingly fast, and although relatively softly spoken, when the occasion called, had a bark that could and did bite. People who took him to be a 'soft touch' quickly found they were mistaken, and he trained prospective knights long and hard, looking for perfection.

In his new role, he was often seen carrying the young Morgan, and sat him in a safe spot so he could observe everything that went on in the training of a knight. Sir John knew that most of it was way beyond the child's understanding, but he hoped subconsciously that some small amount of knowledge would be absorbed, so that when he was ready to begin his training, he would have an advantage over his peers.

Morgan was also present when the Duke did his training with sword and lance. For the sword, he practiced with Sir John, as the knight was the most experienced and skilled man within Invermere, and they tested each other to the limit. In fact, they were so closely matched, one or the other would win a particular session or, they would exhaust each other and have to agree a draw.

A couple of weeks later, Morgan finally took his first steps. Bronwyn almost wept with joy, but the child was concerned at seeing her eyes brimming, even though she was smiling, and placed both hands on the sides of her face, frowning in concentration.

His eyes widened at the love, happiness, and pride, that Bronwyn was conveying to him, and he gave a tentative smile, which did reduce the Duchess to tears, and she hugged him tightly. Now he was mobile, it was time to introduce him to other children he could play with, and she carefully selected those of her ladies she felt she could trust. From that moment onwards, Morgan began to learn to interact with the children, and over the next month, slowly began to emerge from his shell, becoming more vocal as a child of his age should be.

The twelve days of Christmas was the final event of the year. During this period, a role reversal took place, a tradition dating back hundreds of years, where the masters waited on the servants.

Markus, the Duke of Inver's head steward, was appointed Lord of Misrule during this period and organised various festivities, feasting and games to take place. Everyone entered into the spirit of the occasion once the seriousness of the midnight mass had taken place.

The Duke, Duchess, lords and ladies present, took their role very seriously in waiting on their staff, and the atmosphere was relaxed and filled with happiness. Even the children of the servants were allowed to mix freely, but all too soon it ended, and life returned to normal.

Morgan's first birthday arrived in February, and the Duke and Duchess spoilt him with gifts and special treats to eat. Sir John presented him with a small wooden sword to practice with, as he had started wielding an imaginary one when he had been at the Pell with the Master-at-Arms. The child had finally settled in and started to talk more. For one so young, his vocabulary was rather impressive. Bronwyn put that down to him having spent most of his time listening. She had read to him, or told him stories every day, and he had lapped it up.

Now that he was steadier on his feet, he was forever exploring and had turned into an escape artist. Every time his wet nurse—Glesni—turned her back, he took the opportunity to make a break for freedom, which resulted in the young woman running around, frantically searching for him.

On several occasions he had successfully managed to locate Bronwyn in her rooms. She hadn't the heart to chastise him, but instead, sent a page to find Glesni so that she could stop searching...and panicking.

Secretly, she was delighted that Morgan had come looking for her; it made her feel as if he had accepted her as his surrogate mother. Then, as if to confirm this he uttered the most important word: "Mama." Bronwyn had hugged him and cried with happiness.

When he was around fifteen months of age, his Aunt Mereli arrived, with her son, Colin, who was three and a half years old. The two boys seemed to establish a connection right from their first meeting, united by their shared pedigree. Mereli began to tell them about their Kadeau heritage and all that it entailed. She had also used her magic and skills to ascertain how powerful Morgan was likely to be when he was adult, and gasped as she discovered, he was going to be a formidable Kadeau, despite his mixed heritage. It was now vital that he started and remained on the right path going forward, for if he were to become as powerful as she thought, he would prove almost impossible to stop, which was of great concern. He needed to know magic, but he also needed to know when and where to use it. Too little could put both him and the future King in danger; too much and people could look to dispose of him before he became too powerful to stop.

Mereli started to teach him some simple elements of magic; harmless little tricks, and exercises to guide and train his mind, for the Kadeau had to possess a highly disciplined mind to be able to control and perform magic. Bronwyn also attended, so she would be able to teach him until Mereli could return, but the Kadeau had realised that would not be enough, and she took Bronwyn aside one afternoon.

"I sense no fear in you regarding me or my abilities," Mereli said as they sat alone in an arbour.

"Why would I fear you?" Bronwyn responded. "You have done nothing that would warrant any fear."

"Yet you know of our history, of the atrocities that were committed."

"As I recall, atrocities were committed by both sides."

"That is true." Mereli paused before continuing. "It would be better if I could take Morgan back with me, to the north, but I know the King does not wish this. I am concerned it could hamper his development."

"Is there anything I can do to assist or help?" Bronwyn asked.

Mereli smiled at her.

"There is indeed, but it is not for the faint-hearted and it would mean you having to trust me without question, and for no one else to ever know what I am about to propose to you; not even your husband."

Bronwyn swallowed nervously. It was not in fear of what Mereli was going to suggest, but of keeping secrets from her husband, Richard. They had sworn to always be true and honest with each other. Mereli's instructions would be a breach of that promise.

"I sense your unease, please let me explain," Mereli continued. "Morgan is going to be an incredibly powerful Kadeau. To that end, we must ensure he is trained correctly, and is fully disciplined. Without me being here full-time, I cannot guarantee that he will follow the true path, and hence I need to enlist your help. If you will permit me, I will share my knowledge with you, so that you can ensure Morgan develops as he should."

"My unease is not based on fear, but that I would be keeping a secret from my husband. We made a vow to always be honest with one another." She shook her head. "Also, I can't possibly learn what I need to know in so short a time," Bronwyn protested. "Could you and young Colin not stay longer?"

"Alas no, but I wish to share my knowledge. Will you consent? I understand your concern at keeping this sharing of knowledge from your husband, but it is not a permanent situation, it will only be necessary until Morgan is delivered safely to the King."

"How will you share this knowledge?"

"By the temporary joining of minds."

Bronwyn's eyes widened at this news. Up until this point, she had thought the mind reading and sharing was but a story to scare both children and adults. She swallowed slowly and took a deep breath.

"I thought that—"

"It was a tale to scare humans?" Mereli finished. She smiled sadly. "Alas, it is true. The sharing of minds is meant to be a wondrous and glorious thing but, in the past, some Kadeau used it for more insidious reasons. I assure you, that what I ask of you is for the protection of Morgan and the Cantrell royal family."

Bronwyn bit her lip in silent contemplation as she studied her hands that were clasped in her lap. A few moments passed before she looked up at Mereli.

"My duty is to the King above all else," she said in the merest of whispers.

"Then you are agreeable?"

"Yes."

Mereli laid a hand over Bronwyn's and squeezed it reassuringly.

"Know that I will never do anything to harm you. Morgan is my kin; you are tasked with protecting him. It's vital he develops the skills he needs to both survive and defend."

"What do you need me to do?"

"Nothing, as such, but the sooner we do this the better. You will need to get accustomed to the knowledge that I will pass onto you, and we have so little time. Will you allow me to perform the joining now?"

Bronwyn nodded slowly.

Mereli smiled gently.

"All you need to do, is close your eyes, relax, and welcome me into your mind. I will do the rest."

Bronwyn took a deep breath and closed her eyes.

"Good. Now let your mind go completely blank, relax, listen to the silence and my voice. Breathe normally and calmly. Excellent. I am now going to place my fingers on specific points of your face."

Bronwyn felt fingers gently, yet firmly touch her face at the temples, forehead, and chin. A minute or so passed, and then she felt something at the edge of her mind; something warm, friendly.

Bronwyn, it is I, a voice said in her head.

"Mereli?" she questioned.

Yes, but there is no need to speak, simply think about what you want to say. I will hear you.

This is very strange, Bronwyn thought.

I know. Now all you have to do is welcome me. Do not fight or resist. There may be some discomfort, but it will be short lived.

It took a few minutes for Bronwyn to finally understand what she needed to do, and suddenly it all became clear and Mereli was there, in her mind, friendly, soothing.

You will not know I am here in your mind. Once the link is established, we will agree contact times and exchange information. You will update me on Morgan's progress, and I will advise you of the next steps. This may involve some transfer of knowledge, or I may watch, observe and instruct through you. This can be quite strenuous, so if I do this, it will be kept short, and you may feel tired afterwards. I would advise you to rest whenever we finish. Now, are you ready?

Bronwyn nearly nodded and stopped herself in time. *I am ready,* she thought.

Then let us begin.

Mereli worked quietly in the back of Bronwyn's mind, her touch so slight, that Bronwyn thought nothing was happening, but she was laying the foundation of the bond, anchoring it securely, so there was no risk of it breaking.

Bronwyn felt a pressure building in her mind and frowned slightly.

Relax, it is almost done, Mereli said.

A few more minutes passed and then Bronwyn felt Mereli withdraw and leave just the merest of touches behind.

"That's it?" Bronwyn asked.

Mereli smiled. *It is done,* she sent as a thought and Bronwyn gasped.

"I can still hear you!" she exclaimed.

"The link is still open," Mereli explained. "I will close it and only open it at specific times as agreed between us. When the link is closed, have no fear, I will have no idea of what you are thinking, or doing. Your privacy will be maintained."

"That is reassuring!"

Mereli smiled. "Now, shall we see what those two boys have been up to?" she asked.

"I believe that would be a good idea. It has been suspiciously quiet!" Bronwyn replied, and both women laughed softly.

The boys were playing exactly where they had been left.

"I think that is enough for the moment. Are you hungry?" Mereli asked them and smiled as they both nodded vigorously. "Come then, let us eat."

Over the following days, the boys practiced their newfound skills together and even tried some magic on each other, under the strict supervision of Mereli, with Bronwyn helping. They joined the other children to play, and even went down to the mere, where Colin taught his cousin to swim.

Mereli crammed as much Kadeau education in as she could during her stay, and was pleased with their progress, but all too soon, it was time for her and Colin to depart.

The two boys hugged each other tightly as they said their goodbyes, and Mereli promised to return before winter set in to see how Morgan was progressing. She would have liked to have taken him back with her to The Highmeres but understood the danger to his life and why he was to remain where he was, safely within Inver Castle, so she left Bronwyn with instructions as to what he must do until she returned and agreed a timetable for contact to provide updates.

They conversed on a weekly basis. Mereli received Bronwyn's updates, then issued instructions for the next week which occasionally included corrective work if Morgan had not quite grasped exactly what was required.

Morgan's natural ability with the sword soon became evident, even at his tender years, and Sir John ensured this gift was nurtured and encouraged him to practice with both hands so he could develop the skill to wield a weapon with either one. He even had him mounted on his own pony at the age of two and began to teach him how to ride. At this age, he concentrated on improving Morgan's overall balance and controlling the beast using the reins and his legs. Once John was satisfied that the child could handle the horse safely and had developed his balance, he made him do some more advanced exercises, including riding with his arms crossed, without stirrups and even bare-back. With the progress the child made, John was confident that he could start the serious training of teaching Morgan how to control his steed using his legs, feet, hips, and seat, so that his hands remained free to wield his sword and shield before he left for Ellesmere, which would give him a distinct advantage over the other boys of the same age.

Chapter Two

———◆———

It was time, Sir John decided. He adjusted the stirrups on Morgan's saddle before placing the child's feet in them, then stepped back and studied his profile.

"Sit up straight, Morgan," he instructed before moving round to the front of the pony to check that his legs and feet were parallel with the beast's flanks. "Your hands need to be lower...that's better." John walked all the way round the pony, checking from all angles and nodded in satisfaction. "You have a good posture. Make sure you maintain it."

"Yes, Sir John."

Morgan's third birthday had been a couple of days before, and John had decided he was now old enough to start learning how to control his pony without using his hands.

"In mounted battle, you will need both hands to defend yourself, so you need to be able to control your charger with your feet and legs. Romaine here, has been trained in the past by a previous rider, but he's been rather idle in the last few years, and ridden more as a child's palfrey. Let's see what he remembers. The position of the legs and feet are vitally important for the pony to understand what you want him to do. Eventually, when you get your own charger, you will need to train him to obey. The Kadeau may have other ways of controlling their mounts; no doubt Sir Trahaearn will be able to teach you, when you go to Ellesmere."

John idly patted the pony.

"Morgan, are you ready to begin?"

"Yes, Sir John."

"Romaine may need a bit of encouragement to remember, so I will help you. The first command we are going to learn is forward at a walk. Control is all about pressure. Equal pressure on both sides means the horse should move forward. If you want to turn left you increase pressure on the right, as your horse will want to move away from that pressure. To stop, remove pressure and sit back slightly."

"It's a lot to learn, and remember," Morgan said frowning.

"You will practice for thirty minutes every day and eventually, it will become second nature. It's all about posture, position, and pressure. For now, we shall practice straight lines."

John checked Morgan's posture one more time, ensuring there was a straight line down his spine and legs and that the balls of his feet were correctly placed in the stirrups and heels down. The knight took hold of Romaine's bridle.

"Let us begin. Gently squeeze and maintain. Not too much pressure though, we want the horse to walk, and you must also push with your hips." John illustrated the hip movement by over exaggerating it so the boy could clearly see what was required of him. "You don't need to do such a large movement for a walk, but that is in essence what you need to do."

The knight watched the slight movement of Morgan's legs and pulled Romaine forward.

"Walk on," he instructed the horse. "Keep that slight pressure on." He let go of the bridle but kept walking alongside. "Now, release the pressure."

Romaine walked on for a few steps, then stopped.

"Again," John instructed.

It took about four attempts before Romaine started to remember what he was supposed to do, and after another three, he was moving and stopping directly in response to the change in pressure against his flanks.

"Let's see if you can transition into a trot," John said. "Slight pressure to walk and then up a notch to get him into the trot. Don't forget to push with your hips."

Morgan frowned in concentration. Romaine started to walk and on John's order, the child increased the pressure slightly and the horse walked faster. Morgan tried again and Romaine did a couple of paces at a trot, then walked.

"Go on, you're almost there," John encouraged him.

On the third attempt, Romaine broke into a trot and Morgan grinned.

"Very good. Stop, turn around, and then see if you can go from a stand straight into a trot. You will need to push a little harder with your hips."

After a couple of attempts, Morgan finally managed it, and grinned again at John, feeling very pleased with himself.

"Excellent. Now, you must practice every day and build a bond with your mount. Your lives may well depend on each other; not that this little fellow will ever go into battle, but it's good practice."

"Thank you, Sir John. I will practice every day."

Time soon passed, and by his fourth birthday, he was skilfully guiding his horse without using his hands. He had even done some jumping. Sir John was very pleased. None of the other pages would be as advanced as Morgan when they started their training at Ellesmere.

Following Mereli's weekly instructions, Bronwyn had continued Morgan's education in all things related to his Kadeau heritage. She read to him, helped him practice hand movements associated with performing spells, and taught him simple harmless ones to focus his mind.

Aunt Mereli visited twice a year, accompanied by her son, and was currently at Inver again. Morgan had questioned her about mental communication and control of animals, like his pony, and she explained that depending on the animal in question, varying degrees of control was possible, but that great patience and care had to be taken. The shock of mental contact could cause death if not carried out with the lightest of touches.

Morgan had decided to experiment on his pony, and gradually, over the following few weeks, he began to grasp the concept and build a stronger and closer relationship with his steed. During the little leisure time he had, he played with Colin, and they went swimming a number of times.

Every day, after he had finished his studies, he would go and see Bronwyn and explain to her what he had seen, done and learnt; however, he became aware of her slight distraction as time went on, and finally plucked up the courage to ask about it.

"Mama, have I done something to displease you?"

"Never, Morgan." She flashed him a smile, although it did not appear to reach her eyes.

"But there is something wrong, isn't there?" he persisted, seeing sorrow in her face.

Bronwyn pondered for a few moments, then decided to tell him, knowing he would continue to worry that he was the cause of her unhappiness.

"You are the Duke of Rossmere, set to inherit a vast duchy when you come of age. As yet, there is no heir to inherit Invermere. Richard and I have been married just over six years now, and I have failed to produce an heir and a little brother for you to play with."

"You are still young," Morgan replied.

"Yes, but many women my age have had at least one or two children by now. I don't want to fail in my duty, but I fear there may be something wrong with me, and that I cannot produce the heir that Inver needs."

He saw the unshed tears in her eyes, and his heart wept for her. It would be nice to have a playmate of equal standing. He sat by her side, contemplating, and then gave her a hug.

"Babies grow in here, don't they?" he asked, resting a hand on her stomach.

"Yes, that's right, my love."

"I will pray very hard that you get your heir," he whispered into her ear.

"Morgan, bless you, and thank you." She drew back from him, and he saw a lone tear trail its way down her cheek.

"Please don't cry, Mama. It will be all right, you'll see."

"I'm sorry," she apologised.

"It means a lot to you. The continuation of the Coltrane line is important. Aunt Mereli told me that Rossmere and Invermere are the two most trusted duchies of Devonmere and have supported the Cantrell royal family for many generations."

"That is true. And if I cannot produce an heir, then the Cantrell's will lose a supporter, and Rossmere will lose a good neighbour and ally."

Morgan took a deep breath.

"I am sure I will have a baby brother to play with in a little while," he said firmly.

"I do hope so," Bronwyn replied heavily. "Now, my pet, isn't it about time you changed for supper?" She smiled at him again.

"Yes, it is." He hugged her again. "Please don't worry, everything will be all right."

He released her, stood up and flashed her a beaming, confident smile, before turning on a heel and leaving her staring after him.

The innocence of children...I wish I could be as positive as you are, my darling, Bronwyn thought wistfully as she watched him leave.

It was a few days later, when Morgan decided to question Richard about children, when they were out in the fields, inspecting the land, following the tilling of it in preparation for the next sewing of crops. The Duke nearly choked on the mouthful of water he had been taking, at hearing the question, but once he had recovered himself, he decided to answer the boy honestly.

"Yes Morgan, I yearn for a son, but God has seen fit not to grant us our wish for a child yet. There is still time."

The boy knew of sex, for he had seen lambs born, and knew about the ram being allowed in with ewes, the bull with the cows and had started to learn about animal husbandry to improve stock and knights' chargers.

"Do you love Mama?" he asked seriously.

"Yes, I do. From the moment I set eyes upon her. It was an arranged marriage, which King Rhisart had orchestrated. I was very much against it, as I had never seen my intended. I was very fortunate, for she was beautiful, and my heart was lost as soon as she looked at me."

"It is important that you keep trying, Invermere must have its heir, and I must have a good neighbour."

Richard coloured slightly at Morgan's direct words. To hear them uttered by one so young was rather unnerving.

The boy mistook his slight blush as to meaning that he was no longer intimate.

"You don't try anymore?" he questioned, quite taken aback.

Richard's colour heightened further. It was not a subject he expected to be discussing with a boy who was less than five years old.

He opened his mouth, closed it again, then cleared his throat very loudly before answering.

"Yes," he finally said. "We do try."

"Good," Morgan responded. "I have a feeling that things will soon change, and you must believe it too. It will be nice to have a younger brother."

"I will try to believe that God will grant us our wish," Richard replied, then decided to change the subject, as he was finding the current conversation extremely uncomfortable. "It was a good harvest this year, don't you think?"

"Yes. Letting the animals roam the harvested land seems to be working. The people will not starve this winter." The boy shivered as an icy blast of wind whipped by them.

"It's going to be a harsh winter," Richard told him. "There are lots of berries on the trees, but the cold will be a good thing, it will help to kill the bad insects." He looked up at the sky. "Come, it looks like it may snow at some point today or tomorrow, and it's All Hallows Eve. I shall be visiting the Pell tomorrow morning, to see how you are progressing with the sword."

Morgan's eyes lit up at this remark, which Richard saw as he turned his horse. The boy did the same, and they made their way back to the castle.

That evening, they all gave thanks to the saints, ate their evening meal, then Morgan had hugged and kissed Bronwyn and Richard, and retired for the night. The servants had cleared the table a little earlier, leaving just the wine.

Silence reined in the private quarters as the Duke contemplated the contents of his goblet and took a deep draught of the wine it held.

"Something troubles you, husband?" Bronwyn asked.

The sound of her voice roused him from his thoughts, and he smiled weakly at her.

"Morgan asked some rather uncomfortable probing questions today," he finally replied.

Her eyebrows rose in question, but nothing was forthcoming.

"What sort of questions?" she prompted.

"About love and...intimacy."

Bronwyn's mouth dropped open, then she recovered herself and closed it, swallowing nervously.

"Go on."

"He was asking about an heir to Invermere."

"I had a similar conversation a few days ago."

"Really? You didn't say anything. He seems confident, that we will be blessed with a child."

"Do you think he knows something? Could his Kadeau heritage provide him with some kind of...insight?"

"I have no idea," Richard replied. "Do you think it's possible?"

"I haven't read anything about that whilst doing my research, but who knows?" Bronwyn said, rising from her chair, walking to the door and locking it. "However...if you are game, we could give it a try?"

She moved back to him, sat on his lap, and bent her head to kiss him. Richard responded with enthusiasm as she fumbled with the buttons on his jacket, and he grasped her thigh firmly through the material of her dress.

The chair they were sitting on had arms, and was totally unsuitable for their planned antics, so he shifted position, lifted her into his arms, stood up, and sat her on the table, before urgently pulling at the lacings of her dress.

Within a few seconds, he was caressing and kissing her now exposed breasts, her creamy white flesh supple under his touch, as her nipples hardened under the assault.

His jacket fell to the floor, and Bronwyn tugged his shirt from his breeches and pulled it over his head, so that it joined its companion by his feet, before fumbling at the lacings of his breeches, her hands expertly arousing him as she freed his manhood.

Bronwyn saw the fire burning in his brown eyes and the love he held for her in his ruggedly handsome features. She saw him now as she had when she had first laid eyes upon him, clean shaven, square-jawed, honourable, loyal, dependable and madly in love with her.

Standing between her thighs, his hand slowly raised her skirts as his tongue encircled a nipple, causing her to moan as his fingers reached her inner core, making her arch her back and move against him as her passion mounted; then a raging inferno engulfed them, and almost in a frenzy and totally out of control, Richard pushed her back onto the table, sending the flask of wine flying, and entered her, thrusting urgently as if to relieve himself of the fire that had suddenly overtaken him. Bronwyn wrapped her legs around his hips, her hands gripping his biceps tightly as she felt him moving inside her, slowly gathering speed, and then everything exploded, as he climaxed, his seed filling her as she twitched one final time and cried out in an exquisite orgasm.

A few moments passed and the Duke found he was unable to move; trapped within the confines of her body, her legs securely wrapped around his hips. Every little movement he made, caused her to gasp, but he managed to draw back from her enough to view her heaving breasts.

"Oh Richard!" she gasped, "You've not been this much out of control since our wedding night!"

27

"I apologise, my love. I don't know what came over me, just then…" His breath caught in his throat as he continued to view her breasts and knew in that instant, he wanted her again.

"It was… extremely pleasurable," Bronwyn responded, looking at him from under her eyelashes. It was as if she knew what he was thinking, for she released him then, and sat up, drawing a hand seductively down his chest.

Seeing her look, Richard pulled himself together, picked her up and walked purposefully towards the bedchamber.

"We might as well be comfortable," he whispered in her ear, making her shiver with anticipation, as he set her down on her feet and divested her of her clothes, before removing the rest of his, and pushed her down onto the bed.

He surveyed her for a few moments as she lay there, inviting him, and he felt the heat rise in his body once again. Joining her, he gave her pleasure almost beyond reason before claiming her time and time again that night, until exhausted, they both fell asleep in one another's arms in the early hours of the morning.

It was the persistent thumping of a fist on the outer door that finally woke Richard a couple of hours later. He jerked awake, slightly disorientated, and ran a hand through his shoulder-length brown hair, and over his eyes, as if to brush away the cobwebs. Beside him lay Bronwyn, still fast asleep, with a slight smile on her lips. He looked down at her, suddenly shocked to realise that he wanted her again, but as he reached out to touch her, the fist hammered against the outer door once more, and a muffled voice could just be heard.

"Your Grace! Your Grace, is everything all right?"

It was Trystan, his personal steward.

Richard sighed, and carefully slipped from the bed, smiling slightly. Oh yes, Trystan, everything is fine, he thought as he remembered the night of passion he had just shared.

He looked around for his dressing gown and spied it on a chair. Putting it on, he quickly moved to the outer chamber, unlocked the door and opened it.

"Your Grace," Trystan said again.

"Everything is fine, Trystan. Come back in an hour."

His steward saw the smile on his Lord's face, then managed to glimpse the spilt jug of wine, the discarded clothes, and nodded knowingly.

"As you wish, Your Grace, but—" he just about managed to say before the door closed in his face.

Habit ingrained, he bowed at the door and left, pausing a fraction as he heard the key turn in the lock once again.

Richard threw his dressing gown on the floor and slipped between the bedding once again, to caress his wife. His touch was feather light, but after a few minutes, Bronwyn began to utter little moans, and willingly opened her thighs. He was curious to try something he had never done before; something he had overheard one of his knights talking about to a comrade. He threw back the covers and knelt between her thighs. Taking a deep breath to steady his nerves, he bent his head, and used his tongue to arouse her.

Bronwyn's eyes flew open at the sensation, and she moaned loudly, her hips moving against him. His name was wrenched from her lips, and as he glanced up, he saw her knuckles whiten as she gripped the pillow under her head tightly.

Richard was shocked. Never had he seen such a reaction from her, but it had the desired effect on him as well, and painfully aroused, he finally allowed his manhood the release it craved as he entered her once more. The blood pounded in his ears, and the pleasure seemed to last an aeon before he had been emptied, and he had heard her scream with pleasure.

Spent, he collapsed onto her slight body, to regain his breath, and silently offered his thanks to the overheard conversation of the knights.

"Oh, Richard," Bronwyn finally managed to gasp. She was still trembling in the aftermath of the passion, and her body was tingling all over.

Recovered enough to move, he shifted to lie beside her, enveloped them both in the bedsheets and took her in his arms, kissing the top of her head.

"My love, thank you for this past night of pleasure. Words cannot even begin to describe the feelings that were felt."

The Duchess smiled demurely at him from under her lashes, then frowned, as if trying to remember something.

"Aren't you supposed to be watching Morgan this morning, at training, in the Pell?"

Richard froze.

"Oh Lord, yes!"

He threw back the covers again and rose from the bed. Bronwyn watched his lithe, naked form as he ran to the garderobe, feeling a pleasant ache between her thighs at the sight of him. There was a flurry of activity as he then quickly washed, and threw on some clothes, before returning to the bed, to kiss his wife.

"I will see you later!" he said, and literally ran from the room, leaving Bronwyn smiling.

Morgan was practicing with the sword but was not really concentrating. He was looking for Richard, who was supposed to be watching him.

"Morgan!" John said curtly.

The child jumped and had the good grace to look guilty.

"I'm sure Duke Richard will be here shortly. He may have been momentarily detained," John continued more softly. "Now pay attention, the ground is frozen this morning, and footing a little unsure. This is good practice for you; you may not necessarily be on good ground during a sword fight."

Morgan nodded and swallowed, then took up his defensive stance, his wooden sword held securely in his hand.

"Hold," Sir John said, and slowly walked around him, correcting the position of his feet, the line of his shoulders. "Straighten that back, drop your right shoulder more, that's better." He inspected his grip and altered it slightly. "When you are older, you are likely to develop a grip more suited to you, but for now, try to maintain this one, it will stand you in good stead." He stood back and nodded in satisfaction. "Excellent, Morgan. Now let me see you go through your exercises."

The Master-at-arms stepped back further so he could clearly see the boy's movements, and spied the Duke, quickly making his way towards them.

"Back to the starting position, Morgan. His Grace is here."

Eagerly, the young boy took up his previous position, just as Richard arrived.

"Good morning, Your Grace," Sir John said cheerfully.

"Good morning, Sir John, Morgan. My apologies for being late, I was...detained. Please, continue."

Richard stood with arms folded and watched attentively as Sir John put the youngster through his paces.

He may not yet be five, Richard thought to himself, *but he has a grace and a skill I have never seen in one so young. This skill must be nurtured, if he is to be the prince's protector.*

The demonstration lasted for fifteen minutes, then Sir John ordered him to stop.

"Well done, Morgan, you are indeed showing a great deal of promise," Richard told him.

Those words resulted in one of the boy's rare smiles.

"Thank you, Papa."

"His riding is coming along well also, Your Grace, and he has made vast improvements in sword play on his pony. Once he is older and has a more suitable steed, I believe he will improve a great deal. The skill with the sword is unparalleled for his age, but currently, his age and height are against him. By the time he is a knight, I believe he's going to be over six feet tall if he keeps growing the way he is, and if he attains that, he will be unbeatable."

"Now don't let all that news go to your head, young Morgan," Richard said sternly. "A knight must be modest. His acts will show his virtues. Remember that."

"Yes, Papa."

"When you are five, you will start your training properly with the other boys. I can see you're almost ready now, but we will leave it a little longer, to be sure. You are destined for great responsibility, and I must ensure that you remain safe, until you are ready to assume your role. Now, I will see you this afternoon, I am holding court. You need to learn how to govern your duchy, and how to do it justly and wisely." Richard nodded at him and reached for Sir John's hand. "Thank you, Sir John, I am very pleased."

"Thank you, Your Grace."

Richard then ruffled Morgan's hair, smiled, and returned in the direction from which he had come.

That afternoon, Morgan sat alongside Richard as the Duke held court. Morgan had hoped it would be exciting, with lots of thrilling disputes that Richard would have to resolve, but most of what the Duke had to hear was petty, and minor, regarding property, a request for a tenancy, and pleas of hardship. Morgan stared and concentrated on what sounded like a particularly sad case and saw Richard frown.

Suddenly, the boy was overcome with the strongest feeling that the man was lying. He didn't know how he knew, but he was absolutely sure, and fidgeted in his chair. Richard noticed and turned to him.

"Morgan?" he queried.

The child leant closer to him and whispered very quietly. "He's not telling the truth."

"How do you know?" Richard whispered back.

"I... I just know... I can sort of... see it. In fact... he has hidden some coin away... in his barn where he keeps his cow, under one of the wooden boards."

Richard was shocked at this revelation. Mereli said he would be powerful but...?

The Duke called a guard over and issued some orders. The guard immediately disappeared, and Richard addressed the man.

"Cadoc of the Mere, there is some question regarding your honesty. I have despatched a guard to check on the truth of what you have said. You will be held here, until he returns."

He saw the colour drain from the man's face, as he stared first at the Duke, and then at the boy by his side.

The man was pulled aside, and Richard continued holding court. He had just finished when the guard came back, approached the chair on which the Duke was sitting and pulled a small pouch from his jacket, bowing as he handed it to Richard.

"Where did you find this?"

"Exactly where you described, Your Grace. Under one of the wooden boards, where the cow is kept."

Richard opened the pouch and emptied the coins into his hand. He rose an eyebrow as he saw the amount there; it could not have been saved in just one year. He gestured for the guards to bring the man forward.

"Cadoc of the Mere, you have committed wilful perjury against this duchy to avoid paying your taxes. I will remove what is owed from this pouch, the rest I will return to you." Richard counted out the amount owed and indicated for the treasurer to tick the man's name, as having settled his debt. "The amount here could not have been saved in just one year. This is not the first time you have claimed hardship. I consider myself a just ruler of this duchy, asking for a fair price each year. I assume you are taking me to be a fool?"

Cadoc shook his head vehemently.

"No, never, Your Grace."

Richard paused for effect, then threw the pouch at the man. "Take what is left. You have one day to pack your belongings and leave this duchy, never to return. If you are found on this land after one month has past, you will forfeit everything, and further justice will be served upon you."

"But Your Grace..."

"Go, before I shorten the length of time."

Cadoc looked furious and turned his glare upon Morgan.

"You! It was you! You read my mind, you filthy half-breed! You'd better watch your back, young Morgan Bodine, for I will get my revenge, I swear it!"

Richard rose from his chair of state.

"Guards! Arrest this man!"

Two members of the elite guard moved forward, swords in hands, ready to despatch their prisoner if required.

Morgan looked on, trying not to look visibly shaken, but feeling very much so, underneath the stone-faced mask he was gallantly wearing.

"Take him to the dungeon."

"P – Papa, wait, please," the boy said softly.

The Duke turned and looked at him.

"Let him go. There was a family requesting a tenancy; let them have his, along with his cow and whatever other animals are on the farm. He can be escorted from Invermere, can he not?"

"He has made a threat on your life."

"I know, but by the time he will be able to do anything, I will be grown and more than a match for him." The boy's eyes were almost transparent as he stared at Cadoc, and the man drew back, suddenly afraid of the child.

There was a long pause as Richard pondered the request. Finally, he nodded.

"Very well, son, as you wish." He turned back to the guards. "Escort the prisoner from our lands. As punishment, he will go with what he has now, and that pouch of money, there is enough there for him to survive and find a new position. Go."

The guards bowed, grabbed Cadoc by his arms and marched him out of the hall. The man said nothing as he went; realising that far worse was likely to happen to him if he spoke further.

Silence reigned for a few minutes.

"Are you all right, Morgan?" Richard finally asked the boy.

Morgan nodded. "Yes, I am fine," he answered. "Although, this is the first time I have felt the hate that you have tried to prepare me for." He abruptly changed the subject. "Will you send for that family who wished a tenancy?"

"I will do that. They should still be waiting; would you like the pleasure of telling them the good news?"

"Really? May I?"

Richard smiled at him.

"You may." He turned to a steward. "Go and fetch Elwyn and his family."

"At once, Your Grace."

Several minutes passed, and then the door at the end of the chamber opened, and a man, woman and two children, who had put in the request for a tenancy earlier in the day, entered, and nervously approached the bottom of the steps to the dais where Richard and Morgan were sitting.

They bowed and curtseyed in respect. Richard motioned for Morgan to speak.

"Elwyn, we have good news for you and your family. A tenancy has become available. It is yours if you want it," Morgan said, remembering the words that Richard had used on a previous occasion.

"The land is fertile and good. There is a cow and some chickens included," Richard added, and his heart was warmed at the expressions of joy that could be seen on Elwyn's and his wife's face. In fact, the wife was crying with happiness.

"Your Grace, thank you; you won't regret it, we will be good tenants," Elwyn said.

"You will need to make your mark, and the steward will explain what is expected of you whilst you are a tenant. We wish you every happiness in your new life."

"God bless both of you!" The family paid their respects once again and then followed the steward away.

There was no one else to be seen, so court ended. Richard turned to face Morgan once again.

"Well done, my lad. You did very well today."

Morgan smiled at him, then sobered.

"I was angry that Cadoc lied to you. You are a just and fair leader of this duchy and it was wrong of him to do that. Are you annoyed with me for allowing him to go free?"

"No, I'm not annoyed, but it is my responsibility to see you safely to Ellesmere. I will increase the guard for a while at least, to ensure your safety."

"I understand, Papa. Giving the tenancy to that family felt good, though. They were so grateful."

"Aye, they were. I think you have made a friend there."

"Do you think it would be all right, if I were to visit them in a couple of weeks, to see how they are settling in?"

"I'm sure they would welcome such a visit, providing the weather isn't too bad. It will be the middle of November, and we are due snow, I'm sure of it."

"May I take them a gift of some food and other provisions as a kind of welcome?"

"If you wish, yes. Now come, it's time for your afternoon nap."

"Your Grace, I will have the final figures for you at our usual meeting later today," the treasurer said, bowing.

"Thank you, Gruffydd. Until later."

Richard gestured for Morgan to precede him; they left the room, and went to the boy's chambers, where the Duke ensured he was safely tucked up in bed for his nap, in the chilled air of the bedchamber.

Glesni was stoking the fire that would soon radiate its heat around the room and keep Morgan warm.

The Duke headed for his wife's rooms, assuming she would be there, and he was right. He paused at the entrance to her day room, and watched her working on some needlework, a soft smile on her face.

"And pray, what are you smiling about?" he asked her as he entered.

She looked up, her eyes alight with love, and her smile grew in size.

"I think my Lord knows perfectly well what I'm smiling about," she answered, putting her embroidery down. "How did court go today?"

"On the whole, very well."

"What aren't you telling me?" she asked.

"I had Morgan with me today. There was a case of hardship, and he whispered to me that the man was lying. He even told me where this man had some coin hidden, so I despatched a guard to investigate, and it was exactly where Morgan had said it would be. I know Kadeau can read minds, but I thought they had to be in physical contact, and older."

"Mereli did say he was likely to be exceedingly powerful, but I am surprised it is making its appearance so soon. We must be careful how we handle this development."

"Agreed, but that isn't my immediate worry. The man threatened him." Richard paused as he saw one of his wife's hands move to her throat and utter a gasp. "I have had him escorted from Invermere. I was going to throw him in the dungeon for making the threat, but Morgan asked me to let him go. Needless to say, I have increased the guard, and that will remain in force for the rest of the year. Wherever Morgan goes, he must be accompanied."

"Yes, but how did he take it?"

"He was shaken, but he took it well."

"Do I need to go to him?"

"He's sleeping at the moment, but if you like, you can be there when he awakens."

"Thank you, my love, I will do that."

A couple of hours later, Bronwyn was sitting by Morgan's bedside pondering this latest development in his abilities. Mereli would need to know, so she would inform her at their next weekly meeting. Bronwyn gazed at her son and smiled as she waited for him to awaken, admiring his good looks and his blond hair, although she was sure it was a shade or two darker, than it had been.

He gave a little sigh, stretched and opened his eyes. A look of surprise and then pleasure entered them.

"Mama!" he exclaimed, sitting up.

"My pet. Richard has told me, you had some excitement today, at court. Are you all right?"

His heart warmed at the love and concern he heard in her voice, as she reached out and brushed a stray lock of hair from over his right eye.

"I admit I was shaken, but I'm all right now."

"Truly?"

"Yes, truly. The session finished on a high note, with me granting a tenancy to a family. I'm going to visit them in a couple of weeks and take some gifts and provisions to see how they are settling in."

"That is very generous of you."

"They were so grateful. It warmed my heart."

"I'm pleased. Now, it's time you were up; we shall be eating shortly."

03 80 03 80

Chapter Three

———•———

Two weeks later, as he had said he would, Morgan visited the new tenant, Elwyn and his family, on their new farm.

"Now, you mustn't take too much. They may be too proud to accept the gifts," Bronwyn had told him.

"I thought I might take some flour, salt, some winter vegetables and a couple of blankets for the two children. That isn't too much, is it?" he asked.

"I think that sounds just about right. The flour should be most welcome for baking, and the blankets for the children are a kind thought."

Happy, he set off with his small guard. The tenancy was beyond the castle grounds and city, and out on the lower plains, about half an hour's ride away. It was a cold day, a freezing ground fog had formed overnight and still lingered in the hollows, but the weak winter sun was doing its best to slowly disperse it.

Elwyn was busy chopping wood as the small party approached, and initially didn't hear them, until they were practically on top of him. He looked up startled to see the boy and his six guards, but immediately recognised him and hastily put down his axe.

"My Lord!" he exclaimed, slightly nervous, bowing deeply, as the youngster dismounted his pony and walked towards him, followed by one of the guards who was carrying a rather large sack.

"Elwyn, I came to see how you are settling in, and I've brought you a small gift of welcome."

"My Lord is generous. Please, may I invite you in? There is a fire inside that you may warm yourself by, before beginning your return journey."

"Thank you, I will."

"My Lord," the guard began, but the look on Morgan's face stopped him from saying anything further. "Sir Hywel, bring the sack."

"If your guard wish to water their horses, there is a trough by the stable."

Morgan nodded and indicated for his men to take care of their horses, then followed Elwyn into the small farmhouse.

Elwyn's wife turned as the door opened and the guests walked in. She gasped in shock and dropped into a curtsey.

"Please rise," Morgan said. "What is your name?"

"Gwenne, my Lord."

"And your children?"

"Symon and Aelwyn."

Morgan smiled at them, then motioned for Sir Hywel to present the sack to them.

"I come bearing a small welcome gift. I hope that's all right and that you are not offended?"

"You are most generous, my Lord, and we are not offended."

Curious, Gwenne opened the sack and pulled out the flour, salt, vegetables and the two blankets.

"Oh, but we cannot take so much..."

"You can, and you will," Morgan replied.

"In which case, may I offer you some mead, and some newly baked bread? It is still warm. Symon, a chair for his Lord."

Morgan spent a little time, talking with the family, listening to their plans for the farm, and then deciding not to overstay his welcome, bid them farewell, and rose to leave, thanking them for their hospitality.

Outside, Elwyn called after him.

"My Lord, thank you. Know that if you need to call upon me, I will answer that call and do whatever I can, or must, in your service or the Duke of Invermere."

"Thank you Elwyn. I hope the situation never arises where we need to do that, but your pledge means a lot. I wish you all well."

He mounted his pony and prepared to return to the castle with his guard. Elwyn waved goodbye as they left, leaving Morgan with an exceedingly warm feeling in his heart.

☙ ❧ ☙ ❧

All too soon Christmas arrived, along with bitter winds and driving snow. The Coltranes attended midnight mass in the cathedral and then returned to the keep, where they had wine and sweetmeats to warm them up after their ride back.

The New Year brought heavy hoar frosts and temperatures persistently below freezing for a number of weeks. Ice had to be broken on water barrels and outdoor troughs several times a day, so that livestock could drink, but most of the animals were brought inside to protect them from the severe cold.

Richard's court sessions were quieter during this period, so he started to teach Morgan how to play tawlbwrdd. It was a long-established strategy game played on a nine-by-nine board, and the two players consisted of an attacker and defender. The defender had a king and eight defenders placed in the centre of the board. The attacker had sixteen men, placed in a pattern partly surrounding the defenders.

The object of the game was to get the king to a far corner of the board, whilst the attackers tried to stop them. A piece was removed by being surrounded on three sides by the opposing force.

By making a game of it, Richard hoped to start training Morgan's young mind into thinking about battle strategies, and plans, in preparation for adulthood. The boy was still too young to start reading about the history of past battles, for they had been written for grown men and were hard to read; but at least the game would plant the seed of planning and gauging an enemy.

Morgan enjoyed playing it very much. Richard let him defend and attack during their weekly matches, and the child was animated as he related his latest battle to Bronwyn, who encouraged him to continue.

"Remember Morgan, Richard has many years of experience on his side, so he will be bound to beat you for a while yet. You must listen to what he advises afterwards, store it away and make use of it. Eventually you will win, and it will be by your own effort."

Morgan nodded. Her words seemed to make him determined to get the better of Richard eventually.

Then one morning, in early February, Bronwyn did not appear for breakfast.

"She's not feeling very well," Richard said to him.

"Is she ill?" the child had asked, concerned. It was his fifth birthday in a couple of weeks, and he so wanted her to be around on that day.

"I'm sure it's nothing serious," the Duke replied, but Morgan could see that he was worried about her.

"May I see her?"

"Perhaps a little later. Let's see how the morning goes."

He was finally allowed to visit her after lunch and expressed his concern.

"Do not worry, my pet. It may just have been something I ate, that has disagreed with me. I'm sure it will soon pass," she reassured him.

But it didn't. She continued to be ill and spent a lot of her days in bed for the next week, so a physician was called.

Richard had waited impatiently, for the physician to carry out his examination to get to the root cause of her ailment, and had not let Morgan stay with him, just in case it turned out to be something serious or life threatening.

Eventually, the physician emerged from Bronwyn's chambers, smiling.

"What news?" Richard demanded.

"Your Grace, congratulations, the Duchess is with child."

The news was like receiving a body blow to the stomach. They had waited so long to hear this news, that now it had actually been said, Richard could not believe it.

"What? Are you sure?" he had asked tentatively.

"Yes, your Grace. I estimate thirteen or fourteen weeks. I believe the child should be born around the beginning of August."

The physician could see that Richard was almost overcome by the news and smiled broadly. "Why not go see her, Your Grace. She is asking for you. I wish you both all happiness for the future event." The physician bowed and left.

It took a few minutes for the news to still sink in, then Richard shook himself and eagerly knocked on the door.

Bronwyn's personal maid, Dilys, opened it and bade him enter.

"Her Grace is resting in bed," she said and indicated for him to go through to the bedchamber.

The Duke moved swiftly to the door and paused at the threshold. His wife was resting quietly in bed, her eyes closed, but seemed to sense his presence and opened them, giving him a smile of welcome.

He hastily moved to her bedside and sat down on a chair. "Oh, my love," he said with feeling, grasping her hands and leaning forward to kiss her.

"Finally," she whispered back.

"It is wonderful news indeed, but how are you feeling?"

"The truth?"

"But of course."

"Dreadful. I had no idea being with child was going to be so debilitating. Morgan must think I've deserted him!"

Richard shook his head.

"He would never think that. All he knows at present is that you are ill. Now, will you tell him the good news, or shall I?"

"Let me tell him, it's the least I can do...let him know he will soon have a brother...or sister."

"I don't care what it is, as long as it is healthy, and you come through the ordeal safely."

A couple of tears escaped from his eyes, which he tried to brush away, but Bronwyn beat him to it.

"Oh, my love, I hope they are tears of happiness. It will be a joyous occasion, but you must forgive me; the physician has ordered that I rest whenever I can, especially if I feel ill. It seems it is not unheard of to be very unwell in the early days. Alas, I am one of those unfortunate women. Now, will you send Morgan up, he must be worried to death."

"I will do as you ask." He leant forward and kissed her again. "Well done, my dearest."

The Duke rose, and reluctantly left her to go in search of young Morgan.

☙ ❧ ☙ ❧

Bronwyn raised her head as there was a knock on the door.

"Come in," she said rather softly. She was feeling tired, and a little unwell and hadn't expected to feel so incapacitated. She watched as the door opened and Morgan poked his head round. "Morgan, my darling, come in."

He smiled slightly, entered, shut the door behind him and approached Bronwyn's bedside.

"You are not well?" the child questioned as he reached her.

"Come sit here, by me; I have something to tell you." She patted a space on the bed and Morgan did as she asked. "Don't be alarmed," she added hastily, seeing his worried expression. "Now, you know the Duchies rely on family to keep them going over the years. So far, I have failed to produce an heir for Inver but...that time is now possibly over. Morgan, you will shortly have a brother or sister, for I am with child."

"I am so pleased for you Mama," Morgan replied seriously, "but I sense, all is not well?"

"You are very perceptive, and you are correct. The pregnancy is difficult. I had no idea it would affect me as it has, and the physician has ordered me to rest a lot."

"I wish I could help you somehow."

"You support me by being here. I just want to apologise in advance. I am finding some days better than others. One day I feel almost like my old self and can get up and move around, and yet, on other days I can hardly lift my head without feeling very ill. I do not want you to think I am neglecting you, for I do love you as my own and always will. I hope you can understand what I am trying to say. I will always have time for you my dearest, but it could be on the odd day when I am feeling below par, that you get the impression I am not interested in what you have done. I am always eager to hear about your day and what you have learnt, or seen, even though I may be laying here with my eyes closed."

"I do understand, Mama. I am so sorry to hear you are suffering, but when the baby comes, I will help you look after it," he told her solemnly, his pale eyes huge.

"I will need all the help I can get, Morgan," she responded, "and I will most certainly take you up on your offer, bless you." She hugged him tightly and kissed his cheek. "Now, tell me about your day."

She listened as the boy recounted his activities, making Bronwyn laugh at some points, which pleased Morgan no end, that he had managed to cheer her up, before he left.

Bronwyn's days were most certainly up and down, and she prayed she would be on one of her 'good days' on Morgan's birthday.

On the whole, fortune was with her. She had been a little ill in the morning, but apart from that, she felt almost like her old self, so had gone with Richard to see what Morgan had felt about one of his birthday presents; a new pony, as he had outgrown his existing one. It was only just a pony, standing at fourteen and a half hands, and Richard had purposely selected a steed that was too tall for the lad, so he could "grow into it", and have it a little longer, to build a partnership. He seemed to be shooting up in height, and as a result also needed new clothes. The downside of his spurt of growth, was that he lost some of his coordination with the sword, and felt he had to start almost from scratch. It was like taking one step forward and two steps back.

Sir John did his best to lift his spirits by telling him, that if he grew just a few more inches, he would have his reach, and probably start winning the majority of his sword matches against the other pages.

This cheered him up, and he dutifully mounted his new horse with assistance from the Master-at-Arms, and walked it round in the small paddock, to see what it felt like. Being taller, its stride was longer and took some getting used to, but again, he reached out with his mind, to gently make contact with his steed, to start to form a bond. Within fifteen minutes, they appeared to have made a connection, and the horse performed willingly under his instruction.

"What will you call him?" Richard asked, patting the pony's neck, as Morgan reined in by the fence.

The boy sat and contemplated for a while.

"I think I shall call him Flint, to go with his grey colour," he finally said. "May I take him for a canter?"

"Not on your own," Richard replied instantly.

"If you will give me a few minutes, your Grace, I will saddle up and accompany him," Sir John said.

Richard nodded and the knight moved swiftly to the stables, returning in just a few minutes with his steed.

"Not too long now," Richard ordered. "Just enough time to see how he covers the ground."

"Yes, Your Grace," Sir John replied.

"Morgan, when you get back, please go to your rooms and we will meet you there."

"Very well, Papa."

Sir John leant over and unfastened the gate, so Morgan could urge Flint out. Richard and Bronwyn watched as the two of them walked sedately away, then the Duke offered his arm to his wife.

"May I escort you back to the keep, my love?"

"You may, indeed," she replied, smiling.

"I'm glad to see you are feeling a little better today."

"So am I!" she retorted. "Today, is a good day, and I'm so pleased. I would have hated to have been ill on Morgan's birthday."

"Still, you must not overdo things. Gentle exercise when you are able."

"You're beginning to sound like the physician!"

Richard laughed. It was a deep, rich sound, and Bronwyn snuggled closer as they made their way back, enjoying his company.

Now out of the castle, Morgan and Sir John, trotted sedately along the main street until they were outside of Inver, then let the horses have free rein.

Morgan had never travelled so fast before on a horse and found it invigorating. Flint was swift, and covered the ground well, unlike his old pony, who he felt had shaken his teeth loose with its short stride on what seemed like stubby little legs. Now he was impatient to be grown and sit upon his own charger and feel the power and speed that creature would possess.

All too soon, Sir John put an end to his freedom and insisted they return. The days were still short, and a freezing fog was starting to appear, slowly swirling around, making it seem as if their horses had no legs. They slowed to a trot, and then a walk as the fog thickened, and an eerie silence descended as it seemed to deaden all sound.

It took them longer to get back, and Morgan insisted on making sure his new mount was safely delivered to his stall, and fresh hay and water provided. As a parting gesture, he had hugged the beast, whilst Sir John stood back, and smiled.

"Come, Morgan, his Grace will be concerned as to where you've got to."

"I'm coming," the boy replied. "Night night, Flint. See you tomorrow."

The pony snorted softly at him, then started munching on its hay.

They turned to leave, and as they drew level with Morgan's old pony, the boy stopped.

"Sir John, what will become of Romaine?"

"He will go out to pasture with the other horses, until the next child can learn to ride on him."

"So, he won't be lonely. That's good. I just need a few moments with him. I won't be long." The boy entered the stall and stroked Romaine, who seemed more intent on eating his feed. Morgan grabbed the pony's halter and forced his head up. He then laid his palm on its forehead, closed his eyes and reached out. Romaine snorted but did not move. "Romaine, I release you from our bond. Be happy and I thank you for your faithful service."

The pony nuzzled him briefly, then as the boy let go of the halter, Romaine dropped his head and began feeding again. Satisfied that all was well, the youngster left.

When Morgan finally entered his rooms, he saw Richard and Bronwyn sitting at the table, waiting for him.

"There you are!" Richard proclaimed. "We were becoming concerned."

"A ground fog started forming, so we had to slow down coming back."

The Duke nodded in understanding.

"And then I had to make sure Flint was bedded down all right. Thank you for my new horse. He is a much smoother ride."

"We are pleased you like him. He should serve you for a number of years. He's actually too big for you at the moment, but you seemed to handle him well enough."

"My biggest problem will be mounting him for a while," Morgan said. "It's a long way up to his back."

Bronwyn laughed kindly at that.

"The way you are growing my boy, you'll be able to mount him on your own soon enough!" she exclaimed. "Go through to your bedchamber, we have provided you with some other things."

Morgan did as he was told, and returned a little while later, beaming.

"New clothes! Thank you, both of you!"

He hugged them, tightly.

"I do love you, so much," he mumbled, slightly embarrassed at his show of emotion.

"Know that we love you too," Bronwyn whispered back, fondly ruffling his hair.

She sighed in contentment. *All we need now is for this baby to be delivered safely, for me to prove my ability to produce an heir,* she thought to herself.

CB & CB &

Chapter Four

The pregnancy had not been an easy one; Bronwyn had suffered severe morning sickness and spent a great deal of time resting in her rooms, but throughout, she had continued with Morgan's training, under Mereli's supervision.

Morgan had visited her whenever he could, and he told her about what he had done that day; what he had learnt and seen. No matter how poorly she felt, she always responded to his stories with enthusiasm. He felt it was his duty to cheer her up and always tried to tell her an amusing story, to lift her spirits. One time he became very concerned as she had pulled a face.

"What's wrong, Mama?" he had asked.

She smiled at him. "The baby is kicking. We are getting close."

"Why is the baby kicking you? That's not a very nice thing to do."

"Ah, my pet, the baby is telling me it is almost ready to make an appearance and is running out of room to grow much more. Oh! That was a hefty kick, it must surely be a boy." She studied Morgan's frowning features. "Give me your hand," she said to him, and he obeyed willingly. Bronwyn placed his hand on her swollen abdomen and held it there.

"Oh!" he suddenly said, as he felt a sharp kick under his hand. There was an expression of awe on his face, as he continued to hold his hand in the same place, feeling more blows. "Does it hurt?" he asked.

"No, my darling; but I will confess it can be a little uncomfortable. Now, off you go, it's time for your supper."

Bronwyn had fought hard not to go into the birthing chamber a month before she was due to deliver, as all women of status were supposed to do, for she felt Morgan would think she was deserting him, and so, although Richard was forbidden entry, she insisted the child be allowed to visit. She also demanded that more light be allowed into the room, which would usually have been kept dimly lit, with cheerful tapestries covering the majority of the windows, and only one being allowed to let the light and fresh air in. Being summer, the heat was sometimes stifling and oppressive, so she had won her battle.

She kissed Morgan's cheek and hugged him as best she could before he left the room; but when he came back to say goodnight; he was refused entry.

The Duke took him aside. "I'm sorry Morgan, you cannot go in. Bronwyn is in labour; the baby is coming."

"How long will it take?" he asked, then gave a gasp of anguish as a cry of pain was heard from behind the solid door. "It hurts?" he questioned.

"Come, Morgan," Richard insisted, taking his hand and leading him away.

"But I want to help!" he protested, dragging his heels.

"This is women's work, son. We must leave them to do what must be done; the midwives are with her, and it's time you were in bed."

"No! No, I promised I would help!" Morgan dug his heels in as best as he could to stop the Duke from taking him away from Bronwyn.

In the end, Richard had to pick him up and carry him to his rooms, as the child had protested vehemently, continuing to state he had promised Bronwyn, he would help her, but the Duke kept walking, and eventually, with Glesni's assistance, managed to settle him down for the night. He had then gone to his own rooms for a brief respite, before returning to pace the corridors outside Bronwyn's, then not able to stand the sound of her cries, he went to the main hall and paced up and down there instead.

Sleep did not come for Morgan. He lay in the darkness, chewing his lip with worry; scared that Bronwyn would not survive. He had been told about his mother; that she had been too young to be with child. Bronwyn was a grown woman, but it still scared him. He tossed and turned in his bed, then stopped and suddenly lay very still, concentrating. Closing his eyes and breathing slowly and deeply, he reached out with his mind, searching for the woman who, to him, was to all intent and purpose, his mother.

In the darkness, he frowned deeply, his mind searching, practicing the techniques his aunt had started to teach him. Bronwyn was not Kadeau, but Aunt Mereli had told him that it was possible to reach out to the human mind, providing he concentrated hard enough, and for the fleetest of moments, he managed the barest of touches; but all he felt was pain, that made him cry out, and he withdrew; tears in his eyes.

Unable to sleep, he made his way to the birthing chamber, but was refused entry, and not allowed to see Bronwyn at all, so instead, he went in search of Richard, who he finally found pacing the main hall.

"Papa?" he had asked.

The Duke stopped his pacing and turned to face him; seeing his own worry reflected in the young child's eyes, and Morgan was clearly concerned for Bronwyn.

"Morgan, you should be asleep in bed."

"I couldn't sleep. Is...is Mama going to be all right?"

Richard took a knee, to be at his height. "I hope so. We are all praying that she comes through the ordeal safely, but it is hard for her."

"I don't want her to die."

"We are all in the hands of God, child. What He decrees will be. Come, will you pray with me?"

They made their way to the chapel and spent the next hour in their own thoughts and praying that Bronwyn would survive, before sitting quietly, waiting for news.

Morgan eventually fell asleep, cradled in Richard's arms, and he sat there most of the night, lost in thought, about what he would do if things went horribly wrong. Idly, he softly stroked the boy's hair, and fretted.

Childbirth was the most dangerous event for a woman, the mortality rate was high, especially in the lower classes. But being rich and powerful was no guarantee of survival. So much could go wrong both during, and after the birth of the child. Richard had no idea what he would do, should something happen to his wife and the child; it did not bear thinking about.

He glanced down at Morgan, sound asleep, his head now resting on the Duke's lap, and for a moment, wished the child really was his son. In a way, he was, for he had raised him since he had arrived almost five years ago. He was going to be a great knight and leader, of that Richard was certain, as long as they could continue to teach him to use his powers carefully. Mereli McCloud was proving to be invaluable in that regard, and her regular visits to educate and check on Morgan's progress was beginning to pay dividends. She had sensed great power within him; power that needed to be nurtured, trained and disciplined so that it would be used for the good of the kingdom.

There was a lot of responsibility riding on the youngster's shoulders that he was still far too young to understand. Protecting the Prince and future King was going to be a huge burden and on top of that, he would also have his own duchy to govern. For now, that at least had been taken care of, with the careful selection of people to run it until Morgan was old enough to rule it himself.

Richard felt his eyelids growing heavy, and shut them, just for a few minutes respite. The next thing he was aware of, was the sound of running footsteps and someone shouting.

"Your Grace! Your Grace!" Markus sounded out of breath as he hurriedly approached them.

Both Richard and Morgan jerked awake and glanced worriedly at each other before rising from their seats.

"What news, Markus?" the Duke asked, his heart suddenly thumping hard in his chest.

"Your Grace, you have a daughter!"

Richard briefly closed his eyes and took a deep breath; holding it for several seconds before he released it.

"A girl!" Morgan exclaimed. "I was sure it was going to be a boy, by the way it kicked!" He sounded somewhat disappointed at the news. He had wanted a play mate.

"And what of the Duchess?" Richard asked cautiously.

"Her Grace is exhausted but appears well. She is asking for you... for both of you."

Richard nodded in satisfaction and took Morgan's hand.

"Very well. Thank you, Markus." He looked down at the boy. "Well Morgan, shall we go and see Bronwyn and your new sister?"

The youngster's eyes lit up. "Yes please!" he enthused.

They made their way eagerly to the birthing chamber, nearly forgetting to knock. Standing outside, they both took deep breaths and knocked on the door. It was opened by one of the midwives, who curtsied.

"Your Grace; we have been expecting you. Please, enter." She stood back, allowing them both access into the room.

Bronwyn was sitting, propped up in bed, looking tired, but happy, a wrapped bundle in her arms.

"Bronwyn, my love." Richard moved swiftly to her bedside where he leant down and kissed her fondly.

In return, she held the baby out for him to take.

"Our daughter, Richard," she said softly.

He took the offered child and looked down into the angelic face, with vivid blue-green eyes and a mass of short, chestnut hair.

"She is beautiful, just like her mother," he whispered quietly, staring intently at the baby. "She is healthy?" he questioned, knowing the difficult pregnancy his wife had suffered.

"She is perfect and possesses a hearty set of lungs."

Richard smiled at this and turned to Morgan, who was waiting patiently.

"Hold out your arms, Morgan," the Duke instructed.

The boy did as he was told, and seconds later, Richard had placed the baby in them. He had been ready to turn his nose up at this, but when his eyes met the baby's, all thoughts of scorn flew out of his head, and instead, he gasped.

"Meet your sister, Morgan; Colwyn Eilwen Anghared Coltrane."

"Colwyn," he repeated softly. "Know that I will protect you always and keep you safe from harm to the best of my ability," he said seriously, almost mesmerised by the stare she was giving him. "I give you, my word."

"Bless you, Morgan. I can be at ease, knowing you will protect her," Bronwyn said solemnly. "You have no idea how much that means to me."

He tore his eyes from Colwyn's gaze, to look at his adopted mother. He could literally feel the love emanating from her, and his heart felt warmed. Even though he had lived at Inver for most of his short life, and been surrounded by love, deep down, he knew that he had also suffered hate. He had asked about his parents and both Bronwyn and Mereli had told him he would be told when he came of age, which was still a few years away. He was impatient to know, but the adults had been united and firm in their decision. The only piece of information he had was that his mother had been very young when he was born.

Morgan smiled at Bronwyn, and she immediately returned it, knowing he did not do it very often, then held out her arms, and he returned Colwyn to her.

"Come Morgan, we must let mother and baby rest now. Bronwyn, my dear, when will you be returning to your rooms?" Richard asked.

"Tomorrow, I hope. I just need to regain my strength. A decent night's sleep will do me the world of good," she replied, then whispered, "and this room is so dark! I'm dying to see the light again!"

Richard leant forward and kissed her once more. Not to be outdone, Morgan did the same.

"Come, let us celebrate, Morgan. I'll even allow you a little watered wine!"

"Really?"

Bronwyn smiled after them as they left.

"Your Grace, the wet nurse, Sarah, will arrive tomorrow, now that your daughter has been safely delivered."

"Her circumstances?"

"Widowed when with child, and unfortunately, the baby died recently."

"That is very sad."

"With no family to support her, she is grateful for this chance."

"I'm sure she is. I will see her when she arrives."

"As you wish, Your Grace. Now, will you feed your child?"

"Yes," Bronwyn replied, allowing the midwife to prepare her, and settling Colwyn on a breast.

"Now, Your Grace, be patient, the milk will only start once your daughter starts feeding, it may take a few minutes, so stay calm."

The midwife was correct, nothing was forthcoming for the first minute or so, but the suckling motion of the baby stimulated the glands and the milk started to flow.

It was a euphoric feeling, having the baby feeding, whilst she looked up at her with complete trust. Bronwyn wondered whether she should feed the child regardless, to set the bond of kinship, family, and love, but women of her station did not usually do such things; there again, Bronwyn did have the habit of not always following protocol, so she decided to ponder on this overnight.

Finally, having taken her fill, Colwyn was placed in her crib which—at Bronwyn's insistence—was placed close to her bed. She freely admitted she had hoped for a son, but the sight of her beautiful baby girl, dispelled her slight disappointment of not producing a male heir on her first attempt. Her daughter would be loved, and educated; not only in reading, writing and mathematics, but in politics, and how to be a fair and just ruler of a Duchy; just in case. It was always better to be prepared.

In Richard's private rooms, Morgan sipped his small goblet of wine as the Duke offered a toast to the new member of the family.

"So, my lad, what did you think of your new sister," he asked him.

"I will confess, I was disappointed she was not a boy; but when I saw her, so tiny and yet, so beautiful, I knew I had to protect her from that moment."

"You will make a fine knight when you are older," Richard told him. "Sir John tells me you are continuing to improve in the use of the sword, and your lance work is much better since we gave you your new horse. He is very proud of you."

Morgan's chest swelled with pride at these words. "I am planning to be the best swordsman in the Kingdom."

"And from what I hear, and have seen, I believe you can—and will be. Come, off to bed with you. Now that you are Colwyn's protector, you must ensure you get plenty of rest. It is a hard and demanding job."

The following morning, after Bronwyn had again fed her baby, Sarah, the new wet nurse arrived. The Duchess had decided that if a strange woman was to be employed to look after her daughter, she had the right to inspect her, to ensure her baby would be safe, loved and looked after. Lady Nerys, wife of one of the knights, brought the young woman to the duchess's birthing chamber, then discretely waited outside.

Sarah approached Bronwyn's bed nervously, and curtseyed, averting her eyes from the direct stare the Duchess was giving her.

Bronwyn saw she was young, perhaps just sixteen years of age, with brown hair and eyes, and a sorrowful expression.

"Sarah," the Duchess began. "Welcome to Inver Castle. Be seated." She waited until the young woman had done as she was instructed. "I am sorry that you come to us in such sad circumstances. I understand you have no family to support you now?"

"No, Your Grace, I have no one."

Bronwyn nodded, then indicated for the young woman to pick the baby up.

"This is my daughter, Colwyn. We have waited a number of years to be blessed with a child, so you can imagine, I am very protective of her."

"I understand, Your Grace. She is a beautiful baby. I will love and cherish her as if she were my own, I swear, on the graves of my husband and child."

Smiling kindly, Bronwyn studied her a fraction longer. "Very well. Please do not be offended if I visit often, I was beginning to think that I may have been barren, so I will need to keep reassuring myself this whole thing isn't a dream."

Sarah nodded. "It is your right, you will be most welcome whenever you visit, Your Grace."

"In which case, know that I fed Colwyn about an hour ago. She has her own rooms, which Lady Nerys will escort you to. You have also been allocated a room there as well."

"Thank you, Your Grace." Sarah curtseyed, as Bronwyn called for Nerys, and instructed her to escort the wet nurse to her new home.

Morgan arrived with a bunch of roses that he had stolen from the garden. He liked it there, it was peaceful and quiet and he had found himself a secret corner that he sometimes hid in when he felt the pressure growing on him too much.

"Oh, my darling, they are beautiful, thank you," she said to him, giving him a warm hug. He was pleased that she liked them.

Richard had presented her with a gold, jewel encrusted bracelet to show his love for her and the fact she had delivered to him a healthy baby.

Bronwyn fed Colwyn once a day, to help build the relationship with her child, and Sarah took care of the baby the rest of the time. The Duchess did her best not to make a nuisance of herself, but visited at least once a day, until she was more comfortable with what Sarah was doing, and trust had been established between all of them.

ଓଃ ଅଡ ଓଃ ଅଡ

Over the next few months, Morgan tried to visit Colwyn and Bronwyn every day. He even played with the child, under Sarah's watchful gaze and sung to her, and once she was able to sit up and crawl, he took her riding on his pony, much to her wet nurse's concern.

The pair seemed almost inseparable in their devotion to each other. Morgan sensed love and complete trust in her, whenever he dared to gently probe her mind.

What really amazed him was the colour of her eyes; for they had changed, now that she was older and had turned the most beautiful shade of green. They were most definitely not hazel, but emerald.

Concern had been felt when Colwyn had failed to start walking, and continued to crawl, but she had given Morgan a lovely surprise on his seventh birthday and, at the age of eighteen months, had taken her first steps. From that moment on, she followed him around like a devoted puppy.

But Bronwyn was worried; Morgan would be leaving in a few months' time, to begin his formal training for knighthood, and the Prince's protector. The parting was going to be exceedingly painful for Colwyn, who would be too young to understand what was happening and was likely to result in her flying into a temper. It had become apparent right from the very start, that she had a formidable one, even at just a few months and it was normally brought on when she did not get her way, or if she was frustrated when trying to do or solve something and it wasn't working as fast as she wanted. It was strange though, she never seemed to lose it around Morgan. He appeared to have some kind of calming effect on her, for which Bronwyn and Sarah were both very grateful for, but they wondered how they would cope once the boy left for Ellesmere.

The parting would also be hard for Morgan, who had known nothing but love whilst at Inver. He would be subjected to hate and fear when he reached Ellesmere. She had done her very best to teach him of Kadeau ways and magic under Mereli's instruction and hoped the Kadeau Duchess would be able to prepare Morgan for this next step in his life.

His aunt arrived with her son, Colin, in May, to spend a few weeks. She was pleased with Morgan's progress, and rather surprised at the level of his abilities, considering his age and the very limited amount of real Kadeau instruction he had received directly from her, and confirmed he was going to be more powerful than they first anticipated. This meant even more care would be required to ensure he stayed on the right path and did not descend towards the black arts.

She taught him the history of his people; told him of the bad things they had done in the past, and of the persecution they had suffered as a result; instilling in him the requirement to be just and honest, but also not to be taken advantage of. The Kadeau had the ear and friendship of the Cantrell royal family. This had to be maintained at all costs. Kadeau had to be the purest of heart, loyal, but also a little feared. Magic was to be used as a last resort to keep themselves and the royal family safe.

Mereli also told him about his impending role as the protector of the future King; and, if he was good enough, King's Champion; perhaps even more. She told him of his heritage, that he was a Duke, with his own castle and lands. He had tried once again to find out about his parents, but Mereli diverted his attention with a little magic of her own.

It was a lot for his young mind to take in, but he absorbed it all, filing it away for future reference, but the doubt started; his future frightened him, so he had taken himself off into his secret place in the rose garden where no one could find him—except Colwyn. She refused to leave him, sensing his uncertainty and self-doubt and hugged him as tightly as she was able, trying to make him feel better.

After an hour or so, he felt he was back under control. Colwyn sensed his change of mood and kissed his cheek. "Better now," she said in her limited vocabulary.

"Yes, thank you, Colwyn." He hugged her back. "Come on, we'd better return before everyone gets worried."

They crawled from their hiding place and returned to the keep.

Morgan practiced his magic with Colin during the weeks of their stay, and once his aunt and cousin left, he entertained Colwyn with some new tricks, making her laugh and clap her hands in delight, and sung a lullaby to her when she was put to bed for the evening.

Then, before he knew it, July had arrived, and he found himself selecting clothes to be packed. Joining the royal household, he would also be issued with livery, that he would wear whilst learning his craft, until he was knighted at the age of sixteen.

Richard, Sir John MacKenzie, and a small guard escorted him to Ellesmere.

Morgan had hugged Bronwyn tightly and she had done the same to him. He felt her sorrow at his having to leave and was warmed once again by her love.

"Know that you will always be welcome here," she whispered in his ear. "Even when you are Duke of Rossmere, I hope you will still continue to visit and stay when you are able."

He had swallowed hard at that point, then he had hugged Colwyn. She knew something was happening but was unsure what. She could feel the tension in the air and refused to let go of him. That had almost broken his composure, until he saw Richard look at him. He gulped, took a huge breath, and finally managed to free himself of her arms.

Slowly he turned and walked towards his pony.

"Morgan! Morgan!" she shouted, sounding desperate.

He knew in that instant she was going to fly into one of her tantrums and acted quickly.

I love you! He sent back to her in his mind. *I will come back, I promise! I will write! Please stay calm for me. Calm... Colwyn, please.*

He felt the tears prick his eyes at her heartfelt cries, which had gradually faded as they left Inver Castle, but he sensed she had done as he asked and remained relatively calm but deeply upset.

Richard glanced at the boy as they travelled, and saw him sitting straight in the saddle, the expression on his face carefully neutral and unreadable.

"Well done, Morgan," he said quietly to him. "I know the parting was difficult, but you handled it. During your life, many challenging things will be asked of you. That is the way of things. How you deal with them shows the measure of you as a man. That was your first challenge."

The boy looked up at him and nodded in understanding. "Am I... am I permitted to write letters?" he asked tentatively.

"Of course, you are. In fact, we are all looking forward to hearing about your progress in them; and we in turn will write to you."

They arrived at Ellesmere six days later. Morgan was initially totally overawed by the sheer presence of the castle; its size, its elegance, far out stripped Inver, with its white dolomite walls and its eight towers giving it a clear view of the land in all directions. The moat had been created by creating a cut-off from the river, and a second ditch had been dug to provide two barriers to any attacking force. The castle itself was perched high atop of the hill above the river, which made it truly imposing, as if it were surveying the entire kingdom of Devonmere.

On arrival, they were summoned by the King to the throne room, where he and the young Prince Stuart were waiting.

Richard and Morgan bowed respectfully before King Rhisart and the Prince.

"Arise Duke Richard, Lord Morgan," Rhisart said, his deep voice resonating around the room.

Morgan dared to look at his King, and saw the tall, imposing figure with black, shoulder-length hair, just beginning to grey at the temples, the short beard and deep brown piercing eyes. He quickly averted them as the King rose from the throne and walked down the steps towards them.

"So, this is the young Morgan," he said conversationally, and glanced at his son. "What do you think Stuart? Will he do?"

The young Prince joined his father and scrutinized the golden-haired, grey-eyed boy.

"I believe he will, father."

"He's certainly looking a lot better than when I last saw him." He looked at Richard. "There have been no lingering after effects since that incident?" he questioned.

"None Sire. Mereli McLeod has confirmed he is likely to be extremely powerful. She has been teaching him and telling him about his heritage and what will be expected of him."

Morgan glanced up at the King again, then across to the Prince. He found it unnerving to be spoken about as if he were invisible and totally ignored; his eyes flashed a silvery grey in annoyance, but there was also a question in them.

Stuart saw the look and smiled kindly at him.

"Morgan, welcome to Ellesmere."

"Thank you, Prince Stuart," he responded quietly. "May I... may I ask a question please?"

"What is it you wish to ask?" Stuart queried.

"What incident?"

Rhisart raised his eyebrows.

"He doesn't know?" he asked Richard.

"No Sire. He will be told when he reaches the age of ten, when he will be old enough to fully understand the implications, and be adult enough not to seek revenge, or drift into dark magic."

"I'm old enough now!" Morgan retorted. "I have a right to know!"

Rhisart turned his dark gaze on the boy. If the King had expected him to back down and avert his eyes, he was going to be disappointed.

"Morgan!" Richard snapped sharply. "Forgive him Sire, it is his first time at court; we have had a long journey, and he is overtired."

Stuart re-appraised the child and smiled inwardly. He had spirit, that was obvious, and it heartened him to know that his future protector seemed almost fearless, even at just seven years of age. He spoke up before the King could respond.

"Father, I will take Morgan now, with your permission of course."

"Yes, take him. I need to speak to Richard privately about another matter."

"Yes Sire," Richard responded. "If you will grant me a few minutes to say goodbye."

"Of course."

Richard placed a hand on Morgan's shoulder.

"Morgan, I know you will make us all proud of your achievements. Please write and tell us how you are getting on. Colwyn and your mother will love to hear from you." He ruffled the golden hair affectionately. "Be brave, be respectful, be just and fair—even though those around you may not be. Never lower yourself to their level, as it could lead you down a dark path, and yours is to be one of light."

He then hugged him, and Morgan felt the love of a father.

"I will do what you say, Papa. I would never wish to bring shame or disgrace to you, especially after you have taken me into your home and shown me nothing but love."

"Good lad. I know I can count on you."

"Come with me, Morgan, I will escort you to your rooms. As my future protector, you have been allocated rooms next to mine." Once out of ear shot, Stuart added, "I hope we will become good friends as well."

"But you are the future King," Morgan replied.

"May be, but even a King needs friends he can trust."

"I would be honoured to be your friend."

Morgan scrutinized the Prince. He wasn't at all as he expected a member of the royal family to be. Stuart took after his father in looks and colouring, but his eyes were hazel, and seemed to change colour depending on how the light struck them. He was tall and regal in stature, but at the same time, gave a feeling of openness that put the boy very much at ease.

Stuart grinned at him. He may have been ten years older than Morgan, but he instinctively liked the boy. The Cantrells were not Kadeau but were trained and exhibited some magic. Stuart was particularly astute when it came to judging people, and it struck him that Morgan was completely trustworthy, but far too serious for his age. He knew what had happened to him as a baby; that his father had saved Morgan's life and placed him under the protection of the Duke of Invermere who, it seemed, had done a fine job of raising him, so far.

They reached the rooms that were to be Morgan's home for the next nine years. Stuart looked on as the boy explored his new home.

"We need to get you your livery," Stuart told him, "And I will introduce you to your personal steward. You are a Duke, although not officially recognised yet, but you have been allocated a steward as befitting your station. He's waiting downstairs to gather clothes and equipment." The prince studied him critically. "I believe you are a little tall for your age, come."

"But you are a Prince," Morgan whispered. "You should not be guiding me about the castle."

"True, but we need to get to know one another. Our lives are now entwined, and we are dependent on each other. My life may well be in your hands in a few years."

Morgan gulped as the realisation hit him. Up until that point, it had all been just words, but now, hearing them from Prince Stuart, seemed to bring his situation right to the fore.

"Who protects you now?" Morgan asked.

"Trahaearn, the King's Champion. You will meet him tomorrow to begin your training. Duke Richard has been praising you regarding your ability with the sword. We shall practice together; as we need to know how we both perform and move, should we ever be in the situation where our lives really do depend on each other."

As they walked out into the corridor, a younger version of Stuart came from around the corner, moving in a rather hasty fashion. He skidded to a halt in front of them.

"Stuart," he began and shifted his gaze to the boy at his side.

"This is the future Duke of Rossmere, Morgan Bodine," Stuart informed him, then turned to Morgan. "Morgan, this is my younger brother, Prince Michael."

"Your Highness," Morgan replied bowing.

"Welcome, Morgan. I do hope you enjoy your time with us. If my brother is too much of a bully, tell me and I will sort him out!"

Morgan could tell, by the cheeky grin on Michael's face, that he was teasing him slightly but could sense it was all in good fun and not malicious in any way.

"Forgive my brother," Stuart said, smirking slightly. "He still has to grow up and act as befits his station!"

Michael simply laughed and sauntered off to continue on his original quest.

"See you at supper!" he called, as he disappeared into a room further along the corridor.

The rest of their walk continued in silence, as Morgan absorbed the news about him practicing his skills with Stuart. He was beginning to grasp the concept of relationships in battle and believed he understood what the Prince was saying to him.

Below, he was provided with Ellesmere livery, a sword, shield, armour and a lance. As Stuart has stated, Morgan was slightly taller than average, and some adjustment to his clothing would hastily be required.

His personal steward was presented to him. Ioan was nineteen. He was of average height and slight build, his dark hair cropped short. He had kind, brown eyes and a calm demeanour. He could not be called handsome, but his features were not unpleasant. Not fit enough for knightly duties, he still wanted to be within the castle, and Stuart had personally selected him. Ioan was not averse to the Kadeau; Stuart had carefully probed his mind and was satisfied at what he sensed and felt. The boy would be safe in his hands.

Ioan accompanied them back to Morgan's rooms, his arms laden with his livery and other accoutrements he would need going forward. His first task was to adjust the length of sleeves of various pieces of clothing that the boy would be wearing.

For today, Morgan was being allowed to settle in, and his training would begin in earnest, the following morning.

That night, as he prepared for bed, he decided to question Ioan about his past.

"Ioan," Morgan began, as he settled into the huge four poster bed. "Do you know what happened to my parents?"

"Why yes, of course, Your Grace. Your father, the Duke, was killed in battle, shortly after you were born, I believe. I was but a boy at the time, but King Rhisart said your father had won him the day. He was grieved at the loss."

"I see... and my mother?"

"She was very young when you were born; some say that perhaps she had been too young to be with child, but I did hear a rumour that she had in fact been poisoned—as you were."

"Me? Poisoned? Why?"

"Because of what you are, my Lord; Kadeau. I heard the King managed to save you, but unfortunately not your mother, the Duchess Eirian. Your wet nurse was executed by order of the King, and you were sent to Invermere to be raised by the Duke and Duchess. My Lord, did you not know these facts?"

Morgan thought furiously. "Y-yes Ioan, I just wondered if it was common knowledge," he finally said.

"It is not widely known, Your Grace."

"She must have hated my mother and me very much."

"Some say her family suffered in the past, during the Reign of Terror, and wished for revenge."

"My people did do some terrible things, I know... but then, so did—"

"Alas, 'tis all true. For some, the hate runs deep." Ioan glanced at the young boy, who suddenly seemed rather subdued. "Have no fear, my Lord, whilst I am with you, I will help keep you safe. You are but an innocent child, and it is wrong to seek vengeance on the innocent."

"Thank you, Ioan, that means a great deal to me. I have known only love at Inver, but my senses tell me I am about to find out about the hate." He stopped and looked up at his steward.

"The Prince and I will protect you. Now sleep, you have much to learn, starting tomorrow!"

Ioan tucked him in, then smiled reassuringly and left, leaving Morgan with this new knowledge.

He unexpectedly felt very small and alone in his strange new bed, in an equally strange room and castle, and wished with all his heart that Bronwyn would suddenly appear, to give him a hug, and take away all his fears; but she was many miles away, as was Richard. He was on his own and felt like crying. Suddenly he felt very homesick.

᎒ Ꮛ ᎒ Ꮛ

Chapter Five

Morgan's education and training began in earnest the next day, and it was very hard work. In the mornings he studied, improving his reading, writing and mathematics; but on top of that was history, politics and even languages.

The afternoons were taken up with his duties practicing swordsmanship, horsemanship and even battle strategy. Within the first day, his ability with the sword was recognised and special tuition arranged. In between all of this, he accompanied the Prince, ran errands for him, and was educated in court etiquette and manners. He also had to find the time to hone his Kadeau powers with Trahaearn, the King's Champion, who he was introduced to on his first day after arriving at the castle.

Trahaearn was more the King's age, which at Morgan's tender years, seemed ancient! However, he was extremely experienced, and knowledgeable, so the young Duke expected to learn a great deal from him, not just in regard technical fighting skills, but also in relation to Kadeau magic.

The days were long and exhausting. Many a night in the first few weeks, Ioan found his charge half undressed, collapsed on his bed, often at peculiar angles. With infinite care, he had continued the task and put the child to bed, properly.

So far, Morgan had been kept so busy, he had not noticed any hostile attitude towards him; but gradually, as his mind and body adjusted to the new regime, he became aware of a faction within the pages and squires, who were definitely anti-Kadeau. Considering they were training within a castle where his kind had favour with the King, it seemed totally illogical to Morgan.

He was to remember Richard's parting words and quote them to himself many a time over the next few weeks. Ioan tried to help as best he could, but he was not a Kadeau and did not understand. Trahaearn was of more assistance, offering advice and guidance, teaching him the art of mental discipline that he would need in his life. It was at this time, that Morgan began to cultivate a slightly sinister air. Serious at the best of times, he became even more so, and his grey eyes were often silver or transparent and tended to unnerve those around him.

Stuart, Ioan and Trahaearn recognised what he was doing, and did their best to make him feel comfortable in his surroundings; but Morgan grew to be a boy of few words, and he began a careful study of people; their gestures, habits, those tale-tell signs that indicated their mood, or if they were uneasy, frightened or even lying.

Morgan also listened—a lot—and practiced his art under the supervision of Trahaearn, or on his own, somewhere quiet, out of view.

With everything going on in his life, the arrival of a letter from Inver suddenly reminded him that he had not written home. That evening, after Stuart had dismissed him from his duties, he returned to his room to read it.

My dearest Morgan

We grow worried at not hearing from you since you arrived in Ellesmere. We all miss you very much, especially Colwyn, who asks after you every day. We all hope you are beginning to settle in now, and that you are learning the craft that will make you a King's Champion, and a just ruler of your Duchy when you are older.

Please do write soon, we long to hear from you; what you have been up to; to know that you are safe and well and enjoying your new life. We hope you still believe that you are loved and cherished.

Bronwyn, Richard and Colwyn.

Even though it was just a short letter, he could feel the love within the words. Tears crept into his eyes, and one escaped when he saw the extremely unsteady meandering scribble that was clearly Colwyn's attempt at writing her name. It was totally unintelligible, but the fact that she had even attempted it made him smile and feel very homesick again.

In bed that night, he dared to reach out with his mind to see if he could reach hers. He managed it, after a fashion, for she was still a very young child, and sleeping.

The following morning, just before his studies were due to start, he made his way to the library, to see what was available to him, regarding Kadeau magic, history and even fantasy. Noting where these books were stored, he went to class.

The faction of Kadeau haters were in full voice before their scholar arrived. Morgan did his best to ignore them, but when they accused him of being afraid, he knew he could not let that pass unchallenged.

He stood up and drew himself to his full height. A couple of his accusers were older and taller, but that did not deter him. With the best malevolent gaze he could muster, he stared long and hard at the so-called leader of the group and spoke softly, but menacingly.

"Do you really wish to make an enemy of me, knowing what I am and what I am capable of?" he asked, his eyes almost transparent. "I caution you not to anger me." He raised his hand and began to whisper something when the scholar entered.

Morgan continued to raise his hand to his head in a fluid movement and pushed a lock of hair out of his eyes, smiling, as he saw the ringleader swallow nervously and hastily sit down. Morgan smoothed his tunic and also sat, leaving the scholar none the wiser as to what had almost occurred.

His desk partner leant towards him. "Morgan," Cuthbert whispered, "you weren't really going to cast a spell on him, were you?"

"No; but he doesn't know that!"

Cuthbert grinned at him, before returning his attention to what the scholar was saying.

The afternoon did not improve. Following some strenuous sword play and lance practice, Morgan was cornered in the stable.

Owain, the ringleader of the little group, blocked his escape. He was nine years older than Morgan and over a foot taller.

"You may be favoured by the Cantrell family, Kadeau, but they aren't here to protect you. My ancestors were tortured by your kind."

"I can't be blamed for what happened hundreds of years ago," Morgan replied, preparing himself for the inevitable battle.

"You're Kadeau, that's the only excuse I need," Owain retorted. He turned to one of his cohorts. "Taylor, go keep watch. I don't want to be interrupted."

"But Owain, I—"

"Do as you're told, or you'll get the same as this Kadeau brat is going to receive. Go!" He watched Taylor take up his post at the entrance, then turned to Morgan. "I'm going to enjoy this!"

Morgan had not been taught how to wrestle. It was a commoners' sport; and not something royalty engaged in; but he had seen it and tried his best. He even managed to land some blows and made Owain's nose bleed, which incensed the youth, and he laid into the young Kadeau with everything he had. Morgan fought bravely, and well, considering his disadvantage in age, weight, and height. His spirit would not allow him to give in, and he dragged himself to his feet once again to face his opponent; cut, bruised and bleeding.

"Stay down Morgan!" one of the youths shouted. "Owain, he's had enough, stop!"

"He's still getting to his feet!" Owain retorted, as he swung again.

Morgan managed to duck and kick out, knocking Owain back, to land on his backside in the straw.

Oliver, who had been the one pleading with Morgan to stay down, gave a gasp, and was now seriously worried, and for good reason.

"Hold him!" Owain shouted to his companions, and a couple stepped forward and managed to grab Morgan's arms. "Oh, you're going to pay for that!" he spat, as he got up from his undignified position on the floor.

Oliver worked his way back, out of the way and sidled towards the side door of the stable. The beating had gone far enough, but he knew he would not be able to stop Owain on his own, so he slipped out without being seen. Desperately he looked around for someone— anyone—who would be willing to help the Kadeau. He ran towards the keep, and suddenly saw a rather angry Prince Stuart heading roughly in his direction, Trahaearn following behind.

Stuart spotted him.

"You! Boy! Come here!"

Oliver did as he was told.

"Have you seen Morgan? He should have reported to me some time ago."

Forgetting all etiquette, Oliver launched into his plea.

"Prince Stuart! Please help! Morgan is in the stable, being set upon by some squires! Please hurry, I don't think he can take much more!"

79

The lack of etiquette was forgotten as both Stuart and Trahaearn broke into a run, followed by Oliver.

Taylor saw them coming and shouted a warning. Owain hit the now unconscious Morgan a final time, nodded at his companions, who let go of their prisoner, and they all fled via the side door.

Stuart burst through the main door, pushing it back.

"Morgan! Morgan!"

There was no response.

"Back here, Your Highness," Oliver said, running past them to the rear of the stable.

The two men followed him, and Stuart initially skidded to a halt, seeing the crumpled figure laying in the straw.

"Morgan!" Stuart knelt beside him and went to pull him into his arms, but Trahaearn stayed his hands.

"My Prince, best check for broken bones before moving him."

Stuart froze, as Trahaearn carefully felt Morgan's limbs and nodded in satisfaction.

"Nothing broken, your highness."

The Prince let go of the breath he had been holding, and gently turned the boy over, his expression hardening as he saw the blood and vivid bruises already forming. Morgan had been well and truly beaten, but, by the state of his bloodied knuckles; so, had his opponent.

"Who did this?" Stuart demanded of Oliver.

The young page shook his head. He seemed to be more frightened of the other boys than of his future King.

Stuart nodded at Trahaearn, who acknowledged the signal and took hold of Oliver's hands and stared hard at him. The boy's eyes widened, then his face went totally blank. Trahaearn probed his young mind and easily obtained the information he sought. He released the boy who blinked a number of times and did not remember a thing of the past couple of minutes.

"You may leave us," Stuart ordered.

Oliver bobbed his head in respect and ran for his life.

"Who was it?" the prince asked, looking at Trahaearn.

"Owain Prescott."

Stuart nodded. "Find Master Stephen and tell him to come to Morgan's quarters immediately."

"At once, Your Highness." Trahaearn nodded respectfully, got to his feet, and left the stable.

Stuart looked down at the bruised and bloodied face of his future protector.

"For now, young Morgan, it is I who must protect you, and I apologise, for I have failed you. It will not happen again."

Carefully, he got to his feet, cradling the still unconscious Morgan in his arms, exited the stable and strode back to the keep.

People stared as he walked past with the limp form in his arms; initially thinking the child was dead, as his arms swung freely; his head back.

As he reached the Kadeau's rooms, Morgan began to stir, moaning softly.

"Shush," Stuart said softly. "You're safe now." He walked in to find a white-faced Ioan, Trahaearn, and Master Stephen—Stuart's battle surgeon—waiting.

Ioan pulled back the covers on the bed, quickly fetched some water that was heating over a small fire, and placed it on the bedside table, before beginning to undress his charge. Trahaearn went to assist him, but Stuart stopped him.

"I'll help," was all he said.

"But my Prince—"

"I'll do it!"

Together, Ioan and Stuart stripped him, and Master Stephen saw to the wounds, bruises, and generally cleaned him up, before pulling the covers up over him.

Morgan's eyelids flickered; he frowned, moaned, and slowly opened his eyes, to find four worried faces staring at him.

Seeing that one was the Prince, he attempted to get up to show respect, but found he was unable to do so, and a gasp forced its way past his lips.

"Don't move, Morgan," Master Stephen said softly. "You've had a severe beating."

"I will see that your attackers are severely punished," Stuart said.

"P - please d-don't," Morgan whispered.

"This action cannot go unpunished."

"I - I will deal with it," Morgan replied softly. "It is my battle to win."

"Morgan, Owain is nine years older than you, a lot taller, heavier and more experienced," Trahaearn said.

"Father told me that life often isn't fair or just, and that I must learn to fight my own battles. How I handle the challenges set before me, will identify how I am measured as a man...I...I guess I will just have to start earlier than I anticipated."

Stuart's expression softened, and his heart wrenched at the words the boy had spoken.

"Such a wise head on those young shoulders," he said, as Morgan stared up at him from his bed. The Prince took a deep breath. "Very well Morgan, we shall do as you ask but..." and he stared hard at him to make his next words very clear. "...if it gets out of hand, I will intervene; understood?"

Morgan nodded slowly.

"If you please, my Prince, I think that is enough talking for now. The boy must rest," Master Stephen interrupted.

"Very well. Light duties only for the next day or so," Stuart replied. "Next week, you will practice the sword with me."

Morgan nodded, but he was finding it increasingly difficult to keep his eyes open.

"Sleep, young Morgan. When you awake, I shall feed you some rich broth," Ioan said quietly, tucking him in.

Stuart nodded in satisfaction and left, deep in thought. He was loath to leave the situation as it was, but he also wanted to respect Morgan's request. He was buried so deep in his contemplation he did not hear his father calling him.

"Stuart!"

The firm voice finally broke through his reverie, and he turned to see his father striding purposefully towards him.

"Sire," he said respectfully, bowing. "I apologise, I was elsewhere with my thoughts."

"So I saw. It wasn't perchance related to your young protector, was it?"

Stuart's eyebrows rose. News certainly travelled fast in this castle.

"How did you know?" he finally asked his father.

"The heir to the throne of Devonmere, walking across a main thoroughfare with a young boy's body in his arms, is not commonplace. He is still alive, I take it?"

"Yes father. It was a severe beating, but fortunately, nothing was broken."

"What action is being taken?"

"Young Morgan has requested to take care of the situation himself."

King Rhisart frowned. "I will not tolerate such actions in this castle, Stuart. I expect all my subjects to be safe here. What concerns me more, however, is my choice of protector for you. Do you wish me to find another? If Morgan cannot defend himself, how can I expect him to protect you?"

"Sire, Morgan is but seven. His attacker is sixteen and to be knighted at the next ceremony."

"What!" Anger flashed in Rhisart's dark eyes. "I'll not have a knight within these walls who acts without honour. Who was it?"

"Owain Prescott."

Rhisart took a deep breath. "I realise his family were almost wiped out by the Kadeau Reign of Terror, but that was generations ago. I will send for him."

"Sire, what do you plan to do, if I may ask?"

"He will be sent home. There will be no knighting."

"With respect, if you do that, you will simply add fuel to the fire; Morgan has said he will deal with it."

"He's too young to settle this matter."

"It will bring disgrace to both sides, Sire; to the Prescott family and to the Duke of Rossmere; people will say that others fight his battles for him."

"He is a child and not yet formally recognised as Duke; and how will it look if I allow the beating of the boy to go unpunished?"

Stuart opened his mouth and promptly shut it again. No matter what decision was made; it would offend someone. At the end of the day, Rhisart was King, and what he said, or ordered, was the law.

The King spied a page walking towards them along the corridor and beckoned him over.

"Find Owain Prescott and bring him to the throne room, immediately."

"Yes Sire." The page bowed and ran off down the corridor.

"You are welcome to join me, Stuart."

The young Prince decided he'd better be present, so he could at least jump to Morgan's defence, if required.

They walked in silence, and Stuart stood by his father's side as the King sat down on the throne.

A few minutes later, a rather pale-faced Owain entered, approached the throne and bowed somewhat nervously.

"Sire," he said, his voice shaking slightly.

"Owain, is there anything you wish to tell me?" Rhisart asked the squire, fixing him with an unblinking stare, noting the cut lip, black eye and bruised knuckles, and acknowledged that Morgan had conducted himself with honour in managing to inflict some damage on a youth that was several years his senior. "Think carefully, before you answer," he added as a warning.

The squire opened his mouth and abruptly shut it again. The King could almost see the wheels turning in his brain as he fought for the right words. For a mere second, Stuart almost took pity on him, then remembered the state Morgan had been left in, and decided to add his own glare of displeasure.

Owain swallowed slowly and decided to confess.

"For – forgive me Sire, I have acted in an unknightly fashion."

He stopped and Rhisart waited. The silence that followed was almost deafening.

"Well?" he finally prompted the squire.

"I...I attacked a page."

"Attacked?"

"I...my family were persecuted by the Kadeau!"

"And was it this particular Kadeau that did the deed?"

"No, of course not, Sire, it was done hundreds of years ago."

"But you thought to seek revenge on an innocent child?"

"He is Kadeau! The Kadeau are not innocent!"

"All are welcome within the walls of Ellesmere. The Kadeau have favour with the house of Cantrell."

"I forgot myself."

"I see no remorse in your eyes, for what you have done to the child."

"I'm sorry, I shouldn't have done it," Owain responded, but it sounded far from sincere.

"I expect everyone within these walls to be safe. You have shown that my words are meaningless to others. That cannot go unpunished. As long as the Cantrells rule this Kingdom, all, including the Kadeau are welcome here."

"Sire, what is my punishment?"

"I plan to send you home."

"After the knighting ceremony?"

"You expect me to knight you after your conduct?"

"But I will bring disgrace on my family."

"You should have thought of that before your dishonourable behaviour today. You will leave first thing in the morning."

"Please, Sire, my family. I beg you, please reconsider!"

"My word is my oath. You will leave in the morning."

Owain's face looked stricken, then the anger came forth.

"Know this then, Rhisart Cantrell, your rule will end shortly. The Cantrells will be overthrown, the Kadeau executed, and I vow to help this happen with every breath in my body!"

"Hold your tongue!" Rhisart spat. "One more word and it is you who will be executed for your treasonous remarks!"

The young squire turned almost purple in his rage and flew towards the King, drawing the small dagger that hung at his belt. Owain made it as far as the bottom step to the dais before Stuart drew his sword and stopped him dead with the blade pointing at his throat.

Knowing he had now gone too far to ever be forgiven, and seeing Rhisart's guards approaching quickly from their positions, Owain gave a final cry and lunged, and Stuart's sword cut into his neck.

A scarlet ribbon of blood arched out from the wound creating an ever-increasing pool on the stone floor. Owain desperately clutched at his neck and coughed, choking on the blood in his throat, the horrible bubbling sound of him struggling to breathe filled the vast room as he staggered a couple of steps closer to the King, dropped his small dagger and slowly collapsed, his body giving a final couple of twitches as the life left his form. The brown eyes, stared, unseeing, the light slowly fading from them as death took hold.

Stuart looked at his bloodstained sword, then to his father.

"I – I'm sorry father, I – I didn't expect him to lunge onto my sword. I was aiming to just wound him..."

"What's done is done," Rhisart said remarkably calmly. "It was not your fault, Stuart. The boy did this to himself."

"But Owain's family is a powerful one. They rule the Marches, I may well have started a war!"

"War was coming anyway," Rhisart said heavily. "The Marches and Prescott's supporters have been planning to try and overthrow the Cantrells for years. This incident will bring it to the fore. Probably for the better."

"How can you stay so calm?" Stuart demanded. He was still shaken by what he had done.

"Because I am older, wiser, and know the situation within the kingdom. If it hadn't been this event, it would have been another. I know the Prescott's have a supporter in Cottesmere."

"But that borders Rossmere—"

"Exactly, and our fledgling Duke is as yet too young to be recognised in that title. Stuart, war is coming whether we like it or not. Perhaps this unfortunate incident will force their hand when they are not quite prepared for it. I have been planning for such a situation for the last year or so."

"But you haven't said anything."

"No, I did not want to alarm you." Rhisart paused as a couple of stewards entered to take the body away. He motioned for them to carry on with their duties, then continued. "I will send a messenger to Owain's father in the Eastern Marches, and we shall see what the response is. I suspect the worst. Leave me for now, Stuart, I need to send messages to my supporters, and arrange for the boy's body to be returned to his father. I will send for you when I have made my decisions regarding the next steps. In the meantime, you need to concentrate on Morgan's training. He needs to be prepared."

"He's too young to go to war, surely."

"Yes, he is, but he will need to accompany you regardless."

"Very well, father."

Stuart bowed and left. The Prince felt extremely guilty about what he had done to the squire, but it had been a purely instinctive reaction, to protect his King and father.

Rhisart watched him go, knowing what his son was feeling, then went to his private rooms. He had messages to pen to call his supporters to arms, just in case, as well as a very difficult message to write to the Prescott family.

He chose the words he wrote to the family with great care, informing them of the death of their son, and that his body was being prepared for the journey home and used wax to seal the contents. That task complete, he sent for a messenger, who would travel to the Eastern Marches and deliver it.

When the messenger arrived, he gave him instructions to deliver the message into the hands of Arnell Prescott himself, and also to be careful whilst he was there. The messenger was to return with any reply that the Duke of the Eastern Marches penned.

With a heavy heart, Rhisart prepared the message for the call to arms, and listed the duchies it would be delivered to. It was a warning that their support may be required if Arnell Prescott declared war. Beacons displaying red coloured fire would be lit across the kingdom if this were the case, and his supporters would travel to Ellesmere as soon as possible.

Once the messages had been scribed, and the King had placed his seal upon them, messengers were sent for.

They arrived several minutes later, dressed and ready for their journeys. One headed south-west to Invermere, another west-south-west, to Rossmere, one south to Kenneth Dernley, the Duke of Strathmere, and another north, to Morgan's uncle, Rodric McLeod, Duke of the High Meres.

Prescott would be able to call upon his supporters north-west in Stallesmere and the Duke of Cottesmere.

All they could do now was wait, and plan for the worst.

ଓଃ ଙ ଓଃ ଙ

Chapter Six

———◆———

M organ slept through the night, blissfully unaware of what had happened in the throne room. The following morning, he awoke, finding it extremely painful to move. Every muscle he possessed seemed to either ache or be very tender. A grimace and sharp exclamation were forced from his lips and Ioan rushed into his bedchamber.

"My Lord, you are in pain. Shall I summon Master Stephen?" his steward asked, concerned.

Morgan shook his head.

"No, Ioan. I'll be all right in a moment. I was caught off guard." He gave another grimace as he pulled himself into a sitting position.

Immediately, his steward fluffed up the pillows behind him to make him more comfortable.

"Perhaps you should stay in bed today," he suggested.

"I think, if I do that, I won't be able to move at all, I can feel myself stiffening up."

"Then let me fetch you a hearty breakfast and I will assist you to rise and dress."

"I really don't feel that hungry, Ioan."

"Nonsense! It will do you good to get something in you. You haven't eaten since noon yesterday. Now just lie there and relax, I will return shortly."

Ioan bowed, and left, and Morgan did as he suggested, closed his eyes and relaxed.

A number of minutes passed and there was a knock on the bedchamber door.

"Come in Ioan," Morgan called, his eyes still shut.

"And how is my protector this morning?" a deep and very familiar voice asked.

Morgan's eyes flew open to behold the sight of his Prince approaching his bedside.

"Your Highness!" He attempted to rise, but battered and badly bruised muscles protested vehemently, and his breath hissed from between clenched teeth.

"Morgan! Don't move!" Stuart commanded. "My battle surgeon will be here shortly to tend to you. I don't believe you're even fit for light duties today, and perhaps should stay in bed."

"But I feel I'm beginning to stiffen up. If I stay here, I won't be able to move at all tomorrow!"

"Let us see what Master Stephen says. In the meantime, can I get you anything? A book, some fruit?"

"No, I..." Morgan suddenly stopped. If he was going to be ordered to stay in bed, then he could make use of the time by doing some reading. "Would you mind...I mean, is it all right if I ask Ioan to go and get some books from the library?"

"Do you know what titles you want?" Stuart asked.

"Yes. I've written them down, there's a small piece of parchment on my writing desk."

Stuart moved to where the boy had indicated and quickly located the parchment. He read it and his eyebrows rose in surprise.

"You want these?" he questioned.

"If I may."

"I will fetch them. One of these is in the restricted section, so Ioan would not be able to go in there." Stuart put the parchment in his jacket pocket. "So, you are going to read up on Kadeau magic."

"Yes. Everyone keeps on saying I'm going to be powerful, but it's all I can do, to conjure up the blue fire-light. I seem to be very weak. I thought if I did some reading, it might help more, and Sir Trahaearn would not be so displeased with my efforts."

"Is he being hard on you?"

"A little, but he has to be, otherwise I won't be ready to be your protector when I am knighted."

"In which case, I will get the books, and if you like, you can practice some of your techniques on me."

"But suppose I... I get something wrong?"

"You had better make sure you do not!"

Stuart sobered, suddenly thinking, things have already gone terribly wrong, and Morgan picked up on it immediately.

"What is it? What's wrong?"

"I will tell you later," Stuart said heavily.

"No, Your Highness, now. I can sense something is not right."

"You can?"

Morgan nodded.

"May I?" Stuart asked, indicating the child's bedside. Morgan nodded again, and the Prince sat down. He seemed at a loss for words, or searching for the correct ones, and was silent for what seemed like an aeon.

"Something's happened, hasn't it?"

"You are indeed perceptive." Stuart sighed again. "It's about Owain Prescott."

"I said I would take care of it," Morgan interrupted.

"I'm afraid you can't, my friend."

The boy frowned. "What do you mean?"

"The King sent for him yesterday after we all left you and...well to cut to the end, he threatened my father, drew a knife, attacked and I... killed him," Stuart finished quietly.

Morgan's eyes widened and his mouthed 'oh', was never uttered.

"Y-your Highness, I-I'm sorry. This is my fault."

"No, it's not! It's Owain Prescott's fault!" Stuart snapped more sharply than intended. He was still very angry at himself for not wounding the squire. "Morgan, I may have just plunged us into war!"

"What...what did the King say?"

"He said it wasn't my fault; that war was coming anyway, this... unfortunate incident may be the trigger, but by pushing our enemies earlier, they may not be ready for it, which will give us the advantage."

"What happens now?"

"The King has dispatched messengers to our supporters, and one to the Eastern Marches. Owain's body is being prepared so it can be returned to his family."

"I – I will fight by your side," Morgan said gallantly, but Stuart shook his head.

"You will be coming with me, but you will not fight. You are too young and inexperienced still, but I will need your help."

"You may ask anything of me."

"I had hoped to spare you this until you were older. The sights of war are not meant for those of your age. You may be subjected to some horrendous scenes. I will do my best to shield you, but..."

Morgan dared to lay a hand on Stuart's arm.

"We will get through this together, for as you said, our lives are now entwined."

Stuart nodded and gave him a weak smile.

"You must not dwell on this, Morgan. What's done is done. It wasn't your fault. Now you must rest and get well."

"How long do you think we have before..."

"I honestly don't know. Both sides will need time to muster their forces. We shall have to wait and see, but we shall be prepared, have no fear."

The conversation got no further, as Master Stephen arrived on the scene. Stuart stood back out of the way, as the surgeon applied witch hazel to the bruises, and thoroughly checked the boy over, noting the responses to his skilled touch.

"Mmmmm," he finally said. "I recommend you stay in bed, at least for the morning. Then, if you can manage it, get up and move around a little each hour. I will leave this witch hazel for Ioan to apply to your bruises. It will help to bring them out faster. Now, can you see all right? That left eye is rather swollen."

"Yes, I can see," Morgan responded.

"Very well." Stephen mixed a potion in some watered wine. "Drink this," he ordered.

Morgan eyed it suspiciously.

"What is it?"

"Something to ease the pain, and help you relax. I am not going to poison you, young Morgan! You can trust me, after all, I am Prince Stuart's battle surgeon!"

Morgan did as he was told.

"Now, have you eaten this morning?"

"Ioan is just bringing me something."

"Good. Get that down you, then relax for the morning and I will come back at noon to see how you are and help get you out of bed."

"Thank you."

Stephen packed up his bag of medical supplies and stood up, bowing to his Prince.

"Your Highness."

"Thank you, Stephen," Stuart answered, and then stepped forward to touch Morgan's shoulder. "Rest, and that is my order. I will return shortly with your requested books." He smiled, then left.

Morgan had no time to digest all the information, as Ioan came back with his breakfast. The boy had totally lost his appetite now, and simply picked at his food.

"What ails you, My Lord?" Ioan asked him, concerned.

"Have you heard the news...about Owain Prescott?"

"I heard when I went down to the kitchens. It's all over the castle, that he threatened and attacked the King, and Prince Stuart killed him. 'Tis a bad business indeed, but unrest has been growing for a number of years, or so they say. The King is mustering his supporters."

"I know. Ioan, is it...is it cowardly to be scared?"

"Oh no, My Lord. 'Tis not cowardly at all, it is perfectly natural. It's how you conduct yourself that shows your measure."

"I'm...scared, Ioan."

"That is understandable, My Lord. We shall look after one another, never fear. Now, eat that breakfast and rest!"

Morgan did as he was told. Stuart returned at noon with the requested books for him to read, and Master Stephen arrived to check on how he was feeling.

Ioan helped him wash and dress, and the Prince assisted the boy to walk around his rooms, then insisted he at least sit down, and make use of his time to start reading the books. Morgan smiled gratefully at him, and did as he was told, memorising some simple spells and trying to improve his concentration so they worked more effectively, but deep in the recesses of his mind, he could not stop thinking about Owain Prescott, and his concentration wavered.

Sir Trahaearn visited him in the afternoon, to tell him he looked better than he had the night before, then stayed and practiced mental control with him. They had spent an hour simply holding hands and Trahaearn had used his mind to speak to the boy. He had also gently probed his mind, sensed the worry, and set a subtle barrier against it, so Morgan could concentrate on what he really needed to do.

They practiced probing each other's minds, blocking, breathing exercises, instilling calmness and recovering control when things seemed fraught, and at the end of the session, Morgan had felt a new power within, and a calmness he had never known before.

"You must find this place in your mind when a situation is getting out of hand, or you feel you are losing control. A Kadeau must exhibit and practice constraint at all times."

"But what if I feel...fit to burst about something?" Morgan asked.

"You must find that place of calm and maintain it, until you can be totally alone. A Kadeau is not expected to hold everything within, it would be madness to do so, but you must be able to hold onto the rage, anger, sorrow, whatever it is that threatens to overwhelm you, until you are somewhere you can safely let go without anyone else seeing. It is difficult. Sometimes, it will feel almost impossible, but a Kadeau who releases that pent up emotion in the wrong place, can cause irreparable damage; even destroy. That is what our ancestors did and that is why mental control and discipline is now so important.

"There may be times when you really feel anger and rage and the urge to cause harm, but you must not. There is a difference between justice, and vengeance, and you must never act out of revenge."

Morgan nodded slowly.

"There are also times where you must show mercy, and this too comes in many forms. A man may choose not to kill another, or he may choose to assist in the death of another."

"I don't understand."

Trahaearn gave a heavy sigh, formulating his words before he spoke.

"I...once assisted a fellow Kadeau to die. He was being burned at the stake for heresy. No one deserves to die that way, no matter who they are, or what they have done. I eased his passing, and his pain as the smoke and flames took him, to spare the agony of what he was enduring."

The knight stopped as he saw Morgan's eyes widen with a mixture of awe, terror and sorrow.

"I – I'm sorry Sir Trahaearn, that must have been unimaginable."

"I take comfort, that he was spared that torturous death. It happened a long time ago now when I was newly knighted. The situation for the Kadeau has improved, but war is in the air, it is vital that King Rhisart win, or black days will be ahead of us once more."

This news seemed to invigorate Morgan, and he threw himself fully into his studies of the Kadeau and practicing magic, although Trahaearn had told him to slow down, and learn to walk before running at full pelt into the unknown.

CB   ∞   CB   ∞

Chapter Seven

————◆————

A week passed before Morgan was allowed to resume any physical training, so he had spent most of his days in the company of Trahaearn, continuing to learn about the Kadeau heritage, practicing magic and mental discipline. When he wasn't with the knight he was with Stuart, as the Prince wouldn't even let him attend normal classes with the master, but taught Morgan himself. He didn't want the rest of the students to see the state his young protector was in and wanted to give the boy a chance to do some healing.

Morgan also carried out simple exercises with the Prince to start working his damaged muscles, and was even allowed to sit and observe King Rhisart hold court, all valuable learning experiences.

Cuthbert visited him every day and seemed eager to be his friend. Morgan wasn't sure if it was genuine or not, but cautiously accepted the friendly advance, although he decided to remain guarded until he had developed his mental skills enough to discover if Cuthbert's offer of friendship was sincere.

He broached the subject with Trahaearn at their next training session.

"Trahaearn, Cuthbert wants to be my friend. I know I need friends, but I need to know which ones are genuine. Would you teach me how to discover if a gift of friendship is genuine or not?"

"You are correct when you say you need friends, and for a Kadeau it is vitally important that you know if that offer is genuine, or one of deception. We need to work hard on your mental abilities, and the discipline required. A skilled Kadeau can detect what is in another's thoughts without that person knowing. You are not yet at that level and must work hard to attain it. When I think you have gained enough experience, I will allow you to try and read my mind. If he is willing, we will see if Ioan will also allow you to read his."

"Did you read Ioan's mind before he was appointed my personal steward?" Morgan asked.

"Yes, I did. He is one of the most genuine people I have ever read. The Prince and I knew you would be safe with him. I will read Cuthbert, but I will not tell you what I find, that will provide you with the incentive to become good enough to read him yourself. Now, let us continue with today's lesson."

Trahaearn indicated for the boy to make himself comfortable on the chair beside him.

"I'm sure your Aunt Mereli has told you this on more than one occasion, but I'm going to say it many times as well, Morgan," Trahaearn began. "Imagining what you want to achieve when casting spells and more importantly—believing what you want to achieve—is key to helping you make those spells work and work well. Let me give you an example..." The knight paused for a few moments as he thought about what spell to cast. "Something really simple, like the fire-light. I'm going to conjure it without conviction...watch."

He uttered the words quietly to himself, without feeling or belief.

"*Ignite lumine ignis.*"

The blue flame appeared on his left hand, reasonably bright. He extinguished it.

"Now, as if I really mean it." He repeated the phrase, saying it with feeling and as if his life depended on it. The resulting blue flame almost blinded Morgan with the strength of its luminance.

The boy gasped, and Trahaearn extinguished it.

"You must mean it and feel it here..." he placed a hand on Morgan's chest. "...in your heart, and here..." he then touched his head. "Be genuine. Now, you try. Take a few moments to gather yourself. Don't rush."

The youngster swallowed slowly and took a couple of deep breaths, trying to focus his mind.

"Say it like you mean it."

"*Ignite lumine ignis*," Morgan uttered with feeling. The result was the brightest flame he had ever produced but was still nowhere near as bright as Trahaearn's had been.

Encouraged by his first attempt, Morgan extinguished the flame, took another couple of breaths and tried again. The flame was brighter still. He stared at it, willing it to become brighter and larger, and it responded.

"Good! Very good!" Trahaearn enthused. "I'm going to set you some reading when we have finished for the day, and I want you to practice the spells. They are relatively harmless ones, so you won't be able to do much damage if they go wrong! In the meantime, we will spend a little longer on spells, break for something to eat, and practice with the sword afterwards. Come."

Morgan was now becoming used to the longer days and the hard training, but he was still finding the mental discipline required to conjure successful and powerful spells exhausting.

He had managed to bond successfully with his pony, Flint, which gave them both a distinct advantage in the field. The control of his horse was exceptional, and it made learning control of the lance so much easier. Stuart was delighted with his progress and enthused to his father that the child had indeed been the correct choice of protector.

"The only thing I can tell you," Trahaearn told Morgan on one occasion, "Is to practice, practice and practice. It will become easier as your mind becomes accustomed to it, believe me. Eventually it will be like second nature to you, and you'll wonder what all the fuss was about."

"Really?" Morgan sounded somewhat sceptical.

"Yes! It is still draining, especially if you have to do a lot of magic, but on a day-to-day basis, it will be like child's play."

"Thank you Trahaearn, your words of encouragement mean a lot to me."

"Good. You know, I think you are ready."

"Ready?"

"Yes, ready to see if I am friend or foe."

Trahaearn slowly went through the steps of what to do to read someone's mind without them knowing and repeated them three times.

"As this is your first time, you will need to do this very slowly. I will detect you but don't let that worry you. You are going to attempt to gently persuade me to divulge what I think of you. Now, deep breaths, follow the instructions I have given you, and slowly, gently, touch my mind."

Morgan took a few deep breaths, and then reached out gently, as he had learnt to do with his horse, and paused as he made the initial contact, allowing Trahaearn to grow accustomed to the touch at the edge of his mind.

Trahaearn said nothing, and let the boy find his own way through the minefield of thoughts, waiting for the subtle hint to touch his mind.

Eventually it came, gossamer thin and almost invisible, but Trahaearn was an old hand at this, and immediately recognised it was there. Then came the vaguest of suggestions, about what he thought of the young Duke of Rossmere, and he let the reply go out.

He glanced sidewards at Morgan and saw the boy's eyes widen as he received Trahaearn's response to the question.

Shaken, Morgan carefully withdrew and sat, awed at what he had learnt.

"That was very good, Morgan, but you need to keep your face neutral. This was your first attempt, so the concentration on your face and your expression of what you learnt I will forgive, this time."

"S – Sir Trahaearn..." Morgan was struggling to find the words he needed. "D – do you really think I will make a fine knight and protector?"

"Morgan, I think you will surprise even yourself at what you can accomplish. Now, you need to practice this, and keep your face neutral. I knew exactly what you were thinking, by the expressions on your face. You have a gentle and subtle touch. Non Kadeau will not even know you are in their minds, providing you don't give it away. Come, try it on me again. This time, I will turn away from you."

Morgan attempted the mind probe again.

"Don't be impatient," Trahaearn suddenly said. "Take your time, lighten your touch."

The boy immediately withdrew and started again. Trahaearn said nothing until Morgan had completed his second attempt.

"Better. I will now watch you again and see what I can read in your face."

Trahaearn turned and stared at the boy, which unnerved him somewhat, so Morgan took on a faraway look as if he were thinking, or was somewhere else, deep in thought.

Again, Trahaearn said nothing until he had finished.

"That was even better. Not an expression crossed your face. Where were you?"

"I – I'm not sure, I attempted to empty my mind totally before I started. What did it look like to you?"

"It looked as if you were alone with your thoughts, living a memory perhaps, or planning something. That seems to work for you, so use it."

"Did I look sad?"

"No, not at all. Your face was totally blank, as if you were off in another place and time."

Morgan smiled almost sadly. "Sometimes I wish I was," he muttered.

"Enough of that! Now, practice! If you keep this up, you will be able to read Cuthbert very soon if you continue to improve."

☙ ❧ ☙ ❧

Morgan returned to normal classes the following week. Regular treatments from Master Stephen had reduced the bruising a great deal so they were hardly noticeable. Although Cuthbert had visited him every evening, the boy was pleased to see him back in classes, and they also paired up for sword training, although Morgan was already too good for his young sparring partner.

Stuart watched unobtrusively from the sidelines and nodded to himself in satisfaction. His protector was coming along very well but needed a better opponent. The older pages were too tall for Morgan to beat them, but he did possess that lithe agility that could even up the odds. However, he was concerned they may get a little carried away in their enthusiasm to beat the young Kadeau, so he decided to keep to the regime of having Morgan practice with him as well.

Autumn was well under way, the temperature was beginning to drop, but outdoor training continued, no matter the weather. As their instructor informed them, battles didn't only take place when it was warm and sunny. They practiced in the sun, rain, fog, frosty mornings, and even at dusk, to get them used to fighting in all weathers and conditions. Once winter set in, they would also practice in the snow and ice.

Morgan's most pressing decision at that precise moment, was deciding when and where to try reading Cuthbert's mind, and if his offer of friendship was genuine or not. He left it for a couple of days before deciding to attempt it during a meal. Cuthbert would be distracted by the food and with luck, Morgan would be able to probe his mind and find the information he needed.

It turned out, Cuthbert was a bit like an open book. He was a rather insecure child who craved friendship, camaraderie, approval and openly wanted friendship.

Morgan was relieved. It would be nice to have a genuine friend of his own age within the castle, but before he accepted it, he knew he had to confirm his findings with Trahaearn.

"Well?" the knight asked, pulling him aside at the end of the training session for the day.

"The offer is as genuine as Cuthbert believes," Morgan said quietly.

Trahaearn nodded. "Anything else?"

"He is desperate for friendship and insecure. I found it rather sad."

"Excellent work, Morgan. Beware though, Cuthbert's insecurity may make him unreliable, because of his own self-doubt. He will question himself over and over during his life. He lacks confidence, that could lead to danger. Do you understand what I'm saying?"

"I think so. The way he feels about himself could make him a liability."

"Sometimes, with the insight you are showing at your age, I begin to think you don't need me at all."

"Never, Trahaearn! I have so much to learn from you."

The knight placed a hand on Morgan's shoulder.

"You know, if I had ever married and had a son, you would be that son."

Morgan blushed at these words. Trahaearn was such a private person. For him to divulge such personal information showed the trust he was already putting in the boy.

"I would be proud to call you my son and have you by my side in peace and war."

There were a few moments silence before Trahaearn spoke again, suddenly self-conscious about the information he had revealed.

"Come, I believe Prince Stuart will be expecting you to assist him. Let us go find him and see what duties he has for us to do this evening."

They walked companionably towards the keep, finally completely comfortable with each other's company, and the future ahead.

ౚ ౚ ౚ ౚ

Chapter Eight

The messengers Rhisart had despatched for the possible call to arms were from the elite guard, and not the regular couriers that were sent routinely to the duchies in Devonmere, who transported various documents, contracts, and correspondence, so Morgan finally sat down and wrote his letter back to his family. He had decided he would tell them about the attack, in case Bronwyn heard about it via a rumour and it got blown out of all proportion. It took him at least three attempts before he was happy with the content, and he read it back one last time.

Dear Mama, Papa and Colwyn

Please accept my most sincere apologies for not replying sooner. I have no excuse really, except to say, I found the first few months very trying and tiring.

Prince Stuart is very kind and patient, and I believe we have already built up a form of rapport. Prince Michael is also very kind and funny.

Sir Trahaearn is of great assistance, and my Kadeau abilities are being carefully schooled under his tuition. He is a great knight, just and fair. I know I am very lucky to have him looking after me.

We practice with the sword, bow and lance, and I have special tuition regarding the sword. I also practice regularly with Prince Stuart, as he says we need to know how each other fight, so we can depend on one another in battle.

I keep getting told that once I have gained height and reach, I will be almost impossible to defeat, just as Sir John said back at Inver. I wish I would grow faster! Would you also tell Sir John that the riding lessons he gave me have put me in good stead.

I miss you all so very much; it was particularly hard in the early days, and I confess, I did feel rather homesick. The first night, I wished you were here, Mama, to tuck me up in bed, but I am better now.

This next piece of news, I need you to hear from me, in case you hear rumours. Do not be alarmed, I am all right, but I was set upon by some older squires, who do not like Kadeau. As I said, I am all right, Master Stephen (Prince Stuart's battle surgeon) took very good care of me, and I am well again. I did not disgrace myself and put up a good fight!

I appear to have finally made a friend. His name is Cuthbert, and he came to visit me every day after the attack. Sir Trahaearn has confirmed the offer of friendship is genuine. It will be nice to have a friend my own age.

It looks like I will not be home to see you in the near future. I wish I had something of you to remember you by, rather than just your favours you gave me the day I left, although I cherish them and keep them safe.

I bet Colwyn is growing into a beautiful young lady, just like her mother, but I hope her temper is improving. Colwyn, you must learn to keep your temper under control, as I must keep myself under control. Please try hard for me.

Until I manage to get to Inver, look after yourselves. I miss you every day.

With all my love
Morgan

He rolled the parchment, melted some wax and used his signet ring to seal it. Then he went in search of the Invermere Courier, and handed it to him, so it could be safely delivered to Inver when he next journeyed there.

Master Stephen's ministrations, and the use of various potions and witch hazel, had successfully done their work and the bruises had vanished, so regular meetings in the Pell for private training sessions with Prince Stuart increased in their intensity.

Having trained with Sir John and the older pages back at Inver, he knew he was greatly disadvantaged due to his age and height, but Stuart was very patient and clever, and Morgan found he had more success than ever before. The Prince was also highly skilled in the use of the sword, and even taught him some new moves that he could practice, although Sir Trahaearn frowned with some disdain, saying he should not be trying to wield a sword in that way until he was stronger, older and fully grown.

One thing that had changed, was the attitude of the other pages and squires towards him. The open hatred seemed to have disappeared, but Morgan knew it was still bubbling under the surface. The death of Owain Prescott seemed to have curbed the enthusiasm for violence against the boy Duke for the moment. Some—like Cuthbert—approached him in a friendly manner, and using his newly developed skills, he ascertained those that were genuine, and those who were just pretending. The former he encouraged slightly, deciding it would be a good idea to have his own body of supporters around him, and the others he kept at a distance. He was always polite but did not encourage them.

⁂

The mood became sombre within the castle as the King awaited the response from the Eastern Marches. Scouts had been given the task of keeping a watch on Arnell's supporters. They were despatched in pairs, with one reporting back every couple of days, and replaced by another. If any supporters started to prepare for war, one of the scouts would return immediately with this news, rather than wait for the appointed time, and Rhisart would light the beacons to summon his own allies.

The King hoped the Duke would think long and hard before coming to a decision. However, a nagging doubt dwelt in the back of his mind which he tried to suppress without success.

Stuart immediately noticed the change of mood in his father and instantly knew the cause. The King was more worried about the situation than he had admitted, and Stuart also found himself becoming more subdued as the days passed.

Rhisart ordered Owain's body to be treated with respect as it was prepared for transport. The lead-lined coffin would be conveyed on a wagon back to his home. His belongings were carefully packed, placed with the coffin and on a misty, chilly morning in mid-October, the wagon, a small guard, and a courier, carrying another letter to Arnell from the King, left Ellesmere and began the journey to the Eastern Marches.

Everyone seemed to hold their breath, waiting to hear the response to the message the King had sent.

Eventually, the escort returned safely, along with the original messenger, bearing a letter. Rhisart had spoken in private with the courier who explained that Duke Arnell Prescott had been deeply upset and angered, and at one point, the messenger had been concerned for his own safety, but the Duke had not taken vengeance on the person bearing the message and instead, ordered him to convey the reply back to his King.

Rhisart took the offered letter, broke the seal and carefully keeping his face neutral, began to read the reply from the Duke of the Eastern Marches. Having finished it, he carefully rolled it up again and indicated for the courier to leave, then he sat down and digested the information.

Duke Arnell was acting out of pure grief, and not thinking logically. No one in their right mind would usually go to war with winter almost upon them, but he had chosen to do so. In response, the beacons were lit, and spread across the kingdom; a signal for Rhisart's supporters to head for Ellesmere.

The Marches would be particularly unpleasant at this time of year. Wet, boggy, the peaty ground soft and life-sucking to both man and beast. Rhisart's plan was to draw the Duke further away from the Marches, or at least battle on the edges of it, with his men having the solid ground, causing Prescott to be disadvantaged. The Marches were also known to give off a gas that could be ignited. If needs must, then Rhisart would light it, although it was harder to get it to burn in the cold.

The King expected his supporters to start arriving in the next week or so, with some of their armies, whilst the rest defended their home duchies. The battle would need careful planning however, as Rhisart did not want to be caught between two opposing forces and fight a war on two fronts. As yet, none of the scouts had returned with news of supporters preparing for war. Further scouts were sent towards the

Eastern Marches to keep a watch on developments. They would return once they saw Arnell preparing to mobilise his forces.

Duke Richard Coltrane was the first to arrive, eight days later, due to the deteriorating weather, with half of Inver's army. He immediately reported to Rhisart, pledging his support.

"Arise Richard," Rhisart said, taking his hand in a firm grip of friendship as the Duke rose to his feet. "It is good to see you, but not under these circumstances."

"What's happened, Sire? I received Morgan's letter telling me that he had been set upon by some older squires, but nothing about the younger Prescott's death, until your courier arrived."

"Morgan received a very severe beating, but he has recovered now. I summoned the young Prescott to address the situation and told him that he would not be knighted for his unknightly actions. He took offence to this and went to attack me with his knife. Stuart drew his sword and we thought Owain would realise his foolish action, but then went to strike, and Stuart's sword pierced his neck."

"He committed treason, attacking you, Sire."

"The foolishness of youth. Stuart was horrified at what he had done and blames himself, but war was coming anyway. It was only a matter of time. Maybe it's better it happens now, before winter really sets in. My plan is to fight on firmer ground, with Prescott's army forced into the Marches."

Richard nodded.

"Whatever you need of me, Sire, my army and I are at your disposal."

"As always you are a loyal supporter. Once the rest of the armies arrive, we will meet and discuss the battle strategy. Providing all goes to plan, we leave in a week."

The Duke nodded. "Strike fast and hard," was all he said. "I assume you have scouts deployed, keeping an eye on Prescott and McDowell?"

"Yes. I am receiving regular messages from them. Prescott's supporters are massing around his castle. Surprisingly, there has been no movement from McDowell, or Allbright from Stallesmere."

"None?"

"Nothing. It appears they are staying neutral on this occasion. But I will ensure they are watched, just in case they attempt to attack Ellesmere whilst we are at the Marches. Come, I will arrange food and wine to be provided for you."

"Thank you Sire, although I would like to see Morgan first, to see for myself that he is fit and well. Bronwyn was most concerned when his letter arrived."

"Of course. Morgan is settling in well now, Sir Trahaearn and Prince Stuart are pleased with his progress so far."

"That is good to hear, Sire. Thank you. With your permission."

"Yes, I will see you later at supper."

Richard bowed respectfully and made his way quickly to his room to remove his surcoat, hauberk and replaced his aketon for a jacket, retrieving a small package from his saddlebags, before going to Morgan's rooms.

Ioan opened the door in answer to the forceful knock and his eyes widened in surprise and pleasure at seeing the Duke of Invermere standing there.

"Your Grace! Come in. Morgan shouldn't be too long; he will be so pleased to see you. May I get you some wine, or would you prefer a hot toddy?"

"Thank you, Ioan, a hot toddy would be most welcome after the long ride."

Ioan indicated for him to take a seat at the table, whilst he fetched some wine, placed a bag of herbs and spices in a goblet, filled it with the wine, and then used the red-hot poker to heat the liquid. He hadn't long placed it before the Duke, when the door opened and Morgan came in, looking pleased with himself.

He halted for a moment, seeing the stranger sitting at his table, until he realised who it was.

"Papa!" He ran to the Duke and hugged him tightly. "I'm so pleased to see you, though not because of the circumstances."

"Morgan, my boy, I think you've grown a couple of inches already. Let me take a proper look at you."

Richard stood up and held the boy at arm's length, critically appraising him. There was nothing to indicate that the child was still suffering any after effects from the attack, so he would be able to reassure Bronwyn that Morgan was fit and well.

"You're looking well. No remaining after effects?" Richard asked him.

"None."

"Good. Sit, join me, I have something for you."

Curious, the boy sat and waited patiently, whilst Richard delved into an inside pocket of his jacket and retrieved a small, wrapped package, which he handed to him.

"You said in your letter, that you only had favours which you cherished. We hope this will serve you even better," the Duke said as he watched the boy eagerly unwrap the package.

It was a gold locket on a chain. Carefully, Morgan opened it, to reveal miniature paintings of Bronwyn and Colwyn. He gasped.

"I decided you didn't need one of me, as I am a relatively regular visitor to Ellesmere. Here, let me assist you with the clasp."

Richard held out his hand for the locket, carefully undid the clasp and then fastened it around Morgan's neck.

"There. Now Bronwyn and Colwyn will be with you at all times."

114

Idly, Morgan fingered the locket lovingly, then carefully hid it beneath his clothing.

"I will wear it always. Thank you."

"Bronwyn will be delighted you are so pleased with it. Now, if you will forgive me, I need to change. The journey from Inver doesn't get any shorter!" He finished his hot toddy, placed a hand briefly on Morgan's shoulder, then rose. "I will see you later, at supper, no doubt."

"Yes. Papa..."

The Duke paused, his hand on the door and turned to face the boy.

"...thank you for this." Morgan placed a hand on where the locket lay against his chest. "It means a great deal to me."

Richard smiled and nodded. "You are most welcome."

CB & CB &

Ellesmere Castle was full to bursting by the time supper was served. Morgan's uncle, Duke Rodric McLeod had arrived with his army from the High Meres, along with Duke Kenneth Dernley from Strathmere and the Captain of the Guard—Lord Martyn Welles—at Rossmere had also arrived with a considerable force.

King Rhisart welcomed his allies and toasted their good health, then they all ate. Morgan, as the waiting Duke of Rossmere was seated with the other Dukes, between Richard and Rodric. Richard formally introduced the young Duke to his uncle.

"Your Aunt Mereli sends her regards to you, young Morgan," Rodric said. "And Colin says he is looking forward to seeing you again."

"Thank you, uncle," Morgan replied. "I too am looking forward to seeing both of them, soon, I hope."

Rodric nodded and smiled. "It's good to finally meet you. Your Aunt Mereli has been keeping me updated on your progress and development of your Kadeau powers."

"I still have so much to learn, but Aunt Mereli and Bronwyn have helped me a great deal."

Rodric nodded and ruffled the boy's hair affectionately.

The meal was eaten in relative silence, as the reason they were there played on everyone's mind. They all hoped it would be a short battle, for it was almost winter, and the weather was beginning to deteriorate, with frosts appearing in the morning, rapidly dropping temperatures, rain and cold winds. In a few weeks it would probably start snowing too.

Once they had supped, Rhisart let them all relax, deciding that the planning could wait until the morning. His allies had ridden a long way, and ridden hard to reach Ellesmere, it was the least he could do.

Cʒ ♊ Cʒ ♊

After breakfast the following morning, Rhisart invited his supporters into the antechamber, where a map of the Eastern Marches was laid out on the table, and dressed with models that represented the various ducal armies.

His General of the Armies, Lord Dafydd Hughes, outlined the plan of campaign. Stuart had brought Morgan with him, deciding he might as well start learning about battle strategy based on the upcoming conflict.

A reasonably wide escarpment approximately one hundred feet high, dropped half that height to form a narrow ledge that overlooked a long but relatively constricted plain before the actual Marches began; marked by a slim line of exceedingly bright green mossy ground. Behind the escarpment, the ground rose up again sharply to form a line of mountains that on their western side dropped down almost vertically, through which the River Elles ran. On the other side of the river there was a ledge several feet above the water level that was just about wide enough for two wagons to pass that provided a way through the gorge. The High Hills then rose steeply, and dropped away more gently. Over thousands and thousands of years, the river had cut through the rock to form the gorge and path between the mountains and hills.

During the summer, the land to the east of the narrow plain dried out and became firmer but was intersected by numerous channels that usually still held water. The ground was peaty, and where any water stood, bubbles could be seen rising up through it to the surface. It was able to hold large amounts of water, but over the winter months, it became saturated and turned sticky and boggy and had claimed many an unwary traveller. It rarely froze unless the temperature plummeted far below the norm for that time of year. The area smelt of death, there was an unpleasant odour at all times, but more so during the cold, wet months, that made all those that dared to travel there think of fetid decay. There were two safe paths through, but these were narrow, treacherous and wound several miles until the peat gave way to more stable and firm ground in which Arnell Prescott resided in his castle.

Dafydd had no intention of entering the Marches. If Arnell wanted war, he would have to cross them and meet Stuart's army on the narrow plain, where the general would either drive the enemy back into the Marches, to be bogged down in the saturated, sticky ground, or drowned in the numerous deep pools. Or, if Arnell split his forces, they would surround them and force them to fight on two fronts. Archers would be lined up along the lower escarpment to take down as many opponents as they could before they reached Rhisart's knights and foot soldiers.

During his explanation, Dafydd used models to illustrate the movement of the King's army, so the supporters could see how the plan would progress.

Morgan paid avid attention as the finer details were discussed and learnt that holding the higher ground was of vital importance in any battle.

Explanations complete, work began on preparing weapons and supplies for the movement east and the engagement with Arnell Prescott and his supporters. Stuart instructed Morgan to pack his saddlebags for the journey, advising him to make sure he took his heaviest cloak and warmest clothes, as the weather was likely to deteriorate more as the end of the year approached.

"Prince Stuart, how long do you think this will last?" Morgan had asked him, as they walked along a corridor towards their rooms.

"I honestly don't know, Morgan. It would be advantageous if it were to end sooner rather than later. It depends on how eager Arnell and his supporters are to prolong their inevitable defeat and how many men they are prepared to lose."

Morgan nodded grimly. He was both excited and terrified at the same time. Although still within Ellesmere castle, already his mouth felt dry, and despite the cool temperature, he could feel a trickle of sweat running down his back. So, this is what fear really feels like? he asked himself.

Stuart glanced at the boy and saw his unease. "Morgan, it's all right to be scared. I'm scared, and I feel this is all my fault. I was the one who killed Owain."

"Really? You're scared too?" Morgan whispered back. "And it's not your fault, you were defending the King."

"Thank you for that. Father did say that war was inevitable, I just... caused it to arrive sooner." Stuart took a deep breath. "As to your duties, you will not be going to war, you will stay at camp, aid me, run errands, help the battle surgeons, carry water, that sort of thing. My steward, Aiden will look after cleaning my armour and weapons, fetch my food."

Morgan nodded.

"I'd advise you to get an early night," Stuart continued. "Sleep out in the field can be rather sporadic. No need to attend me tonight, no errands need running. I'll see you in the morning."

"Goodnight, Your Highness," the boy said as he reached his rooms.

Stuart gave him a wave of his hand and disappeared through the door to his own chambers.

Ioan had already made a start on packing clothes for the forthcoming journey, so he could double check he hadn't forgotten anything. Their departure was still a couple of days away, but he wanted to make sure he had everything the boy would need for at least a month. Secretly he really hoped it would be over before Christmas.

Ↄ ⁊ Ↄ ⁊

The next couple of days flew past as everyone hurried to get all the preparations completed. It had to be well organised due to the sheer numbers of men and supplies that would be required. The list seemed endless, clothes, food, water, checking the horses, checking and cleaning armour, the weapons, supplies of arrows and lances, tents, bedding, blankets, medical supplies, firewood, flints, maps. Morgan's brain was befuddled with it all, but he attempted to absorb all the details, and file it away for future reference.

Dafydd had spent almost the entire week sorting out whose army was going to be where in the plan of the campaign, which archers were to be deployed on the lower escarpment, which knights would make up the central force that would meet Arnell's army as it reached the narrow plain, where they would have little space to fight or manoeuvre before being forced into the peat bogs, or drawn along the plain to Rhisart's waiting forces.

Scouts were despatched ahead of the main body, to ensure Arnell had not arranged any ambushes on the journey to the battlefield, the foot soldiers left shortly after that, accompanied by part of the supply chain and finally, almost a week later, on a freezing November morning, with poor visibility due to fog, and breath from both horses and men condensing in the low temperatures, the knights prepared to leave.

Morgan glanced across to his guardian. It was the first time he had seen Richard in full battle armour, complete with fur-trimmed winter cloak, and he cut an imposing, regal figure. The Duke took Morgan aside and re-introduced him to Martyn Welles, Captain of the Rossmere Guard. Sir John MacKenzie also reacquainted himself with the boy and remarked that he had most definitely grown since he had last seen him.

With final preparations complete, they set off at an easy pace just after dawn. The journey to the Eastern Marches would take approximately four days, depending on the weather.

The foot soldiers split into three divisions, to approach the Eastern Marches from the north, south and through the narrow pass. The archers all headed through the narrow pass, and then climbed up the sides of the valley to gain the height advantage that the lower escarpment offered.

There were only two ways out of the Eastern Marches and Dafydd had both of them covered. The central division was going to form the barrier that would effectively trap Arnell's men, forcing him to fight on two fronts. Rhisart had decided to fight hard, and this plan of attack was designed to decimate the opposing army in as short a time as possible.

The main camp was set up on the higher escarpment that backed onto the mountains. From that vantage point, the King and his general would be able to view a great deal of the narrow plain and the Eastern Marches and would also be able to see Arnell coming from a far distance, providing the weather was clear.

By the time the knights arrived, the three camps had been set up and organised. Food was being prepared, tents and shelter raised. Dafydd set up the plan and maps in Rhisart's tent, on the long table that had been assembled. Noblemen and Captains of the various guards attended a meeting that very same evening, to confirm the plan remained unchanged, and would be put in final place once Arnell's army was spotted crossing the Marches. Now all Rhisart could do, was wait for Arnell's forces to make an appearance.

It was three days later when the first scout returned. Lookouts spotted the lone rider way before he reached the narrow plain, coming in via the northern route, and once he reached it, he was guided up to the plateau and Rhisart's tent to deliver his report.

Arnell had split his forces in half, each of them travelling on the two routes out of the Marches. The northern force was being led by Arnell's general. Dafydd nodded, and it was then Stuart suggested a small feint that consisted of sending two small contingents to meet both halves of Arnell's forces and then turn and run them into a trap. The archers would take out as many as they could, then the mid-force would split and go north and south to cut off any escape.

The second scout arrived eleven hours later during the middle of the night from the southern route, to report that Arnell himself was leading the group and were about a day and a half behind him.

"Stuart, as it was your idea, would you like the honour of leading the northern feint? Let them chase you north."

"Sire, I would be honoured to lead."

"Once you get beyond the archers, they will let fly with their arrows. Carry on and join up with Rossmere and High Mere armies. Take control of the Rossmere army. Martyn Welles will be your deputy. Once the Prescott force is following you, half of our army will move to block off their retreat."

"Yes, Sire."

Rhisart turned to Richard.

"Richard, I would like you to lead the southern feint, lead Arnell south, towards your army and Strathmere. I will lead the other half of my army to block the southern retreat."

"Thank you, my Liege, I would be honoured," Richard replied. "If all goes to plan, this could all be over within a day."

"I don't believe Arnell has thought this campaign through at all. McDowell has stayed neutral, and Eairdsidh Allbright of Stallesmere has made no move to assist Arnell either. I will move south tomorrow to get into position. We will gather before dawn for prayer, then move to our respective positions. I recommend we all get some sleep. The next few days are going to be... hectic."

"Yes Sire."

The two men bowed to their King and left him to reflect on the plans for the coming days.

Stuart returned to his tent to find Aiden tip-toeing around preparing the Prince's sleeping alcove as Morgan had dozed off, propped up awkwardly in a chair. He smiled. It had been a hard few days for the boy, it wasn't surprising that the strain and long hours had finally caught up with him.

The Prince stood looking down at him for a few moments, then gently reached forward and shook him.

"Morgan, wake up," he said softly.

The youngster awoke with a start, jumped to his feet, then bowed.

"My Prince, apologies."

"Don't apologise, Morgan, you must be exhausted. Go on, off to bed with you."

"But I need to help you—"

"Do as I say. Aiden can assist me. Go on. It's going to be a busy few days for you. You will stay here until I return. I'm heading north tomorrow morning; the King and Richard will be riding south. Master Stephen will be staying here, to assist with any injured that may arrive. So he may need you to run errands for him or other battle surgeons."

"Do you know how long you will be gone?"

"No, not really. Our enemy is still about a day's march away, but the King seems to think they are very disorganised, and their supporters have not arrived to assist, so this may actually be over in a couple of days."

"I hope so."

"Now go on, bed. I will wake you in the morning. Sleep well, Morgan."

"And you, Prince Stuart."

The boy had a little alcove within Stuart's tent, with a cot. It was nowhere as comfortable as his bed back at the castle, but he was so tired. Ioan helped him prepare for bed and he was asleep before his head reached the pillow.

ᘓ ᘔ ᘓ ᘔ

The next thing the boy was aware of, was something touching his hair. It took him a moment or two to awaken, and he opened his eyes to find Richard kneeling by his cot.

"Papa!" he exclaimed, sitting up. The Duke was once again in full battle dress, and did not look like the gentle, kind man that Morgan had known almost all of his life.

"I'm sorry to have disturbed you," his guardian said. "But I couldn't leave without saying goodbye. War is fickle and uncertain, brutal and cruel. No one knows what fate awaits them. I want you to remember your training, to be loyal, truthful, gallant. Uphold good and defeat evil."

Fear appeared in Morgan's eyes, fear that Richard would not be returning from the engagement.

"Papa..." he said again.

"Do not worry, my boy. I am planning on returning, but there is always that chance, so you must be prepared."

The rarely emotional Morgan suddenly threw his arms around Richard's neck.

"Please come back," he mumbled into the Duke's neck, "I couldn't bear to lose you."

Richard was quite taken aback by the unexpected show of emotion and returned the hug.

"I will do my utmost to return safely."

A discreet cough made them break apart. Stuart stood at the entry to the tiny alcove.

"It is time," was all he said.

Richard got to his feet.

"Please be careful, both of you."

"We will, Morgan. Take care of yourself as well. Follow any instructions you are given whilst we are away. Help where you can, and don't forget to keep practicing with your sword."

"I will, Prince Stuart."

Morgan watched as both men smiled reassuringly at him, then turned and left, leaving him feeling very alone.

Unable to sleep, he got up and went to the entrance of the tent to watch the knights mount up and leave. It was a breathtaking sight, as they left the camp, heading for the centre path. Once on the plain the division led by the prince would turn towards the northern end, the division led by Richard would head to the southern end, and Rhisart would divide his army to follow both divisions once the archers on the high ground had done their work, the other half led by Dafydd.

The colour of the surcoats, steel glinting in the feeble sun and the odd neigh of a horse breaking through the sound of hooves and jangle of metal, resounded in the air as they gradually disappeared from sight.

The knights rode hard from camp, wanting to reach their destinations as soon as possible, so they could rest their horses before the engagement was due to take place.

More scouts had been despatched to keep a watch for the opposing forces and reported back at regular intervals as to how fast Arnell's army was progressing through the Marches. Rhisart received the news that they were still approximately thirty-two hours from reaching the narrow plain.

It was on a murky, cold, damp morning that both Stuart and Richard led a modest contingent of knights towards the two trails that crossed the Marches. They were pretending to be two small forces who would 'accidentally stumble' across Arnell's men. Vastly outnumbered, they would make a run north and south to lead the two groups, straight back to the awaiting armies. General Hughes and King Rhisart would lead the central group forward, through the narrow pass and cut off the retreat, once Arnell's forces discovered the ruse.

Stuart's force briefly engaged with the emerging force from the Marches, then made a run for the north, with Arnell's knights in hot pursuit. Their general had thought he had caught the smaller force by surprise and fell for the feint. Stuart encouraged them to carry on pursuing, by slowing down and letting them get closer, before leading them on, straight into the range of the archers, hiding on the high ground. As soon as Stuart and his men were clear, they let fly with arrows, and the pursuing knights started to drop.

Stuart reined in as the chasing knights stopped, turned and started to run south. A beacon was lit and the remaining knights to the north moved south. The pursuer was now the pursued.

The identical ruse was carried out by Richard, although with Arnell leading this group, they did not immediately fall for the trap and Richard realised he would have to get a lot closer and probably engage them to some extent.

They clashed swords, as soon as the knights entered the narrow plain. As the trail was not very wide, knights could only get onto the plain a few at a time, and Richard's force was able to engage in relative safety for a number of minutes, until they became outnumbered. The Duke kept a careful watch, then deciding they were outnumbered enough called the retreat, and Arnell fell for it.

Richard's knights were not as far ahead of their pursuers as Stuart's had been, so a significant number of Arnell's men managed to get past the archers on the high ground before they could let fly with their arrows, but their number was still reduced. Another beacon was lit, and a further legion left the centre pass, leaving about half behind in case any stragglers or a smaller force tried to make it through that narrow passage.

Kenneth and John saw Richard and the knights approaching and readied the rest of their horsemen and foot soldiers. They let Richard's knights get to within four hundred yards, then gave the signal and the two armies moved forward to meet them. The King had given orders that Arnell was to be left to him to deal with.

At both ends of the narrow plain, the armies clashed, and a fierce battle ensued. The ground turned red with the blood of fallen comrades. Slowly but surely, the army of the Eastern Marches was driven back. A few of Arnell's own archers managed to let fly with arrows but were cut down by Rhisart's.

The King spotted Arnell and fought his way towards him, Trahaearn by his side. The remaining knights did their best to stop them, to no avail, and the inevitable finally happened.

Rhisart decided to give Arnell the option to surrender.

"Arnell, yield and I will let you live!"

"You murdered my son!"

"Owain committed treason by attacking me, my son acted in my defence."

"No!"

Arnell pushed forward with his attack. Rhisart ordered Trahaearn to stay back and moved forward to engage.

Swords clashed together and against shields, sparks flying. Rhisart knocked Arnell from his horse and dismounted to continue the fight. The two men circled one another, studying each other, then Arnell lunged. Rhisart realised the Duke wasn't thinking logically at all. His moves were all emotional, not measured and the King easily parried them. He attempted to get Arnell to surrender again, but his request was in vain, and the King realised it was only going to end one way, so increased the ferocity of his attack to end this battle before too many men were killed. Using a complex series of moves, he disarmed the Duke and held his sword against Arnell's throat.

"One last chance Arnell, yield."

Arnell glared at him, anger and grief visible in his eyes. He blinked once, swallowed and lunged forward, causing Rhisart's sword to cut his throat in an almost identical way that Stuart had done to Owain.

As it had back at Ellesmere, a scarlet ribbon of blood arched out from the wound. Arnell's eyes locked with Rhisart's for what seemed like an eternity, and then the Duke collapsed, his lifeless eyes staring at nothing.

The King heaved a huge breath and went to sheath his sword, when two fallen Marches soldiers gained their feet and with their last breaths lunged at Rhisart.

"My liege!" Trahaearn shouted and leapt forward, receiving the thrust of one of the swords that had been meant for his King. He managed to despatch the attacker but was too late to prevent the other from inflicting a wound on Rhisart. Trahaearn staggered forward, and killed the other soldier, before dropping to his knees clutching at his ribs.

Seeing that Arnell was dead, the remaining members of his army threw down their arms in surrender, enabling Richard to get through to his King.

"Sire!" The Duke dismounted and limped towards him.

"Richard, you are injured?" the King asked.

"It's not serious, Sire. Where are you hurt?"

Rhisart removed a hand from his chest and saw the blood covered gauntlet. He coughed and blood appeared on his lips.

Richard went pale.

"We must get you back to camp, get Rhohan to examine you!" The Duke looked around for some fellow knights.

"Help me mount up," Rhisart said. "The men must not know. We have won a victory today, it is a time of reflection and celebration, that they will return home to their families. Please Richard, say nothing, just help me."

The Duke took a deep breath, then nodded. He limped to where the King's horse stood, grabbed the reins, led him back and assisted the King into the saddle. He then turned to Trahaearn.

"Can you ride, Trahaearn?"

He nodded. Richard retrieved the knight's horse, helped Trahaearn to his feet, then hoisted him into the saddle, before mounting his own charger. They joined up with the rest of the knights and headed north towards the central pass, which was the quickest way back to the main camp.

Rhisart ordered messengers to go north to tell Prince Stuart that Arnell was dead, that the war was over, and that Arnell's remaining army could collect their wounded and dead. He also sent a messenger ahead to the main camp with the good news. They had been fortunate. Due to Arnell's poor planning, it was all over before it had really begun.

He also ordered a couple of experienced knights to check the fallen horses. Any that were seriously injured and still alive were to be killed to prevent further suffering, and slowly the screaming and moaning of the wounded chargers diminished as their lives were extinguished.

The first of the casualties arrived a few hours before the King and his knights returned, and Morgan was kept busy fetching water for the battle surgeons who were treating various degrees of wounds, mopping up and disposing of bloodstained cloths in the numerous camp fires.

Rhisart had brought hostlers with him, and they examined the knights' chargers as they came into camp, treating any wounds the horses had suffered, ensuring they also received food and water.

It was Morgan's first experience of the consequences of war; of death, of blood, wounds, the cries and screams of the wounded, the smell that only blood had, that metallic aroma and his stomach churned. He saw sights a seven year old boy should never see, and he knew it would be forever ingrained in his memory, and now understood why the rulers of Devonmere tried so hard to keep the kingdom at peace. But his mind strayed to thoughts of Richard and Stuart. Were they all right? Had they survived?

He obtained part of his answer a number of hours later, when Rhisart and Richard returned to the camp, accompanied by Dafydd and Trahaearn, heads held high, and at first glance looked reasonably well. The Duke dismounted first. Morgan noticed the mud and blood on his guardian's face, and the fact he was favouring his left leg and realised he had sustained an injury. The child wanted to go to him and confirm he was all right, but a surgeon was shouting for him, and he had to run to fetch fresh water yet again.

Richard called for assistance for the King and Trahaearn. Kenneth Dernley arrived at that point and ran to assist, along with Sir John MacKenzie. With Dafydd also assisting, they disappeared into the King's tent, and Rhohan, the King's battle surgeon arrived shortly after.

It had taken the four of them to remove the King's armour, and Rhohan took a deep breath. The wound was bad and appeared to have punctured a lung, which was causing Rhisart to cough up blood. The battle surgeon swept everything off the table and indicated for the King to be placed on it. He packed the wound as a temporary measure, got a squire to stoke the fire, and placed a knife within the flames.

"Sire, I need to cauterise the wound now, before you lose too much blood. You've been bleeding a while; you can't keep losing blood like this."

"P – pack it. I will not succumb to unconsciousness until I have spoken to Stuart."

"But my Liege, if I don't do this, you may not live long enough to see your son!"

"I said no! I will greet him conscious, not half dead!"

Rhohan looked around at the assembled nobles, his eyes pleading with them to try and change the King's mind, but he still refused.

Rodric arrived from the north and Richard asked him if he had seen Stuart.

"He's a couple of hours away still."

Richard nodded and turned to his King.

"Sire, Prince Stuart is still hours away, you must let the surgeon do his work!"

"No, I forbid it. I must speak to Stuart first."

Richard felt helpless.

"I will get someone to watch out for him then and order him to come here immediately he arrives."

"Yes, proceed."

"By your leave, Sire." Richard bowed and limped out of the tent, looking for Morgan, and spied him delivering a bucket of water to another surgeon's tent.

"Morgan!" he called. The boy turned and hurried over to his guardian. "When you've delivered that water, I have a very important task for you."

Morgan nodded, hurried to finish his task, then ran to Richard.

"Papa, you're hurt, how may I help" the boy asked.

"It's nothing. I need you to keep a lookout for Prince Stuart. He is still a couple of hours away, but it is imperative you get him to report to the King's tent immediately he returns. Do not let him delay, do you understand me?"

Morgan saw the grim expression on his guardian's face and realised something was wrong. He did not ask what, but simply nodded and said "I understand. As soon as he arrives in camp, no matter his state."

"Good boy." Richard laid a hand on his shoulder, and gave him a feeble smile, before he turned and limped back to the King's tent.

As the King would not let Rhohan treat him, the surgeon turned his attention to Trahaearn. The stewards had assisted in removing his armour, and he was dressing his wound when Richard re-entered. Now bandaged, the knight was sleeping on his cot in another corner of the tent.

"Your Grace, your turn," Rhohan said pointing at the Duke's leg.

"It's nothing," Richard replied, but Rhohan refused to back down.

"You are still bleeding. Let me take a look and dress it."

"Richard, do it," Rhodric said to him. "The sooner you get it treated, the better."

The Duke sighed and reluctantly nodded. John MacKenzie came forward and assisted him out of his chausses, then the Duke sat on the edge of a chair as Rhohan approached with another knife, knelt down and cut the blood-soaked breeches to expose the wound. There were two; an entry and exit point.

"An arrow," Rhohan stated calmly. "You pushed it all the way through?"

"Yes," Richard replied wincing as the surgeon examined it.

"You have been lucky. It's missed the artery." He stood up, poured some powder into a small bowl of water, picked up some clean cloths and returned to clean the injuries. Richard pulled a face as the fluid found its way into the wounds. He'd forgotten how much it stung.

Satisfied, Rhohan, returned to the fire, retrieved the heated knife and returned to Richard's side. From his bag he obtained a round piece of stick and handed it to the Duke. Richard took a deep breath and bit down on it, then nodded.

The Duke screwed his eyes shut, his body tensed and he groaned as the knife seared the first wound. He was breathing heavily and felt the bile rise at the pain. Fighting it down, the surgeon gave him a couple of minutes to get himself under control, then seared the other wound.

Richard groaned again and suddenly felt light headed. John reached out and steadied him, easing him back in the chair. Another couple of minutes passed, then Rhohan reached up and took the stick from the Duke's mouth.

Richard's eyes were still closed as he attempted to slow the thud of his heart. Rhohan studied him for another couple of minutes, then dressed the wounds and bandaged his thigh.

"You can do no more until Prince Stuart returns, I recommend you rest the leg for a couple of hours." The surgeon reached out, grabbed a nearby chair, carefully elevated the Duke's leg onto it and stood up. "I also recommend some wine...for all of you," he finished, then wiped the discarded knife down and placed it near the fire in readiness.

John disappeared for a few minutes, and returned with a sealed jug, which he opened, and poured into goblets that were standing on a smaller table. He handed them out to Kenneth, Rodric, and Richard.

"Master Rhohan, I think you have more than earned a goblet. Will the King take some?" John asked and handed two goblets to him.

"It will help to ease the pain, let me dissolve this powder into it. Would someone assist me, please?" He quickly measured out some painkiller and stirred it into the wine.

John assisted by lifting the King's head slightly so Rhohan could place the goblet against his lips.

"Sire, it is wine with something that should help to take the edge off the pain. Take some sips, slowly now. Once Prince Stuart arrives and you have spoken to him, I will complete your treatment."

Rhisart took a good portion of the wine, before John laid his head back, then turned a picked up the final goblet. Rhohan covered the King with some blankets to help keep him warm and stated he would keep a careful watch on him, as he would need to repack the wound at regular intervals but all they could do now, was wait for Stuart's return.

Chapter Nine

———◆———

Morgan stood anxiously, nervously biting his lip, as he waited for Stuart and his men to return to the camp. He knew something was seriously wrong, for Richard had had a very grim expression on his face, as he had approached the boy and given him the task of bringing Stuart to the King's tent as soon as he returned; with the explicit orders that he must not delay.

The boy wondered what it was, as he had heard that King Rhisart had been victorious in the battle. Perhaps it wasn't over, and they would have to fight on, even though he had seen the triumphant look of the King and his men.

What Morgan didn't know, was that Rhisart had been seriously wounded during the final battle. He had seen him ride proudly into the encampment, but that had been a ruse, to ensure his army kept their spirits high and could celebrate the victory.

Dafydd came out of the tent and began circulating amongst the members of the army who had returned, offering support, or congratulating them on contributing to the victory. John also came outside and went to check on the Invermere army.

Eventually, as the sun began its journey towards the horizon for the day, Morgan saw a group of horsemen approaching. As they got closer, he recognised Stuart at the front and left his vantage point, to greet the Prince.

As they rode into camp, Morgan observed they were tired, filthy and somewhat bloodied after their successful battle. Stuart would want to clean himself up before visiting his father, but Richard had been insistent the prince report to the King's tent immediately.

Stuart dismounted and Morgan approached, bowing respectfully.

"Your Highness, it is ordered you report to the King's tent, immediately," the boy said quietly.

"Thank you, Morgan," Stuart replied, sounding weary. "As soon as I have made myself presentable, I'll be there."

"No, my Prince, you must go now; this very second."

Stuart frowned at him, suddenly concerned; an unease settling around his heart.

"Surely—"

"Now! At once!" Morgan interrupted rather rudely.

Even with the dirt, mud and blood on the Prince's face, Morgan saw the colour drain from it. He literally threw his horse's reins at the boy and strode away quickly.

He wanted to run, but he dared not, so instead took long, purposeful strides. Morgan watched him go and was suddenly fearful. He could sense Stuart's heightened unease.

Richard turned his head sharply as the tent flap moved and sighed in relief as Stuart entered. The Duke gave a grimace as pain shot through his thigh as he struggled to his feet and bowed in respect.

"Richard, Morgan told me to report here directly..." His voice trailed off as he looked around for his father. "The King?" he questioned.

"Master Rhohan is with your father," Richard replied. "Prince Stuart, you need to prepare..."

His voice trailed off as he saw the prince's eyes widen, before he turned and strode to the back room of the large tent. Sweeping the heavy curtain aside, he stopped dead as he saw Rhohan working furiously on his father, who lay on the table, still trying to stop the bleeding from a wound inflicted by a broadsword. Blood-soaked cloths littered the floor and Dukes Rodric and Kenneth stood to one side, waiting.

Rhohan glanced round and heaved a sigh of relief at seeing the Prince. He leant over Rhisart.

"Your Majesty, Prince Stuart is here." He put the discarded knife back in the fire.

"S-Stuart..." The King's voice was weak, but the authority was still there.

Stuart approached his side. Rhisart lifted a hand, which the Prince took hold of.

"I – I am sorry. I had hoped to rule longer, to give you more time to prepare for your future. Today's battle is won. Duke Arnell Prescott is dead, the Eastern Marches will fall to the second son, but you will have much work to do."

"Majesty," Stuart began. "You are still alive, Master Rhohan—"

"I know I am dying, no matter what Rhohan does."

"No!" Stuart raised his head and looked at the battle surgeon. "Is there nothing you can do?" he pleaded."

"There is one last thing," Rhohan said, "but His Majesty would not let me touch him until you returned, in case it did not work."

"Whatever it is, do it! Do it now!"

Rhohan nodded. "I will need Duke Richard's assistance as well," he said quietly as he reached for a generous goblet of un-watered wine with a liberal amount of opium in it and held it to the King's lips. "Drink, your majesty, it will help dull the pain."

The King did as he was told and gulped the goblet of wine down.

"Richard!" Stuart called, and the Duke appeared a few seconds later. It was then that the Prince noticed the Duke was limping heavily. "You're hurt," he stated.

The Duke shook his head. It wasn't important.

"It is time?" Richard questioned and Rhohan nodded as he turned to check the knife heating in a small fire. It was glowing red.

"Please, take your places," he said to the other dukes.

They immediately moved to the table. Rodric and Kenneth held the King's legs, Richard put firm pressure on one shoulder, and indicated for the Prince to do the same on the other.

Rhohan took the round cylinder of wood and placed it in the King's mouth. "Are you ready, Your Majesty?"

Rhisart nodded, took several deep breaths and closed his eyes, as Rhohan removed the hot knife from the fire, pulled the latest blood-soaked dressing from the open wound and lay the knife on it. The King went rigid whilst his son and the three dukes held him down as he strained against them. His face showed the agony, the veins in his neck stood out as he fought those who held him down. He did his best not to make a sound, but a long low groan forced its way out past the teeth-clenched piece of wood.

The smell of burning flesh assailed everyone's nostrils. The knife seemed to stay against the King's skin for an aeon, but it was only a few seconds. Time seemed to slow almost to a standstill, and then Rhohan removed the blade and inspected the wound. The knife had cauterised it, the skin was red and thoroughly seared, but it appeared to have stopped the bleeding.

Rhisart's body suddenly went limp as he passed out. The battle surgeon quickly checked to make sure he was still alive, and he nodded, but didn't smile.

The three dukes stood back and waited.

"What happens now?" Stuart asked, his face white.

"The next few hours will be critical. He will either live...or die. His Majesty has lost a lot of blood; he wouldn't let me do this until he had spoken to you, Prince Stuart. I just hope it hasn't been too long." Rhohan reached for the blankets again and draped them carefully over the King's body to help keep him warm.

Stuart stood by his father's side and looked down at the pale features. A frown was etched on the King's rugged face even in his unconsciousness, but the Prince didn't see that, his mind was drifting off at a tangent. His father had to survive, he wasn't ready for ruling an entire kingdom, he still had too much to learn. He bowed his head and prayed with all his might that his father would live.

But it was not to be. Rhisart never regained consciousness and died just four hours later. Richard's wound prevented him from kneeling before the dead King, so he stood, his head bowed and offered up a prayer. He closed his eyes, fighting not to be overcome with grief and took several deep breaths before he opened them and straightened up. Turning, he came face to face with Stuart's stricken expression.

"Your Majesty," he said quietly. "May I be the first to offer my sincere condolences at your loss."

Stuart said nothing, but just continued to stare at the face of his dead father, the expression now at peace.

"Sire, what is your command?"

That question brought Stuart back to reality with a start. *Sire!* He was King of Devonmere now. He swallowed slowly, and tried to speak, but his throat constricted, and he felt like he was choking. He swallowed again and cleared his throat.

"Ga – gather the men. We need to announce the death of... of the King."

Richard nodded.

"I will deal with it, Sire. With your permission..."

Stuart nodded and waved a hand. He couldn't speak anymore.

Richard bowed, turned and limped away to find squires to spread the word for the men to gather in front of the King's tent.

It didn't take the squires long to get the message passed to the majority of the army, and they began to gather, as they had been ordered, expecting to hear from their King about the glorious victory. They stood waiting patiently for their sovereign to emerge from his tent. Morgan had joined them and was standing right at the front.

Suddenly, the tent flaps moved, and Stuart came out, followed by Richard, Rodric, Kenneth and Dafydd. They all looked haggard and strained, but the Prince had the expression of a man who was carrying the weight of the whole world upon his youthful shoulders.

They stopped. Richard took a deep breath and then spoke to the eager, waiting men. "The King is dead...Long live the King!" His voice wavered slightly. Rhisart had been twelve when the Duke had first met him—though being just two, he didn't remember much of the first meeting—and their association covered most of his life. Now, he had a new King. The waiting men were shocked to hear the news, and it took them a few seconds to make the expected response.

"Long live the King! Long live the King!" the army shouted and, as one, they all took a knee and bowed their heads in respect.

From somewhere, deep inside, Stuart found the resolve to speak firmly.

"Arise, men." He paused as everyone got to their feet. "Victory is ours, but at great cost. We must take comfort that my father knew he had succeeded in quelling the uprising from the Eastern Marches, at least for the moment. We have peace again in the Kingdom and, going forward, I hope I can count on the continued support that you gave so willingly to my father."

Beside him, Richard withdrew his sword from its scabbard and held it vertically against his chest, as he said loudly: "With respect and honour, Sire!"

Taking the hint, the rest of the men followed the gesture.

"With respect and honour, Sire!" they repeated.

Stuart raised a hand in acknowledgement.

"Tomorrow morning, we will finish collecting our dead, make preparations to break camp and head back to Ellesmere, but tonight we celebrate the life of King Rhisart, and our victory."

The men cheered and shouted, "King Rhisart and victory!"

Stuart acknowledged them once again; indicated for Morgan to follow him and turned to re-enter the tent. Richard held the flap open and motioned for the boy to precede him inside.

The young Duke had seen more than his fair share of war and death, that should be seen by any boy of his age, and now he was to view the body of the dead King, who was laying on the table, covered with a rich blanket. The only sign that anything untoward had happened were the blood stains on the rug on which the table was standing.

Rhisart's face seemed at peace, but Morgan noticed how grey it looked, especially with the black hair and beard. Self-consciously, he gave a small bow of respect and followed Stuart, to assist him out of his armour.

"Sire," Morgan said softly. "Shall I send for Aiden to assist you?"

Stuart shook his head. He didn't want his steward to witness any weakness he may show. He'd sooner it be Morgan who saw if he couldn't maintain control until he was alone.

"Then I will fetch you some water to refresh yourself."

"Thank you, Morgan. That would be most welcome."

The boy bowed and disappeared to complete his task. He returned shortly with a basin of warm water which he placed on the table within what was now Stuart's bedchamber. He then disappeared again.

The new King was just easing out of his silk shirt when Morgan returned with a generous goblet of wine. He accepted it gratefully and took a large mouthful, before handing it back to Morgan and bending over to wash his face.

Morgan put the goblet down, and reached for a cloth which he placed in the bowl whilst Stuart dried his face, wrung it out, and handed to Stuart to continue to wash his chest.

The King gave him a fleeting smile and nodded his thanks. Task completed; Morgan fetched him a clean shirt.

"Is...is there anything else I can do for you, my Liege?" the child asked.

"Send Richard in. I think I need to order him to rest that leg. I don't want to lose my most trusted ally with loss of blood."

"At once, Sire."

Richard came through a few seconds later.

"Sire, I will make arrangements to transport King Rhisart back to Ellesmere."

"Thank you Richard, but it can wait a few hours. I order you to rest that leg. I will have need of your wisdom and guidance in the coming days and weeks. I couldn't bear for something to happen to you as well."

"'Tis but a small wound, Sire."

"Your limp says otherwise. It is my decree that you rest. Tell Rodric to prepare the wagon, then I expect you to go to your tent and rest for the night. Do not disobey me."

"I will obey, my Liege. I will find Rodric, give him your order and retire." He bowed and left; his limp slightly more pronounced.

Stuart addressed Morgan.

"Ask Rhohan to visit Duke Richard and provide him with pain relief so he gets a good night's sleep. Then, go to bed, Morgan. You look exhausted. Tell Aiden to attend me in the morning."

"Sire, surely I must—"

"Do as you're told, Morgan."

The child bowed and left, suddenly realising that his new King required some time to himself to work through the loss of his father and King. Somehow, he also knew the next few months were going to be very taxing for his Liege.

Having given Rodric the instructions to prepare transport for the King's body back to the city, Richard retired to his tent and dropped his chausses on the nearest chair, making a dozing Trystan jump at the noise. He stood, went to pick them up, then looked at the Duke. His master looked tired to the bone, so instead he assisted him out of the rest of his armour and placed it on top of the chausses. Once Richard was settled, he would take care of it.

The Duke was sad, but his comfort was that Stuart was safe and that Duke Arnell had been killed in battle.

However, the kingdom was still a troubled one, and with Stuart being almost eighteen, it could be that others would try to usurp him from his new position. Thankfully, Trahaearn was still alive, although seriously wounded, and once recovered would transfer his allegiance to the new King; but it also put more pressure on Morgan, to attain the required level of skill to become Stuart's protector and champion. No one had expected this situation to arise so soon. All had hoped to see Rhisart in power at least until Morgan had attained knighthood. As it was, he was still not of the age to be officially recognised as Duke of Rossmere. That title was still over two years away.

Richard stretched his aching muscles. He was so tired. The long hard ride to the Marches, to get into position for the battle, the battle itself, his injury and the ride back to the main camp, had all taken their toll.

"Your Grace..." Trystan asked concerned.

The Duke sat down heavily on his cot, just as Rhohan arrived.

"Your Grace, His Majesty has ordered you drink this." He held out a goblet.

"What is it?" Richard asked suspiciously.

"Just something to ease the pain and give you a good night's sleep." He waited for the Duke to take the goblet. When Richard made no move to take it, he added, "It is by order of the King, Your Grace."

The Duke took a deep breath and then accepted the offered goblet and took a sip.

"All of it," Rhohan ordered, standing over him.

Richard looked up at the surgeon, noticed the expression on his face, and did as he was told.

Rhohan took the goblet off him, put it on a nearby low table, then lifted the Duke's legs onto the cot and stood guard until Richard had laid down. He fought the drug, but his eyes grew heavier and heavier until he succumbed to sleep.

The surgeon nodded in satisfaction, reached for a blanket and covered him, to keep out the chill of the winter night.

"Make sure he stays there until morning," Rhohan told Trystan who nodded.

Outside, the knights and foot soldiers had been rewarded with wine, mead and sweetmeats and although sad at the loss of their fellow comrades and their King, were also in a jovial mood. Lookouts were still posted, as the rest of the army settled down for the night.

In the King's tent, Stuart finally surrendered himself to the King's cot, not wanting to be too far from his father. Grief threatened to overwhelm him, but he couldn't let it win the battle, not when there were others close by. He had to stay strong, at least until they got home. He rubbed a hand wearily across his face and shut his eyes. His body took this as a signal to induce sleep, and it was how Rhohan found him a little while later. Again, he grabbed a nearby blanket and covered his new King, before retiring himself.

ය ∞ ය ∞

By the next morning, Rodric had organised transport for Rhisart's body, using what they had close at hand to try and make it acceptable to convey their departed monarch back to the Devonmere capital.

Stuart and Richard awoke to a cold, frosty morning, with a temperature around freezing. Dafydd had already started organising the breakdown of the camp, ordering the men to be as quiet as possible until the King appeared, but they still made enough noise to wake their sovereign.

Morgan, who was already up and about, returned to the King's tent with some food for Stuart, when he emerged from the small alcove.

"My Liege, I have brought you breakfast."

Stuart's stomach churned at the mere thought of eating anything, and he shook his head.

"You eat it," he replied.

"But Sire, you need to—"

"I'm not hungry. I'll have something later."

Morgan nodded and changed the subject.

"Duke Rodric has prepared the transport for the King," he said, almost in a whisper.

Stuart let a flash of pain cross his face for a few seconds before he pulled himself together again.

"And General Hughes is currently overseeing the breakdown of the camp. He says we should be ready to leave in a couple of hours. Men have been despatched to collect our dead."

Stuart nodded.

"Very well. We will return to Ellesmere once they have returned."

"Your majesty," a call came from just outside the tent.

Stuart recognised the voice immediately.

"Enter, Richard."

The flap of the tent moved, and Richard limped in. If anything, he was moving worse now, than he had been the day before.

"Apologies Sire, I confess to having some difficulty walking this morning," the Duke said.

"Are you well enough to ride?" Stuart asked in concern.

"I will be all right, I just need to keep moving, although I may require some assistance mounting my horse." Richard looked rather embarrassed at that admission.

Stuart looked critically at the Duke's leg. He was still wearing the same breeches, but he had a clean dressing and bandage over the wound.

"You've had a visit from Master Rhohan, I see," Stuart said.

"Yes, Sire. About an hour ago. Has Morgan updated you on our current situation?"

"Yes, he has, and very aptly too."

Richard nodded with approval. "In which case, with your permission, I will assist Dafydd and Rodric with His Majesty. I believe we should allow the wagon to leave now, with a small detachment. Their progress will be slow, and it will not take us too long to catch them up."

Moving the dead King's body to the wagon seemed to make it 'final' and the end of an era, but a new chapter was beginning, the rise of

Stuart Cantrell. Stuart had insisted on lending a hand, after all it was his father they were placing on the wagon.

Dafydd draped a clean surcoat with the coat of arms over the blanket, then placed the King's sword and shield on top.

This isn't happening...it can't be happening, Stuart thought to himself. *It's just a nightmare and I'll wake up shortly.*

But he didn't wake up, he couldn't, because he was already awake, and it was all horribly real. At that precise moment, he wanted to run away, hide and scream, but the royal family did not succumb to such weaknesses.

Richard guided everyone away from the wagon to leave Stuart alone. The new King needed to grieve, but this was neither the time nor the place. All Richard could offer him was a few moments alone with his deceased father before the wagon left with its escort.

The Duke turned away and saw Morgan standing just a few steps from him. He limped up to him and lay a hand on the boy's shoulder. Morgan looked up at him, his eyes searching those of his guardian.

"Are you all right, Morgan?" the Duke asked him.

"Yes, thank you, Papa."

"You have a huge responsibility now. Trahaearn will help you until you are ready, but it means a lot of hard work, as you are now page to the new King."

The boy nodded. "Will you be returning home soon?" he asked.

"Once the King is buried. It will take time to plan Stuart's coronation and with winter here, I surmise it will not take place until spring next year. Why do you ask?"

"I just wanted you to give Mama and Colwyn my love. When I am recognised as Duke of Rossmere, I hope I will have the opportunity to visit again."

"I'm sure you will. If you wish to write a letter, I will gladly take it back with me."

"Thank you, Papa. That would be most agreeable."

Richard smiled fondly at him and returned to watching his new King who was still standing by the wagon.

Stuart finally lifted his head, took a deep breath and straightened up. He wasn't ready for the responsibility of Kingship—of ruling an entire kingdom—and if he was honest with himself; the prospect terrified him. At that moment, he wished his mother was still alive, and that Morgan was older, so that the young Duke could help him.

Abruptly, he stopped that train of thought. What was he thinking? He was King now; he had to be strong, for his people; for the Kingdom. Then another thought came to him. Michael, he had to tell his brother that their father was dead. The teenager was going to be sixteen next year and was looking forward to being knighted by his father. Now the only close relation he had left was the new King. Rhisart had been a stern father, but he had been the foundation of the family; solid, reliable, fair, supportive, and very strict. Now he was gone.

Stuart wondered how on earth he was going to tell Michael and also support him during the grieving period when there was so much to do. He looked up to see Richard looking at him, sympathy written in his features. The Duke walked over to him and whispered in a very low voice.

"My Liege, I will do all that I can to support you in the early days," he said.

Stuart suddenly felt like crying, hearing the unwavering support offered by his father's most trusted supporter. He swallowed and turned away, taking a deep breath to gain back control of his emotions. A few seconds passed and then he turned back.

"Th – thank you, Richard, that means a great deal to me. I – I will have to tell Michael..." His voice trailed off.

"I will tell him, if you prefer," Richard offered.

Stuart shook his head.

"Thank you, but...I think it will need to be me that tells him."

Richard nodded in understanding.

"Whatever you need from me, please do not hesitate to ask."

"Thank you." He took a deep breath and cleared his throat. "Instruct the guard to leave for Ellesmere." He stopped talking again, fighting to maintain control, then carried on. "Richard, please excuse me." He turned to enter the King's tent. "Morgan, attend me."

"At once, Sire."

03 80 03 80

The journey back to Ellesmere was somewhat subdued and became even more so once they had caught up with the wagon transporting Rhisart's body. His charger was tethered to the back of the wagon and was walking quietly, the King's helm hung from the pommel of the saddle. Trahaearn was in another wagon, deemed by Rhohan as too badly wounded to sit astride his horse.

As the army finally approached Ellesmere a narrow black pennant was added underneath the King's to denote that death had occurred, and it was then that Stuart realised that a herald would be blown announcing their return and his brother was likely to be at the entrance of the keep to welcome them, without the new King being able to pre-warn him of the tragic news.

He glanced at Richard, trying to catch his eye. The Duke saw a movement and turned his head. Stuart leant towards him slightly.

"The...the pennant...Michael will see the pennant," he whispered.

"You cannot go ahead, Sire. You must remain to escort the King's body. With your permission, I will ride ahead and break the news."

Stuart nodded.

"As soon as we are through the town and begin the ascent, I will go ahead."

The people of the town were silent and bowed their heads as the wagon led the way, escorted by Stuart, Richard, Rodric, Kenneth and Morgan. Behind them, the knights were led by Dafydd. They were followed by the foot soldiers and archers, then bringing up the rear were the supply wagons, many of them carrying the wounded and the dead.

As the front of the column reached the foot of the hill, Richard spurred his horse onwards, cantering upwards over the drawbridge of the moat, the zig-zag path, over the drawbridge of the ditch and towards the Barbican.

The Duke crossed the Lower Bailey, went under the Gatehouse and into the Main Bailey. As he looked ahead, he saw Prince Michael waiting with various stewards. Taking a deep breath, the Duke approached the youngster and halted at the bottom of the steps.

Michael frowned at him in confusion, not understanding why he wasn't with the main column and watched as Richard dismounted with difficulty and limped towards him, taking one step at a time.

Reaching the younger Prince, the Duke bowed.

"Prince Michael," he began.

"The battle, did we win?"

"Yes, Your Highness."

Michael smiled, but then it faded as Richard's expression remained grave.

"What's wrong? What's happened?" Michael suddenly asked. "Why have you come ahead of the column?" The questions tumbled over one another.

Richard took a deep breath. He was not a stranger to breaking bad news, but it never got any easier, especially when he had to deal with wives, and especially children of the fallen.

"Prince Michael, please..." He gestured for the boy to precede him into the keep.

"What is it? Is it father? He's been hurt, hasn't he?"

Richard kept his voice low and calm.

"I'm afraid I bear grave news, my Prince." He paused as he saw Michael's eyes widen with uncertainty. "We were successful, but at a cost. Your father, the King, defeated and killed Arnell Prescott, but... unfortunately he was...mortally wounded." Richard paused again, as he saw Michael's bottom lip tremble. "I'm sorry," the Duke continued, "but it is with the deepest regret that I must inform you that the King died of his injuries."

Michael fought bravely to maintain control of his emotions, as he had been trained to do, but he was failing. Disregarding all etiquette, Richard stepped forward and hugged the boy as he succumbed to his grief, burying his head against the Duke's shoulder.

Richard said nothing, but simply held him, offering support, letting him cry for as long as he could, before finally speaking again, as he heard the herald announce the arrival of the column.

"My Prince, you must be strong," he whispered. "Your father, the King is here. You must greet him and accompany him to the private chapel."

Richard felt the youth take a number of deep breaths and wipe a hand across his eyes to dry them, before he straightened up, nodded and dared to meet the Duke's eyes.

"Come, Your Highness, he will soon be here." He indicated for Michael to precede him back outside onto the steps of the keep.

Richard stood directly behind Michael and unobtrusively placed a hand on his shoulder to offer moral support as the wagon approached with Stuart, Rodric, Kenneth and Morgan directly behind, and the elite Ellesmere guard behind them. As they halted in front of the keep, Stuart dismounted and walked to the bottom step. He saw Richard whisper something to Michael, who slowly came down the steps.

The two brothers stood and looked at one another for a few moments. Stuart saw the pain and the struggle to maintain composure in Michael's eyes and reached out. They hugged tightly, trying to offer solace to each other. No one interrupted them, they waited until they separated, then Stuart guided Michael and they walked behind the wagon as it continued its journey towards the private chapel, with Richard just behind them.

Outside the chapel, one member of the elite guard lifted Rhisart's shield and sword from the body, then another six carefully lifted the dead King from the wagon and carried it on their shoulders into the chapel. As a temporary measure, he was placed on the altar and Rhohan carefully made sure Rhisart was laid as required. The sword was placed on top of his body, his fingers wrapped around the hilt, and the shield on top, then the six guards took their place to stand watch. They would be swapped every four hours until Rhisart was ready to be transported to the cathedral for buriel.

Bishop James Douglas arrived and made his way to the altar, offering a prayer over the King. Everyone present stood with bowed heads and uttered an amen when he had finished. Then he went to the King's two sons and offered his condolences.

"I will begin the necessary preparations," he said softly.

Stuart cleared his throat before speaking. "Thank you, bishop."

James bowed and retreated to begin work on the state funeral.

Stuart and Michael stood a while longer, bowed their heads once more, then turned and left the chapel, followed by the dukes and Rhohan.

The mood was still sombre, as Rhohan ordered Richard to rest. Stuart, who wanted some time alone with his brother, instructed Morgan to accompany his guardian, and everyone dispersed. Battle surgeons checked the wounded, those who felt like eating, ate. Those who needed rest, slept.

ㆍ ㆍ ㆍ ㆍ

Rhisart's tomb was already prepared. He had ordered it to be created when his queen had died a number of years ago. The accompanying sarcophagus had been built to hold both of them, and the King's effigy was already there, although not quite finished, next to that of his queen. Shortly, they would be reunited once the state funeral had taken place.

The people came to pay their respects over the next few days, filing past the King's body. The flag flying from the top of the castle keep had been lowered to half-mast and everyone dressed in sombre colours for the period of official mourning.

It would usually have been custom to await the arrival of dignitaries from all corners of the land, but with winter approaching, the weather was beginning to deteriorate quickly. If the funeral did not take place soon, Rodric would be unable to get home until the spring, and Stuart did not want him stranded so far from home, so it was agreed it would take place as soon as possible.

Thus, on a freezing, cloudy morning that threatened snow, the procession left the castle. Half of the elite guard headed the procession, followed by a more ornate open carriage that carried a lead-lined beautifully carved coffin. Behind that were Rhisart's two sons, then the dukes of the kingdom that were either already present or had managed to journey to Ellesmere having seen the beacons, lesser earls and lords, and finally the other half of the elite guard. All were in dress uniforms with black armbands.

They travelled at a slow pace. People were once again lining the route to the cathedral, and bowed their heads as the procession went past. Some then joined it, walking behind the rear guard.

The ceremony was long, as the bishop wanted to celebrate Rhisart's life as well as commit his body to the tomb. Both Stuart and Michael found it hard to get through, but the reassuring presence of Richard by their side provided them with the support they so desperately needed in their grief.

Eventually the service finished, and Richard ushered everyone except the two brothers out of the cathedral, to give them time on their own. In the background, the main cathedral bell tolled solemnly for a couple of minutes.

After around ten minutes Stuart and Michael exited the cathedral. Half the elite guard had remained to escort them back, and Richard was waiting patiently at the bottom of the steps, despite the fact that it had begun to snow. Having descended the steps, Stuart gave the Duke a weak smile.

"Thank you, Richard." He paused to look at the falling snow, which couldn't make up its mind whether it was going to settle or not. "It looks like winter has finally arrived. Everyone needs to get home before conditions get too bad and they get stranded in Ellesmere." He paused again.

"Would you like me to stay, Sire?" Richard finally asked.

He could see by the expression in the young King's eyes, that he desperately wanted the Duke to remain with him a while longer, but he shook his head.

"You have a young daughter. I have no right to keep you here unnecessarily. You should be home with them, especially as Christmas is fast approaching."

"Thank you, Sire. I will stay if you want me to. Bronwyn will understand."

"But Colwyn won't, she is too young. No, you must head home, but if you would return in the spring, to help me prepare for the coronation, that would be most welcome."

Richard nodded.

"Please come and see me before you leave."

"But of course, my Liege."

He stood back as the King mounted up. Michael stopped by Richard's side, then suddenly threw his arms round the startled Duke and hugged him.

"Thank you, Richard," he whispered, then straightened up, and also got onto his horse.

Richard bowed before turning to his own mount. One of the elite guard gave him a leg up into the saddle, as his wound still prevented him from bending his knee to get his foot in the stirrup, and then they returned to the castle.

Richard went in search of Morgan once they arrived back, and found him in his rooms. The boy smiled a warm welcome and gave his guardian a hug.

"I am returning to Inver tomorrow morning," Richard told the boy. "The King has told me to go home, although I know he would prefer it if I stayed. If you compose your letter, I will take it with me."

"I will write it straight away... How is your leg? You're still limping."

"I will admit that it's sore," the Duke replied. "The most inconvenient aspect of it, is I can't get on my horse without help. I will visit you before I leave."

"I will come and see you off," Morgan said.

"Your first few months here have been very eventful. I hope things quieten down for you, at least for a while. You're looking tired."

"I confess, I have found it exhausting, and with practicing my magic...Trahaearn says it will get easier as I become used to it."

Richard nodded. "I'm sure it will. Well, I have a few duties to perform still, but I will see you later."

ೞ   ಲ   ೞ   ಲ

The following morning, Richard was in the King's chambers saying goodbye.

"Sire, turn to Bishop Douglas, he is wise, and also to your general. They will assist you over the coming months... but I can stay if you so wish."

"No," Stuart said, shaking his head. "You must return home, as much as I would appreciate you staying, it's not fair. So, I will wish you a safe journey and see you in the spring, the first week in April, weather permitting. I am planning the coronation for May. That will give everyone plenty of time to prepare and make the journey."

Stuart looked around self-consciously and, confirming there was just the two of them in the room, succumbed and threw his arms around Richard in a fierce hug.

"I can't thank you enough for the support you showed my father, and me and...for Michael. He told me of your meeting when we arrived back from the Marches."

"Know that you can always count on my continued support, Sire, for as long as I live. I don't pretend to completely understand what you are feeling right now... overwhelmed, frightened, nervous, and perhaps even alone. But know that you will never be alone. You have

156

your brother, you have me, Trahaearn, the bishop, the general and, also Morgan."

"And for that I feel blessed, but a King's position is lonely...and I am frightened, Richard. Everything I say and do from now on affects the kingdom and the people. If I make a wrong decision..."

"That's why you have advisors, older and wiser. Think before acting, do not make rash decisions, think it through to its conclusion and the possible consequences. You can do no more. Be just, but firm. Serve your people well."

"As always, your words provide me with comfort. Thank you. Now, best you leave, I have seen more snow in the clouds, it feels colder and may start to settle, and you need to get home safely. I believe the Rossmere army will be travelling with you until you get through the pass."

He hugged Richard once more, then stood back and shook his hand.

"I will see you in April, Sire."

The Duke turned and left. Morgan was waiting for him on the steps of the keep, wrapped up against the cold.

"Morgan, Stuart will need your support more than ever over the coming months. He was not expecting to be King so soon. Forgive him, if his temper is short, he is trying to find his way in his new position. The responsibilities will lie very heavily on him. I will not be here, but you will be. You must be my eyes and ears and help the King until I return in April."

"I will do my best, Papa."

"As I know you always do. Have you got something for me?"

"Oh! My letter! Yes." The boy handed it over and watched as Richard placed it safely in one of his saddlebags.

An Invermere knight assisted the Duke into the saddle, and with a final wave, Richard and Martyn Welles, led their armies home.

 G & G &

Chapter Ten

The Rossmere and Invermere armies travelled together until they reached the other side of the narrow pass between the High Hills. Already the temperature was staying close to freezing, even during the day and the snow that fell was beginning to settle, so they pushed on hard, as they knew if they lingered, they would be in danger of not reaching their destinations before the trails became snowed under and impassable.

Richard shook Martyn's hand and bid him safe passage as they parted ways and continued on their separate journeys. The going became more difficult as the days went by, and keeping up the hard pace became dangerous but necessary. It also caused severe discomfort to the Duke as the wounds on his thigh were continuously aggravated.

His own battle surgeon, Master Gethin, kept a close watch on his master, growing more concerned as time went on.

Three days away from Inver in camp that evening, Gethin voiced his concerns.

"Your Grace, the wound isn't healing, the chaffing of the saddle has undone the work of the cauterising, and you are continuing to lose blood. Will you at least ride in one of the wagons to give your leg a chance to start healing?"

"Many of the wounded have no option but to ride their horses," Richard said, wincing as his battle surgeon re-dressed the wounds and bound them tightly. "I will not take the easy way out when my men have no choice. We only have three more days to go, then we will be home, and I can rest."

By the time they reached the River Wyvern, the snow was over a foot deep, the wind was howling and the river itself beginning to freeze at the edges. The one consolation was as the temperatures had dropped early before the clouds had started to release their moisture, and the wet season had started, most of the moisture was trapped, frozen in the High Hills and mountains, resulting in the level of the river being at a reasonable depth for a safe crossing.

Once everyone was safely across, spirits rose, two days and they would at last be home, and in time to enjoy the twelve days of Christmas.

Finally, Inver Castle came into view, and it was a most welcome sight. Despite the appalling weather, people came out of their houses and lined the streets, cheering the returning army, which lifted the knights' spirits further, and half an hour later they were in the Main Bailey.

Richard continued on to the steps of the keep, where Bronwyn and Markus were waiting, wrapped up warm against the bitter wind. He saw the look of sheer relief on his wife's face at having him home safe again. As he carefully dismounted, she ran down the steps and threw her arms around him, not caring he was mud spattered, and carrying a growth of beard.

"Richard! Thank goodness you're home, I was becoming so worried..."

Any further conversation was cut off as the Duke kissed her fiercely, ignoring etiquette as he crushed her to him. There had been times, when he thought he wasn't going to make it back, and his show of emotion in front of his knights was the release of the stress, strain, grief and relief that they were home.

"My darling," he finally whispered against her lips as the kiss ended. He was so tired and weary, and needed to let go, but he knew he had to hold himself together a little while longer, for his men.

He held Bronwyn at arm's length, seeing the love and concern in her eyes, then turned to his knights.

"Men, we have reached home." His voice was thick with emotion. "I thank you as always for your service. We will honour our dead, care for the wounded, but we will also celebrate victory over the forthcoming days. Let it be known that our dead contributed greatly to us being victorious. Their sacrifice will never be forgotten, as we fight to maintain peace in the kingdom of Devonmere.

"The pages will take care of your horses; the surgeons will look after the wounded. Check on your men, then go home and be with your families. Those of you without family who are staying, food and wine are being prepared for you in the main hall. Thank you for your continued service to me and the King. God save King Stuart!"

"God save King Stuart!" the men shouted, and then one of them called out:

"God bless Duke Richard!" and the shout was taken up and repeated three times.

The Duke acknowledged them with a wave of his hand, then looked down at his wife as she gripped his arm tightly and saw her look of shock and sorrow.

"Rhisart is dead?" she asked in a choked whisper.

He nodded but couldn't speak. Hearing her say those words, caused grief to well up in him again.

"Oh Richard, I am so sorry. I know the two of you were close..." she let her voice trail off as she saw the pain in his eyes and instead started to lead him up the steps to the keep, pausing as she realised he could only take them one at a time. As his heavy cloak moved, she spotted the bloodstained bandage around his leg. "You're hurt!" she exclaimed.

"'Tis nothing," he replied, but his leaning on her quite heavily for support hinted otherwise.

Bronwyn was about to call for Master Gethin when he appeared at the Duke's other side and assisted him up the steps.

"I have sent Trystan ahead to get hot water ready. You will do no more today," Gethin said firmly. "You will permit me to change the dressings, and then you will rest on your bed. No arguments."

Richard was now too exhausted to argue, but from somewhere he found the strength to ask one final question.

"Where is my little angel?" he asked Bronwyn.

"She is inside with Sarah. I thought it wise not to let her be on the steps with me, just in case."

"Will you bring her to me, once Gethin has finished his work?"

"Of course I will."

"You must rest, Your Grace," Gethin interrupted.

"I will see my daughter!" Richard snapped more harshly than intended.

Safely in his rooms, Gethin and Trystan removed the Duke's armour and his clothes. Bronwyn had insisted on staying, wanting to see for herself, that the leg injury was the only one he was suffering, and that he was not hiding any others from her.

Trystan bathed and shaved the Duke whilst Bronwyn observed, noting several fading bruises on her husband's body along with some minor cuts and abrasions, he had also lost a little weight. She sighed, realising he had survived the battle relatively unscathed.

Clean again, Trystan assisted him with his robe, then guided him to a chair so Gethin could complete the task of redressing his wounds.

"Your Grace, the aggravation the wounds have suffered will leave a larger scar than hoped," the surgeon said softly.

Despite the discomfort, Richard attempted to make light of it.

"Gethin, women love men with scars, it shows them to be brave and fearless." He looked pointedly at Bronwyn and saw the fire flare up in her eyes.

"No we do not!" she snapped, rising to the bait. She was angry, for she knew her husband would have thrown himself into the battle, leading his men, putting himself at risk. That's why they followed him, because he never asked them to do anything he would not do himself.

Tasks completed, the two men assisted Richard into bed and drew the bedclothes up around him, as the room still had a chill in the air, because the fire had only recently been lit.

Gethin placed a goblet of wine containing pain relief and something to make the Duke sleep, on the bedside table but he refused to take it.

"I will see Colwyn first," he stated.

Bronwyn moved to the door of the outer chamber and ordered a passing page to get Sarah to bring Colwyn to her immediately.

A number of minutes passed before they arrived in Richard's day room. Sarah gingerly walked towards the bedchamber and was met at the door by Bronwyn.

"Thank you Sarah. I will bring Colwyn back to you."

"As you wish, Your Grace." Sarah curtsied and left, but not before she had managed a glimpse of the Duke, who she thought looked exhausted and ill.

Bronwyn addressed her daughter.

"Your father is home safe but—" she paused as Colwyn's eyes lit up in anticipation of seeing him. "—he has been injured. It's not serious, but you must be careful. He has a bad leg. Do you understand what I am saying?"

Colwyn nodded furiously, even though she didn't completely comprehend what her mother was telling her. Her papa was home!

"Come then." She took her daughter's hand and led her into the Duke's bedchamber.

"Papa! Papa!" she cried, breaking free from her mother and running towards the bed.

"Colwyn, my darling," Richard said holding out his arms.

The two year old ran into them, and he lifted her up onto his lap, burying his head against her shoulder as she hugged him with all her might.

"Papa! I love you."

The Duke's resolve almost broke at that point. Bronwyn saw him screw his eyes shut as he fought to maintain control of his emotions.

Colwyn felt him tense and drew back concerned.

"Papa hurt. I make better," she said innocently, and kissed his cheek. "Papa better now?"

Richard cleared his throat before speaking.

"All better," he managed to say. "Thank you, my darling."

"Make sure," she added and kissed him again.

Bronwyn saw he was losing the battle with his emotions, and stepped forward, taking their daughter in her arms.

"Papa must rest, Colwyn," she said, "He is very tired after his long journey home."

He nodded at her gratefully.

"Papa rest, get better. Come back later," Colwyn said blowing him a kiss.

Bronwyn shifted her so one hand was free and held it out to her husband. He took it as she mouthed, I love you. The look he gave her said it all, and she smiled, pulled her hand reluctantly from his grasp, turned, and left the room.

Gethin immediately pounced, picked up the goblet and thrust it into Richard's hand.

"Drink, now," he ordered and stood arms folded, watching as the Duke did as he was told.

Satisfied, the surgeon took the goblet and put it down on the side table, then removed a couple of pillows, so Richard could lie slightly flatter, and stood back again, not moving until the Duke had succumbed to the sleeping draught in the wine, and his eyes closed.

"He should be asleep until tomorrow morning," he told Trystan. "Please check on him every now and again. I'll be back in the morning to change the dressing." Gethin nodded to the steward and left. He had other patients to check before he managed to get some sleep himself.

ଓ ଚ ଓ ଚ

The following morning, Richard awoke to find Bronwyn sitting by his bedside, holding one of his hands. She smiled lovingly at him, as he opened his eyes.

"Good morning my husband, you are looking better than you did yesterday. A good night's sleep has done you the world of good, but I can see you are still tired."

It was true, he was still very tired, but he was feeling better. The grief was still there, but not as pronounced and he surmised it was exhaustion that had made it feel so much worse yesterday. He smiled at his wife and pulled her towards him.

"Bronwyn, my love…" he kissed her thoroughly, knowing the effect it would have on her. She pulled away from him.

"Do not start anything you cannot finish," she said huskily, running a hand teasingly over his chest and smiling as she heard his sudden intake of breath.

"I can finish what I start," he whispered in her ear, making her tremble in anticipation, but she drew back from him.

"No, you can't. Your leg...I don't want you doing anything that may cause it to take longer to heal... You will have something to look forward to," she added demurely.

He was about to reach for her again when there was a knock on the door. Bronwyn's lips twitched in amusement as she saw his eyes flash momentarily with annoyance at the interruption.

"Come in," she called.

The door opened and Sarah came in holding Colwyn.

"Forgive the interruption," she said curtseying, "but Colwyn is refusing to do anything until she has seen His Grace."

Richard held out his arms and Sarah handed her over.

"If I may be so bold, you are looking a little better this morning, Your Grace," Sarah added, swallowing nervously. It was the first time she had ever been in his bedchamber and seen him in such a state of undress. He was good looking, and his hair in disarray gave him a rather roguish appearance.

"Thank you, Sarah."

She curtseyed and left in rather a hurry.

Bronwyn watched her go, then turned to her husband and gave him a knowing look.

Richard met her gaze in between hugging his daughter.

"What?" he finally asked.

"You still have it," his wife said.

He frowned. "Have what?"

"That roguish, disarming way that can wrap a woman round your little finger."

"Roguish?"

"Oh I've heard the stories. The Queen told me some good tales about you and the King before we were wed." Bronwyn started to laugh at the expression on his face.

"Papa better this morning?" Colwyn asked before he could defend himself.

"Yes, my darling, Papa is feeling much better, especially after seeing your beautiful face." He kissed her forehead and she giggled. He cuddled her and looked at his wife. "Did she behave herself whilst I was away?"

"I was a good girl," Colwyn interrupted. "Wasn't I Mama?"

"Yes, my darling, you were."

"Good. Oh, Bronwyn, in my saddlebags is a letter from Morgan."

"Morgan coming home?" Colwyn asked.

"Not yet, but hopefully quite soon," the Duke answered.

"I miss him."

"We all miss him," Bronwyn said rising from her seat and going to the outer room to find the saddlebags and the letter.

She returned a few minutes later and sat down again.

"How is he, truly?" she asked Richard.

"He is well; at least two inches taller, I'm sure. And before you ask, there are no after effects from...you know..." He didn't want to use the word 'beating' in front of Colwyn.

"None? Are you sure?"

"I am sure. He conducted himself with honour at the battle camp. He's seen sights a child should never see, but he has come through it. He misses you both, but what does he say in his letter?"

Bronwyn broke the seal and unfolded the parchment to read the letter aloud. In it he told them that his magic was improving, that his studies were going well, and that he had a good relationship with Stuart and Trahaearn. He thanked them for the beautiful pendant that he wore almost all the time. He had purposely left it back at Ellesmere when they had gone to the Eastern Marches, as he had been scared of losing it, but now it was again around his neck and close to his heart. He also told them about his new friends and that they were genuine, so he wasn't as lonely as he had been, but he still missed them and Inver, and looked forward to the day when he could come home for a visit.

"I am happy he has some friends now and I do hope he will be able to visit soon."

"Stuart has some hard adjustments to make, so it may be longer than we anticipated. No one was expecting him to be king yet. He still has to find his way in his new role."

"I'm surprised you didn't offer to stay."

"I did offer," Richard confessed, "But he insisted I return to you and Colwyn. I have to return to Ellesmere in April to help him prepare for the coronation. It's been a while since you left the castle, my love. You must attend the coronation with me. For now though, I am home, and we can look forward to the twelve days of Christmas. I think Colwyn is now old enough to begin to appreciate it."

"Appre...appresheate, Papa?" Colwyn asked, making a gallant attempt at a new word.

"A very special time of year, my darling, when we celebrate the birth of our Lord and give thanks for His coming."

There was another knock at the outer door, and Gethin came in. Bronwyn took that as a signal to remove her daughter from the room so the battle surgeon could do his work.

The wounds were redressed, and Richard took that as a sign to get out of bed.

"Where does His Grace think he's going?" Gethin asked.

Richard froze.

"You are to stay in bed, apart from...how can I put this...personal ablutions," Gethin finished.

"Gethin, I have a duchy to rule. I can't stay here, in bed."

"With respect, Your Grace, the Duchess Bronwyn appears to have managed perfectly well without you." Gethin knew he was pushing the boundaries, but he knew Richard would understand his concern, even though he may fight against the surgeon's ruling. "If you stay in bed you will recover faster. If you insist on rising, you must rest with that leg elevated. Once the wound begins to knit properly, you may move around, slowly and gently. Ignore my recommendations and you will be out of action even longer."

Richard opened his mouth and promptly shut it again.

"I will follow your advice," he finally replied and Gethin looked triumphantly at him.

ℭ ℬ ℭ ℬ

Richard was up and about just in time for the twelve days of Christmas, and the role reversal. Markus once again served as Lord of Misrule, a role he greatly enjoyed. It was a happy time, although Morgan was missed, especially by Colwyn. The family all hoped he was enjoying his first Christmas at Ellesmere.

On twelfth night, Bronwyn crept into the Duke's bedchamber and slipped naked under the covers, waking him with a start.

"Bronwyn?" he questioned, "is something wrong?"

"Now my husband is well again, I did promise him something to look forward to," she breathed into his ear, as her hand meandered its way down his body to rest on his manhood.

Richard's sudden jagged intake of breath was all the encouragement she needed to continue her attack...

Normality returned after twelfth night, as far as it was able, for the bitter weather continued into March, and best laid plans for crops were delayed until the snow disappeared and the ground began to warm.

Thoughts also turned to the forthcoming coronation. As soon as the passes were clear, messengers arrived informing the various duchies that it was planned for May when travel within the kingdom would be relatively easy.

ༀ ༀ ༀ ༀ

Morgan's first Christmas away from home proved quite difficult. Once again, he felt terribly homesick and missed the joy of being in a real family at this special time of year. What happened at Ellesmere though was quite similar; he attended midnight mass, Ellesmere's head steward was Master of Misrule and in a weird switch round, because being a page meant he had served the King and been under his beck and call, over the twelve days, Stuart and his brother Michael, had waited on him and the other pages and squires.

Having some genuine friends did help ease the melancholy he had felt, and small tokens had been exchanged. Stuart and Trahaearn had surprised him also with some larger token gifts.

All too soon life returned to normal, and in addition to all his regular studies, he, along with seven other pages, had been selected to take an active part in the coronation and thus started rehearsing their roles so it would be perfect when the actual day arrived.

ༀ ༀ ༀ ༀ

Chapter Eleven

———◆———

Stuart stared at himself in the long mirror. Was the young man with the haunted expression really him? His hazel eyes reflected the worry and uncertainty he was still feeling. Today was the day; the day he would be crowned King; King of all Devonmere.

Several months had passed since King Rhisart had been killed. In that time, aides had arranged his burial, and the ceremony for the crowning of the new King. Stone masons had put the final touches on the effigy that was mounted on Rhisart's tomb. Stuart had turned to Richard and Bishop James Douglas, to help him make the various necessary decisions as to what it should look like, along with the invitations for the ceremonies of his forthcoming coronation and the knighting ceremony in June.

In between all that had been Christmas, and Morgan's eighth birthday in the February. Richard had returned as requested in April to help with the final preparations for the coronation. Now it was May.

Bronwyn and Colwyn, accompanied by Dilys, Sarah and an escort, had arrived the day before the coronation was due to take place. It was the first time Colwyn had been away from home, and she had travelled reasonably well, only losing her temper towards the end of the journey due to over tiredness and being subjected to many new experiences that had overwhelmed her.

Richard had been at the entrance to the keep to greet them and escorted them to their rooms. Sarah had immediately prepared Colwyn for bed and laid her down, before unpacking everything.

Dilys had done the same with Bronwyn's clothes, poured some wine, then left her mistress alone with the Duke.

"You are looking tired, husband," Bronwyn said to Richard as she sipped her wine.

"Things have been hectic," he admitted. "Morgan will be so pleased to see you and Colwyn. He's talked of nothing else since he realised you would be here."

"I can't wait to see him."

"You will see him tonight at supper. For now, I think you too should rest, so you are prepared for this evening."

Bronwyn's hand lingered on his chest.

"You cannot stay a while?" she asked looking up at him, her lips parting invitingly.

Richard succumbed and kissed her thoroughly before drawing back.

"I'm afraid that will have to do...for now..."

He kissed her once more.

"I have more errands to run, but I will return to escort you down to the banqueting hall this evening. For now, rest." He smiled at her, his eyes twinkling, then left her staring after him.

As he promised, Richard escorted his wife down to the banqueting hall that evening, where an eager Morgan had thrown himself at the Duchess, hugging her with all his might.

"Mama, I'm so pleased to see you!" he enthused, treating her to a huge smile.

"Morgan!" she gasped, overcome by his welcome. "I hardly recognised you! How you've grown!"

"I would have come to see you earlier, but my duties prevented me. Is Colwyn here? I so want to see her."

"Yes, she is here. Hopefully you can see her tomorrow, before the coronation begins?"

"I will do so. I may only have a small amount of time free, but I must see her too."

"Come, let us go to our places," Richard said, "the banquet is due to begin, Stuart is on his way."

They had just taken their positions at the top table when Stuart arrived, looking nervous. Richard had told him not to stay too long, as it was going to be a very long day tomorrow. The King welcomed his guests, thanked them for coming, bade them sit, eat and drink.

Musicians played whilst they ate. Richard and Bronwyn took to the floor after eating and danced. Stuart excused himself after a couple of hours, taking Morgan with him but encouraged his guests to carry on. Richard and Bronwyn left shortly after.

The Duke had escorted his wife back to her rooms, and then at her invitation stayed for an enjoyable night of pleasure, leaving early in the morning to get ready for the coronation.

Morgan had risen early and rushed to Colwyn's rooms to see his sister. She had squealed in delight at seeing him and hugged him with all her might. The little girl had grown considerably in the ten months since he had left Inver. Her beautiful green eyes seemed even more green than he remembered, and her chestnut hair had grown to be almost down to her waist. Instinctively he just knew she was going to be very beautiful when she grew up.

Reluctantly he said he had to go, but that he would see her later, and left Sarah to prepare her charge for the forthcoming event.

☙ ❧ ☙ ❧

Aiden had done an excellent job in dressing his master. Stuart was dressed in white, from the delicate silk shirt, jacket and breeches, all decorated in the finest filigree gold thread in intricate designs. The jacket was also quilted in a diamond-shaped pattern and finished off with a jewel-encrusted belt. The long white boots were also trimmed with a thick gold cord. His black hair shone and fell about his shoulders. Stuart may have looked very regal, but he was feeling far from it. There were butterflies in his stomach, and he felt nauseous. He swallowed hard, in an effort to quell the feelings, but failed miserably. Not wanting Aiden to see his nerves, he had dismissed him.

Suddenly, a discreet cough caught his attention, and he shifted his gaze to see Morgan standing a little way behind him, a goblet in his hand. The boy had grown another couple of inches since the death of Rhisart.

"Sire, would you like some wine, to see if this will ease your nerves?"

Stuart turned to face him; his expression rather sad.

"You used to call me Stuart, when we were alone, as we are now," he said to the boy.

"You are my King now. It would be disrespectful of me to address you so informally," Morgan replied, holding out the goblet, and pointedly ignoring the fact that Stuart's hand was shaking slightly as he reached out and took it from him.

Stuart nodded slowly and took a deep draught. He needed someone to ground him going forward; to keep his feet firmly on the ground. The informal address he had allowed Morgan to use, made him feel 'normal'. Going forward, at least for the moment, he would have to rely on his younger brother to help keep him sane. Perhaps, once Morgan was older, and a knight, he would be able to address Stuart by his first name again.

A knock on the door brought him out of his wondering thoughts.

"Come," Stuart responded, and Osian Thomason, the Master-of-the-Robes, entered.

He bowed respectfully.

"Sire, the time is almost upon us." He moved to Stuart's bed where the opulent Robe of State lay, carefully spread out. It was made of a heavy, rich crimson silk, lined with ermine and decorated with delicate handmade gold lace from the Duchy of Invermere.

The Master-of-the-Robes carefully picked it up and Stuart moved closer, so that it could be placed around his shoulders and the ornately decorated gold clasps were fastened.

There was another firm knock on the door, and Richard entered, dressed in all his finery. Stuart silently gave a sigh of relief. A steady calm descended on him as the Duke approached.

"Are you ready, my Liege?" he asked, smiling kindly, as if he knew how the young king-to-be was feeling.

Stuart straightened up, took a huge, steadying breath, and nodded slowly.

"I am ready," he confirmed.

Richard looked at Morgan, who was in the dress livery of Devonmere.

"You know what you must do, Morgan?" he questioned.

The boy nodded.

"I have rehearsed for weeks with the Master of Ceremonies," he confirmed, his face serious as always.

"With your permission, Sire," the Master-of-the-Robes said, and at Stuart's nod, he clapped his hands, and four pages entered the bed chamber. They immediately moved behind Stuart and carefully lifted the Robe of State.

Richard gestured with his left hand for his King to precede him from the room, and the small procession made its way along the corridor, carefully down several steps, along more corridors and out of the keep. More steps were taken down to where the royal coach stood waiting. Four Devonmere-Grey horses stood patiently. Their black leather had been cleaned and polished; the brass glinted in the light. Manes and tails had been carefully plaited and tied with gold ribbon, and their coats shone. Hooves had been washed and oiled.

A footman opened the door to the carriage, Stuart stepped in, and the Master-of-the-Robes supervised the loading of the fourteen-foot-long Robe of State, before the door was closed. Prince Michael joined him from the other side.

Satisfied all was in order, Richard moved to the rear of the coach where a page was holding his horse and mounted. Ahead and behind the coach were the Devonmere elite guard, resplendent in their dress uniforms. In front of the procession was another coach, containing the royal regalia, guarded by knights, and immediately behind, rode Morgan and seven other pages.

Everyone moved slowly out of the castle, down the winding road, over the moat, the ditch and through the city towards the cathedral. People lined the entire route, waving and cheering. The noise was deafening, 'God save the King' could be heard from many quarters and lifted Stuart's heart.

The eight pages dismounted first and moved to the coach that was carrying the royal regalia, which consisted of two royal maces, the Sword of Mercy, the Sword of Spiritual and Temporal Justice, the Sword of State, the orb, St Dafydd's staff and St Dafydd's crown.

Whilst the pages sorted out their order of procession, Stuart was assisted from the coach and the ornate Robe of State was spread out on the ground behind him, visible for all to see.

With a nod from Richard, they all started to walk slowly up the steps towards the main cathedral entrance, every footfall in unison as the crowds eagerly watched, a herald announcing to those already within, that the royal party approached.

Arriving at the top of the steps, the bishop blessed the royal regalia, then led the procession slowly down the aisle, to the altar, where the pages very carefully deposited the items, before moving to the side.

Stuart inclined his head and moved to sit in the Chair of Estate, whilst the rest of the royal party took their seats. The pews were lined with Dukes and Duchesses from the twelve duchies of Devonmere, their families, and dignitaries from surrounding islands and countries. All were dressed in their best finery as befitting the coronation of a new king. The families of the two duchies that were taking an active part in the ceremony had the honour of being placed on the front rows of the pews. This included Bronwyn and Colwyn.

Bishop Douglas turned to the congregation, and welcomed them to this auspicious occasion, recognising the various visiting dignitaries. He then motioned for Stuart to move and stand before the Coronation Chair, that was situated facing the high altar.

The coronation ceremony consisted of several stages. The first was the recognition. The bishop and the other three members of the clergy presented Stuart to the four corners of the coronation theatre, starting with the east, then south, west and finally, north. The congregation gave shouts of joy.

The next stage was the oath. Bishop Douglas nodded at Morgan, who retrieved the Sword of State and moved to stand in front of Stuart, the sword held upright in salute. He turned his back on the sovereign and solemnly walked towards the altar, Stuart following him. On reaching it, Morgan turned, keeping the sword in its upright position as Stuart placed his right hand on the Holy Bible.

Bishop Douglas, standing before him, spoke slowly in a deep, rich voice.

"Stuart Rhisart Aiden Eurion Cantrell, will you solemnly promise and swear to govern the peoples of Devonmere according to the laws and customs of the Kingdom?"

Stuart cleared his throat nervously.

"I will," he replied.

"Will you, in your power, cause law and justice in mercy, to be executed in all your judgements?"

"I will."

"Will you, to the utmost of your power, maintain the laws of God and the true profession of the Gospel? Will you maintain and preserve inviolably, the settlement of the Church, and the doctrine, worship and discipline and government thereof, as by the law established in Devonmere? And will you preserve unto the bishops and clergy of Devonmere, and to all the churches there committed to their charge, all such rights and privileges, as by law do, or shall appertain to them or any of them?"

"I will."

Stuart then moved and kissed the bible.

Bishop Aulean of Inver handed him a scribe and Stuart signed the written oath.

Bishop Douglas nodded in satisfaction and opened a marked page within the bible and began to read a passage to all those present. A hymn followed, then another reading, a hymn, and a prayer that Stuart would be a just and fair King, protect the innocent and weak, defend the honour of his people, and combat evil and vile doers.

The next part of the ceremony consisted of the anointing. The Master-of-the-Robes stepped forward and divested Stuart of all celebrated symbols of status and dressed him in an anointing gown consisting of a simple white linen bliaut with a white belt that he wrapped twice around Stuart's waist and tied in a simple knot at the front. The gown's official name was the Colobium Sindonis and was to symbolise the future King divesting himself of all worldly vanity, to stand bare before God.

Stuart then moved to the coronation chair and four knights approached with a pall made of silk, to shield the congregation from the next part of the ceremony.

Bishop Douglas picked up the Ampulla and coronation spoon from the altar and stood before Stuart. He poured some Holy Oil into the spoon and anointed the young King's hands, chest and head, before handing the Ampulla and spoon to one of his companions. Indicating for Stuart to kneel, the bishop placed his left hand on the young man's head and raised his right one as he gave the blessing.

"Stuart Rhisart Aiden Eurion Cantrell, you kneel before God, divested of all your worldly vanity to receive His blessing. May God keep you, protect you and guide you in the ruling of the Kingdom as you are crowned this day. Seek His wisdom in times of trouble, put your trust in His hands and in your peers and people that they may serve you with reverence and respect. Amen."

"Amen," Stuart repeated quietly.

The four knights removed the pall and walked away, then Stuart stood in preparation for the actual investiture.

Osian approached with the Supertunica, a long flowing coat of golden silk, and expansive sleeves trimmed in golden lace, decorated with the national symbols of Devonmere. He dressed Stuart in the coat, and then fastened it with a gold buckle that was adorned with roses and the Devonmere lion.

Two squires then presented the Pallium Regale or robe royal which was also embroidered with the national symbols and the royal lion in silver thread in the corners of the four-square mantel. This robe designated the divine nature of kingship.

Morgan knelt before Stuart and presented the gold spurs, before first fitting the right one, and then the left. He bowed his head and then rose and moved out of the way to retrieve the sword of state, which he presented to Stuart, bowing again as he did so. The young boy bowed once more, and then moved aside, as Stuart held the sword upright before him then sheathed it in the scabbard at his side. He then sat in the Coronation chair, and another page presented him with St Dafydd's Staff and the Orb. The Coronation ring was placed on the fourth finger of his right hand, and finally, he received the sceptre with the cross, and the rod with the dove.

Bishop Douglas picked up the Crown of St Dafydd and turned to stand directly in front of the seated Stuart.

"We beseech thee O Lord, to invest thy servant, Stuart, Rhisart Aiden Eurion Cantrell, with wisdom and justice, so that he may serve his people firmly, yet kindly. That he will rid the Kingdom of thine enemies, and those who would do evil against the people of Devonmere. That he will protect the innocent and weak and defend the virtue of women."

He paused as he raised the crown above Stuart's head then continued.

"By the power of God and the Holy Church, I crown thee King of Devonmere." The crown was placed upon Stuart's head.

At the same time, all the peers present, placed their own crowns and coronets on their heads and shouted, "God save the King!" which made Colwyn jump in fright.

This was immediately followed by the peeling of the cathedral bells, heralding that the new King had been crowned and was now ruler of them all.

Bishop Douglas paid homage to the new King and pledged his support, followed by the other bishops and clergy present. Richard then stepped forward, bowed deeply and accepted the sceptre and the rod from Stuart and placed them on the altar. Prince Michael came forward to bow in respect and pledge his support and was then followed by the dukes of Devonmere, including Morgan, who was the last to do so, as it was his duty to accept the crown and place it back on the altar.

Communion followed, then Stuart knelt before the Coronation Chair whilst Richard and Duke Kenneth Dernley of Strathmere, removed the Pallium Regale, the Supertunica and the Colobium Sindonis. The passing of these items to a number of pages was supervised by the Master-of-the-Robes.

Bishop Douglas then said another prayer and ended that part of the ceremony with a blessing for the new King.

That completed, the final part of the ceremony was the recessional. Stuart rose from his knees and walked into the private chapel, with Richard and Osian. A number of minutes passed, and then Stuart emerged, wearing the Imperial State Crown, and the Imperial Robe, which was made of a heavy purple silk, eighteen feet long, trimmed with ermine, and with a sumptuous ermine cape. He held the sceptre in his right hand, the orb in his left, and slowly walked along the aisle to the huge double doors of the cathedral, to meet his subjects. Behind him followed Prince Michael, the clergy and the peers.

A dozen members of the elite guard stayed behind to collect the royal regalia that was on the altar and deposited it in its coach for transport back to the castle, whilst Stuart stood on the steps of the cathedral to acknowledge the people standing before him.

After several minutes had passed, he descended the steps to his waiting carriage, and was assisted inside; the heavy Imperial Robe was lifted and carefully arranged around him. Prince Michael joined him, and they were driven back to the castle.

As befitting such a grand ceremony, there was to be a feast and entertainment that evening, so Stuart would have a couple of hours to himself before the festivities started. To him, the whole ceremony seemed to have passed him by and he couldn't remember a single thing after he had arrived at the cathedral, until he had returned to the castle.

He was King. He closed his eyes for a few moments to let it all sink in.

"Sire?" Michael asked. "Is everything all right?"

Stuart opened his eyes and turned his head to look at his brother.

"Michael, when we're alone, please call me Stuart. I need you to keep me grounded. We're brothers and we need to support each other."

"Very well, Stuart, as you wish." Michael grinned at him. "What does it feel like, to be officially crowned King of Devonmere?"

"You want the truth? I'm terrified! Everything now rests on me. One wrong word or deed, I could plunge us into war. If I'm too soft, there are others who would try to take advantage of me, or even try to take the crown; if I'm too hard, the people will see me as cruel..."

"It is a fine line that you must tread."

"But how do I know?"

"That's where your advisors come in. Duke Richard Coltrane has always been a Cantrell supporter and father thought a lot of him. I'm sure he would be pleased to offer you advice if you needed it."

Stuart looked down at the floor, pondering.

"I must not appear weak or indecisive, and I must be able to make decisions and face the consequences when I am wrong."

"You attended father when he held court, I'm sure some of his wisdom must have rubbed off on you."

Stuart did not reply, but simply frowned in concentration.

"And for goodness sake, remember to smile now and again, otherwise I will think my brother has been replaced by Morgan!"

Stuart smiled then, albeit briefly.

"We wouldn't want that now, would we?" Michael continued, chuckling.

"You can't blame Morgan for being how he is," Stuart said, jumping to the young Duke's defence. "I'm just thankful that Richard and Bronwyn did such a good job of raising him. Can you imagine what would have happened if he had started down the path of darkness?"

Michael shuddered at the thought.

"He may be just a boy still, but Sir Trahaearn did say he was going to be incredibly powerful. The Kingdom would be plunged into darkness and fear if he ever faltered," Michael whispered.

"Then we must make sure he never does." Stuart paused. "Would you mind leaving me, Michael? I could do with some time alone, to digest my new position."

"Of course. I will leave you in peace, and see you tonight, at the banquet. Do you need me to find Morgan and send him to you?"

"No. I think I can cope for a couple of hours! I will see you in the banqueting hall this evening."

Michael bowed respectfully, and left Stuart alone in his new rooms. He had avoided coming to what had been his father's rooms until after the coronation today. In the months since his father had died, they had been redecorated to Stuart's preference and, as he looked around, he realised he had put his own stamp and identity on them. It was clear to see they reflected everything that made Stuart the man he was.

He had also insisted that Morgan be moved closer as well. Trahaearn was still on the other side of the King's rooms as befitting the position of royal protector.

Stuart sighed and loosened the buttons on his jacket. The padding made it feel so restrictive, he could hardly breathe in it. Moving to the table, he poured himself a generous goblet of wine and took a large mouthful. It was a disgraceful way to treat a good wine, but it helped relax him as it hit his stomach and sent a warmth radiating outwards. And with that warmth came a feeling of calm and peace. He closed his eyes and breathed it all in. His heart rate began to slow, and with it came a form of clarity of where he stood in the universe.

Opening his eyes, he moved to the window and surveyed the view of his kingdom. *My kingdom*, he mused. The land was well on the way to bursting into life. Spring flowers were on the wane, crops were being sown, or had already been planted. The ewes had their lambs, life was everywhere. He lost himself in the moment, and the next thing he was aware of, was a knock on the door.

"Enter," he called, and turned to see Richard walking towards him. "Richard..."

"Sire, the festivities are about to begin, and our guest of honour is missing."

"It's time already?"

"It is."

"Don't let me drink too much, Richard. It wouldn't do for the King to make a fool of himself at his first official engagement!"

The Duke smiled and laughed, his eyes taking on a faraway look as he remembered a distant and fond memory.

"What is it?" Stuart queried. "What memory has amused you so?"

"We were wilder back then," Richard said, shaking his head, but still smiling.

"'We'?"

"Your father and I."

"You? Wild? Never! I don't believe it."

"It's true, Sire. Before he was crowned, your father and I had many a wild evening, drinking far too much and not behaving as due our station."

"When we have time, you must tell me about some of these wild adventures. I think I have missed out on enjoying myself!"

Richard smiled almost roguishly at his King, which piqued Stuart's curiosity even more, and he made a mental note to interrogate his supporter at a more opportune moment. For now, it was time for him to attend the banquet in the hall below.

ᘓ ᘔ ᘓ ᘔ

The tables in the banqueting hall were full of dignitaries from the far reaches of the kingdom and nearer oversea lands. Stuart paused at the double doors and took a deep breath. He then nodded to the two guards who opened them.

"His Majesty, the King," one of the guards announced.

The room fell quiet, and everyone stood as he entered, observing him as he strode along the walkway, and up to the dais and the top table. He was followed by Prince Michael, Richard, Rodric, Kenneth, Morgan, Dafydd, Bishop Douglas and Trahaearn. Bronwyn— holding Colwyn— and Mereli were already standing at the top table. Stuart's brother and supporters took their places whilst the King stood and surveyed the expectant faces below.

"My lords, ladies and gentlemen. Welcome to this coronation banquet. I thank you for your support and to continued peace upon our lands. This is a day of celebration," he said in a firm voice. "I hope I will serve you as well as my father did. Know that I will be a just and fair King, defending the weak, following the teachings of God, and continue to defeat evil and those who would do harm to you all. This I pledge with my life."

"God save the King!" Richard said loudly.

"God save the King! God save the King! God save the King!" the assembled audience repeated.

Stuart acknowledged them and sat down.

"You may all be seated," Richard said, and everyone did so.

Musicians at the side of the room began playing softly, whilst squires and pages began serving food and wine. There was a huge assortment of both, and the mood was jovial as the guests ate and drank their fill.

Stuart noticed there weren't that many women guests present. The few that were, consisted mainly of wives of the other lords and the occasional daughter, who all kept glancing at him, as if to attract his attentions, but they were wasting their time. Stuart was too busy concentrating on not making a fool of himself to let any guard down, however he did agree to Richard's suggestion of dancing with at least a couple of the wives, and began with Bronwyn, who handed Colwyn to Richard.

"Bronwyn, it is good to see you again. I feel I must both thank you and apologise to you."

"Thank me and apologise, Sire? I don't understand."

"I thank you for allowing Richard to aid me whilst I find my way. Also, for the aid he gave my father, and I must apologise for keeping him away from you and your beautiful daughter for such long periods of time."

"Sire, we are honoured that you have such a high regard for the House of Coltrane, and we are proud to do our duty to the kingdom."

"Know that it will never be forgotten."

The dance finished and Stuart returned her to Richard, thanking him for allowing him to dance with her. Then he moved onto Mereli McLeod.

Morgan held Colwyn whilst Richard danced with his wife, enjoying having her close, talking to her, feeding her treats, and bouncing her on his knees. Eventually though, she grew tired and ready for bed.

On returning from her dancing, Bronwyn summoned Sarah who arrived and took the child back to her rooms to sleep.

The celebrations went on well into the night, and the amount of wine consumed led to a drop in some inhibitions, but Stuart managed to stay sober. Richard gave him a nod of approval, then glanced at Morgan, who had been relatively quiet all evening after Colwyn had left, and was currently doing his best to stay awake, and beginning to fail miserably. It had been a very long day for the eight year old and it was way past his bedtime.

"Sire," the Duke began, leaning slightly towards the King. "With your permission, I would like to get Morgan to bed," he whispered, nodding in the boy's direction.

Stuart's expression softened as he watched his page gallantly trying to stay awake, but every now and again his head dropped.

"Of course, how thoughtless of me. I will retire also, then my guests can relax and enjoy themselves without their King passing judgement." He rose, and everyone stopped what they were doing and got to their feet. Silence descended. "Please, continue to enjoy yourselves. I will withdraw now." He nodded at Richard, who moved and picked Morgan up.

The boy stirred, but Richard shushed him and with Bronwyn beside him, took the child to his rooms, where they left Ioan to take care of him and put him to bed, then escorted his wife to her chambers before heading for his.

187

CR ᗷ CR ᗷ

In his own rooms, Trystan was waiting for the Duke of Invermere, and helped him out of his jacket. He then poured the Duke a goblet of wine and went through to turn down the covers on the bed.

Richard took a long draught from the goblet then heaved a huge sigh, mainly in relief that the day had gone well, and that one obstacle had been overcome.

"Is everything all right, Your Grace?" Trystan asked as he came back from the bed chamber.

"Everything is fine, Trystan. It's just been a long day!"

"That it has," Trystan agreed as he came forward to assist the Duke to prepare for bed.

"We have the celebration tournament to get through and then hopefully we can head for Inver."

"Another long couple of days, Your Grace. I have polished your armour in readiness."

"Thank you Trystan. I'm getting too old for this sort of thing."

"Begging your pardon, but you're only just in your thirties, Your Grace. I would call that your prime!"

"You certainly know how to make a man feel good about themselves! Thank you for that."

Trystan poured some water into a basin, then held out his hand for the Duke's shirt. Richard obliged by pulling it over his head and handing it to him, and the steward stood patiently whilst his lord washed.

The Duke was still in excellent physical condition, his skin marred only by a couple of scars that had been obtained in battle. The most recent ones on his thigh had healed well but were still quite vivid. Trystan shuddered at the thought of having to do what his master had done; having been shot by an arrow, he had pushed it out through the other side of his leg. That took real courage, but then, Richard was royalty and a knight.

Trystan knew many of the common people thought those of station had an easy life. Some did, he knew that, but his lord had suffered the hardship and horror of battle many a time so far in his life and was likely to suffer more in the future. He worked hard at keeping peace in the duchy, serving justice, holding court. It wasn't an easy life. Far from it, but the Duke accepted it.

Richard straightened up, the muscles in his arms flexing as he ran his hands through his hair before he turned and took the offered towel to dry himself.

"Do you require your robe, Your Grace, or are you retiring immediately?" Trystan asked.

"Well, as it's the tournament tomorrow, I suppose I had better get some sleep!" He smiled ruefully at his steward. "What do you think my chances are, Trystan?"

"Well, my lord, it depends on whether Sir Trahaearn has fully recovered from his injury. If he hasn't, I believe you have a good chance of winning."

"Trystan, you're biased! I've never won a tournament in my life!"

"You came close last time, you were runner-up."

Richard stopped and pondered.

"I was, wasn't I?"

"Yes, Your Grace. So, if Sir Trahaearn isn't back to full fitness, you are in with a very good chance."

Richard grinned.

"I think Morgan would be very pleased if I won. I will most certainly do my best. Thank you for giving my ego a boost. I'll take my wine and retire, you get some sleep, Trystan, I'll see you in the morning.

Would you bring me breakfast when you come, I'd sooner eat alone and prepare myself mentally."

"Very well, Your Grace. Sleep well." Trystan made a little bow and retired to his own room next door, leaving the Duke in peace.

ଔ ଊ ଔ ଊ

The following morning dawned bright and clear. Richard was still fast asleep when Trystan returned to lay his armour out in readiness, then disappeared to fetch the Duke some breakfast.

The kitchens had been a hive of frenzied activity as they prepared food for all the guests, and Trystan had gotten in and out as fast as he was able, so he wasn't in their way. With breakfast laid out neatly on the small table, he went through to the bedchamber and pulled back the heavy curtains.

Richard didn't stir, which was unusual for him, as he was a light sleeper, but then he took a deep breath and woke.

"Good morning, Your Grace. It is a beautiful day. Your breakfast awaits you."

The Duke wiped a hand across his eyes, stretched, pushed the bed covers down and sighed heavily.

"Morning already?" he moaned.

Trystan grinned at him.

"I'm afraid so, Your Grace. But it is a beautiful morning." The steward picked up the robe that was draped casually on the nearby chair and held it up, ready.

The Duke threw the covers back and swung his legs over the edge of the bed. There wasn't an ounce of spare flesh anywhere on his body, despite the fact he didn't see quite as much action nowadays, Trystan mused, as his lord accepted his help to put on the robe.

"I believe the odds of your success may have increased this morning," Trystan continued.

"How so?" Richard asked as he fastened the belt on his robe.

"It appears the coronation celebrations continued until the early hours of this morning, and many of the competitors may have...over indulged. The castle is exceedingly quiet at the moment."

A smirk caressed the Duke's lips. Eighteen to twenty years ago, he would have been one of the over indulgers. His smirk turned to a grin as Trystan raised an eyebrow and allowed his own lips to twitch as he too remembered Richard's wilder days.

The Duke decided to eat before he washed and got dressed for the tournament. Breakfast finished, Trystan helped him get ready, assisting him with the hauberk once he had finished his ablutions and donned his silk shirt, breeches, chausses and aketon. He then knelt down and attached the spurs before standing and helping him with the surcoat. Next came the surcoat belt and the sword belt. Trystan retrieved the Duke's sword from the table, letting Richard inspect it before he sheathed it.

"With your permission, I will meet you in the warmup area with your shield and helm," the steward said.

Richard nodded and left his rooms, heading towards Morgan's chambers. The youngster would have a bit of a dilemma. Of course, he would want to support his guardian, but he may also feel some loyalty to his mentor, Sir Trahaearn. If it turned out they met before the final, poor Morgan would have a difficult decision to make.

Ioan answered the knock on the door and opened it to find the Duke standing there.

"Your Grace! Good morning to you. My Lord is awake and dressed. He was about to come and find you."

"I'm going into the practice rings to warm up, so thought I would say good morning now, before things get too hectic."

"Of course. Please, come in." Ioan stepped back out of the way.

"Papa!" Morgan ran to his guardian, who knelt to receive the bear-hug of a welcome. "Did you carry me to bed last night?"

"Yes, I did."

"I apologise for my falling asleep."

"Morgan it was well past your bedtime, you did well to last as long as you did."

"You always make me feel so good. Thank you."

"You're welcome. I am going to warm up in the practice rings."

"May I come with you?"

"Won't the King require your presence?"

"No, he left a message with Ioan. I think he knew I would want to be with you first thing this morning."

"Very well, although I am going via Bronwyn's rooms. Shall we go?"

They walked like father and son as they made their way to Bronwyn's chambers. Richard knocked firmly on the door, and it was opened by Dilys.

"Your Grace, Lord Morgan, welcome. Her Grace is up and in her day room. Please come in."

They entered and went through to where Bronwyn was sitting, with Colwyn on her knee. Colwyn gave a squeal and struggled to get down so she could run to them.

"Papa! Morgan!"

She reached them and Richard bent down and picked her up, twirling her around in a circle before hugging her and receiving a kiss from her. Then he placed her back down on the ground and she immediately hugged Morgan tightly. He picked her up and she clung to his neck, kissing his cheek.

"I love you both," she said with feeling.

Bronwyn came to them.

"Richard," she said. "You look as handsome as the day I first saw you." She reached up on tiptoe to kiss him.

"And you as beautiful," he replied, returning her kiss. "Will I see you at the tournament shortly?"

"Of course you will. I must support my husband, and champion."

He smiled kindly at her.

"Morgan and I are on our way to the practice rings. I will watch out for you, my love."

"Sir, take this favour to protect you and bring you luck." She handed him a silk embroidered handkerchief which he placed safely within the sleeve of his aketon. He then bowed to her and looked down at Morgan.

"We must leave now. Come, young man, we must go."

Bronwyn reached out, indicating for Morgan to hand Colwyn over. Before doing so, he gave his 'sister' one last hug and chaste kiss, and followed Richard out.

They made their way down to the practice rings. Morgan hadn't seen Richard's swordsmanship for quite a while and was eager to see how well he handled a sword.

The practice rings were deserted.

"Where is everyone?" Morgan asked more to himself.

"Trystan said most of the guests over indulged last night and are feeling a little worse for wear this morning."

"You didn't though, did you?"

"My days of sowing wild oats are long gone," Richard replied without thinking, and he closed his eyes briefly as Morgan's mouth dropped open at this revelation.

"You?" the child queried.

"Perhaps I will tell you when you're older," Richard replied. He pulled his sword from its scabbard and was about to start his warmup exercises when he caught Morgan staring at him in a whole new light. "What?" he finally asked the boy.

"I'm just trying to imagine you being wild and reckless," the child replied.

"Meaning?"

"You've always been so calm, collected, measured. I just can't imagine you being..."

"Young?" Richard said as a suggestion.

"But you are young."

Richard laughed kindly.

"Thank you, Morgan."

"But it's true. You aren't as old as...Trahaearn."

"That is also true," the Duke replied starting his exercises. "Who will you be cheering today?"

"You, of course, who else would I support?"

"Your mentor?"

"Oh...well I can cheer for both of you."

"What will you do if we come up against one another?"

"I hadn't thought of that...you are my father...but..." Morgan frowned, torn between his loyalties.

Richard smiled kindly at him, as he continued his exercises.

The boy watched avidly as the Duke skilfully twirled his sword around his head and carried out some intricate manoeuvres with it and tried to fathom out the movements of the Duke's wrist as the sword rotated in a figure of eight.

"You'll learn this eventually," Richard said, seeing the expression on the child's face.

"How are you doing that?" Morgan asked.

Richard stopped, held his sword in his left hand and demonstrated the wrist movement in slow motion with his right. Morgan attempted to imitate it.

"You have a good eye, you almost have it, you need to be more flexible...that's it. Now you've got it. If you are going to attempt this, I suggest you forget about trying to perform it with anything in your hand until you have perfected the movement first. Once you can perform it at speed, I suggest you start with a stick...it will be safer! Build back up to speed with that, and then try it with a blunt sword before a sharp one."

"Thank you, Papa," Morgan said, still practicing.

"I recommend you practice with left and right hands. I've seen a couple of knights manage to do this with two swords at the same time. It's known as Florentine."

"At the same time?" The boy frowned. He was having enough of a problem remembering to do the wrist movement correctly with just one hand. Then he gasped as Richard started the movement with his left wrist, transferred the sword to his right, and then swapped back to the left.

"I shall deny ever showing you this movement if Trahaearn tells you off for using it at your age," Richard said grinning, a glint in his eye.

Morgan assured him he had no intention of telling anyone and would practice in secret, but a challenge had been set, he would practice and learn to perform Florentine.

A few other knights started to appear, some looking a little worse for wear after the festivities of the previous evening.

Richard and Morgan stopped and observed them for a few minutes.

"You'll win," Morgan finally said, and Richard laughed out loud. "I'm serious," the boy continued. "It's all they can do to stand up straight!"

Richard managed to stop laughing and indicated with his head.

"Here comes your uncle...Good morning Rodric!"

"Stop shouting!" Rodric said and winced. "I believe there is a man with a blacksmith's hammer striking an anvil in my head!"

Richard and Morgan glanced at one another, and the Duke had to put a considerable amount of effort into not laughing as the boy pulled a face and mouthed silently, "See, told you... you'll win!"

"Go on, off you go," Richard finally managed to say. "We'll be starting shortly."

Morgan skipped off happily towards the main arena, humming to himself, whilst Richard continued with his warmup exercises, finally stopping when Trystan arrived with his shield and helm.

The tournament got underway an hour later and up on the royal dais, Stuart sat with Kenneth, Morgan, Bronwyn and Mereli, who had cornered the Duke-in-waiting to enquire after both his health and his education. She appeared pleased with what she had ascertained when she had touched his face and nodded, smiling.

The King made a speech and then the activities started.

Morgan dutifully cheered both Richard and Trahaearn through their rounds and was still convinced his guardian had a chance of winning, as Trahaearn still seemed a little stiff and inflexible after recovering from the wounds he had received back in November.

Stuart looked at Kenneth.

"So, Kenneth, who's going to make the final?"

"Well Sire, I do believe Richard may actually reach it again this time."

"So do I. Who do you think will be his opponent?"

"I can see that Trahaearn is still recovering, he's still very stiff. Rodric is obviously suffering from his overindulgence last night... if

196

I had known the two of them were this bad, I might have entered myself!"

Stuart tried not to laugh but failed miserably.

"I guess it will depend if Rodric's sore head makes him lose his concentration."

Morgan watched as Richard defeated another knight and reached the final. The youngster cheered, and the Duke gave him a little bow in acknowledgement.

The battle for the other place in the final was between Rodric and Trahaearn. As the two men moved around the arena trading blows, it was evident they were both suffering, but in the end, Trahaearn's experience won, and he sent Rodric staggering back, knocked him to the floor with his shield and that was that.

Morgan cheered again and Stuart looked at him.

"So, Morgan, what are you going to do now? You can't cheer for both of them."

The child frowned and glanced at Bronwyn before facing the King again.

"I – I don't know, Sire. Richard is my father, so of course I want to support him, but Trahaearn is my mentor and teacher..." He sat quietly, trying to figure out what he was going to do, and was still thinking whilst some acrobats came into the arena to entertain the crowd to give the finalists some time to recover.

Then it was time. Richard and Trahaearn entered, saluted their King, and then each other. Everyone cheered, then it went quiet, and the King gave the signal for them to begin.

Morgan watched, his face a picture of concentration as the two opponents circled one another, then attacked. There followed a volley of blows from the two men, that was supported by the noise of the crowd. It was all very polite as the two men took measure of each other, testing, teasing, enquiring, then they got down to the business in hand: winning.

Trahaearn was moving stiffly, but he had superior strength. Richard was agile and flexible and thus able to avoid many of the heavy blows Trahaearn was attempting to deliver whilst landing a good number of his own.

The crowd were cheering continuously for both men were popular. Blow after blow was traded and time wore on. Stuart decided they had fought long enough and was about to call a draw, realising the champion was not yet back to full fitness when Richard made one final gallant effort and drove the knight back so fiercely that he lost his balance and fell.

Trahaearn looked up at Richard and nodded acquiesce. Richard froze in shock. He had actually won!

Grinning like a teenager, he sheathed his sword, pulled off his helm and held out a hand to assist Trahaearn to his feet. The knight accepted the offer, sheathed his own sword, removed his helm and the two men stood looking at one another for a few moments, then gave one another a hug. The crowd roared.

"Well done, Your Grace. A most deserved win," Trahaearn said, shaking Richard's hand once again.

"Only because you are not fully recovered," the Duke replied.

Together they walked back to the raised dais where the King was now standing and faced him. The two opponents unsheathed their swords briefly to salute their King who was clapping his hands with approval, before they saluted each other, then followed the King's instructions and came up the steps to the dais.

Once there, they knelt before their sovereign as Richard was awarded the crown, and Trahaearn with some gold. They then stood and Stuart presented both of them to the crowd of onlookers.

"Well done, both of you," the King said.

"Sire, I only won because Trahaearn is not back to full fitness," Richard replied.

"Do not underestimate your own skill, Your Grace," Trahaearn countered. "It was a worthy win. Who knows, I may get my revenge back tomorrow, in the jousting."

Richard smiled warmly. "Indeed, you may."

They shook hands again, and Morgan approached to congratulate them both.

"Go with your guardian, Morgan," Trahaearn instructed.

The boy gave a polite bow and paused as Richard held out his hand to his wife, who gracefully accepted it and stood, then all three made their way back to the Duke's rooms.

"I am so proud of you," the boy said.

"As am I," Bronwyn added.

"Thank you. I think I am still in shock!"

"Your Grace! Well done!" Trystan enthused as they entered the chambers and immediately came forward to assist the Duke out of his armour.

"Thank you, Trystan." Richard flexed his right arm. "Oh, I'm going to be stiff for the joust tomorrow!"

"I will arrange a hot bath for you, Your Grace, to help you relax."

"And I suppose I should let you rest," Morgan said, hugging Richard around the waist.

"You may stay if you want. I'm aching, not tired."

Richard sighed wistfully as he eased out of the aketon, pulled off his silk shirt and stretched his aching muscles, whilst Trystan ran off to sort out the hot water.

Morgan moved to the table and poured two generous goblets of wine, which he handed to the Duke and Duchess.

"Thank you," Richard said, taking a large mouthful and absorbing the pleasurable feeling as it spread warmly through his body. Bronwyn of course, was more refined in taking a sip from her goblet.

Trystan returned some minutes later and assisted the Duke into his robe, stating the water would be arriving in around thirty minutes or so.

Forty minutes later, Richard was relaxing in his tub of hot water, letting it soothe his muscles for a while before he allowed Trystan to wash him.

Morgan sat on a chair a little way away, so Trystan had full access all the way around the tub and spoke in an animated voice about the tournament and how exciting it had been. He understood it all much better now that he was a little older and because he had family and friends taking part.

Bronwyn smiled indulgently at his enthusiasm and sat quietly, absorbing the sight of her husband as he relaxed in his bath.

Richard's eyes were closed and his head rested against the back of the tub, but he was making all the right sounds in the appropriate places and also answering questions, so Morgan knew he was listening.

Having washed and rinsed his master, Trystan moved to Richard's right and began to massage the Duke's shoulder firmly, causing him to pull a face.

"Does it hurt?" Morgan asked in concern.

"No, it's just a little sore." After several minutes had passed, he flexed his arm a few times and nodded in satisfaction. "You have worked your magic as usual, Trystan."

"Thank you, My Lord." Trystan reached for Richard's robe and held it ready as the Duke got out of the tub and eased into it.

Morgan noticed the scars on Richard's left thigh were still quite vivid and mentally hoped that he would have as much courage to do what his guardian had done should he ever be in the same situation.

Shaking himself out of his reverie, he smiled at the Duke.

"I'm pleased you have suffered no injuries. I will leave you now, so you may get some rest."

"Very well, Morgan. Would you care to join us for a meal this evening, or has the King summoned you?"

"I am free this evening and would love to dine with you," Morgan replied eagerly. If he was lucky, the Duke just might provide him with more instruction on the move he had shown him earlier.

"Excellent. Shall we agree to an hour after sunset?"

"Agreed." Morgan went to Richard and gave him another hug. "Until later," he added, then left.

Richard turned to Trystan.

"Why don't you take some time to see what else is happening, Trystan."

"If you're sure, Your Grace."

"I'm sure. Off you go."

Richard waited until the door closed then turned to his wife. He smiled warmly.

"I also have a reward for my champion," Bronwyn said demurely.

"Oh?"

"Would you like to know what it is?"

"I would."

Bronwyn took another sip of her wine before putting it down on the table, then turned and made her way into the bed chamber.

"It's in here," she said over her shoulder.

He followed her, shutting the door behind him.

Reaching the bed, she stopped, unobtrusively loosened the lacings of her dress, turned and waited for him to get near.

"Would you like to know what reward I have for you?"

Richard saw the loosened lacings, swallowed and took a pretty good guess at what it was going to be. "Yes, very much," he replied, deciding to go along with her little game.

She reached out a hand and sensuously drew it down the V in his robe, parting it as she went, then ran her hands seductively over his chest, her lips following in their wake. Richard closed his eyes and absorbed the pleasant feelings that were already starting to invade his body.

Bronwyn's hands crept up, pushing the robe from his shoulders and then fastened around the back of his neck to pull his head down so she could kiss him. Richard's eyes opened as their lips parted and she indicated with her head for him to assist her with her clothing. Willingly he obliged, sliding her dress from her shoulders, down over her breasts, allowing it to drop to the floor before he pulled her shift up over her head.

"Does my lord wish to receive his reward?" she whispered and smiled as she saw the fire flare up in his brown eyes.

"Very much," he replied, his voice dropping in pitch.

She turned away from him and leant back against his chest, then took his hands and placed them on her breasts. Needing no further bidding Richard gently squeezed them as she moved against him. He nuzzled her neck, gently nipped an ear lobe and allowed a hand to snake down her body to gently touch her intimately, enjoying the sound of her heavy breathing as she continued to arouse him as she rubbed herself against him.

When she moaned, he turned her around, placed his hands under her buttocks and lifted her. She immediately wrapped her legs around his hips, and he walked the last few steps to the bed, carefully knelt on it and then lowered her.

Their love making was slow and passionate as they took their time, savouring the touch and feel of each other. When Bronwyn started moaning, he claimed his final reward as she welcomed him into her body, gasping as he thrust strongly, tirelessly and sent them both over the edge of a cliff, to fly in the height of their passion. Richard groaned with the pleasure of his climax as his wife sighed in utter contentment.

They lay, bodies entwined for a while, Bronwyn's head lay on his shoulder, and she felt the rhythm of his breathing change as it slowed and deepened and realised he had fallen asleep. She smiled kindly. It wasn't surprising, he had had a busy couple of days, it had taken a lot of energy to defeat his opponents in the tournament, and there had been quite a few. For a moment, Bronwyn wondered if she had been selfish, inviting him to make love to her, she realised he could have said no, but he hadn't. He had wanted it as much as she.

Carefully she lifted herself from his body and looked down at him. His lips were slightly parted, and his brown hair was untidy, a lock hanging dangerously close to his right eye. *Roguish!* Bronwyn thought, smiling as she gently placed a kiss on his lips, then rose from the bed. She carefully covered him with a blanket, got dressed, and quietly left to return to her chambers to prepare for their meal that was to take place shortly.

Trystan returned a few minutes later to help prepare his master to dress. Not finding him in the day room, he moved quietly to the bedchamber. The door was open, so he peered in and saw the Duke asleep on the bed. He looked so peaceful, Trystan hated to disturb him, but his family would be arriving for supper soon, and he needed to get his lord ready to receive them.

"Your Grace," Trystan said softly, then repeated it slightly louder. "Your Grace, time to wake up."

Richard gave a large sigh and smiled, then gradually opened his eyes.

"Your Grace, time to get ready."

The Duke nodded and looked down, seeing the blanket. "Did you..."

"No, Your Grace, you were covered when I came in."

The Duke's smile broadened as he threw the blanket aside and rose from the bed. Trystan hastily picked his robe up from the floor and assisted Richard into it.

"Do you have any preference for what you would like to wear this evening, Your Grace?"

"I won today, Trystan, so let's go for something with a little colour."

"As you wish, Your Grace."

Within thirty minutes, the Duke was dressed in clean black breeches, a white silk shirt, and a red jacket decorated with gold thread. He took a sip of wine as he waited for his family to arrive for supper, and they appeared a few minutes later.

Morgan was carrying Colwyn, who was chatting away happily. Richard kissed his wife, then they all sat at the table, with Colwyn now sitting on the Duke's lap. There was a lot of chatter, and laughter throughout. Morgan asked how Colwyn was doing in his absence, and the Duke told him that she was turning out to be rather rebellious. The little girl made no response, she was too busy playing with a toy that her mother had brought with her.

"She should have been born a boy," Morgan said.

"Most definitely," Richard agreed, "But I wouldn't trade her for the world. She is as beautiful as her mother, but not as sweet tempered." He smiled lovingly at his wife.

"So she gets her temper from you?"

"Certainly not!" Richard retorted. "Have you ever seen me fly off into a tantrum?"

"No, but if it's not from you or from Bronwyn, where has it come from? I mean, you did mention about sewing wild oats earlier."

Richard coughed loudly and Colwyn stopped what she was doing. "Who's sewing wild oats?" she asked.

"No one darling, it's just a figure of speech, carry on playing with your toy," Bronwyn said, smiling broadly.

"I have no idea where the temper has come from. It must be in Bronwyn's ancestry somewhere, plus that red hair of hers doesn't help!" The Duke looked almost teasingly at his wife, daring her to rise to the bait, but she just responded by sitting more straight in her chair, and looked down her nose at him in a rather superior attitude which made Richard's lips twitch in amusement. He changed the subject. "But enough of Colwyn, tell me how things are with you."

Morgan told him the hostility had diminished somewhat since the death of Owain, and also that he now had a few more genuine friends, which pleased Richard immensely.

"We're so glad you have friends, Morgan. We were desperately worried about you. Now we can relax a little."

The boy gave him a rare smile. He then went on to describe his developing magic skills and even performed a few simple spells to show how he was progressing, and proudly announced that in his studies, swordsmanship and riding, he was the top of his class.

"Modesty," Richard gently reminded him, but Morgan could see in the Duke's eyes that he was as proud as a father could be about it. "Stuart is pleased with your progress and states you are very mature for your age. Trahaearn thinks the world of you."

The four of them had a pleasant evening, but Morgan left relatively early so Richard could be fully rested for the joust tomorrow. The tournament had presented Morgan with the first opportunity to see his guardian fight, although it had been very gentlemanly. Of course he had seen him at the Eastern Marches last November, but he had not witnessed him engage in battle. The tournament had given Morgan the ambition to be as good, or even better than the Duke when he was finally grown. He also thought about how Richard conducted himself in public. He was not overstated, but there was something about him. He treated even the most lowly with respect, and he was a kind and generous ruler, but Morgan had also seen the other side of him, when he held court. The soft brown eyes hardened like the strongest dark wood, his voice changed, along with his demeanour. The aura crackled around him when he served tough justice. Richard was Morgan's hero in every sense of the word.

Bronwyn, carrying Colwyn, left early too, telling her husband he needed a good night's sleep to prepare for the jousting in the morning.

"If I win... does that permit me another reward?" he asked roguishly. Bronwyn simply smiled demurely and left him wondering.

CB   CB

The morning was overcast, there was a heavy dew on the ground and the sun was fighting to break through when Morgan awoke. Ioan had already collected his breakfast and it awaited the boy on the table in the outer chamber.

The youngster groaned and squinted as Ioan opened the drapes.

"Good morning, My Lord," Ioan said brightly. "Did you sleep well?"

"I suppose I must have," came the sleepy reply.

"Your breakfast is on the table, when you are ready."

Ioan held the boy's robe ready for him as he got out of bed. There was still a bit of a chill in the air, and Morgan gratefully wrapped it tightly around his body and made his way to the outer chamber.

Elsewhere in the castle, more people were stirring. There had been further festivities, and many of the guests had been more interested in eating and drinking rather than taking part in the tournament. When the King's food and drink were on offer, the guests made the most of it.

By the time the tournament was ready to start, the sun had managed to evaporate the dew and was valiantly burning off what was left of the cloud that was attempting to block its view of the forthcoming proceedings.

Colourful pennants adorned all available posts, and all the chargers were wearing caparisons with the colours and coats of arms that were on the competitors' shields and surcoats.

Stuart was once again sitting with Kenneth, Morgan, Bronwyn and Mereli.

"Good morning Kenneth, so you weren't tempted to enter the joust?" Stuart asked.

"My days of jousting are over, Sire! That is most definitely for the younger men."

Stuart grinned at him, then turned his attention to the knight marshal who was ready to begin. His collection of judges were stationed beneath the dais and ready to score. The King nodded, gave a wave of his hand and indicated for the tournament to start.

The knight marshal gave a short introduction, and the first opponents entered the ring. Again, Morgan watched avidly, trying to pick up hints and tips as the competition progressed.

Trahaearn entered on his chestnut charger to face his opponent. Stewards presented them with lances, a signal flag was dropped, and the two riders raced towards each other, bringing the lances to bear. It was all over in an instant as Trahaearn's lance knocked his opponent clear out of the saddle to land in an undignified heap on the grass. The crowd cheered. Morgan was concentrating so hard, he didn't make a sound, then realised and clapped.

The jousting continued. Richard appeared, his powerful bay stallion prancing so much in anticipation that his steward had problems handing him a lance. In the end, Richard had to make a grab for it and adjust it on the run, but he still managed to hit his target, and the knight toppled off sideways.

The competition continued and the rounds got progressively harder as the more experienced knights dispatched the more unskilled ones. Single runs went to two, then three, then four. Somehow Richard found himself facing Trahaearn again. He did his best, but Trahaearn was far more experienced. The Duke managed to stay in the saddle, but Trahaearn won on points.

Once again they ascended the steps but this time the knight received the crown and Richard the coin. The two men shook hands and patted each other on the back, before turning to acknowledge the crowd.

One final competition remained, the infamous pillow fight, where all the riders entered the arena and attempted to batter everyone else to death with a feather pillow. Last man in the saddle was the winner.

Within five minutes, feathers were flying everywhere, raucous laughing could be heard, both from the competitors and the crowd, and some underhand cheating took place, with the knights trying to pull one another from their saddles. The crowd were crying "Foul!" but the word was lost amongst the laughter and cheering.

With all the knights covered in feathers, it was proving difficult to identify whom was who. Feathers stuck to their hair, their faces, their clothes, they all started to look like giant geese.

Morgan was laughing so hard he was crying, but in the end, one man remained on a dun horse. Rodric McLeod.

He mounted the dais to receive his crown.

"Is that Rodric under all those feathers?" Stuart asked grinning.

"Yes Sire, it's me."

He knelt before his King, who pulled some of the feathers from his hair, before placing the crown on his head.

"Arise, pillow king!" Stuart said causing more laughter, and thus the tournament ended.

Rodric left the dais and a trail of feathers behind him.

The following day, the guests began to leave and castle life returned to normal. Richard was the last to depart, with Bronwyn and Colwyn.

೮ ೮ ೮ ೮

Chapter Twelve

It took a number of days for the regular regime to be restored, and once again the pages were practicing the sword, lance, riding and studying back in class,. Morgan spent his spare time with Trahaearn continuing to learn his trade, and even more time with Stuart learning to govern. There was very little time to actually relax and do all the things a boy of his age should do, have fun, play and just be a normal eight year old. This was where the mental training became so vitally important, but Trahaearn knew he couldn't let the boy keep all his pent up emotion bottled up inside, he had to have the freedom to let it out, or it would surely drive him insane.

So, it was for this reason that the knight cleared his plans with the King, made Morgan pack a saddlebag with a couple of days supplies, and they disappeared to the north. Trahaearn refused to tell him where they were going and swore him to secrecy.

Morgan had never been so far north before. They travelled through a vast forest, growing on continually rising ground, then left the trail and went east to arrive at the base of a cliff. Trahaearn turned north, followed it, moving through increasingly dense wood and shrubs to a small kink that went east, and then there it was, a cave entrance.

"What is this place?" Morgan asked somewhat nervously.

"This is my...retreat," Trahaearn answered, dismounting. "This is where I come to release the cork from the bottle, you might say. Remember I told you that a Kadeau cannot be expected to keep everything locked up inside and must have a place of safety where they can freely express themselves in whatever way they see fit. It is well off any track, secluded. There is no fear of someone stumbling across us."

Morgan was feeling decidedly uneasy. Trahaearn paused from lifting off his saddle bags and turned to look at him.

"I sense your unease, Morgan, but you have nothing to fear. Apart from letting go of any pent up emotions, I thought you might like to try some more adventurous magic?"

The boy's eyes lit up at this point and he eagerly dismounted.

"We'll set up camp, have something to eat, and do a little magic."

It didn't take them long, as Trahaearn had already set up a fire the last time he had visited, so all he had to do, was light it. At the back of the cave, water trickled down one wall into a pool. Using fire-light, Morgan could see the water was crystal clear, so he collected some in a pot which the knight placed on the fire. Meat and vegetables were added and the whole thing left to heat, whilst moss and leaves were collected to make two beds upon which they placed their blankets, about halfway back in the cave.

Having eaten their fill and cleaned up, Trahaearn suddenly smiled, mumbled something and disappeared right in front of Morgan's eyes. To say the child was startled was an understatement and he jumped to his feet, his eyes darting in all directions. Then he nearly leapt out of his skin as something touched his shoulder and Trahaearn reappeared.

"Wh – what...how?"

"It's a good one to learn. You never quite know when it may be of use. As with all the magic we use, you simply think or say what you want to do. In this case it's *Invisibilia me*. Now practice saying it so you get the pronunciation right."

"*Invisibilia me*." Morgan repeated it at least half a dozen times to make sure he was saying it correctly.

Trahaearn nodded in approval.

"Your pronunciation is sound. You know what to do; say it with conviction, as if it is the most important thing in the world to you. Take your time, do not hurry."

Morgan swallowed a couple of times, took some deep breaths and uttered the spell. He looked at his hands as he spoke it and saw them flicker out of sight then back in.

"That was better than I expected for your first attempt," Trahaearn said sounding impressed. "Try again."

Morgan did as he was told and for a couple of seconds, succeeded in disappearing from sight.

"Believe it with all your soul. Again."

He achieved four seconds.

"How long can you hold this for?" the boy asked. "I'm feeling tired already."

"Depending on your strength, a few minutes. Like all magic, it takes time. One more attempt, then you can have a rest and then we will do some sword practice."

The boy tried with all his might and managed six seconds.

"You are maintaining it longer on each attempt. Now sit, recover for a few minutes. There is another piece of magic I will show you at some point. It can temporarily provide you with additional energy, but that really does take its toll and you would need a good night's sleep to recover from it. It should only be used in dire emergencies because of how much energy it initially gives to you, then takes away."

"So, once I am trained, I know there will always be more to learn, but with the magic, if I think about it hard enough, I can make it happen?"

"It depends on how powerful you turn out to be, but in theory, yes. In reality, no. No one is that powerful. But that is why you must be so disciplined. You can be powerful, but without that control, you could do great harm."

"What harm?"

"Kill," Trahaearn said simply. "That is not what the Kadeau are about. We are a peaceful people, that live in harmony with all that surrounds us, but we will fight to defeat evil and defend good. We rarely think of ourselves. God created us to be the protectors of the world. Those few like you and me have the most difficult task of all, for we do kill—usually without magic—to carry out our duty to the King and the kingdom. The path we tread is narrow and filled with danger. Now do you understand why control is so important and also, why being able to release frustrations and anger far away from anyone is vital."

"But what if I'm not good enough?" Morgan asked, suddenly fearful.

The knight laid a comforting hand on the boy's shoulder.

"It is natural to have self-doubt, and I am pleased that you have that, rather than being over confident in your abilities. You are so very young, with much to learn, but already I can see you have what it takes. The Duke and Duchess raised you well and have provided you with a good, solid foundation in your core makeup. I will guide and teach you for as long as I am able. I have every confidence in you, Morgan Bodine. I know you will do me proud."

Morgan was suddenly choked and overcome by what Trahaearn had said. The knight had complete faith in him, but as yet he felt so small and insignificant. Without speaking, he turned and hugged the knight tightly. That spoke more than words could ever do and moved Trahaearn greatly.

"I hope you're not going all soft on me now," he finally joked, to ease the electricity that seemed to be in the air, all around them.

Morgan drew back and looked at him.

"Soft? I'll show you who's soft when we start our sword practice!"

Trahaearn roared with laughter.

"That's the spirit!" he enthused. "Come then, show me you are not soft!"

They spent an hour or so going through various exercises, then Trahaearn decided they would finish with a proper sword 'fight'. He let Morgan take the lead, and just defended his ripostes initially, then he stepped things up by putting in his own gentle attack, to test the boy's defences. Morgan was definitely showing improvement, so the knight pressed harder, watching the boy's expression. Within a few minutes Morgan was frowning with increased concentration as he tried to stop Trahaearn pushing him back.

"Show me how good you really are," the knight said, launching a rather ferocious attack.

Morgan gasped with the effort as he attempted to parry the assault. Trahaearn was stronger, heavier and taller and, for the first time, Morgan tasted real fear as the knight pressed him further, back onto uneven ground. The child desperately tried to feel his footing as he was forced to retreat, then a loose rock moved under his boot, and he fell heavily.

Usually, Trahaearn stopped the exercise at this point, but not this time and Morgan tried to fight him from the ground. His mentor's face was unreadable as he continued the attack on the disadvantaged youth.

"Trahaearn!" he shrieked as the knight's sword came down, and somehow, Morgan managed to roll out of the way as the sword pierced the ground where he had just been laying. He scrambled to his feet, but he was fighting a losing battle, for suddenly his mentor had disarmed him with a vicious circular motion that caused his weapon to fly away from his hand and pinned him back against a tree, the knight's sword against his throat.

Morgan was shaking with a mixture of fear and the effort of the exertion. His heart was thumping so fast in his chest he could hardly breathe, and he nearly choked himself as he attempted to swallow.

"Is the blood pounding through your veins?" Trahaearn asked him quietly. "Has your mouth gone dry? Are you having trouble breathing?"

Morgan nodded the affirmative in answer to all of those questions, still gasping for breath, his eyes wide.

"I see fear in your eyes, boy. A Kadeau may feel fear, but he will never show it."

There was a long period of silence, then Trahaearn smiled suddenly and sheathed his sword.

"But that was not bad, not bad at all. Thirsty?"

Morgan was still frozen against the tree, trying to fathom what had just happened and gradually came to realise it had been a test. He swallowed and closed his eyes trying to get his breathing under control, then swallowed again and opened them, but found he couldn't move. He was sure his legs were trembling uncontrollably and if he attempted to take a step they would give out under him.

"Are you going to hug that tree all day?" Trahaearn asked him.

Morgan took a step and as expected, his legs crumpled under him. Trahaearn caught him before he landed on the ground and held him up as the boy clung to him.

"You have tasted real fear, young Morgan. You know what it is now. Going forward you must conquer it, so that it does not rule you."

Trahaearn could see that the boy was thoroughly shaken by the experience, but that had been the whole intention. The exercises at the castle were simply that, exercises. To improve and develop they had to fight, and to also know what it really meant to be afraid, to know that they were going to lose, but to still fight with every last breath in their body.

"Are you hurt?" Trahaearn asked him gently.

"N – no, just a little winded," he managed to reply, wishing he could stop shaking, and tensed as the knight picked him up, carried him back into the cave and sat him down on a log by the fire.

"Know that I would never intentionally hurt you, Morgan, but this is all part of your training as the King's protector. You have to be the best, and I will do my utmost to make you the finest knight in the kingdom." Trahaearn went to his saddle bag and pulled out two goblets and a small amphorae containing malmsey red wine, that was rich and sweet with hints of spice. He poured them both a small goblet and handed one to the youngster. "Here, drink this. You've earned it."

Morgan took a rather large gulp and nearly choked on it.

"Steady," Trahaearn soothed, sitting down beside him. "Small sips. That will calm you."

A few minutes went by before Trahaearn spoke again.

"Tell me how you are feeling," he said.

"I don't understand," Morgan replied.

"How are you feeling inside? Have you pent up emotions that are bursting to get out, or are you now feeling calm and collected?"

"I..." Morgan stopped and analysed how he felt. The fear had gone and now that his heart rate was back to normal, he was actually feeling fine. "I feel...calm."

Trahaearn nodded.

"Any frustrations or anger you still need to vent?"

Realisation dawned on the boy's face.

"No...I feel...fine."

Trahaearn smiled at him.

"There's nothing like a good battle to free you of all those pent up emotions and frustrations. Or a good shout."

"Shout?"

"Aaarrrgggghhhhhhhh!" Trahaearn shouted as loud as he was able, making Morgan jump. "Aaarrrgggghhhhhhhh! Try it."

"That's silly."

"Try it!"

"Aargh!" Morgan shouted not very convincingly.

Trahaearn was not impressed. He turned to face the child, leant towards him so their heads were less than an inch apart and shouted.

"Aarrggghhhhhhh!"

Morgan joined in, and soon they were screaming at each other at the top of their voices until they were almost hoarse.

Trahaearn pulled back and raised an eyebrow. Morgan started to giggle.

"That was fun," he finally managed to say, and Trahaearn shrugged his shoulders in a kind of 'I told you so', attitude.

"Now it's time for your next lesson," he said. "You may have heard the rumours that we can make people do what we command. It is true for some Kadeau, but not all. I have taught you to read others, but there is also control. We will practice together. You must try and stop me making you do something against your will, and then you will try and make me do something I do not want to do. The key against being made to do something is to build a mental barrier. It can be a wall, a screen, a castle, anything that you feel makes you invincible against bending to the will of another. So, build your wall and nod when you are ready."

Morgan closed his eyes for a few moments, took some deep breaths and envisaged a thick and sturdy stone wall. With it in place, he nodded at Trahaearn, who seemed to look straight through him. At first, nothing happened, but then Morgan found his left hand moving towards the flame of the small fire. He ordered his hand to stop, which it did, then it moved closer. He swallowed nervously and threw everything he had into willing his hand to stop and move away from the heat. His hand stopped moving again, then it began to shake as Trahaearn's mind tried to take over again. Morgan gritted his teeth and tried even harder, his hand moved away a little, then stopped.

"Trahaearn..." he gasped. "I – I can't..." His eyes widened in horror as his hand started moving towards the flame. "No!" he screamed and suddenly his hand obeyed him fully and he almost fell backwards as it flew back away from the fire.

It took him a few minutes for him to get himself back under control and look at Trahaearn, who was studying him thoughtfully. Finally, the knight spoke.

"That was rather impressive, young Morgan. A very good effort for your first attempt."

"I – I thought you were going to force my hand into the fire."

"I was."

Morgan paled.

"What better way to concentrate your efforts than put you in perceived real jeopardy." Trahaearn smiled. "Take a breather, then you can try to make me do something."

Morgan tried his hardest and did manage to make Trahaearn's hand shake a couple of times, but that was as far as it got for his first attempt. The knight slapped him on the shoulder, indicating he was satisfied at the endeavour.

Next followed more sword training, and finally some mental discipline to relax them for the coming evening.

By the time they had eaten, Morgan was yawning, and Trahaearn thought it was the perfect time to teach him the revitalising spell, as he would be going to sleep soon anyway.

"Tired?" he asked the boy.

"Yes, I am."

"Then try this. Pinch the top of your nose, here, and say *vivifica me*."

Morgan practiced saying the words a few times, and then tried it for real.

"*Vivifica me*." The surge of resulting energy he received, almost felt like he'd been given some kind of magic potion or something. "Oh!" he exclaimed standing up. "Oh! I feel like I can take on the world!"

"Steady," Trahaearn warned. "It can drop off very suddenly when you're not used to it. It probably won't last long for your first time."

He was right, it lasted about three minutes, and then Morgan wilted. Trahaearn helped him to bed, and he went out like a light.

In the quiet and growing darkness, Trahaearn took the time to sit and ponder the day that had just gone. It had been a good one. Morgan was progressing well, and in his swordsmanship, he was doing better than the knight expected for his age. As for his magic, to have even managed to make himself invisible, even for only a few seconds showed he was really beginning to focus his young mind. King Stuart would be pleased with his report when he got back to the castle.

Trahaearn permitted himself a little smile. In regard to the sword attack, he had done exactly the same thing to Stuart at around the same age. Thinking about it, their reactions had been pretty similar as well.

He looked over at his sleeping student and smiled to himself. They would have another fierce swordfight tomorrow. Of course Morgan would think that he would ease off, like he had today, but he would be in for a little shock. With that thought in his mind, Trahaearn retired for the night as well.

The following morning was overcast, but not too cold. They had something to eat and drink and did some warm up exercises, then

Trahaearn blindfolded Morgan. This was to try and develop his other senses, his hearing and the Kadeau sixth sense.

"I want you to stay still and listen for a little while, then I will ask you what you have heard and can hear."

Morgan stood still and listened. He could hear some birds calling, the breeze in the trees, other than that it seemed very quiet. He did not hear his mentor come up to him.

"Well," Trahaearn said, and the boy pulled the blindfold off to find his teacher standing very close. "What did you hear?"

"Birds, the wind in the trees."

"Anything else?"

"N - no," came the tentative answer that implied he knew he should have heard more.

"You didn't hear your own heart beating? Or the leaf fall from the tree, the mouse scuttle across the ground, or me approaching?"

The look on Morgan's face said it all. Failure.

"You have relied on your eyes too much. You must use all your senses. What would you do if you suddenly lost your sight for some reason? You must use hearing, touch, smell, the sixth sense. Any one of those may save your life. Let me show you. I shall close my eyes, and I want you to try and creep up on me. Every few seconds, I will point to where you are standing." He took the blindfold from Morgan and placed it over his own eyes. "I will put my hands over my ears so I do not know what direction you have gone in, then I will put them down, and you must try to reach me without me hearing you."

He placed his hands over his ears.

"Move away."

Morgan did as he was told, then crept around so he was in a different starting position.

"Begin," Trahaearn instructed.

The knight counted silently to three, then pointed in Morgan's direction. The boy changed track and Trahaearn pointed at him again. Morgan pulled a face, then smiled and didn't move.

"You haven't moved," Trahaearn said.

"What! How are you doing that?"

"I'm listening," Trahaearn said grinning. "I can even hear you breathing. Come, try again."

Morgan still couldn't manage it and after a few more tries, gave up in frustration.

Trahaearn sat him down and they tried a few mental exercises and Morgan tried again. He managed to get closer a couple of times, but not all the way up to his mentor. Then they swapped again. Morgan tried to find that inner peace, that would enable him to concentrate on his other senses. It felt more like a 'feeling' than actually sensing it, but something made him point to his right.

"Well done," Trahaearn said, and Morgan wondered if that was it, that 'feeling'.

He tried again and just felt like turning and pointing behind him.

"Right again. One more and we will stop, as it does drain you."

The third attempt was just a fraction out, but Trahaearn was still pleased with his attempt.

"Let us have a break and we will do some more work with the sword," Trahaearn said. This next lesson was going to be particularly unpleasant for the boy, but it was meant to be, if he was going to be the King's protector and the best swordsman in Devonmere, it had to be done away from the castle, in private. Trahaearn was going to see if he could get the young Duke to fall back on some magic to help him. There was no way he would ever defeat Trahaearn being only eight years old, but he needed him to be able to call upon magic. So far, they had only done one or the other.

He wasn't expecting Morgan's attempt to be perfect; he might even be a little young to attempt it, but Trahaearn thought he might just be able to manage it, and he was going to give him a rather harsh incentive to try.

"You have now received some instruction in magic, and in swordsmanship. There may be occasions where you need to combine the two. Remember, your duty above all else is to protect the King when he calls upon you to do so. You will shortly understand why I have stressed the importance of mental discipline. We are alone here so you can freely practice your new found skills away from prying eyes. The final test for today is about to follow. Defend yourself, young Morgan."

As had happened yesterday, Trahaearn let the boy ease into the exercise, then slowly upped the intensity and pressure of the attack. Morgan handled the first part well. It was difficult, but he was just about managing to hold his own. Of course he knew Trahaearn could easily kill him, due to his height, weight, experience and strength, so he was not unduly worried, and the knight said he would never harm him intentionally.

However, the pressure grew, Morgan was driven steadily back beyond the marked arena onto the uneven ground once more. Determined not to fall again, he attempted to fight even harder to get back onto the more even terrain, but Trahaearn would not let him gain any ground, and if anything, drove him back further.

The boy stumbled a few times, almost wrenched his ankle, but stayed upright, gritting his teeth at the growing pain in his arms as Trahaearn's attack continued. He gasped and grunted a couple of times, then the knight knocked him completely off his feet and he landed heavily winded and could not prevent a cry as a particularly sharp rock dug into his back.

"Defend yourself!" Trahaearn growled as he raised his sword to deliver another blow.

Morgan brought his sword across and managed to deflect the knight's thrust, but Trahaearn came after him again.

His mouth suddenly dry, Morgan deflected the downward travelling sword again, but it caught his arm, and he felt the blade cut his skin.

Shocked, he lay frozen as Trahaearn's eyes took on a dangerous glitter.

"I said, defend yourself!" the knight roared.

Morgan felt a moment of sheer panic and then, as if his life depended on it, uttered, "*Invisibilia me!*" and rolled desperately away from the blade which missed him by a fraction. He managed to scramble to his feet and get back onto the even ground before he became visible, and Trahaearn was right behind him.

Exhausted beyond belief, Morgan felt himself losing his grip on reality. His right arm was burning with the effort of defending himself, his left was throbbing from the wound, and then Trahaearn knocked him off his feet again. With a supreme effort, he tried one more time with a final desperate spell.

"*Vivifica me!*" The adrenalin surged through his body, and he fought back from the ground, jumped to his feet and attacked. But it couldn't last and just a few minutes later, due to the effort he was putting in to defending himself, it suddenly left him.

His legs refused to hold him, they buckled, and he collapsed. Barely conscious, he watched as Trahaearn advanced on him. Every limb felt like lead, and he was unable to lift his sword as the knight reached him.

Trahaearn sheathed his sword and knelt by Morgan's side.

"Don't move," the knight soothed, "don't talk. Rest. You have done very well."

Morgan fought to keep his eyes open, but even that was too much effort and he let them close. Vaguely he was aware of being lifted, carried back into the cave and placed on his bed.

Trahaearn left him to pour a small goblet of wine and returned, gently lifting Morgan's head and placing the goblet against his lips.

"Drink, slowly," the knight ordered, and the boy did as he was told.

Once he had had his fill, Trahaearn put the goblet aside, then shifted Morgan into a sitting position to remove his aketon, and shirt, so he could examine the wound he had inflicted. It was oozing blood but was not serious. Trahaearn retrieved the medical supplies from his saddle bag, then returned to clean the wound and bandage his arm. Finally, he made him lay down again, covered the boy with a blanket, then stood and began a few chores, placing more wood on the fire, preparing the next meal and tending the horses.

Trahaearn then sat and pondered. They would return to the castle tomorrow morning. King Stuart would be eager to hear how the training session had gone, and Trahaearn would be able to tell him that it had gone better than he expected. In the last few months, Morgan had improved a great deal. His mind was beginning to understand what it was supposed to be doing with magic, and both his mental and physical stamina had grown.

The knight regretted inflicting the wound on his pupil, but it had been of vital importance to get Morgan to call on all his skills to defend himself and realise how they could be used, both in defence and attack.

The smell of food pervaded Morgan's senses, causing him to stir. For a few seconds, he couldn't think where he was, then realised he was back in the cave. He fidgeted, then groaned as his left arm throbbed. He looked down and found a bandage on it, then froze as Trahaearn knelt by his side.

"You've done very well, these past couple of days. I am proud of you."

"You - you said you'd never intentionally hurt me."

"I know. Forgive me, but I saw no other way to force you to use all the skills you have at your bidding. You successfully used magic to defend yourself, despite only just learning to use those two difficult spells I taught you. Now we will need to build up your stamina, so you can maintain any spell you do, for a longer period. Do you feel up to eating?"

Trahaearn helped him to sit up, and put his shirt back on, before helping him to his feet. Morgan still felt wobbly, so the knight assisted him to sit by the fire, where they ate in relative silence, whilst the child digested what Trahaearn had said to him.

"You're very quiet," the knight finally said.

"I'm tired," Morgan responded. It was a true statement, but he didn't want to admit that he felt slightly uncertain about his relationship with the knight at that precise moment. The ferocity of Trahaearn's attack had shaken him, but on thinking about it further, he realised that in his role, he had to be ready for anything, and that the knight was trying to prepare him the best way he knew how.

"Have I lost your trust, young Morgan?" the knight asked softly.

He didn't answer immediately.

"I'm doing my best to understand why," Morgan said simply.

"Because your life is not going to be easy. Yes, I know you are a Duke—or will be very shortly—but you will still have enemies because you are Kadeau. You have made some friends, and you need to try and keep the genuine ones but remember, the King also has enemies, powerful ones, and you need to be as powerful, if not more so to keep your King safe. I know I've said this before, and I will continue to say it. You are going to be a powerful Kadeau, Morgan Bodine. Better than I could ever be and thus you need to be prepared."

Morgan's head jerked up at the last sentence.

Better than Trahaearn, he thought in awe.

"I trust you, Trahaearn. I realise now that you're doing your best to prepare me. By telling me what you're planning isn't necessarily the right way for me to learn, hence those..." His voice trailed off.

"There is no shame in being afraid. It is how you conduct yourself whilst afraid. You performed admirably and you will learn more from this experience than any exercise could teach you. Now, I think you should get a good night's sleep. We return to Ellesmere tomorrow."

Morgan nodded, prepared himself for bed, and retired. Trahaearn made sure he was tucked up nice and warm, checked the fire one last time, then got some sleep.

It took the boy some time to drift off as his mind refused to relax but exhaustion finally won the battle and he succumbed to the needs of his body.

� ꙮ ꙮ ꙮ

Morgan and Trahaearn left the cave relatively early the following morning and arrived at Ellesmere castle just after midday. The knight instructed the boy to go to his rooms and make himself respectable, as he was sure the King would be requesting his presence at some point.

Ioan was pleased to see him as he opened the door and walked in, carrying his saddlebags, but noticed the boy seemed a little tired, and he gave an exclamation as he saw the bruises and the bandage on his arm and asked what had happened, but Morgan refused to divulge any information, much to his steward's annoyance.

Master Stephen arrived.

"Sir Trahaearn has told me you were slightly injured so the King has ordered me to check you over. Come, sit, let me look at you."

Stephen prodded and poked him, re-bandaged his arm and treated his bruises with witch hazel. He left a small bottle with Ioan, to administer to the bruises at regular intervals, and left, satisfied that the boy was fine.

Morgan was summoned to Stuart's rooms an hour later, and he wasted no time in reporting to the King in the antechamber.

"Sire," Morgan said, bowing before his King.

Stuart acknowledged him and motioned for him to sit on a chair opposite him.

"How was your trip away?" he asked.

"Eventful," Morgan answered after a pause.

Stuart smiled, remembering his own experience at the hands of Trahaearn.

"Master Stephen has told me you have some bruises and a cut on your arm."

"Yes."

"Trahaearn frightened the wits out of me the first time I went to his sanctuary. I honestly thought he was going to murder me."

"Really?" Morgan relaxed a little. "Hearing that makes me feel better. I thought I may have disgraced myself, but Trahaearn said he was pleased with my achievements."

"He has given me a full report. Well done. I am more than pleased with your progress. I know it hasn't been easy for you, but you have coped far better than any of us thought you might. Now, it's back to normal for you for a few days, but your training with me and Trahaearn will become more intense. I know you are still to win against either one of us, but it will come, Morgan. Be patient, you still have some growing to do. I estimate, by the way you are growing, come the age of fifteen, you'll be winning."

"That's almost seven years away!"

"I know, but you must be patient. Your time will come, then watch out anyone who crosses you!"

Morgan dared to smile.

"So, back to classes in the morning, some training with the other pages, and then you'll join either me or Trahaearn. And you will continue to join me whilst I hold court."

"Thank you, Sire. I—"

He got no further as there was a knock on the door.

"Enter," Stuart replied.

The door opened and Bishop Douglas appeared.

"Your pardon, Sire," the bishop said bowing, before coming forward. "I need—" he stopped as he saw Morgan present. "If it is inconvenient, I can return at another time."

"No, I think Morgan and I have finished our discussion. Is there a problem?"

The bishop looked rather uncomfortable.

"I need to speak to you about a delicate matter..." his voice trailed off.

It was obvious to Stuart that his bishop wasn't going to say anything more with Morgan present.

"Morgan, I don't need you anymore today. Make the most of your freedom and I will see you tomorrow," Stuart said to the boy.

"As you wish, Sire." He bowed to both the King and the bishop and left the room.

Stuart waited until the door had closed behind Morgan, then turned to the bishop.

"What is this delicate matter you wish to discuss?"

James took a deep breath, he had already set in motion the information gathering he was about to discuss with his King, and responses were starting to arrive. He took another deep breath and broached the subject of his visit.

"Sire, we need to think about a future heir to the throne of Devonmere. Should something happen to you, then Prince Michael would become King, and he is yet, unmarried as are you."

"Married!" Stuart exclaimed. It was the last thing on his mind, he was still getting used to ruling the kingdom. "James, I've only just become King! At least let me settle into the role first, before trying to marry me off!"

"My apologies Sire, but we cannot afford to dally for too long. Whomever is chosen, must be for the good of the kingdom. It is whether you wish to strengthen an alliance within Devonmere, or with one of the islands or lands across the sea. You cannot marry just anyone, Sire. We must tread carefully and select the most suitable bride that will bring stability and peace to the kingdom and provide Devonmere with the heir it so desperately needs."

James was right of course, and Stuart knew this, but he was feeling 'set upon' for want of a more apt description. He was being pulled in every direction; decrees to sign, decisions to be made, wars to avert, the running of the castle, the kingdom, relationships to be built upon and now...marriage! Stuart so desperately wanted some time to himself, time to process everything; get himself under control, but it seemed as if the whole world was against him or vying for his time and attention. He held a hand against his forehead, suddenly feeling weary and tired.

"Later," Stuart finally said, taking a deep breath to try and calm himself.

"But my Liege—"

"I said later!" the King snapped more harshly than he intended. "Leave me." He waved a hand in dismissal, but the bishop stood his ground.

"Sire, let me at least—"

"Get out!"

James physically jumped. Stuart had never spoken to him like that before, and he suddenly realised the young King was feeling the strain of his position.

"Very well, Sire. With your permission, I shall draw up a list of suitable candidates for you to look at when you are...more settled." He bowed deeply and moved towards the door.

Stuart realised the bishop had gently chastised him for his behaviour, took a very deep breath, and held it for several seconds before letting it out. He spoke, just as James reached the door.

"James, I'm sorry," he said softly.

The bishop stopped, hand poised on the latch of the door and turned back to face him.

"My King, never apologise."

"I was rude and ungrateful. I know you are trying to help me in these early days."

James smiled slightly.

"And I have been pushing a little too hard, methinks. These past few weeks have been exhausting for you. You are tired. If I may be so bold, you should get some rest."

"I still have much to do today."

"Nothing that cannot wait until the morrow, Sire. Permit me to send for Sir Trahaearn, to assist you, as he did your father."

Stuart shook his head.

"I can manage, James. I will give your... request, some thought, but not tonight."

"Very well, Sire. Do not dally too long in this matter. Sleep well."
The bishop bowed and left.

Sleep? How am I expected to sleep after that conversation! I've been crowned just a few days and he's trying to marry me off! Stuart shuddered. There was just way too much else to sort out and do before he could think about marriage. He shuddered again and began to get ready for bed, expecting a restless night.

Chapter Thirteen

Bishop James Douglas stopped when he got outside the King's rooms. That, he decided had not gone quite to plan. It was why he had not confessed to have started to look for a bride as soon as he'd found out King Rhisart was dead. It took time to find a suitable wife for a King. In a perfect world, Stuart should have been married already, but he had successfully avoided any involvements that his father had tried to set up. Now there was no excuse. He had to marry, the sooner the better.

Couriers regularly arrived at the castle from within the kingdom of Devonmere, and from overseas. Some of these included information from foreign monarchs looking to find a match for their daughters. So he already had information on some available brides and had used this knowledge to inform them that there was a new King of Devonmere, who was looking for a suitable wife.

He was currently awaiting the arrival of replies from those countries further afield, which were due any day now. Once they arrived, he would go through them and create a shortlist for the king to peruse. Another month and the last courier should arrive back.

☙ ❧ ☙ ❧

Stuart had a restless night, filled with nightmares about being pursued by numerous women all wanting to be his queen. He'd woken in a sweat after one turned out to have horns, a forked tongue and claws for hands and shuddered at the memory of her reaching for him and attempting to devour him.

Agitated he prowled his rooms, then he poured himself a goblet of wine and gulped it down before returning to bed, only to wake a couple of hours later, to the sunrise and he groaned. There was so much to do today; tasks he hadn't completed the day before, the continued planning of the knighting ceremony, which was just over a month away, training with Morgan, the daily court session, the council meeting, papers to sign, decisions to make, maintaining the peace in the kingdom... the list went on. How had his father managed everything?

Aiden arrived with his breakfast and assisted him to dress. Just as that task was completed, there was a knock on the door. Stuart sighed, closed his eyes and took some long deep breaths. *Oh, what I would give for the chance to escape this duty, even if just for a day*, he thought.

"Come."

The door opened to admit Morgan.

"Good morning, Sire," the boy said bowing.

"Morgan." The King flashed him a smile of welcome. "What trials and tribulations have you brought me today?"

"I come bearing messages."

"Of course you do," Stuart said wearily. "That was beneath me. Come, sit. You can tell me the messages over breakfast." He turned to Aiden. "That will be all for now."

"My Liege," Aiden said bowing and left.

They sat together at the King's table and feasted.

"Sire, what ails you? Can I be of assistance?"

Stuart sighed heavily.

"Oh, that you could, my dearest Morgan. But come, tell me the messages."

"The bishop wishes to finalise the preparations for the night of vigil and the knighting ceremony, the high steward wants to discuss the tournament and celebrations, the scribes need your approval on the wording of the gifting to Prince Michael for the title of Duke of Connamere after his knighting. There are also a number of issues to address at court this morning."

"Stop! No more!" Stuart could feel the pressure building, and his control slipping. He also realised Morgan would be no match for what he required. "Do you know what Trahaearn's plans are this morning?"

"He will be in the Pell, helping to train the squires."

"Assist me with my armour."

"But Sire, you have a meeting with—"

"It can wait. If I don't vent some energy, I will explode. Quickly."

Morgan did as he was told, and within a few minutes, Stuart was ready for battle.

"Forgive me, Morgan, but today I need to fight, I will surely injure you if you train with me."

"I understand, Sire. But may I accompany you?"

Stuart nodded, handed the boy his helm and shield, and strode swiftly away, causing Morgan to have to do the occasional running step to keep up with him. They did not slacken in pace until they reached the Pell. Trahaearn saw them approach and frowned. Was there something wrong? Stuart was suited up for battle.

"Cease!" Trahaearn commanded of the squires who were practicing their swordsmanship.

He moved away from them to greet his King.

"My Liege," Trahaearn said, bowing. "What has happened? What's wrong?"

"Trahaearn, I have use of your services this morning. I am fit to explode," Stuart said.

The knight nodded in understanding.

"Let me suit up fully, Sire," Trahaearn said. He turned and walked to a bench where his sword, shield and helm had been placed and quickly completed dressing. Done, he returned to the King.

"Try not to kill me, but do not hold back. That is an order."

"But... yes Sire, by your command."

The two men made their way into the adjacent training ring next to where the squires were standing. The young men all looked at one another, and dared to move to the fence to get a closer look at what was about to take place.

Morgan handed Stuart his helm, which the King put on, and then took the offered shield.

"Back behind the fence, Morgan," Trahaearn ordered.

Safely behind the barrier, Morgan waited with bated breath. The two men often trained together, but this sounded as if it was going to be something more...heated.

Stuart and Trahaearn drew their swords, saluted each other, then began circling one another. Morgan watched as the King swung his sword in a circle, much like Richard had shown him, loosening any tension in his wrist. Trahaearn did the same.

The two men sized one another up with some experimental strikes, as if carrying out warming up exercises, to ensure their muscles were prepared for what was to come, then all hell broke loose and Stuart put in an almost frenzied attack on his protector, driving him back towards the barrier. Trahaearn defended, gathered himself and created the opportunity for his own riposte back on his opponent. Sparks flew as the swords clashed, and the thud of sword against shield sounded very loud with the force of the blows.

Morgan watched avidly as they continued to fight, looking as if they meant for every blow to end the life of the other, and suddenly the youngster understood properly what Trahaearn had been trying to teach him at the sanctuary. No training could ever replace a real battle situation. The fear, battling against an opponent, the adrenalin, fighting for your very life and trying to deprive another of theirs.

For half an hour they kept at it, neither giving ground, then Trahaearn carried a particularly vicious attack and knocked Stuart to the ground with his shield. The sword followed, and the King was forced to defend from his position on his back as Trahaearn continued the violent assault.

Stuart was forced to switch to battle tactics and kicked out with a foot, catching Trahaearn at the hip and sending him staggering backwards. It provided the King with enough time to get to his feet, and he laid in with his own frenzied attack.

By now, the swords were moving so fast against each other, that they were all a blur. Both the collection of squires and Morgan were now standing, mouths agape, having never seen anything like it before.

Suddenly, Stuart kicked out again, and the momentum knocked the knight completely off balance, and it was his turn to be on his back on the ground, defending with all his might as the King continued his merciless attack. The penultimate blow wrenched Trahaearn's shield from his arm and as the final thrust of the sword came down, making the audience shriek, the knight managed to roll out of the way, and the sword plunged into the ground, and became stuck, due to the force Stuart had exerted.

It was at that moment, the King yelled.

"Aarrrrggghhhhhh!" He straightened up, breathing heavily at the exertion.

Trahaearn studied him from his position on the ground. He too was gasping for breath, and after a few moments found the energy to speak.

"D - does m - my Liege feel better now?" he asked.

Stuart's chest was heaving as he desperately drew in lungful's of air, then he nodded, walked up to his protector and held out a hand which the knight grasped, allowing Stuart to pull him to his feet.

Trahaearn sheathed his sword, then they both placed their hands around the hilt of Stuart's and pulled it out of the ground. The King placed it back in its sheath.

"Thank... thank you Trahaearn. I needed that."

"Indeed you did, Sire."

Stuart placed a hand on the knight's shoulder and then caught sight of the gaping squires who were still standing transfixed.

"I hope you all learnt something today," he said to them. They all jumped to attention, still awed by what they had just witnessed. Then some of them managed to nod and look at one another.

Trahaearn looked at Morgan and raised an eyebrow, as if to say, *see, even the King shouts when he needs to.* Then turned back to his King and bowed.

Stuart acknowledged him, then turned and left the ring.

"Morgan!" he commanded as he strode back towards the keep, and the boy ran after him.

ᙝ ᙞ ᙝ ᙞ

Finally the details of all the possible future queens arrived. Bishop Douglas took his time, studying the details of the candidates that were spread across his table and frowned, deep in thought. Out of fourteen possible unions, he had at last managed to narrow it down to three, which he deemed to be the most suitable to maintain the stability of Devonmere and the House of Cantrell.

Miniature portraits of the prospective women had been included from all the candidates and he studied his final three with some scepticism. They were either all incredibly beautiful and James had been fortunate in his choice or, there had been a degree of 'artistic licence' in the painting of the portraits, and the Bishop suspected the latter.

With King Stuart's permission he hoped to arrange for his Liege to embark on a tour to visit his three possible brides and make a choice for one to be his Queen. The whole situation was proving to be a rather touchy subject and extremely hard work. The Bishop knew he had to make Stuart see sense and get the matter sorted sooner, rather than later, especially with Morgan still being a child and unable to fulfil his role as protector until he was at least another eight years older. The untimely death of Rhisart had caused a number of problems.

James studied the portraits one more time, then gathered the papers together. He would present them to Stuart after he had eaten that evening.

It was after supper when the Bishop squared his shoulders and requested an audience with the King. Carrying the documents and miniature portraits of the three women, James bowed before his King, then moved to the table, a curious Stuart and Morgan following behind.

"James, what have you got there, that needs my attention this evening?" the King asked rather jovially.

James took a deep breath as he set the items down on the table, wondering if he was going to ruin the King's good spirits with the conversation he was about to embark on.

"Sire, I have short-listed three possible brides that will enhance the stability of Devonmere," the Bishop said without any preamble.

"James, I said I didn't want to discuss this."

"With respect, Sire, you cannot afford not to. You must have a Queen and heir as soon as possible. At least cast your eyes over them, please." He gestured for his King to start on the first set of documents.

Stuart gave a sharp sigh of annoyance but did as he was asked. The first candidate was Princess Annalise from Malandalia, across the sea and far to the south. He skimmed the contents of the documents, and the dowry on offer. All was in order; her pedigree was sound, the dowry generous—perhaps too generous, as if her father was eager to be rid of her. He indicated for James to pass him the miniature portrait. Dark haired, dark eyed, with an olive complexion, she had the appearance of being rather exotic. She was pleasing to the eye but...he looked down at Morgan and handed him the painting.

"What do you think?" he asked the youngster.

"Sire!" James protested, but Stuart just wagged a finger at him.

Morgan studied the portrait and pulled a bit of a face. That was good enough for Stuart.

"My thoughts exactly," the King replied and moved onto the next one.

According to the papers of the second candidate, her ancestry led back to one of the oldest families of Devonmere, yet she was of the Western Isles of Isatiri. Fair-haired, blue-eyed with full red lips in an oval face. Her complexion was fair, and Stuart found himself staring. He studied her pedigree again as Morgan attempted to get a glimpse of her.

Stuart looked at the portrait again, and James looked hopeful.

Morgan finally managed to view the portrait. "She is very beautiful, Sire," he said.

"Yes, she is, isn't she...providing the painting is accurate, but her line is based on the Ulrich family."

Morgan frowned at him.

"The Kadeau almost wiped the family out during the Reign of Terror, forcing them from Devonmere, and I have Kadeau in my court."

"That was several hundred years ago, my Liege," James interjected. "If a grudge was still held, why send her credentials over for scrutiny? Surely enough time will have passed for the memory to have faded."

"Perhaps not enough, if your family was almost annihilated and those left were forced to flee for their lives, never to return to Devonmere. Only last year we had evidence that the hate still exists." He looked at Morgan as he spoke the last sentence.

"Sire, I will leave this court if you so wish, so you may wed the princess," Morgan said softly. "If that's what you want to do."

Stuart shook his head. "You will do no such thing, Morgan. If I do find her favourable, and her father agrees to the union, then she will do as she is told." He looked at the portrait again. "Princess Alexandra, are you the one?" he almost muttered to himself.

"Sire, the third possibility," James said indicating to the table once more.

Stuart pulled himself together and concentrated on the third and final possible future Queen. The woman was slightly older than the previous two with light brown hair brown eyes and a pleasing disposition, but the King found he wasn't really paying as much attention as he should. Again, her ancestry was impeccable, she was well bred and would make a fine Queen, but his eyes wandered back to Alexandra.

James watched him carefully and held his breath.

"Sire?" he prompted.

"James, we're going to Isatiri."

The Bishop smiled broadly and bowed. "I shall send word first thing in the morning and start on preparations for the journey, but do you wish me to include a visit to one of the others?"

"No."

The Bishop bowed again and took his leave.

Stuart looked at Morgan. "Have you ever been on a ship?" he asked the boy.

"Only once. I was sick," Morgan replied remembering how he'd spent most of his sailing adventure hanging over the side, retching. The whole experience had made him feel light-headed and out of sorts. He'd since been on the River Wyvern in a small boat a number of times, but never again on the open sea. "How long will it take to get to Isatiri?"

"Oh, about two weeks," the King replied, then quickly asked, "are you feeling all right?" as Morgan had turned a delicate shade of green at the thought of spending fourteen days on a ship, with huge waves crashing over the deck.

"I shall be dead before we arrive," he whispered.

Stuart laughed kindly. "No you won't. You'll get your sea legs in a day or so, and then you'll be fine and wonder what all the fuss was about! I believe we will be ready to set sail in about a month." He studied his future protector. "Have you ever played tawlbwrdd?"

"Yes Sire. Father taught me, but I haven't played a game since I arrived here."

"Then we must rectify that." Stuart went to a wooden cabinet, opened a door a retrieved the board and a bag that contained the pieces.

They managed two games that evening. Stuart won the first one, but the second one neither managed to win so they eventually called it a draw.

⁓ ⁀ ⁓ ⁀

The month passed quickly, during which time Stuart conducted his first knighting ceremony. It went smoothly, Richard had returned once again to Ellesmere to ensure everything had been arranged correctly and Stuart had sighed in relief once it had finished. His proudest moment had been when he had knighted his brother and then at a separate ceremony had appointed him Duke of Connamere just to the north of Ellesmere. As per Rhisart's tradition there was a tournament for the newly appointed knights, the winner or winners of which were invited to participate in the experienced knights' tournament if they so wished. The novices exited at round two of the swordsmanship and round three in the jousting. Richard, to his utmost surprise won the swordsmanship and Stuart had teased him up on the dais, asking him if he had now reached his peak and was starting a winning streak. As before, his win had been exceedingly popular with the spectators. In the month since the coronation, he had worked hard on his jousting and won that as well. The King also asked him jokingly, if he was vying for position as King's Champion or protector, which of course the Duke emphatically denied. His latest wins did at least make him feel that his previous success had not been so much of a stroke of luck.

Finally the day arrived when they were to set sail for Isatiri. Morgan's dread of the journey had grown day by day, until he almost made himself ill. He had voiced on several occasions that it would be better if he didn't go, due to him being Kadeau, but Stuart refused to listen and insisted he accompany him on the journey and so, on a sunny July day, they left the castle and journeyed to Inver, the main port of Devonmere to sail to the lands of Isatiri.

They had stayed overnight with the Duke and Duchess of Invermere, where Morgan had spent part of the evening playing with Colwyn, but he'd had to say good bye at the same time, as they were setting sail with the dawn tide.

The sun was just breaking the horizon when they made their way down to board the ship.

In the safety of the harbour the waters were calm, but beyond the curvature of the bay, beyond the breakwaters, the breeze was teasing the waves, creating white horses and a fair swell.

Morgan looked nervously out to sea. He really didn't want to travel to the lands of Isatiri, but his King had demanded his presence, so here he was, but he couldn't stop himself from lingering and falling to the back of the small guard that was to accompany the King to visit the young woman who he hoped to take for his bride.

Trahaearn suddenly appeared by his side.

"Are you thinking of deserting us, young Morgan?" he teased.

The youth had the good grace to blush slightly, as if guilty of the voiced question.

"I don't like ships, Trahaearn," Morgan confessed. "The last time I was on one, I was ill the entire time. We have two weeks of sailing...I will surely die!"

The knight laughed good naturedly. "And pray tell, how long was your last trip?"

"Two days. Two days of continuous torture."

"Aha!" Trahaearn exclaimed. "You did not have sufficient time to gain your sea legs. You may be unwell for a day or two, but then you will get used to it and wonder what all the fuss was about."

"That's what the King said."

"Do you doubt the word of your King?"

"Never! But...look at the sea beyond the bay! It's wild. We will surely founder!"

"'Tis but a slight swell, no more than eight feet. The ship will be fine and so will you." He paused as he saw the King looking around, as if searching for someone. "Methinks the King is looking for you, Morgan. You'd best return to your rightful place. I will escort you forward. Come."

Morgan sighed heavily, nodded, and reluctantly followed Trahaearn forward to his rightful place.

"Something wrong?" Stuart asked as they drew almost level with him.

"No, Sire. Let us just say young Morgan was feeling a little apprehensive about his sea trip and needed a little reassurance."

The King nodded knowingly but said nothing more.

A few minutes later, they reached the quay, where they dismounted. Squires came forward to take charge of the horses and take them back to the stables at Inver Castle. Ioan and Aiden carried the saddlebags aboard and they were shown to the cabins the King, Morgan and Bishop Douglas were to occupy. Trahaearn followed to check the cabins, and his own. Master Stephen was also given one. The small guard were assigned shared cabins.

Morgan's stomach started to churn as soon as they left the shelter of the harbour, and he took to his cabin, with a bucket to retch into. When he did not appear in the stateroom to eat, Stephen went to him and prepared a mild potion. The smell of it made Morgan retch again.

"I – I can't..." he mumbled trying to push the goblet away.

"You can and you must," Stephen said firmly.

"No!" Desperately he turned away and Stephen knew he would need assistance to get the potion down him.

The surgeon rose from his bedside and went in search of Trahaearn, who accompanied him back to Morgan's cabin and held the child down whilst Stephen administered the potion. Morgan choked on half of it, tried to retch again, but the foul liquid stayed down. He partly heaved another couple of times but again, nothing came up, then he strained against the hands holding him down, but they refused to relinquish their hold.

"Calmly now," Trahaearn said softly. "Surrender to it, it will make you feel better."

The fight left him, and he collapsed back against the pillows.

"That's more like it. You will feel perfectly well by tomorrow, but you should eat or at least drink something."

Morgan shook his head and closed his eyes. The rocking motion of the ship and the potion caused him to sleep. Trahaearn released his hold on him and stood up.

"I think we should leave him to sleep," Stephen whispered. "He should feel a lot better when he awakens."

Trahaearn nodded, and they left the boy to his dreams.

As predicted, Morgan had recovered by the morning and was fine for the rest of the voyage. After two weeks, they entered the port of Makara on Isatiri. Carriages awaited them and transported them to Makara Castle situated on a cliff top above the port. It was a grand structure, built of local sandstone with four towers that faced inland. When they passed under the gatehouse into what should have been the bailey, they instead entered a large courtyard in front of what was more a palace than a castle.

Standing on the steps in front of grand double doors were a regal looking man and woman accompanied by a couple of guards resplendent in colourful uniforms. Behind them were a number of pages, waiting to escort the visitors to appropriate chambers. Another two guards stood on the bottom step standing at attention.

As the main carriage stopped at the bottom of the steps, one of the guards moved and opened the door then saluted as Stuart, wearing a simple gold band on his head, emerged. He took a couple of steps forward and waited until Trahaearn, Morgan and the bishop joined him before ascending the steps towards what he assumed were the King and Queen of Isatiri. Bishop Douglas had briefed him on names and etiquette of the land which was similar to their own.

When they reached the top step they stopped and bowed to the King and Queen as a mark of respect, and this was returned.

"Welcome to Isatiri, King Stuart. For the duration of your stay, our home is your home."

"Thank you King Alwyn," Stuart replied as the two men shook hands in a gesture of friendship. Alwyn was tall and blond, with hair just past his shoulders, blue eyed, square jawed and ruggedly handsome.

"May I present my wife, Queen Iola."

"Your majesty," Stuart said as he took her hand and kissed the back of it.

"King Stuart, welcome." Her voice was soft, which matched her beautiful features. Fair-haired, grey eyed, with high cheek bones and full red lips and, if Stuart was not mistaken, expecting a child, as she was only just beginning to show.

"May I present, my bishop, James Douglas, the future Duke of Rossmere, Morgan Bodine and my protector and champion, Sir Trahaearn."

"Gentlemen, welcome to Isatiri."

James, Morgan and Trahaearn bowed and straightened up. There was no mention of Kadeau for which everyone was thankful.

"Alwyn, I have brought you some caskets of wine from our finest vineyards in Devonmere as a gesture of goodwill."

"You are most kind. My steward will arrange for it to be moved to storage. Now, you must all be tired after your journey. My pages will escort you to your chambers so you may refresh yourselves and rest.

We sup one hour after sunset. I will arrange for escorts to collect you and bring you to the banqueting hall.." Alwyn gestured with a hand, and the pages came forward to carry out their duties.

Aiden and Ioan unpacked clothes and hung them in the wardrobes in Stuart and Morgan's chambers, before moving to the balcony doors and opening them to allow in some fresh air. The day was pleasantly warm and the view from the balcony overlooked a beautiful formal garden, beyond which were fields of ripening crops. In the distance beyond that were mountains which seemed to glisten in the sunlight.

Stuart joined Aiden on the balcony and took in the sight.

"It's beautiful, Sire," Aiden said.

"Very different from Ellesmere, that's for certain. The weather here seems milder than at home."

"I assume my liege wishes to refresh himself, and I have prepared bathing facilities."

"Perfect Aiden, thank you."

Stuart re-entered the day room and with Aiden's assistance stripped to wash the salty air from his body before putting on a robe and investigating the bedchamber. It was bright and airy, with heavy drapes, and a huge four-poster bed that was dressed not in similar heavy curtains, but a light, almost transparent cloth. Stuart frowned.

"The drapes on the bed are pulled at night to prevent insect bites, I was told by the page who escorted me here," Aiden told him. "They appear to be quite annoying during the summer months here, especially at night."

"Oh, I see. Thank you. I think I will rest a while. Go and get some sleep yourself Aiden. Return at sunset."

His steward bowed and left. Stuart made himself comfortable on the bed. It was softer than he was used to, but exceedingly relaxing and he felt himself start to doze.

In Morgan's chambers, Ioan had done the same thing for his lord, although Morgan seemed transfixed by the view from his balcony.

"Your Grace, you should get some rest, so you are prepared for this evening's festivities," Ioan told him.

"Look at that garden, Ioan. Have you ever seen anything like it?"

"No Your Grace, I haven't."

"It's beautiful. I wonder if Belvoir has anything like it."

"I doubt it, Your Grace. I've never seen many of the plants before. I assume they are natural to this region. They don't appear to serve any practical purpose. Nothing looks edible."

"You're right, but it does look beautiful, even though it may be impractical."

"Come, Your Grace, you should take a nap." Ioan guided his master through to the bedchamber and saw him safely to bed. He wasn't at all surprised when Morgan fell almost instantly asleep.

౮ ౪ ౮ ౪

On waking, Stuart had managed to get rather tense about the forthcoming evening. He was to meet his possible bride, and providing he liked what he saw and felt, and that the miniature portrait had not been exaggerated, it was expected after a week or so had passed and they learnt more about one another, that the *sponsalia per verbade future*—the formal announcement of the proposal of marriage—would be announced. Dates would then have to be agreed for the actual wedding to take place back at Ellesmere, but Stuart was thinking of the following September, as the ceremony would have to be arranged, invites sent out, it would take time, and winter would get in the way. But that was thinking too far ahead. He had yet to meet the Princess Alexandra.

Pages arrived a little before the hour after sunset to escort the guests to the banqueting hall. It was to be a small scale affair because the idea was to ensure that the Princess and the King of Devonmere were well matched.

Princess Alexandra was fourteen. If the match was successful, by the time the wedding took place, she would be a year older and more mature for childbirth, but Stuart wanted to enjoy his marriage. He had mainly abstained from indulging in sexual activity since being knighted, but the sight of a pretty face still affected him as it would any young man.

The double doors were opened to admit the guests to the hall. The outside long wall had many doors that opened onto a long and wide terrace, that during daylight hours enjoyed a view and access to the formal garden.

Scented torches were burning, emitting a pleasant odour in the air, their purpose was to keep annoying insects away as well as provide subtle lighting.

The two kings greeted one another quite warmly, then the doors opened again to admit a young woman. Stuart didn't need any prompting to know that it was Princess Alexandra approaching. He knew he was staring, but he couldn't help it. The miniature portrait had done her a great injustice.

As she came closer, Stuart was struck by her glowing, flawless beauty, the pale hair that framed an oval face, with large innocent blue eyes, a beautiful straight nose and full lips very much like her mother's. Her body was maturing into that of a young woman. She was of just above average height and moved with a grace that befitted her station.

Drawing level with them, she dropped into a low curtsey then rose again.

"My daughter, the Princess Alexandra," Alwyn said.

Stuart reached out to take one of her hands and brought it to his lips, bowing as he did so.

"Alexandra, this is King Stuart Cantrell of Devonmere."

"The Princess needed no introduction," he said being most gallant. "But I fear her portrait did her a great injustice."

Alexandra blushed at the compliment.

"Your majesty is too kind," she whispered, slightly embarrassed by the way Stuart was looking at her.

Behind Stuart, both Morgan and Trahaearn nodded their approval at the appearance of the young woman.

"May I introduce you to Bishop Douglas, my champion, Sir Trahaearn, and the future Duke of Rossmere, Morgan Bodine."

Bishop, knight and boy bowed deeply then straightened up.

"Come, be seated, let us enjoy our meal," Alwyn said gesturing towards the long table.

They sat, and food was served. Some dishes were unfamiliar to the guests and Alwyn explained them and invited them to at least try them, which they did.

Throughout the meal, Alexandra was sat next to Stuart, and they talked quite amicably. Stuart was careful to avoid any mention of the fact he had Kadeau in his court. Alwyn must have known yet made no reference to it. Stuart assumed that he was more interested in the joining of their two houses, and perhaps be able to return the family to Devonmere, than who he had in his court. The meal finished without incident, and everyone retired for the night.

Over the next week, Alexandra and Stuart spent a great deal of time in one another's company, always chaperoned at a discreet distance, allowing them to learn more about each other. Stuart was very much smitten with the fourteen year old and at the end of the week, nodded his approval to his Bishop.

There hadn't been much for Trahaearn and Morgan to do during their stay, so they had explored, and trained together out of sight of their hosts and also practiced a little magic to keep their minds tuned and ready.

A few of the young ladies at court had taken a shine to the young Morgan. A couple of them had openly told him they wished he had been just a couple of years older. The sexual insinuation could not be missed, even by the eight year old, and he had blushed at their forward talking, which had enamoured him even more to them and it left him a little shaken to realise that had he been older, they would have wanted to have sex with him.

The formal declaration of intent was delivered to King Alwyn, who seemed delighted at the match and the *sponsalia per verbade future* was made the following day, with a celebratory banquet held that evening and token gifts were exchanged between the King and his future wife.

At the celebratory banquet, ladies in waiting and some local gentry attended to boost the numbers and make the event a little more raucous. A couple of the ladies had tried to get Morgan to dance with them, but he had refused, and had remained uncharacteristically quiet which Trahaearn had picked up on.

Morgan excused himself early saying he was tired and left for his chambers. Trahaearn also gave his apologies and followed him.

"Are you all right, Morgan?" the knight asked him as he caught up with him.

"Yes," was all he said.

"Has something happened?"

"No, nothing's happened, it's just that..." he stopped and took a deep breath. "Trahaearn, do women enjoy...sex?"

The knight opened his mouth and promptly closed it again, noticing the flush on the boy's face.

"What's happened?" Trahaearn finally asked him. "You are innocent, young Morgan, you have nothing to be ashamed of. So what has happened?" he asked again.

"Nothing, I swear. Some of the ladies..."

"Go on."

"They insinuated that had I been older, they would have wanted to have sex with me."

"You are an extremely good looking boy, Morgan and I'm certain you will be a very handsome looking young man when you grow up. I would think a lot of women would want to be...intimate with you. They have paid you a compliment." The knight paused for a few moments before continuing. "I do not have much experience in sexual matters, but what I can tell you is that a woman's enjoyment of the sexual act depends very much on the skill of her husband."

"I don't understand."

"You would be better to ask King Stuart, he has more experience than I in this sort of thing. Having said that, when I was younger, I was witness to...well, let me just say, some men treat their wives no better than the animals on a farm, satisfying the desire of their own bodies without thought of the desires of their partner. Other men are more thoughtful and realise a woman is capable of great passion when their bodies are aroused in the correct manner, that allows them to enjoy the act. I will say no more, you will learn when you are older."

"Thank you, Trahaearn," Morgan finally said. "I will retire now. No, don't call Ioan, I can manage on my own. Good night."

"Are you sure?" Trahaearn asked him.

"Yes. I... I think I want to be alone now."

"Very well, Morgan. Good night."

଼ଷ   ଼ଵ   ଼ଷ   ଼ଵ

Stuart and his party stayed a few more days. During that time, he had been allowed to be with Alexandra on his own and had managed to kiss her. Using the skills he had acquired when his father had arranged for some sexual education, he had left his intended wanting to know more. She was a virgin, untouched by a man, and her body was coming to life as she began to develop into a young woman. He had used his lips to caress her, awakening the new feeling of passion in her body, but left her pure and unsullied.

He had seen the shock at the emotions she was feeling and nodded in satisfaction, knowing that if he treated her correctly she would be a passionate wife. With this knowledge, they had set sail a couple of days later to return to Devonmere, where arrangements for the wedding ceremony were begun and invitations issued, providing plenty of notice of the ceremony.

C３ ８０ C３ ８０

Chapter Fourteen

"Father, you're not a supporter of the House of Cantrell, and yet you stay carefully neutral. I don't understand. You didn't support Arnell Prescott last year following the murder of his son. If you now joined forces with his son Taliesin, we could overthrow Stuart Cantrell," Nigel McDowell, Duke-in-waiting to the Cottesmere duchy said to his father, as they exited the grand hall, where Alisdair McDowell had been holding court.

"Arnell was a fool to call Rhisart out at that time of year. No one in their right mind goes to war on the verge of winter, especially in the Eastern Marches. He was going to be on his own in that battle as soon as he took that emotional decision. We need to be careful and clever about the situation. Stuart has some very powerful allies. Rossmere for one—"

"Shortly to be ruled by a mere boy!" Nigel interrupted rudely. "He is no threat!"

"Invermere for another. Richard Coltrane is very much favoured by the King."

Nigel's eyes narrowed.

"He has a daughter; she will be of marriageable age in seven years or so. I will wed her and take control of the Inver army, who can then fight for our cause."

"Not whilst Richard Coltrane is alive," his father responded.

"Accidents happen," Nigel retorted.

"You will cease this conversation immediately!" Alisdair snapped. "I have nothing against the Coltranes', and although I may not like the Cantrells', I will not commit treason! If we failed, we would lose everything!"

"We should have struck when Stuart first attained the throne!"

"Arnell's army was decimated; we would have had no support!"

"In seven years or so, the Inver army would give us a clear advantage."

"You've yet to marry the girl, and there is no guarantee of that. I forbid any action against Stuart; do you hear me? As long as I am Duke, there will be no more talk of treason!"

Nigel's face flushed red with a mixture of annoyance and frustration, but he wisely bit back the retort he had been about to utter.

"As you wish, Father," he finally replied. "I will not raise the subject again." He carefully masked his features. "By your leave," he added, bowing, and left his father in the long corridor to storm off to his own chambers, plans already beginning to form in his mind.

Oh father, accidents do happen, even here at Cottesmere, he thought to himself as he reached his rooms and found himself standing in front of a mirror.

Nigel McDowell was a handsome young man, a shade under six feet tall, with dark brown hair and eyes, but there was a slightly cruel twist to his mouth, and his expression was often cold and calculating. There was just something about him that made others feel rather uneasy in his presence, which was understandable, as he was rumoured to dabble in the black arts; a dangerous pastime, but for those who knew how to control what they did, it could be very rewarding.

Unfortunately, he had ideas above his current station, and had no qualms about using his dark magic to assist him in his goals. If his father and Duke Taliesin were too afraid to act, he certainly was not.

His thoughts formulated into a brief outline of a plan. He could wed the daughter of the Duke of Invermere. She would give him an heir and, if she protested too violently about his planned ambitions, she too would suffer an unfortunate...accident, as his father would, very shortly.

He straightened his back and studied his reflection, imagining the crown of Devonmere upon his head. He would make a good King, and Colwyn Coltrane, a fine Queen, if she behaved herself and did as she was told.

The child was currently hardly more than a baby, but it was never too soon to do a little courting to indicate his expression of interest.

Mind made up, he sent for his steward and ordered him to pack saddlebags to be ready for the next morning. He would travel to Inver Castle and make his intentions clear. It was important that his father remained totally unaware of his plans, both in regard to his great ambitions and to his own fate.

That night, he dreamt of being King of Devonmere, with his Queen and son beside him, and smiled as he surveyed his kingdom. He would rule with a rod of iron, and all would bow down before him.

ᙯ ᙰ ᙯ ᙰ

Nigel left for Inver Castle the following morning, with a small escort of four men and his personal steward, Celwyn. He had left a note for his father, to be delivered later in the day when they were well into their journey. He knew the Duke would not approve of his actions. By rights, it was his father who should start the process of finding a wife for him, and he knew full well that Colwyn Coltrane was not on the list of possible brides, due to her family being such a close and firm supporter of the Cantrells. Additionally, King Stuart would probably not allow it either.

However, Nigel had everything planned, down to the last detail; the 'accidental' death of his father, his marriage to Colwyn, the downfall of Rossmere and finally, usurping Stuart to take the throne for himself. With a little dabbling in magic, he could see no reason why it could not all come to pass.

The journey to Inver Castle took just over six days of reasonably hard riding and was totally uneventful. During the trip, Nigel had often been pre-occupied with his thoughts of power and ignored the changing scenery they had passed through. The jagged outcrops and steep valley sides of Cottesmere eventually gave way to rolling countryside, filled with crops, or covered with grass and forests. He had crossed through the duchy of Rossmere, with its fertile lands that was home to one of the finest vineyards in Devonmere. It wasn't until he had to concentrate on what he was doing, as they crossed the River Wyvern, that acted as a natural border between Rossmere and Invermere, via the ferry just outside the city of Inver that he realised they were approaching the end of their journey. The ferry was basically a large raft that was attached to both banks by two ropes and was pulled back and forth across the river by two men. There was also a bridge further up that spanned the river, but for the trail he had taken, the ferry was closer.

Three hours later, they rode across the drawbridge, under the barbican, across the lower bailey, under the gatehouse and into the upper bailey and the huge expanse of open ground before the keep.

Their pending arrival had been spotted by lookouts and a herald had sounded to notify Markus, the head steward of Inver, who descended the steps to meet them. He immediately recognised the coat of arms on the surcoats and bowed as Nigel dismounted.

Straightening up, Markus indicated for pages to take charge of their mounts and lead them to the stables.

"My Lord, we were not expecting you."

"No. I did not send word I was coming. Have rooms prepared for myself and my men."

Markus bristled slightly at the arrogant tone but remained polite.

"May I enquire how long you are staying?"

"What business is that of yours?"

The steward took a deep breath before continuing.

"So I may know which rooms to allocate. We are expecting the King and his entourage the day after tomorrow."

"I see." Nigel pondered for a few moments. The news of the King's visit would interfere with his plans, for he had no desire to be in the presence of His Majesty. "I shall be leaving first thing on the morning of the King's arrival," he finally answered.

"Very well, My Lord. If you would care to follow me to the main hall, I will arrange for refreshments whilst your rooms are prepared."

"Lead on," Nigel replied with a nonchalant wave of his hand. "Tell me, are the Duke and Duchess available?"

"The Duke is not here. Her Grace is just finishing daily court."

"Is she now? In which case, you may escort me to the antechamber. I wish to speak to her."

"As you wish, My Lord. Please, follow me."

Markus sent messengers to the kitchen to arrange for food and wine, and another to prepare rooms for the nobleman. Celwyn accompanied the messenger so he could unpack Nigel's saddlebags and lay out a change of clothes.

The escort were led away to the barracks, and Markus led Nigel to the ante chamber.

Bronwyn was just about to leave, having completed hearing requests, complaints, pleas and judging those to be guilty of crimes against the duchy and its people, when the double doors opened, and Markus entered. He bowed.

"Your Grace, Lord Nigel McDowell, son of the Duke of Cottesmere." He straightened, stood aside and Nigel took that as a cue to sweep past him to enter the chamber.

Bronwyn raised an eyebrow, wondering what on earth the young man wanted. She knew the family were not supporters of Stuart, but that did not prevent her from being polite and welcoming.

"Lord Nigel," she said, descending the steps of the dais. "To what do we owe the pleasure?" She extended a hand.

Nigel removed his glove, did the barest of bows, took her hand and briefly kissed it.

"Duchess, pardon my unexpected visit. I have been travelling and thought, as I was passing, it would be rude not to pay my respects."

It was a lie, but Bronwyn did not know that. It was a perfectly plausible story.

"You are welcome here, at Inver. Did our steward inform you the King is due to arrive in a day or so?"

"Yes. My stay will be short, I need to return home. I shall be leaving the morning the King is due."

Bronwyn nodded.

"Have you eaten at all?"

"Your steward is graciously laying on food in the hall."

"Please..." Bronwyn gestured for the young man to accompany her out of the antechamber to the main hall, where a table had been set with plates, food and wine.

A squire poured two goblets of wine, and then Bronwyn dismissed him, so the two could eat and talk alone.

"Duchess, I have not been entirely honest with you, I have actually come to discuss a rather delicate matter," Nigel said, pulling a leg off a cooked chicken.

"Indeed?" the Duchess questioned.

"I was wondering...what are your plans for your daughter, Colwyn?"

Bronwyn's hand paused for a fraction of a second before it continued its journey to place a slice of venison on her plate.

"Plans?"

"For finding her a suitable husband."

"Colwyn is far too young for any thought of marriage. She is just a child, approaching three years old. It will be several years before she is old enough to be married off, and the Duke and I are in complete agreement that she will have a childhood, without the threat of being married and with child before her body is truly ready."

"I understand perfectly," Nigel replied, smiling inwardly. At least there were no other suitors; no one to get in his way. He could wait, and in the meantime, once he became the new Duke of Cottesmere, he could build his army, court the child and marry her. "I would like to express my formal interest in having Colwyn as my wife," he finished.

Bronwyn somehow stopped herself from choking on the mouthful of wine she had just taken. She thought furiously for a suitable reply.

"Thank you for your interest in my daughter, but you haven't even met her and, as I said, there will be no thoughts of marriage for a number of years. Besides, it would also have to have the approval of the King."

Nigel's lips compressed themselves into a thin line, then he caught himself, smiled and inclined his head. It appeared that this part of his plan was going to take a little more hard work than he expected.

"Of course. As you say, there is plenty of time, and we should get to know one another before anything formal is agreed. Perhaps I could see her this evening at supper? At least introduce myself." He fixed Bronwyn with a hard stare, trying to influence her.

Bronwyn took a deep breath. She wanted to deny the young man's request but realised it would be incredibly rude if she did so.

"Very well. If you wish to meet her, we will arrange to eat earlier than usual. At her age, Colwyn eats in her rooms, or with us in our chambers, depending on what is happening that day. I will send for you, say around an hour after sunset?"

"I look forward to it very much."

They ate their meal mainly in silence, with the odd conversation on non-controversial matters, until they had both taken their fill.

"Will you permit me to explore your beautiful castle?" Nigel suddenly asked.

"If you wish. I can arrange for someone to act as your guide—"

"No, that won't be necessary," Nigel interrupted. "I'm sure I'll be able to find my way around."

"Very well. Then I will see you an hour after sunset," Bronwyn said rising from her chair. "No, please do not get up, finish your meal." She gave a small nod and left the nobleman sitting at the table.

Once outside the hall, Bronwyn took several deep breaths. She was angry beyond belief at the audacity of Nigel's request of marriage. Although she had only met him a few times in the past, there was just something about him that made her uneasy and her heart was telling her that she did not want him near her family and most definitely not married into it.

Swiftly, she went to her rooms to regain control of her emotions, wishing that Richard was with her, but he would only just get home before the King was due to arrive back from Isatiri, so for now, she was on her own.

Nigel wandered around part of the castle, avoiding those areas where guards were stationed so as not to arouse any suspicion, then ordered the next page he saw to show him to his allocated rooms, where he rested before changing for the meal and meeting with his future wife. He was convinced that the child would become his bride.

An hour after sunset Nigel made his way to the banqueting hall. Bronwyn was already present, along with a woman who was holding a young girl in her arms. He approached them and made a little bow.

"Duchess Bronwyn," he said politely.

"Lord Nigel. This is my daughter, Colwyn."

Sarah shifted the child in her arms, so that Colwyn could look at the duke-in-waiting.

Nigel was struck by the large, intense green eyes and the long chestnut hair. He had to admit she was a pretty little thing, but he felt rather unnerved by the way she was staring at him. There was no hint of a smile on her face, and she seemed to be almost staring right through him.

"Lady Colwyn," he said stepping forward. "It is a pleasure to meet you at last." He held out his hand to take hers, but she did not offer it, and simply stared at him, not saying a word.

Bronwyn glanced at her daughter.

"Colwyn, manners," she said.

Her daughter looked at her, briefly back at Nigel, then fidgeted so she could bury her head in Sarah's shoulder.

"I'm sorry, Your Grace," Sarah said to Bronwyn. "I believe Colwyn is over tired."

"Give her to me," Nigel demanded. He reached out to take her, and Colwyn started screaming, and carried on screaming…very loudly, whilst clutching Sarah with all her might.

"Sarah, take her out, put her to bed," Bronwyn ordered.

"At once, Your Grace." Sarah turned and walked towards the double doors.

"Wait!" Nigel ordered. Sarah stopped and turned, as he looked at Bronwyn. "You're not going to let your daughter get away with that, are you?"

"I beg your pardon?" Bronwyn asked, starting to bristle.

"The child is totally undisciplined. Give her to me."

"Sarah, take her out. Now!"

Nigel's eyes flashed anger, he had wanted to get his hands on the child to start asserting his influence on her.

"And you, Lord Nigel, kindly remember you are a guest in this castle, not the master!"

Sarah left the room, rather shocked at hearing Bronwyn's tone, but understood it perfectly. Who did Lord Nigel think he was, issuing orders in Inver Castle? The maid took an immediate dislike to the man, and hoped Bronwyn would throw him out. Something had obviously upset Colwyn, as she didn't usually misbehave like she had done just now. It had to be something about Lord McDowell, for as soon as they left the hall, Colwyn stopped screaming and quietened down.

Bronwyn meanwhile was giving Nigel the iciest of stares. His eyes displayed annoyance at having been stopped forming a link with the child, to start to mould her in readiness for when they would eventually wed. He would have to try again. He took a deep breath to get his temper under control and forced a smile.

"Perhaps you are right, the child may be over tired. I apologise, I was so looking forward to meeting her. She is very pretty and obviously gets her looks from her beautiful mother." He gave the Duchess a charming smile, but she didn't fall for it.

Bronwyn's expression clearly indicated he had failed to ingratiate himself back into her favour. The Duchess had suddenly lost her appetite.

"Please help yourself to the food laid out. I will leave you in peace to eat," she said, and walked out, leaving a livid Nigel alone in the banquet hall.

As she made her way to Colwyn's rooms, Markus appeared.

"Your Grace, I heard Colwyn screaming. Is everything all right?"

"Markus, inform the guard I want someone standing watch over Colwyn's rooms until Nigel McDowell leaves this castle. I do not trust that man. It appears that Colwyn does not like him either."

"I will inform the Captain of the Guard of your order right away, Your Grace."

"Thank you, Markus. The sooner that man leaves, the better!"

Bronwyn entered her daughter's chambers, to find Sarah tidying up.

"Your Grace, Colwyn stopped screaming immediately we left the banqueting hall. For some reason, she does not like Lord McDowell."

"I don't think anyone does!" Bronwyn retorted. "The nerve of the man. Anyway, I've come to tell you that there will be a guard outside these chambers until McDowell leaves. How is my daughter?"

"Settled for the night, Your Grace. I am planning to stay close, just in case."

"Thank you, Sarah. Oh, lock the door tonight, please. Good night."

"I will, Your Grace. Good night."

Once the Duchess had left, Sarah locked the door, finished her chores and also retired.

Bronwyn entered her own chambers and slammed the door behind her, making Dilys jump.

"Y – Your Grace? Is anything wrong?"

The Duchess took a deep breath to calm herself.

"Hopefully not for much longer. Apologies Dilys. Everything will be fine once Nigel McDowell leaves this castle."

Dilys helped her mistress to disrobe and get ready for bed.

"I'll be glad when Richard gets back," Bronwyn mumbled as she got into bed. "Good night, Dilys."

"Good night, Your Grace."

ରେ ଚ ରେ ଚ

Nigel slammed the door shut behind him as he entered his chambers. He was angry beyond measure.

"Lord Nigel?" Celwyn questioned.

"Get out!" Those two words were full of venom. Celwyn knew better than to linger, and fled. When his lord was in this kind of mood, it was best to stay as far away from him as a person was able to, or receive a severe beating as his lord vented his anger on those within reach.

Nigel realised there was no point in staying longer on this occasion. He could tell the Duchess was in no mood for his planned antics concerning her daughter. She was another one who could do with being put firmly back in her place. He did have a liking for women with spirit, he liked to deprive them of it in his own special way. Nigel smiled as he thought of how he would divest Bronwyn Coltrane of her spirit and bend her to his will. It was his last thought as he retired for the night.

The following morning, when he awoke, he ordered Celwyn to pack their bags. There was no point in staying this time, but he would return. Nigel was still angry enough to leave without informing Bronwyn directly but left a message with a page to be delivered.

The page in question dutifully delivered the message and Bronwyn smiled, grateful to be rid of the hateful lord. If she could have her way she would bar him from ever coming to Inver Castle ever again, but that unfortunately could not be done.

The castle spent the day preparing for the return of the King from his journey to Isatiri. Bronwyn wondered if it had gone to plan, and that the King had found his future queen. The kingdom desperately needed it, and Stuart needed someone who would eventually love him, be by his side, and provide him with the much needed heir.

It was mid-afternoon when Richard returned with his small escort and Trystan. He'd been in the very south of Invermere, checking on his tenant farmers and visiting gentry. There had been a couple of minor issues he'd had to attend to, but overall, the trip had been successful. He was looking forward to a bath and time with his family.

As usual, Bronwyn was on the steps of the keep to greet him. He dismounted and kissed her, then stepped back.

"What's wrong?" he asked. "You seem...tense."

She smiled apologetically at him.

"I'm sorry husband, I thought I was relaxed now."

"What's happened?" he questioned. "Is Colwyn all right?"

She took his offered arm, and they went inside and to his chambers. Trystan had grabbed his saddlebags and run on ahead to arrange hot water for his master. Richard stripped off his armour with Bronwyn's assistance and stretched in relief before reaching for his wife again.

"Now, tell me, what's happened?"

She looked up into his beautiful brown eyes, and at his handsome features. He looked tired, but she knew he wasn't going to back down from finding out what the issue was, so she told him.

"I had a visit from Nigel McDowell yesterday," she began and paused as she saw her husband frown. "He initially said he was just passing through and thought it would be rude if he did not pay his respects, then confessed he had an ulterior motive... he asked me for Colwyn's hand in marriage."

"He what!"

"Calm down Richard," Bronwyn said hastily. "I told him in no uncertain circumstances that no consideration of marriage would be taken until our daughter has reached a suitable age and that any marriage would have to be approved by the King."

The Duke took a couple of deep breaths and began to relax again.

"He did ask to see Colwyn, which I did allow, but when he went to take her from Sarah, she screamed and screamed and didn't stop until Sarah removed her from the room. He was very angry about that."

"Is he still here?"

"No, he left this morning without informing me directly. I'm telling you now Richard, that man is never going to marry our daughter! There's something about him...something evil. Even Colwyn sensed it."

"The King would never allow it. The McDowell's are not supporters of the House of Cantrell. I will not allow it either. Do not fear."

Bronwyn smiled up at him and Richard took that as an invitation to kiss her. His arms encircled her as the kiss deepened, but the Duchess pushed him away.

"You smell of horse!" she exclaimed, "and I will too!"

The familiar roguish expression filled his eyes, making Bronwyn feel hot and flustered.

"Then perhaps..." he kissed her again, "...we could bathe together..." another kiss, "...to rid us of the smell."

"Richard Coltrane, you are incorrigible!" Bronwyn laughed to hide the fact that her heart had started beating faster at the thought. "Away with you to your bath, so I may get on and finish preparations for the King's arrival!"

He nuzzled into her neck.

"Until later, then," he whispered, then straightened up as Trystan knocked respectfully on the bedchamber door to announce his bath was ready. "Thank you, Trystan, I'll be there shortly." He turned back to his wife. "Last chance," he said to her, the look on his face telling her all she needed to know as she started to undress him.

☙ ❧ ☙ ❧

Chapter Fifteen

The King's ship arrived in the port of Inver earlier than expected the following day due to a favourable wind, but fortunately lookouts had spotted it approaching the sheltered harbour which enabled Richard to get the horses saddled and down to the docks to greet them when they disembarked.

Richard stood on the quay waiting patiently, and smiled a warm welcome as Stuart led his party down the ramp towards him. Everyone looked relaxed and happy, including Morgan, who appeared to have found his sea legs during the trip.

The Duke bowed as Stuart reached him. "My Liege, welcome back. You made good time on your return journey. I hope your visit to Isatiri was fruitful and rewarding?"

They shook hands warmly and Richard noticed the sparkle in his King's eyes.

"Richard, she is beautiful!" Stuart enthused quietly to him. "I am arranging the marriage for September next year. The organisation will take time, and this must be a wedding fit for a King and Queen."

"That is good news indeed," the Duke replied.

Morgan gave Richard a hug. "I got my sea legs, Papa," he said.

"I knew you would," the Duke replied, ruffling his hair affectionately, then greeted Trahaearn, the bishop and Master Stephen.

They began to walk along the quay back to where the horses were waiting.

"Will you also crown her queen the same day?" the Duke asked conversationally.

"As we will have everyone present, it seems the logical thing to do."

Richard nodded in agreement. "Sire, I am pleased you are happy with the arrangement."

Stuart smiled. "On my last night of freedom, I am going to make you tell me about your wilder days with my father!" he teased.

Richard laughed openly at that. "We will see," he replied, his own eyes twinkling.

"Richard, I shall make it a royal decree!"

They both laughed loudly as they mounted their horses and started back on the road up to the castle.

"Will you be staying just tonight, or longer, Sire?" Richard asked.

"I think we will stay two nights. I didn't get the opportunity to meet your beautiful daughter when I arrived before our sailing. I must get acquainted with her, as she is a member of my most loyal house."

"I would be honoured, although I must warn you, she has quite a temper on her."

"Where has that come from? Both Bronwyn and you, are most even tempered."

"I have no idea, Sire, but I assure you it's not from my side!"

Stuart laughed again. "Not even in your wilder days?" he teased. He was happy, relaxed and for once, at peace with his position and role. "But tell me, have things been quiet whilst I have been away?"

"Yes, My Liege. The only...excitement was a visit from Nigel McDowell."

"Nigel? Here at Inver?"

"Yes."

"What did he want?"

"Lady Colwyn's hand in marriage."

Stuart almost pulled up but recovered quickly. "What did you reply?"

"Unfortunately, I wasn't here, but south in the duchy. Bronwyn said no consideration would even be contemplated until she was of marriageable age, and she confessed she gave him short thrift and he left the following morning."

"He will never marry her," Stuart said firmly. "I can see where that union would lead!"

"As can we all, Sire."

As they finally approached the keep, Richard saw Bronwyn already in place outside the keep, waiting to greet the royal guest. Just behind her stood Sarah, with Colwyn in her arms, and the Duke smiled.

They all dismounted. The King walked up the steps, closely followed by the Duke, Morgan, and the rest of their guests, whilst their personal stewards collected the saddle bags and were escorted to the assigned quarters.

"Your majesty," Bronwyn said, curtseying deeply. "Welcome back to Inver. I hope you had a fruitful and successful trip to Isatiri."

Stuart kissed her hand and helped her to rise. "Duchess Bronwyn, thank you as always for your warm welcome." He leant forward and kissed her cheek. "Our visit was successful."

"Oh, I am so pleased for you, Sire. You deserve every happiness."

"Thank you." His eyes strayed to just behind her and slightly to the right. "My goodness, Colwyn has grown these last couple of months since I last saw her at the coronation. She is going to be a beautiful woman when she grows up."

"You are most kind, Sire," Bronwyn said, indicating for Sarah to come forward.

The nursemaid did as she was told and curtseyed, then her eyes widened in surprise as the King requested for Colwyn to be handed

271

to him. Mindful of what had happened with Nigel McDowell, Sarah reluctantly held the child out for the King to take. Colwyn did not make a sound, but studied the King's face for a few moments, then smiled at him.

"Lady Colwyn, I do not believe we have been formally introduced. I am King Stuart."

Colwyn cocked her head on one side. "Stuat," she said confidently. Bronwyn was horrified, but the King just laughed, and Colwyn did too. "Stuat."

"Close enough," Stuart chuckled.

"My apologies, Sire, court etiquette is not yet her forte."

"She is but a babe. It does me good to be brought down to earth now and again."

"Sire, we have food and refreshment in the banqueting hall."

"Then lead on, Bronwyn." Sarah went to take Colwyn back from him. "No, I will carry her," he said. "It will be good practice for when I have children of my own."

They ate in relative silence. Bronwyn took the opportunity to speak to Morgan and enquire how he found the journey there and back, and what he saw.

"I thought I was going to die, I was so ill, but Master Stephen came to my rescue, although Sir Trahaearn had to hold me down to enable him to get the potion into me, but I started feeling better the next day."

"Oh that's good, so you have found your sea legs. Tell me, what was Isatiri like?"

"The climate was warmer, and they had lots of strange plants that I have never seen before. They also had this beautiful garden, arranged in a complicated pattern."

"It was a formal garden, Your Grace," Trahaearn broke in. "Not practical, but beautifully laid out."

"We have a rose garden," Bronwyn countered.

"Yes, but we use the flowers for decoration, the petals for rose water, pot pourri, to eat, we use the hips to make jelly."

"That's true. But it would be nice to have something of pure beauty rather than it having to always be practical. I may give this some consideration. How were the people? Were you treated well?"

"The princess was very beautiful, and everyone was friendly."

"That's good to hear." Bronwyn glanced at Trahaearn and mouthed silently, *despite you both being Kadeau?*

Trahaearn nodded, then mouthed back. *Our heritage was not mentioned.*

Oh, I see.

Morgan went to play with Colwyn and the King, and Trahaearn leant close to Bronwyn.

"It appears, Your Grace, that some of the women were very much drawn to Morgan. Had he been older, I believe they would have..." he let his voice trail off.

Bronwyn's eyes widened and glanced briefly at the boy before giving her full attention to Trahaearn. "Did... did he understand the... innuendo?"

"Yes, Your Grace. But have no fear, it did not frighten him, but he did start asking questions of me."

"Poor Trahaearn, that must have been rather uncomfortable for you."

He nodded. "Somewhat."

"He will shortly be old enough to be told...he knows of the act, for Richard was involving him in the husbandry around breeding good animal stock practically as soon as he could walk. Thank you for telling me. I will speak to my husband about some...further education on the matter. The last thing I would want is for him to be totally ignorant."

"Probably a wise decision, Your Grace. Morgan is a very handsome looking boy. No doubt there will eventually be women closer to home who find his looks irresistible in a year or so."

Everyone spent a relaxing afternoon and evening for a change, and in that atmosphere perhaps a little too much wine was enjoyed, after which the over indulgers staggered off to bed.

Bronwyn was unusually quiet as Richard escorted her to her chambers.

"What troubles you, my love?" he asked as they reached the door to her day room.

"It seems Morgan's adventure to Isatiri was a little more colourful than he has let on. When do you think he will be old enough to be told about the union between a man and a woman?"

The question brought Richard up short, and it took him a moment to recover. "I had planned to...explain everything when he reached ten, why?"

"The women of Isatiri found our adopted son very much to their liking."

Richard blushed, which Bronwyn found enchanting. Her battle hardened husband was suddenly shy and uncomfortable. He cleared his throat. "How much to their liking?" he finally managed to ask.

"Well, let me just say, that had he been a little older..." She let her voice trail off but couldn't help smiling as Richard swallowed. "Perhaps you had better tell him sooner rather than later? I would hate our son to be at a disadvantage." She paused, reached up and kissed her husband and entered her chambers. "Goodnight, my love."

Richard stood staring at the closed door for a few seconds, swallowed again, pulled himself together and headed for his own chambers deep in thought about how he was going to tackle the delicate subject.

ℭ ℬ ℭ ℬ

The following day, Richard invited Morgan to his chambers for a game of tawlbwrdd.

"I'm a bit rusty. I haven't played since those two games I managed to play with the King a month or so before travelling to Isatiri."

"I'll take it easy on you," Richard teased as he set the pieces up, and dismissed Trystan, so there were just the two of them in the room. "I need to talk to you about something," he finally said.

Morgan looked at him curiously.

"I wasn't going to approach the subject until you were older, but it seems circumstances may have forced my hand." He paused as the boy frowned at him. "You're a very handsome boy, Morgan and I've been told you're already beginning to turn a few heads."

"Trahaearn has told you about Isatiri, hasn't he?"

"Yes, he has."

"Nothing happened."

"I know it didn't, but it may in the future."

"I've seen the animals do it, I know what it entails."

Richard shook his head. "That's the problem, you don't. It's different between a man and a woman. I would love for you to find a woman who loves you for who you are, not because it's been arranged, but that could happen. And if it does, you need to be...a good lover. A true husband does not only think of his own pleasure, but that of his wife as well. She should enjoy the act as much as he."

"You mean kissing," Morgan said knowledgably.

Richard paused and took a deep breath. "There's much more than just kissing. There's how you kiss, the touching, finding out what pleases you both, being... intimate, bringing pleasure to your partner, making each other yearn for more. I can't describe it, but when you

275

get it right, it is the most enjoyable experience, you feel like your heart will explode as you reach that moment of fulfilment."

Morgan was suddenly seeing his guardian in a whole new light. Did he do this with Bronwyn? Of course he did, otherwise he would not have the knowledge of it.

"But how do you learn of these things?" Morgan asked.

Richard actually blushed slightly and took a deep breath.

"On my fourteenth birthday, Prince Rhisart, as he was then, took me into the city to a very high class...brothel. A brothel is where—"

"—I know what a brothel is, I've overheard some of the squires talking, when they try to shock us pages."

"Very well. He arranged for me to be...shown various techniques and then how to use them."

"King Rhisart did that?"

"Until he was married, he was quite...wild. But I will tell you, a man with those skills will find them invaluable, and a woman who knows how to pleasure a man is beyond measure."

Silence reigned for a few minutes as Morgan digested the news. Another skill to learn, once he was older, but at the moment, he wasn't really interested in the opposite sex. His most pressing issue was to become the finest knight and be King Stuart's protector and champion.

"Let's play," the boy finally said, moving a piece on the board.

ଓ ଞ ଓ ଞ

Stuart spent another relaxing day at Inver, free from decision making, diplomacy and ruling the kingdom, then left the following morning. Morgan said goodbye to the Coltranes' saying that he hoped to see them again soon, but if not, he hoped to see them at the King's wedding. Bronwyn assured him they would be there, and that nothing would keep them away. He hugged his family, then Richard had given him a leg up onto his pony and they headed for Ellesmere.

Cȝ 𝕏 Cȝ 𝕏

Chapter Sixteen

"Nigel!" Duke Alisdair McDowell's voice carried across the bailey as he spied his son riding under the gatehouse towards the stables.

Nigel stopped his horse, looked over at his father, and changed direction, allowing his mount to amble over to where the Duke stood, on the bottom step leading into the keep. He halted a few feet from him.

"Father."

"What on earth are you playing at?"

For a fleeting moment, Nigel considered being obtuse, then changed his mind. Instead, he shrugged his shoulders. "As I stated in my note to you, I paid a visit to Inver Castle."

"But they are supporters of the King! Why waste your time?"

"I decided to meet the Lady Colwyn and divulge my intentions to her parents."

"I'm sure that was received well!" Alisdair replied sarcastically.

"Only Bronwyn was in residence. Richard was near Strathmere."

"And?"

"Colwyn is a pretty child, but far too undisciplined. She will need to learn her place once we are wed."

"You're telling me Bronwyn said, 'yes' to the marriage?" Alisdair sounded shocked.

"No," Nigel admitted. "But I will wed the brat one way or another."

"The King will never allow it, as it will put Rossmere in a dangerous position."

"Damn the King!" Nigel snapped. "I want Inver, and I shall have it."

"Keep your voice down!" Alisdair said urgently. "Do you want to be executed for treason?"

Nigel almost snorted in disdain. "With the Cottesmere and Inver armies, I will have nothing to fear."

"You haven't got either of them yet. I am still Duke and by the sounds of it, there will never be a union between Cottesmere and Invermere."

The Duke saw his son flash him a malevolent look.

Nigel considered his father to be weak and lacking ambition. More importantly, he was attempting to thwart Nigel's plans. It was perhaps approaching the time for his father to hand the control of Cottesmere over to him; but the only way that was going to happen was when the current Duke died.

Life was hard, even for the gentry, and it was possible his father could suffer a tragic and unfortunate accident. Nigel smiled as he revisited the next steps he would take.

"Are you listening to me?" Alisdair said, slapping his son's leg as hard as he could. He would have slapped his face, had the young man not been mounted.

Anger flashed in Nigel's eyes.

"Don't even think about it," Alisdair said. "I can still knock you senseless. Perhaps I ought to anyway and knock some sense into you, because you've clearly lost what little you had!"

"What do you want, father?" Nigel asked 'innocently'.

"We have guests arriving tomorrow, and I promised them some exciting hunting. I need you to help me keep them entertained."

"Who is it?" Nigel's voice sounded genuinely interested, but not for the reason his father thought.

"The Earl of Dalesmere, his wife, son and daughter. We are looking to improve relationships and promote support for the opposers of the House Cantrell."

"Very wise." Nigel tried to remember what the Earl of Dalesmere's daughter looked like. The visit by the Earl and his family could provide a perfect opportunity for an accident to happen if things were not organised appropriately, and some feminine entertainment if things went to plan.

ೞ ೲ ೞ ೲ

Their guests arrived around midday the following day. Nigel stood with his father to welcome them; his attention firmly fixed on the daughter as she was presented to them.

"Duke, may I present my daughter, the Lady Coira."

Lady Coira was fourteen years old, brown haired, brown eyed, not particularly beautiful, but passable, with full lips that deserved to be kissed. Nigel towered over her, but acted the perfect gentleman as he kissed her hand and smiled warmly.

"Lady Coira, welcome."

"Thank you Lord Nigel." She curtseyed her respect.

Alisdair indicated for servants to come forward and escort the guests to their chambers.

"I assume you will want to refresh yourselves after your journey. We will convene in the banqueting hall, an hour after sunset."

"Thank you, Duke Alisdair." The Earl gave a little bow and followed his assigned servant.

Nigel watched Lady Coira follow her parents. There could be some entertainment in the offing after all...

During supper that evening, Alisdair outlined the agenda for his guest's stay. They would take a day to get over their journey, then would go hunting the day after. Nigel paid avid attention. Hunting... the perfect opportunity... He enquired whereabouts the hunt would take place, on the pretence that he could assist with organising the beaters to drive the game towards the guests so he could put his plans into action.

Nigel decided to be friendly and offered to show the Lady Coira around the castle. She seemed flattered by his attentions, and her father was hopeful that it might lead to something... like a future marriage proposal and improve their station.

Alisdair had indicated on a map where the drive was going to take place and his son carefully worked out a plan that would result in the desired outcome. In celebration of this forthcoming change in the leadership of the duchy, Nigel decided he would like to have a celebration of his own, which would also require some careful planning, so no suspicion could be thrown on him; he would be grief-stricken at the 'accident' and standing watch over his father's body.

During supper the following evening, Coira kept giving Nigel furtive looks and he knew his plan was going to work. His steward would give him a cast iron alibi for the evening following the unfortunate incident, or something unpleasant would occur. He issued instructions to the steward that were to be followed to the letter, and no matter what occurred Coira must not be able to identify him.

The hunt started well, although the weather was a little misty but that would be advantageous. Beaters drove whatever game was in their path to the awaiting gentry. Unfortunately, an arrow hit a deer, but did not kill it.

Dogs were despatched to track it and keep it at bay until they caught up and could put it out of its misery.

"I'll go," Alisdair said, mounting up and following the hounds. At the same time, Nigel went a different way to warn the beaters, and in the beautifully orchestrated confusion, as Alisdair shot the deer, it made one final cry, and crashed through some bushes, just as one of the followers also fired and hit Alisdair's horse.

The animal went down, crushing Alisdair underneath. The Duke was still alive, but the weight of the horse was slowly squeezing the breath out of him. Nigel arrived and looked down at his father.

"S – son... help me!" he pleaded.

Nigel didn't move.

"G – get this horse off me! I can't breathe!"

Nigel went to the horse, it was breathing hard, but it was alive and the wound the arrow had made was not lethal. He grasped the arrow and pulled it out. The animal screamed, thrashed, and eliminated the final breath from Alisdair's body as it fought its way to its feet.

Beaters and followers arrived on the scene.

"An...unfortunate accident," Nigel said, "my father's horse fell on him and crushed him."

"Your Grace! I – I am sorry for your loss."

Nigel put on a brave face. "It – it is no one's fault," he said with supposed difficulty. He checked Alisdair's horse, the wound it had sustained was bleeding slightly, but it could move, so he got a couple of beaters to help hoist his father's body onto the saddle.

A pack horse was used to convey the deer back to the castle. A rider went ahead to deliver a message to the bishop so he could begin preparations for the funeral, another to round up the rest of the hunting party and escort them back to the castle. Nigel rode back quietly, playing the part of the grieving son to perfection.

The bishop was waiting for him when they arrived back and attempted to talk to the new Duke about the arrangements, but Nigel wasn't interested.

"Do what you think best," he simply said. "I can't talk about it now. I leave all the arrangements to you." He turned to his guests. "Forgive me, I am going to my chambers. The stewards will take care of your needs for the rest of today. I need to be alone to come to terms with what has happened." He strode away.

Coira put out a hand to him, but he brushed past her, noting her action.

The castle was very subdued that evening and everyone retired to their rooms early.

Nigel requested his steward get him some wine and then gave him his instructions on bringing the Lady Coira to his chambers. Now that his father was dead, there was no one else occupying that floor of the castle keep.

It was ten minutes later when his steward returned, complete with an unconscious Coira over his shoulder.

"She fainted," the steward whispered very quietly. "I blindfolded her as you instructed, went to gag her and she just fainted."

"Put her on my bed, then wait out here. You have done well, help yourself to some wine, while I... entertain my guest," Nigel whispered back.

The steward did as he was ordered, then came back, poured himself a generous goblet of wine and after the Duke had shut the door to his bedchamber behind him, made himself comfortable on a chair. It had been a while since he had smuggled a woman into Nigel's rooms. He thought those days were over, but apparently not. He assumed the Duke was still smarting from the rebuff he had received from the Duchess of Invermere.

Nigel's visitor had still not regained consciousness. What he didn't want, was for her to try and remove the blindfold. It was important that she would not be able to identify him, so using a couple of his sashes, he tied her hands to the headboard, and waited, studying her. Coira was in her nightgown. He reached out and undid the lacings on it, then removed his own clothes, lay down beside her and began to touch her, curious to know what her body felt like.

She regained consciousness as he was kissing her, and froze, demanding to know what was going on, to be released, or that she would scream. No answers were forthcoming and she struggled as hands touched her breasts through her nightgown, squeezing, massaging, then she panicked and kicked out with her feet as she felt her nightgown being pulled up, hands on her thighs and she screamed, loudly.

Her assailant clamped a hand over her mouth and draped a bare leg over hers to keep her still, as the nightgown was dragged up over her waist, and suddenly she was being touched intimately.

Coira struggled violently. Nigel had decided to be generous and bring her pleasure, but he was growing tired of her trying to scream and struggle. He put up with it a little longer, then struck her sharply. Dazed, she lay there as he continued to play with her body, then needing to satisfy his own needs, he moved over her and thrust savagely into her, making her scream. He did not care about the fact she had never been with a man, and that he was hurting her, he just kept moving until his body reached its ultimate climax and grunted in satisfaction. His victim started to cry pitifully, and Nigel was bored.

Lifting himself from her abused body and getting up from the bed, he looked down at her as she trembled, the nightgown above her waist, blood on her thighs and turned to his dresser to obtain water and a cloth. He cleaned her up, forced some drugged wine down her throat, waited for it to take effect, then opened the door to his bedchamber and ordered his steward to take her back to her chambers and put her to bed.

The steward used the secret passages within the castle to return her. She would wake up in the morning, thinking it had been a nightmare.

The next morning, all hell seemed to break loose, with Coira saying she had been assaulted and raped, and yet, she had been found asleep in her quarters, clean, and apparently unharmed. When she then said she had been tied, no evidence was found on her wrists to back up her claim.

A 'distraught' Nigel heard this and ordered them to go. How dare they claim such a thing when his father had been killed just the day before.

Nigel saw them off, then followed up on the preparations for his father's funeral. Things were in hand. It couldn't be over fast enough as far as he was concerned. The bishop had sent a messenger to Ellesmere as was the law, to inform the King of the death of Alisdair and that Nigel was now the new Duke.

C３ ８０ C３ ８０

Stuart read the proclamation from Cottesmere concerning Alisdair McDowell and the fact that Nigel was now the new Duke and was suspicious. The facts contained in the message from the bishop seemed to confirm that it had been an unfortunate accident, but the King wasn't so sure. However, he had more pressing things to attend to and without any proof, was unable to challenge the matter.

C３ ８０ C３ ８０

Chapter Seventeen

Bronwyn was feeling 'out of sorts' and wondered if it was a reaction to Nigel's visit catching up with her and his outrageous request for the hand of Colwyn in marriage.

It was a couple of days later when she awoke feeling slightly ill and realisation dawned.

"Your Grace," Dilys asked concern, seeing her expression. "What's wrong?"

"Dilys, I...I think I am with child!" Bronwyn's voice sounded awed, yet doubtful. It was possible, but she'd had such issues conceiving Colwyn, that she dared not hope she'd fallen again after just a couple of years.

"Oh, Your Grace, but that's wonderful news!" Dilys exclaimed. "But why the doubt?"

"You know how long it took for me to conceive Colwyn. I have been feeling out of sorts for a week or so, and this morning, I have felt ill, but it's not the same as last time."

"Just because you were so incapacitated the first time, does not mean you will be ill this time. Do you want me to arrange for the physician to visit. He can confirm one way or another."

"I don't want Richard to know, not until I'm certain, I wouldn't want to raise his hopes, only to have them dashed."

"Leave it with me, Your Grace, I will arrange it."

Dilys discretely arranged for the physician to visit whilst the Duke was out in the surrounding countryside, checking on crops being grown by tenant farmers, this time to the east of the duchy.

The physician carried out a thorough examination of the Duchess, and Bronwyn could tell by the expression on his face when he had finished, that he was about to confirm her suspicion.

"Your Grace, you are indeed with child. Allow me to be the first to congratulate you. No extreme sickness at the moment?"

"No, just a little queasy in the mornings, and the odd retch, but nothing like last time."

"Excellent. Well, I still advise plenty of rest and no undue exertion. Should anything cause you concern as you progress, send for me immediately." He bowed and left the Duchess.

Dilys came to her smiling broadly. "Congratulations, Your Grace!" and impulsively took her hands in support, then frowned as tears began to flow from her mistress's eyes. "I hope they are tears of joy, Your Grace."

"Oh Dilys, yes they are. They are!"

Richard returned mid-afternoon and went to see his wife in her rooms. Bronwyn was trying to concentrate on some embroidery, but her mind was elsewhere, trying to work out how to tell her husband the good news.

"Bronwyn, my love," he said as he approached.

He had caught her unawares and unprepared. He saw the expression on her face and immediately went and knelt before her.

"What's wrong?" he asked.

Those two simple words caused the tears to flow.

Seriously worried, he took her hands. "What's happened? Is it Colwyn? Morgan?" His tone of voice clearly conveyed the worry. "What is it?"

She shook her head as he had asked the questions, took a deep breath and then smiled at him, making him frown in confusion.

Bronwyn clasped one of his hands and placed it on her abdomen. "Richard," she began. "I... I am with child," she finally finished.

She watched his expression change, the brown eyes softened with love, and grew bright with the threat of tears.

"Oh, my love, are you sure? Shall I summon a physician?" he asked.

"The physician has already been and confirmed," she replied.

"Why didn't you tell me your suspicions?"

"I didn't want to raise false hopes, I know how much it means to you. I needed to be sure, before imparting the news."

Richard's heart was fit to burst with the information. He hugged her tightly and kissed her with everything he had.

"You are feeling well?" he asked her as their lips parted. "The sickness?"

"I am...surprisingly well at the moment. A little nausea, but nothing like the first time."

"I will take the greatest care of you. Well done, my love." He kissed her again and stood up. "This calls for a celebration." He went and retrieved two goblets and filled them with wine from the container that was always present. Richard then handed her one. "To my beautiful wife and the child within her. May they both stay safe."

☙ ❧ ☙ ❧

The pregnancy progressed, Bronwyn was nowhere near as ill this time around, and as the weeks passed, she dared to hope that everything was going to be all right.

Now almost six months along, Bronwyn realised that they would all be able to attend the King's forthcoming marriage the following

September. The baby would only be around seven months by then, but as long as they were careful, it would be all right to make the journey to Ellesmere.

Autumn had arrived and Bronwyn was lying in bed, when she felt a slight twinge, but thought nothing of it. She had become familiar with the movement of the child within her.

Dilys came in. "Good morning, Your Grace, are you ready to rise?"

The Duchess nodded, so her maid pulled back the covers and assisted her mistress to get out of bed. Dilys's eyes widened in a mixture of shock and fear.

"Whatever's the matter Dilys..." Bronwyn turned to follow her fixed stare and the colour drained from her face as they both stared at the blood on the bedclothes. "No... no not yet! It's too early!"

Dilys pulled herself together. "Lie down, Your Grace, I will send for the physician immediately! Try not to worry, or it may make things worse." She assisted Bronwyn back onto the bed, then ran, searching for a page or other servant.

Finding one, she ordered them to run and fetch the physician, and also the midwives.

The midwives arrived first and took charge of the situation.

The physician arrived next and almost collided with the Duke in his haste to get to Bronwyn's chambers. An icy hand clutched at Richard's heart, and he accompanied the physician as they literally ran to their destination.

The Duke knocked on the door and threw it open, striding in with the physician on his heels, to the bedchamber.

The presence of the midwives, and his wife's stricken expression made him feel as if he was being strangled and he couldn't breathe.

"Bronwyn!" He went to her bedside.

"It's too early! It's too early!" she was crying, panic stricken.

"Shush," he tried to soothe, managing to find his voice, trying to stay calm for her sake. "Let the physician do his work. It may not be as bad as it seems..."

"Your Grace, I must ask you to leave," the physician said as he approached.

He didn't want to go, he wanted to stay and provide Bronwyn with the support she so desperately needed, but he was ushered out by the midwives, and the door shut in his face.

Desperately worried, he continually paced the corridor from one end to the other, waiting, listening. Hours seemed like days. He kept pacing, and then he heard it.

"Nooooooo!" The scream could be heard down the entire length of the corridor and made Richard's blood run cold.

"Bronwyn!" he cried and ran towards her chambers. "Bronwyn!"

He didn't even bother knocking, but burst in. The heavy door swung back and crashed against the wall as he entered. He strode quickly across the room to the bed chamber, stopping at the threshold unable to take in the sight before him.

"Bronwyn!" he said a third time.

There was blood on the sheets, and his wife was clutching a bundle to her breast, sobbing uncontrollably, whilst a midwife tried to remove it from her arms. The physician was washing his blood soaked hands in some water.

Heads turned towards him and for a second he stood, frozen, unable to move.

"Your Grace, you should not be in here," another midwife said, walking towards him and then stopped as she saw the look on his face.

He turned his gaze upon his wife. Her tear-stained face said more than any words could.

"Ric – Richard," she sobbed. "I – I'm sorry. O – our son..."

Something tight squeezed his heart and prevented him from breathing. He moved to her bedside, ignoring the blood on the sheets, on her nightgown, the untidy, perspiration soaked mahogany hair.

"My darling," he finally managed to say as he enfolded her and their dead baby in his arms.

"I'm sorry, so sorry," she kept mumbling into his shoulder.

"You have nothing to apologise for," he said softly, fighting to maintain an iron grip on his grief.

"The baby came too soon to survive, Your Grace," the physician said quietly. "My sincere condolences to you both." He bowed, collected his tools together, then prepared a powder in some wine. "Her Grace should drink this; it will ease her pain and help her sleep." The physician placed the goblet down on the small table by the bed, bowed again and left.

"Your Grace, please pass us the child," said the midwife who had so far unsuccessfully managed to take it from Bronwyn.

"Leave us," Richard said.

"Your Grace—"

"I said leave us!"

The midwives still didn't move.

"Get out!" he shouted, and they fled the room.

"We will return in a little while," one of them said as they shut the door behind them.

Richard kissed the top of his wife's head, and held her as her unrelenting sobbing continued. His own tears of grief ran down his cheeks onto her hair and the relief that Bronwyn was still alive almost overwhelmed him.

"Shush," he soothed. "It's all right, it's not your fault, never will I believe it's your fault." He just held her for several minutes, then moved slightly to look down at the tiny baby in Bronwyn's arms. He was under developed and would have stood no chance of surviving having been born three months or so too early. *My son,* Richard thought, choking on the words.

He wasn't sure how long they stayed trying to comfort one another, but eventually Richard straightened up, reached for the goblet and held it to Bronwyn's lips.

"Drink, my darling," he said encouragingly, and she obediently obeyed. Richard made sure she drank it all and stayed supporting her until her eyelids grew heavy and sleep claimed her. He lay her gently back against the pillows, then took the baby from her arms, got up and walked to the door.

The midwives were waiting just on the other side and curtseyed as Richard opened the door to them. One of the women carefully held out her arms and the Duke handed the baby over.

"Your Grace, be assured, we will prepare the child for burial. He will be treated with reverence."

Richard nodded. "You... you will need assistance with the Duchess. I will help you," he said.

"This is woman's work, Your Grace."

"Her Grace is currently asleep, having taken the physician's potion. I cannot have her wake up surrounded by blood."

He turned and went back into the bed chamber. The remaining midwives followed him and stripped the bed after he had lifted Bronwyn into his arms. Warm water arrived, the Duchess was bathed, dressed in a clean nightgown, then Richard placed her back on the now clean bed and pulled the bedclothes up over her. Finally, he kissed her and left her in the hands of the midwives, whilst he went to the chapel to pray for the dead child and Bronwyn's recovery.

Having spent a considerable amount of time in the chapel trying to get his emotions under control, he knew he should see Colwyn. She would be too young to understand what had happened, so he would simply say that her mother was ill and would be abed for a few days.

"Papa!" Colwyn greeted him happily and hugged him tightly as he lifted her into his arms.

Richard was feeling the grief again, and Colwyn immediately picked up on it. She drew back and looked at him.

"What's wrong Papa? Why are you sad?"

The Duke was surprised at her intuition at her tender years.

"Your mother is poorly, so you may not see her for a few days, but it's nothing to worry about," he told her.

"She will get better?"

"Yes, she will."

"Is the baby all right?"

Richard closed his eyes momentarily. How on earth did he explain this to the child?

Sarah, who was across the room, saw the pain and sorrow in the Duke's eyes and decided to help him. She had heard what had happened.

"Colwyn... God had need of a special helper. It was a great honour bestowed on the baby, and your little brother is now at God's right hand," she said approaching.

"I had a baby brother?"

"You did, and now he is with God."

"Is that good?"

"Yes, it is good."

Colwyn nodded and hugged her father again. "Don't be sad Papa, my brother is with God."

"Y - yes, he is." He turned his gaze to Sarah. "Thank you," he said simply, and she nodded, then held out her arms.

"Come Colwyn, time for your afternoon nap."

Richard kissed his daughter and handed her to Sarah. He desperately needed some time alone and went to his chambers.

Trystan was there and poured the Duke a goblet of wine.

"Your Grace, may I offer my—"

Richard cut him off mid-sentence, took the goblet and downed its contents in a few gulps, then held it out for a refill. Trystan obliged and went to leave the Duke to his grief.

"Leave the wine," Richard said.

"Your Grace, do you think—"

"Leave the wine, and leave me," he said calling on the last reserves of composure.

Trystan bowed and left, closing the door behind him.

The Duke succumbed to his wilder days that afternoon and evening and drank himself into a stupor, drowning his sorrows. He knew it was weak of him, but he felt he had to let go, to preserve his sanity. He had to be strong for Bronwyn, but first he had to deal with his own feelings, and this was the best way he knew.

Trystan returned at sunset and receiving no response to his knocking, dared to open the door and peered in. Richard was sitting on a chair, slumped over the table. The steward shook his head and approached. The Duke had not gotten into this state since he had been married. He reached out a hand and shook his master. There was no response. Trystan went through to the bedchamber and turned down the bedclothes, then went back into the main chamber, took a deep breath and hoisted the Duke over his shoulder. He carried him through to the bed and lowered him down onto it, pulled off his boots, and with difficulty divested him of his clothes, then covered him, leaving him to sleep it off.

It was a sad day, but he would be in the next room, all night if need be, ready to offer any support that was required. He had done it before, when Richard's parents had died and expected this would not be the last.

There was an air of gloom and profound sadness over the castle the next morning as the news spread that the Duchess had lost the son she was carrying. Everyone spoke in quiet whispers, no one laughed, and some of the staff had even shed tears, for the Duke and Duchess were held in much reverence.

Having spent the entire night on a small couch in the day room, Trystan knocked on the door to the Duke's bedchamber. There was no response. The steward actually hadn't expected any. He knocked on the door again. Still no answer, so he opened it and peered in.

The Duke was laying just as Trystan had left him last night, dead to the world. The steward sighed in sadness; it was obvious that the loss had hit his master very hard. Trystan decided to leave him to sleep it off. He would no doubt have a severe headache when he woke up.

The steward tidied up the day chamber, disposed of the wine container, and opened the windows to let in some fresh air. They wouldn't stay open long, just enough to get rid of the stale air and the smell of wine that had oxidised. Then he arranged for some raw eel and bitter almonds to be delivered in readiness to address the Duke's hangover that he was sure to have when he finally awoke.

It was a couple of hours after that when Richard regained consciousness. The first thing he was aware of was the persistent hammering going on in his head. The steady thump that matched the beat of his heart. He groaned, and Trystan prepared a cold damp cloth and was by his bedside in just a couple of seconds.

Knowing how the Duke would be feeling, he kept his voice to a whisper. "Your Grace, steady now, do not move." He placed the cloth on the Duke's forehead.

Richard groaned and a hand went to his head. "Try – Trystan," he mumbled, totally disorientated. His mind was befuddled, he was having problems trying to remember what had occurred. "What – what happened?"

"I'm afraid you over indulged in your wine drinking, Your Grace. I found you slumped unconscious and put you to bed."

Grief and pain hit the Duke full force. It hadn't been a nightmare after all, it had all happened, and he felt his control beginning to slip again.

The Duke had been a young boy when Trystan had first started serving as his steward. He knew Richard's moods inside and out and he also knew when he could take liberties with his position. Now was one of those times.

He laid a hand on the Duke's shoulder. "Richard, it's all right to grieve," he whispered. "I am here to support you at this sad time." He watched as the Duke fought to maintain control of his emotions. "Let go," Trystan soothed. "Let it all go."

Richard was royalty, a Duke. Royalty did not show their emotions, they were bred to be aloof of such things and yet, they were still human, they still felt, they still hurt, they suffered grief and loss like everyone else. Trystan understood that bottling up grief and other destructive emotions was not a good thing. It destroyed.

"I – I need to – to go comfort Bronwyn..." the Duke gasped.

"Not in this state," Trystan stated firmly. "First, you must see to yourself. If you do not do that, you will not be able to comfort the Duchess. Now... there is just the two of us here. Let go."

"It – it is unbefitting—"

"Poppycock!" Trystan exclaimed. "Let go."

Richard fought it, but the more he tried to fight it, the worse it became. "My...son..."

Trystan opened his arms. Richard tried to resist but felt his determination and resolve slipping and gratefully accepted the support.

"That's it," Trystan soothed as he felt the Duke shaking in his arms. "What happens in this room, stays in this room. Release your grief, it will not diminish the sorrow you feel, but will make it bearable, and enable you to help the Duchess in hers."

Neither man were sure how long they had hugged each other, but the Duke straightened up and took a deep shuddering breath and winced as his head started throbbing again.

"How are you feeling?" Trystan asked.

Richard swallowed. "Sick!" came the response.

Trystan grabbed the pot that was under the bed and handed it to him and the Duke obliged by retching a few times.

The steward then got up and left him to carry on retching whilst he sorted out a bath for his lord. He couldn't allow the Duke to visit his wife smelling of wine and other unsavoury odours.

That sorted, he returned to the Duke's side, removed the bowl and cleaned it.

Richard eventually pulled himself together, threw back the bedclothes and got out of bed. His legs crumpled under him, and he collapsed to the floor. Trystan returned, helped him up, into his dressing gown and to the garderobe.

The bath water arrived whilst he was in there, and once it was ready, the steward assisted his lord into the warm water and proceeded to wash him. He also shaved him and finally the Duke started to feel a little more human.

Once again in his dressing gown, Trystan sat him down at the table and placed the raw eel and bitter almonds in front of him. Richard's stomach churned at the sight and smell, and he pushed it away.

"I'd sooner have the hangover," he mumbled, as Trystan prepared his clothes for the day.

Half an hour later the Duke was dressed. He looked at Trystan in some embarrassment.

"Thank you, Trystan," Richard said simply.

Trystan simply nodded. "For what?" he asked. "The matter is forgotten already. Go support the Duchess, Your Grace," he said quietly.

The Duke nodded his thanks and left.

Bronwyn was still sleeping when Richard arrived by her side.

"Dilys?" he questioned the maid.

"Her Grace has slept the entire night through. Whatever the physician gave her, must have been strong."

The Duke sat by his wife's bedside, took hold of one of her hands and waited patiently for her to awaken.

A further hour went by, and then as Bronwyn began to stir, Richard leant forward as she opened her eyes and kissed her gently.

"Bronwyn, my love." His eyes were full of love and compassion.

She stared at him, suddenly felt her abdomen and burst into tears.

He took her in his arms and rocked her gently. "Shush, it's all right," he said softly.

The Duchess clung to him like her life depended on it. "I'm sorry, I'm so sorry," she mumbled into his shoulder, just as she had the previous day. Her heart was heavy and felt like it was breaking.

"You have nothing to apologise for. It...it was God's will. It was nothing you have done. You must believe that."

"But our son..."

"Shush. It's done. He knew he was loved and that is the most important thing. Now you must rest and get well."

She leant back in his arms. "I'm being selfish," she said. "And how is my husband? Are you all right?"

He smiled sadly at her. "I am...back in control," he finally admitted. "Trystan looked after me. I will say no more at this time."

She touched his face with her hand. "You need to grieve too," she whispered and kissed him.

"We have at least learnt something, and can take comfort from it, Bronwyn. You can conceive. Colwyn was not a once in a life miracle. Our time will come, I have every confidence."

"I will try to believe that."

ᘓ ᘔ ᘓ ᘔ

A few days later, Bronwyn was well enough to leave her bed, and decided she wanted to bury their son sooner rather than later, to help the grieving process, so it was that Richard, herself and Colwyn, along with the bishop said a fond farewell to their son, who they had christened Eurion, and he was laid to rest in the crypt in the cathedral.

Life took a number of weeks to return to normal, the Duke and Duchess put on a brave face for the twelve days of Christmas, for Colwyn's sake, and the pain gradually eased.

ᘓ ᘔ ᘓ ᘔ

Chapter Eighteen

With a week to go to the forthcoming wedding, Alexandra, her father, mother, sister, maids, stewards and escort arrived. The baby boy that Iola had given birth to, had been left behind in Isatiri with its wet nurse, as it was deemed too young to make the journey.

The wedding had taken a great deal of organising and planning. Invitations, food, quarters, the actual ceremony, clothes, roles, decorating the cathedral, the list seemed endless. Stuart's biggest headache had been securing a role for Morgan in the proceedings. Alexandra had initially been friendly to the young page, until she had found out about his heritage. The King did his best to shield his young protector from her tirade about it, but he had eventually heard, and it had upset him, to realise that until she knew of his ancestry, she had been warm and kind. Now she ostracised him.

But Stuart did not give up without a fight and created a new role for the boy; ring bearer, a very important duty. Morgan had been measured for new clothes for the occasion and was looking forward to the day, very much.

Richard, Bronwyn and Colwyn had arrived earlier than everyone else, as the Duke was assisting with the proceedings. They had been introduced to Stuart's intended and Bronwyn was asked to accompany his bride, escort her around the castle and act as companion.

Alexandra had fallen instantly in love with four year old Colwyn and insisted she be given a special part for the day, which meant the seamstresses had had to create a gown for her. Colwyn was going to scatter rose petals on the aisle and would head the procession as it approached the altar and the King.

What alarmed Alexandra though, was the fact that Morgan seemed to spend a lot of time in Colwyn's company, something she was against, but Stuart ordered her not to interfere, and explained that they saw one another as brother and sister as they had been raised together.

Bronwyn had been rather emotional when she had seen Morgan, which had alarmed him, and he had immediately asked what was wrong. She had hugged him, and then confessed to what had happened to her late last year, that she had lost the son she was carrying.

He had cried, because she had also cried as she told him and he hugged her tightly, offering his support.

"You will have a son, Mama, I'm sure of it," he had told her, and she drew comfort from the conviction with which he said those words.

Then she had kissed his cheek. "Bless you, my dearest Morgan, what would I do without you?" She held him at arm's length and looked at him. "I swear you gain more height each time I see you! Look at you! I'm so proud of you and I'm even more proud to call you my son, for that's what you are to me."

They had both cried again at that and hugged once more. Then Bronwyn pulled herself together.

"I understand you have a most important duty to perform at the wedding. The ring bearer. The ceremony cannot be completed without your part in it."

"Really?"

"Really. The exchange of rings is one of the most significant parts of the ceremony."

"Now you're making me feel nervous."

Bronwyn gave a little laugh. "Oh Morgan darling, you will excel, and you will make us so proud."

He gave her one of his rare smiles. "Thank you. I have some free time this afternoon, is it all right if I take Colwyn out for a ride? We won't go far, I promise."

"Of course it is, you know you do not need to ask."

"Thank you...mother," he dared to say, and Bronwyn almost started to cry again. Him calling her that, meant more than she could ever express in words.

That afternoon, he went to collect Colwyn from her maid.

"Morgan!" Colwyn squealed as he entered her chambers. She ran across the room and threw herself into his arms as he knelt before her and kissed him on the cheek.

"Colwyn. Every time I see you, you've grown a bit more!"

"So do you!" she replied giggling. "Have you come to play with me?"

"No, I thought we'd do something more exciting. Do you fancy going on an adventure?"

Her eyes lit up. "What sort of adventure?"

"Aha, that's a surprise. Come on." He stood up and took hold of her hand, then spoke to Sarah. "We'll be gone for a few hours, but I will have my sister back before her supper time."

Sarah wanted to protest, but just said, "Very well, My Lord."

Morgan and Colwyn made their way to the stables. He had saddled Flint before going to get his sister, so they could get going straight away. He lifted her up into the saddle, then mounted behind her and just as they were about to make their way out of the castle, Rodric, Mereli and Colin McLeod arrived from the High Meres.

Morgan followed them back to the keep. "Colin!" he shouted. "Uncle Rodric, Aunt Mereli!"

"Morgan!" Colin shouted and turned his pony to be level with them. They gave each other a hug.

"Colwyn, this is my cousin, Colin. Colin, this is my sister, Colwyn."

"Sister? Oh, yes, Lady Colwyn Coltrane. Hello, nice to meet you."

"And you, Colin."

"Where are you going?"

"We're going on an adventure. Do you want to come, or are you tired from your travel?"

"Mama, papa, may I go? I'm not tired."

"Morgan, darling, how lovely to see you again. Colwyn, you are your mother's daughter. Yes you may go."

"We'll be back before supper," Morgan promised. "Come on, Colin," and they may their way out of the castle.

"Where are we going, Morgan?" Colwyn asked him as they made their way along the main street, and then along a path that led to the mere.

"On an adventure," he said simply, urging his horse into a gentle canter, making Colwyn squeal in delight.

"What sort of adventure?" Colin asked.

"Oh, you'll see."

"We're going so fast! Romaine is slow and bumpy," Colwyn said to Morgan.

"Oh, are you on Romaine at home?" Morgan asked. "I started out on him too. Don't worry, when you've outgrown him, you'll get a new pony, just like I did." He idly reached forward and patted Flint's neck.

They travelled a little further and came to an area where the shores of the mere were very shallow, and a couple of trees were growing.

"Here we are," Morgan said, drawing Flint to a halt. "Isn't it beautiful here?"

"It's lovely," Colin agreed, "but it's hot!"

The sun was shining, the sky was blue and the water of the mere also reflected the blue of the sky. It was a very hot day for September, so Morgan headed for the shade of one of the trees to keep his pony out of the sun.

"I thought we could explore, and I've brought a little picnic we can enjoy, after we've searched for the treasure."

"Treasure?" Colin and Colwyn asked together.

Morgan dismounted, then lifted Colwyn down before tying Flint to a convenient branch. Colin also dismounted and fastened his pony in the shade.

"It is hot, like you said, Colin," Colwyn added as she looked around.

"It is, isn't it. We'll try and stay in the shade as much as possible," Colin replied.

"Tell me, Colwyn, how adventurous are you?" Morgan asked of his sister.

"I don't know. Never been on an adventure."

"Have you ever climbed a tree?"

"No."

"Do you fancy having a go?" He pointed at a particularly obliging tree that had some low branches that allowed easy access. "We're going to climb that tree. The treasure is at the top."

"Oooh, yes please!"

Morgan clambered onto a low branch, then reached down, grabbed Colwyn's hand and pulled her up beside him then Colin joined them.

"Now, it's important we take our time and don't rush. You have to imagine this tree is a huge mountain that we have to climb."

"I can do that."

"Good girl. Come on. Colin, would you mind bringing up the rear, just in case Colwyn slips?"

"Of course. Up you go, Colwyn."

Slowly and carefully they climbed the tree. It was more that Morgan climbed, then pulled Colwyn up or Colin gave her a push up, but she still had a go where she could, making her own progress. Eventually they had scaled their mountain and reached the treasure—the most beautiful view of the countryside.

They stayed for a while, admiring the view, until the sun just became too warm, and they reluctantly made their way down. They were all hot and perspiring by the time they reached the ground.

"Morgan, it's so hot! May I paddle in the water?" Colwyn asked.

"Yes, but we'll come with you. I don't know how deep it is. Let's remove our boots first."

They sat down and removed their footwear. Morgan than stripped off his shirt as well and Colin did the same.

"Have you a shift on under your dress?"

"Yes."

"Then let me help you out of that dress. We don't want to get it wet, and your shift will dry quickly in this heat."

Divested of outer clothes, they all held hands and went and paddled in the mere. The water was cool but not unpleasant.

"Can you swim?" Morgan asked her.

"No."

"Right, Colwyn, do you trust us?"

"Of course I do."

"We won't let anything happen to you. When we get out far enough, and when I tell you, I want you to do this with your arms." He demonstrated in the shallow water. "And kick out with your legs. Come." He led her deeper into the water and he and Colin supported her when it became too deep.

"We've got you," Colin said as the two boys lifted her, so she was horizontal in the water. "Now move your arms and legs as Morgan instructed."

She was clumsy as she tried to get her arms and legs to coordinate their movements. Morgan supported her under her hips and Colin just below her shoulders.

"That's it, you're beginning to get it. Carry on," Morgan encouraged.

They carefully shuffled sideward as she at last began to move.

"You're doing really well," Morgan encouraged, and indicated to his cousin to slowly reduce the support they was providing her with, until she was totally unsupported and swimming on her own.

Colwyn was huffing and puffing by now. "May ... I...have a rest?" she asked.

"Yes you may, but have you noticed sister, we're not holding you anymore."

Colwyn panicked at that point, and Morgan came to her rescue, and she clutched his shoulders.

"You were swimming completely on your own," he told her. "Now, if you get tired you can rest on your back." He lay her on her back on the water, with Colin opposite. "Relax, that's it. You can even move your arms and legs and move this way if you like. Try it."

She managed it, and again, the two boys gradually reduced the support, until she was moving on her own and they swam beside her.

After another minor panic attack, Colwyn tried again, and within a short time, they were swimming together in the shallows.

Eventually though, they decided she had had enough for now, and they returned to the shore to eat their picnic. The sun beat down on them, and the gentle breeze quickly dried their clothes.

"That was fun!" Colwyn said. "Can we do it again sometime?"

"Providing the weather is good and warm. Perhaps we'll get a chance to do it again after the wedding." Morgan looked up at the sun. Come on, I think we'd better get you back before someone sends out a search party."

The boys put their shirts back on and made themselves presentable, then went and fetched their ponies and allowed them to drink. That done, they put their boots back on, packed up their picnic, helped Colwyn with her dress and boots, then placed her back on the saddle. Morgan once again sat behind her, and they made their return journey.

Colin hugged his cousin, then went in search of his parents, saying that he hoped to see them later.

Morgan escorted Colwyn back to her chambers and delivered her safely to Sarah.

Colwyn hugged him tightly as he knelt. "Thank you for today, it was fun!" She kissed his cheek, and he kissed her back before leaving.

Sarah looked at her charge. "So what did you get up to?" she asked.

"We went on an adventure and climbed a huge mountain to find some treasure."

"What!"

"Well, it was a tree, but we pretended it was a mountain."

"Colwyn, ladies do not climb trees!"

"It was fun! I liked it, then when we got back down, we were hot, so Morgan taught me how to swim."

"Colwyn!"

"That was fun too. I can swim all on my own now... What's wrong? You've gone a funny colour."

Sarah thought she was going to faint from the shock. Climbing... swimming.... Ladies did not do that kind of thing. What would her mother think!

At supper that evening, it was a small family affair, with the Coltrane family having a quiet meal together because the McLeod's had decided it had been a long day's travelling and they would all go to bed early.

"So what did the two of you do today?" Bronwyn asked Morgan as they ate.

"There were three of us actually, Colin came with us. We went for a ride," the boy started.

"And we had an adventure. We climbed a huge mountain in search of treasure," Colwyn said.

"Really?" Richard asked in some amusement, knowing full well they had done no such thing.

"Well, we pretended a tree was the mountain and climbed that. The treasure was the fantastic view from the top."

"I see," Richard said.

"Then Morgan and Colin taught me to swim," Colwyn said proudly.

"What!"

"Have...have we done wrong?" Morgan asked, suddenly fearful that he had done something very improper. "I wouldn't have done it if..."

"It's not something that ladies do," Richard said.

"I thought it would be a good idea. You live by the sea, surely everyone should be able to swim."

Richard understood his logic. Colwyn was a child, she was curious, rebellious, she was his treasure, he needed to keep her safe but on the other hand, he wasn't always at home, or ever present. Perhaps it wasn't such a bad idea, whilst she was young, to have a little excitement and adventure in her life. After all, he himself had had some hare-brained adventures for several years until he had married Bronwyn.

"I think that was very kind of you to do that, Morgan," he finally said. "I don't think it's such a bad idea. As you say, we live by the sea, accidents happen. Colwyn being able to swim might be a life saver."

"Really?" The relief in Morgan's voice was evident. "I thought I had displeased you for a moment."

"Never displeased, darling," Bronwyn said. "Just surprised."

"I want to do it again," Colwyn said. "It was fun."

"We shall see," was all Richard said, as they enjoyed the rest of their meal.

☙ ❧ ☙ ❧

The following day was the final rehearsal for the wedding. Final tiny issues were sorted out, and they did another run through to ensure everything went perfectly. Bishop Douglas was pleased with the result.

That evening, Stuart celebrated his final night of being a single man. Richard accompanied him along with the other dukes, on a night of celebration, but ensured the King did not drink too much, and escorted him back to the safety of his chambers. The King invited him in, and over a goblet of wine, managed to get Richard to tell him of some tales about his father's and the Duke's wilder adventures.

Although not intoxicated, the amount of wine that had been consumed, had loosened Richard's tongue and he had divulged some amusing stories that had Stuart almost laughing in hysterics, and then shocked him when he had finally admitted an extremely wild night in a high class brothel, and what had gone on. Stuart knew he would never look at Richard in the same light ever again.

"Wait! When was this?" Stuart asked him.

"Oh...a few days before King Rhisart—although he was the prince at the time—was married to your mother. It was...his last night of being a single man."

"And you?"

"I was fourteen. Your father had um...arranged for my...education on my fourteenth birthday, and then later on, just before his wedding, the two of us had gone into the city and...I think he didn't want me to be totally ignorant of what he um...had planned for that last night of freedom." Richard saw the look on Stuart's face. "Know that the King was a faithful and true husband and father," he added. "His wild days stopped the day he married your mother."

"And yours?"

"The day I married Bronwyn." He sighed. "Come my liege, time to get some sleep, you have a very long day tomorrow. By your leave." Richard stood, bowed and left, leaving the King staring after him, wondering what other secrets his most trusted supporter kept close to his chest.

ᥐ ᥑ ᥐ ᥑ

The following morning, after breakfast had been eaten, everyone started to prepare for the wedding, getting dressed in their finest clothes. Sarah took a great deal of time getting Colwyn ready. Her dress was white, with gold trim, and her headdress was made of white flowers and green foliage which were in stark contrast to her chestnut hair. She also had a basket, packed with rose petals that she carried on her left arm, so she could scatter them with her right hand.

Stuart, his brother and Morgan had left for the cathedral already. They were also dressed in white, trimmed with gold braid. Morgan was carrying a small cushion tucked in the front of his jacket that would eventually hold the rings. They had come on horseback; their chargers and Morgan's pony, had been washed and groomed, hooves oiled, leather cleaned and polished. They were escorted by a small contingent of the elite guard, in their dress uniforms as they always were for special occasions, who were also escorting the Queen's crown and all the dukes that had accepted the wedding invitation. The accompanying wives and children had already been conveyed in carriages and were in their seats.

Carriages were standing at the keep. The first one held Bronwyn, Colwyn, Iola and Alexandra's sister, Kenzie. The second one held Alexandra and her father Alwyn. The rest of the elite guard were at the front and back, and Richard was riding at the very front, resplendent in red and black trimmed with gold, his ceremonial sword hanging at his left side.

Precisely a quarter of the hour before midday, the procession moved off. Crowds lined the streets waving and clapping, trying to get a glimpse of the bride, but she was veiled, and they couldn't see her face.

Outside the cathedral, pages opened the carriage doors and assisted the women to descend the two steps to the ground. They got into order for the procession down to the altar; Colwyn, the bride and her father, mother and sister, with Bronwyn and Richard, who had the Queen's crown on a cushion, bringing up the rear. Bishop Douglas would lead everyone down the aisle, and he would take his place at the altar. He was waiting at the double doors of the cathedral for them.

Iola and Kenzie straightened out the long train, made sure everything was in order, then signalled they were ready. Colwyn very solemnly, slowly ascended the steps until she reached the bishop, then she curtseyed. James smiled at her.

He waited until they had all reached the top, inclined his head and turned, slowly walking through the doors and leading the way down the aisle. Colwyn let him take five steps, then started to follow, delicately throwing petals before her. The pews either side were festooned with white roses and other flowers, with greenery providing some colour.

The sun was bravely trying to peek through the clouds to cast light through the stain glass windows and was beginning to win the battle as they walked down the aisle.

At the altar, Stuart, Michael and Morgan turned and watched them approach. Morgan gave a little smile as he saw Colwyn gracefully spreading her petals before them as they walked.

As she reached her final position, she moved to the right, to sit on the side of the King. Alwyn led his daughter to stand directly in front of the altar steps, her mother and sister moved to sit on the left, Bronwyn and Richard to the right, next to Colwyn. Stuart stepped forward to be level with his bride and carefully flicked her veil over the back of her head. Her blue eyes stared at him, and she gave a somewhat nervous smile.

James welcomed everyone to the joyous occasion of the marriage of the King, and asked those present if there was any reason why the two should not be married. Silence followed. The bishop then addressed Stuart and Alexandra. "Do either of you know any reason why this marriage should not take place?"

"There is none," they both answered.

"We are gathered here to witness the sarum marriage liturgy." Prayers were said then James looked at Alexandra's father. "Who giveth this woman into marriage?"

"I do. Alwyn Frederick, William Ulrich of Isatiri," her father responded. He then stepped away to join his wife and other daughter.

"Sire, your vows."

Stuart cleared his throat. "I, Stuart Rhisart Aiden Eurion Cantrell, take thee Alexandra, Kathleen, Iona Ulrich, to be my wedded wife, 'til death us do part, and thereto I plight thee my troth."

"I, Alexandra, Kathleen, Iona Ulrich, take thee, Stuart Rhisart Aiden Eurion Cantrell to be my wedded husband, 'til death us do part, and thereto I plight thee my troth."

James nodded at Morgan, who stepped forward, proudly carrying the two rings on the cushion. He bowed to the bishop and presented them to him. James blessed the rings, then Stuart picked up the smaller one and placed it on the third finger of Alexandra's right hand. She then picked up the other ring and placed that on Stuart's third finger of his right hand.

James then bound their right hands together and gave the final blessing. That completed, he then kissed Stuart, who in turn kissed Alexandra. The binding was removed, and the couple turned to face the waiting congregation.

"You may kiss your bride," the bishop whispered to Stuart, who rather tentatively kissed his new wife.

Everyone in the cathedral gave three cheers, then Stuart escorted his wife to the other side of the altar, where the queen's chair had been placed, and gestured for her to sit, facing the congregation.

Bronwyn took the ring cushion from Morgan and Richard handed him the larger one with the queen's crown on it and nodded.

Morgan walked solemnly towards the chair and stood to attention holding the cushion at chest height.

James moved to stand directly in front of Alexandra and spoke once more. "Alexandra Kathleen, Iona Ulrich Cantrell, do you solemnly swear to support the King, defend the weak, uphold justice, defeat all evil and maintain the laws of God and the true profession of the Gospel?"

"I do."

The bishop then anointed her head with oil and spoke. "We beseech thee O Lord to invest in thy servant Alexandra Kathleen,

Iona Ulrich Cantrell, that she will be true to her King, support him in all ways to uphold righteousness and justice within the kingdom of Devonmere, defend the weak, defeat all evil on behalf of Our Lord."

He paused as he turned to Morgan and lifted the crown and held it above Alexandra's head.

As he lowered the crown, he said, "By the power of God and the Holy Church, I crown thee Queen Consort of Devonmere."

All the peers present, placed their own crowns and coronets on their heads and shouted, "God save the Queen!"

The peeling of the cathedral bells sounded immediately, celebrating both the wedding of the King and the crowning of a new Queen.

Stuart and Alexandra walked back down the aisle, with the sun now streaming through the stained glass, towards the double doors and stood at the top of the steps. Everyone bowed or curtseyed, and the gathered crowd got their first glimpse of the fair-haired blue-eyed Queen and started to cheer.

Stuart escorted his queen down the steps to the waiting carriage, where he assisted her inside, her sister and mother arranged the train, then Stuart joined her. Iola and Kenzie, along with Colwyn, Bronwyn and Alwyn got into the second coach. Richard, Morgan, Prince Michael and the remaining Elite Guard mounted up, and they all made their way back to the castle.

The banqueting hall had been decorated with colourful garlands of flowers and bright tapestries. On the tables were token gifts for all the guests, and of course, gifts for the bride and groom.

The top table had been made longer to accommodate the extra members of the household, namely Alexandra's parents and sister. As Stuart had no parents, he had asked Richard and Bronwyn to stand in, which meant Morgan and Colwyn being there as well as Prince Michael.

When everyone was seated, and goblets filled, Michael stood up and gave a speech, welcoming everyone to the happy occasion, to join in the celebration of the union of the Cantrell and Ulrich houses; wishing Stuart and Alexandra a long and happy life together, and for many children. Then raised his goblet in a toast.

"To the King and Queen," he said.

Everyone raised their goblets and repeated the words, "To the King and Queen!" and drank.

Michael sat down and Stuart stood up. He thanked his brother for his kind words, gave thanks to Alexandra's parents for allowing him to marry their daughter, for his guests, and gave a toast to continued peace within the kingdom, and then invited everyone to eat, drink and be merry.

The food included, chicken, goose, venison, wild boar, vegetables of various kinds. Desserts consisted of a variety of sweet puddings. To drink there was plenty of wine, and mead, and everyone started to become very jolly. Musicians were present, so dancing followed. The King led this, dancing with his Queen. Richard danced with Iola. Alwyn danced with Bronwyn. Michael invited Kenzie—Alexandra's sister—onto the floor and Morgan looked after Colwyn.

Vast quantities of wine were drunk, Richard did his best to moderate Stuart's intake, so that he would enjoy his wedding night, and at the appropriate time, he escorted Alexandra and the King out of the banquet hall, accompanied by the bishop, Iola and Bronwyn.

The King and Queen went to their own chambers to be prepared for the wedding night. This included a bath, and mental preparation for what lay ahead.

When this had all been completed, Richard and the bishop escorted Stuart to Alexandra's chambers. She was standing by a small table, wringing her hands nervously as they knocked and entered, and was wearing a nightgown under a rather heavy dressing gown.

Stuart went to her and held her hands in his, as James blessed them both, and their bed. Then he and Richard bowed and left them alone.

The King released her hands and poured two generous goblets of a heavier, sweeter wine that he hoped would relax his bride. Her hand shook as he handed her the drink.

"Are you nervous?" he asked gently, and she nodded, unable to speak. "If it helps, I am too."

Her features showed surprise. "You, nervous?" she finally managed to say.

"This has got to go right. We don't really know one another. I want to make you happy, Alexandra. We have our whole lives ahead of us. I know you may not necessarily love me, but I hope that will change, for I do love you."

In response, she took a huge gulp of wine and felt it warm her inside as it spread outwards through her body, slowly relaxing her.

Stuart smiled kindly at her as he took a sip of his own wine. He didn't want to drink too much but needed to make sure Alexandra relaxed more. He let her take another gulp, before removing the goblet from her hand and putting both down on the table.

He looked into her face and saw her blue eyes, wide with apprehension.

"You have nothing to fear," he whispered quietly as he cupped her face and gently kissed her full lips. She closed her eyes and trembled. Stuart wasn't sure if it was in fear, or anticipation, so he continued to kiss her and nuzzle her neck, until she gave a little moan, then he pulled back, swept her up into his arms and moved to the bed.

The covers had already been drawn back in preparation, but Stuart deposited her on her feet, pulled at the belt on the dressing gown and swept it off her shoulders to fall to the floor, then eyed the nightgown. Slowly and carefully he loosened the laces on it as Alexandra stood frozen and then blushed furiously as it dropped to the floor at her feet, and closed her eyes in embarrassment.

Stuart stood back and looked at her slender form, held tense. He could tell she was dying to try and cover her body with her arms and hands, but instead stood rigidly to attention. He loosened the belt on his own dressing gown and shrugged out of it.

"Look at me," he commanded. He watched as she swallowed nervously and opened her eyes which grew wide at the sight of his naked body standing before her. If it was possible, she grew even more embarrassed, and her flush deepened. Stuart was broad shouldered, fit and well-muscled, as a result of his training.

He stepped forward, grasped her shoulders and pulled her towards him, kissing her as he did so, and a jolt of electricity seemed to spark between them as their bodies touched.

As they parted, Stuart picked her up and laid her on the bed, straightened up and looked down at her as she lay stiff as a board, awaiting her fate. Then he lay down beside her.

"Relax," he told her. "You'll enjoy it much more if you relax, and I will do my best not to hurt you."

She did not move, but her eyes strayed sideward to look at his face. "I – I've heard the ladies at – at court. They say it hurts."

"What did your mother tell you?" he asked.

"That I must lie here and let you do as you please."

Stuart sighed. That wasn't what he wanted at all. He wanted her willing participation.

"Alexandra, the joining of two bodies can be a wondrous and joyous thing, but it requires participation from both sides to enable us to get the most out of it."

"I – I don't understand," she whispered, frowning at him.

"We will kiss, but we must also touch one another, to awaken our desires. Let me show you the wonders that await you, if you are willing?"

She swallowed again. There was a long pause, and then she nodded.

"W-what do you want me to do?" she asked in a strangled whisper. Having never touched a man's body in her life, she was completely lost and out of her depth.

"Do what I do. I'll go first, to show you what to do."

Stuart began his seduction in earnest, kissing and caressing his way down Alexandra's body. Initially she lay unyielding, staring up at the canopy over the bed. His hands were touching and massaging her breasts, then his mouth was there, licking and sucking at her nipples, as one of his hands moved down over her stomach. He had vowed to only take possession of her body once she started moaning and moving against his touch, but he knew it had to be at some point tonight, his guests were waiting for him down in the banqueting hall.

"Caress me," he ordered her, "gently, take your time." He nuzzled into her neck again as she tentatively ran a hand over his chest, teasing the slight dusting of hair, and gasped as she felt his nipples respond to her touch. "You're doing fine," he encouraged as his hand reached her thigh, teasing her skin, almost tickling her, encouraging her to open her legs, his fingers moving in tantalising circles.

Then she squealed as he touched her where no man had ever touched her before, and tensed up again, but part of her brain was registering the strange feeling that was beginning to centre itself in her womanhood. Part of her wanted him to stop, and the other part to continue, so she could discover where the new, alien sensations would lead.

Stuart continued with his seduction, and finally was rewarded with a twitch of her hips and a tiny moan. Encouraged, he continued, kissing his way down her body, as his fingers teased her womanhood, drawing out the response, and she involuntarily opened her thighs more for him, granting him greater access and he took it.

Her increased cries started to affect him, and he felt himself responding to the sounds she was making as she started to move more insistently against him.

Alexandra was vaguely aware of something nudging against her thigh. She knew she should panic, but a pleasant wave of pleasure was beginning to sweep over her, and she wanted more. Soon she was moving urgently against him, and Stuart took one of her hands and placed it on his manhood, moving his hips against it.

As he thought she might, her eyes flew open and she tried to remove her hand, but he held it there. He was aware of his heartbeat increasing and the heat beginning to centre itself in his groin as he became aroused, whilst his other hand continued to work on her, then suddenly, she was moaning loudly and moving desperately, looking for something, but not knowing what.

Stuart moved and knelt between her thighs, released her hand, so he could guide himself into her. As he thrust gently, she cried out and tensed up again. He spoke to her softly, caressed her, encouraged her to relax, as he slowly began to move within her, and her discomfort gradually gave way to heat, of wanting more, and she was soon writhing beneath him, her moans louder, encouraging him, and he obliged, until it drove them both to that exquisite moment of fulfilment, and for a number of seconds, after she had screamed, she fainted as all the blood left her head and rushed down to the centre of her womanhood. Stuart grunted in satisfaction. It had taken all of his self-control not to rush, as he had not been with a woman since being crowned King of Devonmere.

Taking his weight on his elbows, he kissed his Queen over and over again, telling her she had done well. In response, Alexandra had started to cry.

"I – I never knew...none of the ladies mentioned..." she began in awe, wanting to experience those wonderful feelings again.

As he slipped from her body, he rose from the bed, grabbed his dressing gown from the floor and put it on. He had one more duty to perform this night before his night of pleasure could continue.

"Come, my love," he said gently, retrieving her dressing gown from the floor and holding it ready for her. "You need to bathe, whilst I carry out one final duty."

Her legs were wobbly as she got to her feet and there was a very pleasant ache between her thighs, but as she turned so she could slip her arms into her robe, she saw the blood on the sheet and cried out.

"I'm bleeding? I'm going to die!"

He turned her around to face him and tried to calm her.

"It's all right," he soothed. "It's perfectly normal for a maiden's first time. It simply proves that you have been unknown to a man until tonight. It is proof of your virginity, which I have now claimed. Come." He fastened the belt on her gown and led her toward the other room where her maid would be waiting with another bath to clean her and prepare her for the rest of the night. "I will return soon." He kissed her with everything he possessed and felt her swoon against him before she recovered and went through into the other chamber, where her maid, Rebecca was waiting for her, to bathe her, prepare her for her husband's return, and to refresh the bedding.

Stuart returned to the bed they had just vacated, pulled the bloodstained sheet from it, then headed to the banqueting hall.

A lot of merriment could be heard as he approached the hall, indicating that many of the party goers had drunk more than enough mead and wine. A guard at the door, bowed as Stuart approached, then opened the double doors and announced very loudly, "His Majesty, the King!"

The noise gradually abated as Stuart strode down the length of the room, to the raised dais where the head table was. He climbed up onto the table and presented the soiled sheet to the guests. A huge cheer went up and goblets were raised in a toast to the King and his ex-virgin bride.

"God save the King and Queen!" was heard a few times, then Stuart left the way he had come, to more cheers and returned to his wife's chambers. The night was still relatively young.

CB BO CB BO

Chapter Nineteen

Alexandra was already back in the bed waiting for Stuart when he returned,. He stopped by the table to pick up the goblets of wine then continued to her bedside and handed her one.

She smiled at him still a little nervous, then took a sip of the sweet liquid. Stuart reached out and touched her cheek.

"How is my Queen?" he asked softly. "Tell me what you're feeling."

Alexandra took another sip of her wine and blushed. "I...I feel... different," she finally managed to say.

Stuart cocked his head on one side and frowned. "Different?"

"I can't explain it."

"Did I hurt you?"

"Only when you first...." She blushed again. "Mama never mentioned anything about... she made it sound as if it was a duty, that my part was to simply let you do what you want as I lay in bed. The ladies never said anything either... I...I wasn't expecting to feel... what I felt."

"Did you enjoy it?"

She looked into his hazel eyes briefly before looking away. "Yes," she whispered so softly he almost didn't hear it and took a rather large mouthful of wine, as if to obtain courage from it.

Alexandra placed her goblet on the bedside table then boldy leant forward and kissed him. Stuart was surprised and pleased. He smiled at her, his hazel eyes changing colour to the embers of a fire as he put his own goblet down and shrugged out of his dressing gown, before pushing her gently to lie flat on the bed. He encouraged her to explore his body, to touch and caress and they again reached that ultimate level of fulfilment and finally fell asleep in one another's arms in the early hours.

CB ⁙ CB ⁙

The castle was very quiet the following morning. The majority of guests and residents sleeping in to recover from their hangovers after over indulging at the banquet. A couple of the younger knights hadn't even made it back to their chambers, but were fast asleep on the tables, surrounded by the leftover food, wine and table decorations and didn't even stir as the servants arrived to start cleaning the room up.

Stuart had arranged for a lounging couch to be delivered to Alexandra's day room as a gift for the loss of her virginity. It was an ancient custom, still abided to by royal households. He hoped she would like it. It had been made by the finest cabinet makers in Devonmere.

Morgan, Colin and Colwyn were all wide awake at their normal time. They stumbled across one another outside the banqueting hall whilst the servants were tidying up.

"Where is everyone?" Morgan asked.

"I think they all over indulged last night," Colin said knowledgeably. "Father was staggering around when he came back to the chambers. Mother was giggling. They're sleeping it off."

"Sleeping what off?" Colwyn asked innocently.

"The wine!"

The boys giggled knowingly.

"So what are we going to do to amuse ourselves?"

324

"I don't know. Shall we go for another ride?"

"We could. Where shall we go?"

"How about the forest this time? Build a camp."

"May I come?" Colwyn asked.

"Don't see why not," Colin said, "You did well the other day."

She beamed at him.

"Come on then!"

They ran down to the stables and saddled their horses. As before, Morgan hoisted Colwyn up into the saddle, then leapt up behind her. Colin mounted his horse, and they made their way out of the castle and headed towards the wood that ran northwards bordering the continuation of the High Hills.

ର ଇ ର ଇ

People began to surface just before midday. Stuart awoke to find Alexandra snuggled up close to him, her arm across his waist, and he smiled in contentment. So, she may not love him yet, but he believed he had made progress in the way he had pleasured her. It had taken a little time, but she had gone from the frigid virgin to responsive wife. He lay just looking at her, still not quite believing he was now a married man.

He hoped he hadn't created a child within her, for he wanted to enjoy his new relationship for a while, although the bishop would be nagging him to produce an heir sooner rather than later. Even in having pleasure, he was under pressure! Pushing that thought firmly from his mind, he began to kiss and caress his sleeping queen...

...Richard gave a deep sigh, as he surfaced from sleep. There was an extremely pleasant feeling centring itself in his groin, and he gave a little moan as the feeling increased, and lips caressed his, making him smile.

His eyelids flickered open to find Bronwyn kissing and caressing him, awakening his desires. Fortunately, he hadn't drunk too much wine the previous night and was relatively clear headed enough to enjoy making leisurely love to his wife; giving a fleeting thought to Stuart and hoping his wedding night had gone well...

C3 &O CB &O

It wasn't until the mid-afternoon that Bronwyn and Mereli realised they hadn't seen their children at all. Concerned, Bronwyn went along to Colwyn's chambers to find Sarah preparing the little girl's clothes for the evening and also the following day.

"Is Colwyn here?" Bronwyn asked.

"No, Your Grace. I thought she was with you. I haven't seen her since first thing this morning."

"Have you seen Morgan?"

Sarah shook her head.

"Thank you." Bronwyn left and headed towards Mereli's rooms and met her halfway there.

"Have you seen..." they both said at the same time.

"No one's seen Colin, Morgan or Colwyn since first thing this morning. I'm getting worried," Bronwyn said.

"I'm sure nothing has happened to them," Mereli replied, "I would have sensed if anything were amiss. They are fine."

"Where could they be?"

"Maybe it would be worth checking the stables, if their ponies are missing then we will know that they have left the castle."

The two women walked down to the stables. Sure enough two ponies were missing, and a stable boy reported they had indeed ridden out that morning.

"Well at least they are all together," Mereli said, trying to offer some comfort to Bronwyn. Boys wandering off were one thing, but a little girl...it had to be worrying for her mother. "I'm sure they will be back soon."

"They should have left a message with someone!" Bronwyn said.

"Do you want me to reach out to Colin?" Mereli asked, "and confirm they are all right?"

"Oh Mereli, would you, please?"

She smiled reassuringly at Bronwyn and nodded. "One moment."

Her face took on a faraway look, as she reached out with her mind, searching for her son's thoughts.

Colin! Where are you?

A few moments passed, then he responded. *Mother, we're in the woods.*

Are Morgan and Colwyn with you?

Yes, why? What's wrong?

Nothing, now. You should have told someone! Bronwyn has been frantic about Colwyn.

I'm sorry, mother. We will return shortly.

Make sure you do.

Mereli broke contact and turned to Bronwyn. "They're fine and will be heading back shortly. It seems they are playing in the woods."

Bronwyn shut her eyes briefly in relief, but words would be said when they got back. Colwyn wasn't even five and they had taken her off into the woods on an adventure of some kind.

ᙯ ᙰ ᙯ ᙰ

The children returned mid-afternoon as they said they would and looked rather contrite as they stood before their parents and guardians. Both Richard and Rodric were angry that they could have been so irresponsible to have left the castle without telling anyone where they were going. Mereli wasn't as worried, as she knew they had been safe the entire time.

"What even possessed you to leave the castle without telling anyone?" Richard said as all three of them stood before the adults. "Bronwyn has almost made herself ill with the worry!"

Morgan dared to look up at his father. "I'm sorry, father. We were together, Colin would have been able to contact Mereli if we were in trouble. We were perfectly safe."

"Don't apologise to me, apologise to Bronwyn! I'm very disappointed in all of you, especially you, Morgan. Colwyn isn't even five and you've been gallivanting around the countryside without any consideration that we may have been wondering if you were all lying hurt somewhere. Go to your chambers."

Morgan lowered his eyes. "Yes, father." He turned to leave, then turned back to him. "I'm sorry for my actions. I would never want to cause you any worry, I hope you will forgive me." He turned and left.

Richard looked down at his daughter, who was doing her best not to cry, and failing.

"Papa...p – please don't be angry with Morgan," she pleaded. "I asked to go." She turned her large green eyes on him, in an effort to soften any punishment that might be coming their way.

Richard took a deep breath, held it and let it out slowly.

Rodric turned to Colin. "The same goes for you, young man. Go to your chambers. I think Richard has summed up our feelings perfectly."

"I'm sorry father, mother," the boy replied, head bowed. "I apologise Richard, Bronwyn." He dared to look at them and saw the hard stare the Duke was giving him, then gave a little bow and headed to his chambers as instructed.

"Papa, please don't be angry. We're back safe, that's all that matters," Colwyn said trying to work the magic of her eyes on him but wasn't succeeding this time.

He leant down, picked her up and said over his shoulder, "I'm taking her to her chambers."

The Duke walked in total silence to Colwyn's chambers, ignoring all Colwyn's pleas for forgiveness. He could feel her temper rising because she wasn't getting her own way, and at last said something.

"Don't you dare! You're in enough trouble as it is. If you fly into one of your tantrums, there will be more serious consequences!"

Colwyn kept quiet. She had never seen him so angry, so resorted to tears instead, but that didn't work either.

Arriving at her chambers, he told Sarah in no uncertain terms that Colwyn was confined to her rooms at least until tomorrow morning. She was not allowed to go anywhere on her own, and tomorrow, if he had calmed down by then, he would collect her.

Sarah curtseyed nervously. "Y - yes Your Grace," she said in a worried tone as she took the child from his arms.

"Papa, I'm sorry, Papa!"

But Richard ignored her apology, exited her chambers and slammed the door shut. He leant back against it and took several deep breaths to get himself back under control. He'd lost his son, and for a while there, he thought he may have lost his daughter. He just wouldn't be able to live with that. He had to keep her safe, for at that precise moment, she was his only legacy.

಄ ಐ ಄ ಐ

The wedding breakfast was finally held the following morning. Conspicuous by their absence were Morgan, Colin and Colwyn. The Queen asked Bronwyn if her daughter was all right and was told by Richard that she, along with Colin and Morgan were all confined to their chambers until further notice, as punishment for their thoughtless actions yesterday.

"You will allow them out for the tournament?" Alexandra asked.

"Yes, Your Majesty. Morgan is supposed to be taking part in the exhibition before the tournament." He saw her expression harden. She had heard about what had happened the day before, and had put the blame solely on Morgan, fuelling her hatred of the Kadeau, proving they could not be trusted.

Trahaearn had sought Richard's permission to collect Morgan for the exhibition match before the actual tournament, that would illustrate how the pages and squires were coming along. The Duke was still angry and was tempted to forbid the boy's participation in the event but knew the King would be expecting to see his future protector demonstrate his skills.

"Forgive me, Your Grace, but if I may be so bold," Trahaearn began "...we were all carefree, thoughtless children at some point in our lives."

That stopped the Duke immediately. The knight was correct, Richard had done some incredibly idiotic things in his past, giving no thought of the consequences of his actions, especially as sole heir to Invermere, and his anger disseminated. He nodded at the knight.

"Of course, you are right, Trahaearn. I have overreacted, but losing my son, and then this..."

"What?" Trahaearn exclaimed. "Your Grace, I did not know! I offer my most sincere condolences to you and Her Grace. I thought you had simply not brought the child with you due to its young age. Now I understand your reaction. As parents, you need to keep your children safe. I know I have never married, but I can imagine what it must have been like. With your permission then, I will collect Morgan for the exhibition."

"Thank you, Trahaearn. I will come and see Morgan before it starts. If I don't, he may not perform to his full ability."

The knight nodded. "I think he will be relieved to know he has been forgiven, Your Grace."

They parted ways. Trahaearn to collect his protégé and Richard to get into his armour for the tournament.

Trahaearn knocked on the door to Morgan's chambers and it was opened by Ioan.

"Sir Trahaearn, please come in. I'm hoping you can cheer young Morgan up; he has been very subdued since last night."

Morgan looked up as his mentor entered. Serious at most times, the boy looked almost apprehensively at the knight as he approached.

"Morgan, why are you not dressed? The exhibition is to start in half an hour," Trahaearn asked him.

"I'm confined to my chambers, Trahaearn," the boy responded quietly.

"Well get dressed. I have obtained permission from His Grace to collect you,"

The boy didn't move. "I have never seen him so angry with me as he was yesterday," Morgan said, feeling sorry for himself.

"Morgan, you have to understand, he was so worried. When they couldn't find Colwyn, he thought the worst. Currently, she is his only heir if Bronwyn can't produce a son. Colwyn is his legacy for the Coltrane line."

"I wouldn't have let anything happen to her. I have vowed to protect her with my life."

"But you vanished, with no word, what were they to think. Put yourself in the Duke's shoes. What if it had been your daughter?" He let that sink in for a few moments. "Duke Richard is a compassionate man. He cares greatly for all his family, including you, Morgan. That is the other reason he was angry, because he thought something may have happened to you as well."

The light dawned in the boy's eyes. "If...if Colwyn disappeared and I had no clue where she was, I would be..." his voice trailed off and with wide eyes, he looked at the knight, with the knowledge of understanding. "Especially since...since Bronwyn lost the son she was carrying."

"Exactly. His Grace told you of his loss?"

"Mother told me shortly after they arrived. I could sense they had both been deeply affected by it. They so desperately need a son."

"Yes. You must understand that explains a lot about his actions and how he is feeling. Now, get dressed, His Grace wants to see you before you start the exhibition."

Morgan nodded and stood up so Ioan could help him get dressed and ready for the demonstration of his skills before the King and the crowd.

Richard had returned to his chambers and Trystan assisted him with his armour. "What do you think, Trystan?" the Duke asked him. "Do I have a chance today?"

"It will be harder, Your Grace. Had it been held yesterday, you may have been the only competitor!"

Richard laughed at that. "I guess giving the guests time to recover, I will be competing on even ground. I will be testing my true abilities."

Trystan nodded. "It would be nice if you could win at least one more time, Your Grace. A trio of wins is a respectable record." The steward finished strapping on the Duke's sword belt. "There, done."

"How do I look?" Richard asked.

"As handsome as the day I first set eyes on you," Bronwyn said from the doorway. "My Duke in shining armour." She came to him as he turned to face her, and he crushed her in his arms and kissed her.

"I thought we would collect Colwyn, and go and wish Morgan luck before taking our seats for the tournament...if my husband is agreeable?"

Richard held his wife at arm's length. "I am agreeable. I may have been a little too hard on the boys yesterday," he said, turning to collect his helm, but Trystan stopped him.

"I'll bring your helm and shield, Your Grace."

"Thank you Trystan," Richard said smiling at him, then escorted his wife to Colwyn's chambers.

Colwyn was dressed and ready when her parents arrived to collect her. She was sitting on a chair, stood when Richard and Bronwyn came in, but did not smile and did not run to them. Instead she stood, curtseyed and looked at them apprehensively, not sure what to expect.

"Colwyn," Richard said in a voice that indicated for her to approach them.

Her steps were tentative, and she stopped a few feet away and looked up at her parents, her green eyes large and uncertain. They returned her stare, unsmiling for a few seconds, then Richard held out his arms. She ran to him, and he picked her up.

"Papa, I'm sorry," she whispered as she hugged him around the neck.

He kissed her cheek, and she returned it. Bronwyn stroked her hair and kissed her also.

"Mama," she hugged her mother as well. "I'm sorry."

"All is forgiven," Bronwyn said. She turned to the maid. "Thank you, Sarah. Please feel free to go and enjoy the day's festivities."

"Thank you, Your Grace." Sarah curtseyed and watched them leave.

They walked down to where the pages and squires were warming up, waiting to be called into the main arena by the tournament steward.

Morgan saw the three of them approaching and took a deep breath. Letting him take part in the exhibition of skills must have meant that they had forgiven him to some extent, but he needed to know exactly what his position was.

He stood with head bowed as they came up to him. An awkward silence ensued for a few moments, then Richard put his hand on the boy's shoulder.

"Morgan, look at me," the Duke instructed.

The boy swallowed, took a deep breath and did as Richard asked. "I – I'm sorry about yesterday," Morgan said softly. "Trahaearn made me see it from your side...I would have been angry and worried had my daughter disappeared and I knew nothing of her whereabouts."

Richard smiled kindly at him. "All is forgiven. Trahaearn also reminded me that I too was a boy once, and that I also may have done things without thinking of the possible consequences. Know that we love you Morgan, you're our son, and that we were also worried that something had happened to you."

Morgan hugged them all in turn. "I promise, I won't let you down again," he mumbled.

"In which case," Bronwyn began. "We want you to do your best today. The King will be eager to see how you are progressing."

"Yes mother."

"Good luck, Morgan," Colwyn said.

"Come, Colwyn, the tournament is about to start, Morgan needs to get into position and your father needs to start warming up."

"Yes Mama. I want you both to win," she said to her father and Morgan.

"Mine isn't a competition, it's more a demonstration," Morgan replied, "but thank you."

"And I thank you also. Now off you go," Richard finished. He nodded at Morgan, and headed for the practice rings, whilst his son took his place with the pages.

Bronwyn and Colwyn joined the King and Queen up on the raised dais. The Duchess observed Alexandra to be calm and happy, and surmised her wedding night had been an enlightening one. She managed to obtain a few quiet words before proceedings began, and the Queen assured her all was well.

The King opened the tournament. He welcomed everyone to the celebrations and indicated for the activities to begin. The pages entered the arena to give a demonstration of their skills. Stuart watched Morgan closely and smiled in satisfaction. The child clearly outshone his peers, that much was obvious, and the watching crowd clapped as they finished their demonstration. Morgan then joined Bronwyn and Colwyn on the dais.

Next came the squires, who were more determined to show their prowess with the sword. The next day, both pages and squires would also show their skills with the lance.

Finally, it was time for the sword competition between the lords and knights. Trahaearn was not taking part this time as he had overseen the pages and squires but took the time to wish Richard luck.

The competition was reasonably fierce and hard fought, but Richard was triumphant, defeating Rodric in the sword final. He ascended the dais, and received the golden band from Queen Alexandra, kissing her hand as he knelt before her.

"Well done, Duke Richard," she said. "I understand this is your third win now?"

"Yes, Your Majesty."

"The House of Cantrell is lucky to have your support. I thank you."

Richard stood, bowed and moved to Bronwyn and his daughter and kissed them, before picking Colwyn up and offering his wife his hand. He looked at Morgan and the child rose. They left the dais as a family and returned to the Duke's chambers.

There was another banquet that evening, and the jousting the following day. The pages and squires demonstrated their skill at collecting rings on their lances whilst avoiding being knocked off their horses, and they lanced revolving knights by striking the shields. When struck, these 'knights' then spun and hit the unlucky page or squire on the back, with a large, stuffed leather cylinder on a chain, if they were not quick or skilled enough to avoid it, which usually resulted in the rider being knocked from the saddle.

This was followed by the proper jousting competition, which Richard won yet again. He knew his run of luck couldn't last much longer, and thus debated whether this would be his last entry or not.

The celebrations finally finished, and over the next couple of days, the guests began to leave. Normality once again returned to Ellesmere and the trainees returned to their regular training. The Queen began her instruction into life at the castle and of her required duties. She avoided Morgan whenever possible, which turned out to be rarely, due to his often being in the company of the King.

Time flew. Christmas came and went, as did Morgan's tenth birthday. Fleetingly, the boy wondered if he was mature enough to become recognised as Duke of Rossmere, but his days were so busy with studies and training, that it was forced to the back of his mind.

Bishop Douglas cornered Stuart after the latest council meeting and questioned him about why the Queen was still not with child. The King had simply shrugged. Remembering what had happened to

Morgan's mother he had decided to be careful and wait until Alexandra was older.

"Is there...something wrong with the Queen, My Liege?" James had asked.

"There is nothing wrong with the Queen and...before you ask, there is nothing wrong with me either! It's just not the right time."

"But Sire—"

"Enough, James! No more!" At that point, Stuart had walked out of the room.

Richard returned that April to update the King on the situation west of Ellesmere, and to offer his assistance as always with any issues or problems that Stuart had, and it was in one of these meetings that the King advised the Duke, that he was more than happy with Morgan's progress and maturity and was going to bestow his title on him shortly. He thus requested Richard travel with them to Belvoir for the investiture, and it would also enable the Queen to visit more of Devonmere and renew her acquaintance with Bronwyn at Inver.

The Duke immediately sent word to Inver advising his wife of the forthcoming plans and requested she start preparations for their arrival sometime in May.

ↄ ↄ ↄ ↄ

Chapter Twenty

———◆———

It was April and Colwyn was bored. She had completed her schooling for the day; her father was away in Ellesmere with the King. Her mother was engrossed in other business, and Sarah had tried unsuccessfully to entertain her young charge. In the end, the young duchess-in-waiting, had taken herself off, whilst Sarah's back had been turned.

She was in one of her hot-headed rebellious moods and decided to make her way to an area of the castle that her father had forbidden her to go; namely, the Pell, where all the young boys and men were trained in the use of the sword and other weapons. Her father had told her in no uncertain terms, that it was no place for a woman, and most definitely out-of-bounds to a young lady of breeding like herself; but all that had done was piqued her curiosity and interest even more. So, she had given her maid the slip and headed straight there.

Sir John MacKenzie spotted her within a few seconds of her arriving, but was in the middle of explaining a battle tactic to a group of pages and didn't want to stop until he had reached a natural break; however that idea flew out of the window, as he saw Colwyn pick up a discarded wooden sword and start thrusting and trying to swing it about her head.

A couple of pages noticed her and started to giggle, nudging their neighbours' to make them look. John silenced them with an icy glare and instructed them to pair up and practice their lunges, as their footwork and stance was appalling. He left Lukas, Inver's weapon master, in charge, and walked towards Colwyn,

The young girl stopped what she was doing as the master-at-arms approached.

"Sir John, why can't girls learn to defend themselves?" she asked him.

"The defence of a woman is one of the duties of men," John replied solemnly. "There is no need for a woman to take up arms. In addition, you are not built, or strong enough to bear arms, and a woman's hands are destined for more gentle pursuits associated with their sex."

Colwyn bristled at that response.

"So what happens when the men aren't around to defend the women?"

The knight thought furiously for an answer but couldn't think of anything suitable for a child of her age, and he also became distracted as she started swinging the sword around again, with surprising agility.

"Stop!" he ordered. "Let me see your grip." He ignored the sudden light that appeared in her emerald eyes, and critically assessed her hold, correcting it and ensuring that she maintained it. Next, he made her perform some lunges. For her first attempt, she was actually better than a couple of the boys. What was more, she was enjoying it!

He corrected her shoulders, straightened her back, and nudged her feet into the right position.

After ten minutes had passed, he told her to stop.

"You have done well, my Lady," he praised her softly, so that his voice did not carry. "You handle your weapon well."

"Will you continue to let me attend?" she asked eagerly.

"Your father would not permit it."

"He's not here. Please, Sir John, let me attend. I will practice hard." She turned on the magic her green eyes held, and John found himself nodding, and quickly held up a hand before she could utter the squeal of delight he saw forming on her lips.

Instead, she dropped her sword and hugged him around the waist.

"Thank you, Sir John, I will attend every day!"

"We will also need to teach you to ride, my Lady."

She stepped back and looked up at him indignantly.

"But I can already ride," she retorted.

"As a lady, yes, but you will need to teach your horse to respond to the movement of your legs, and not the reins."

"Oh! There is so much to learn!"

"Your clothing is not really suitable either, and you cannot dress as the boys do."

Her face fell for a moment.

"I can wear hose and adapt one of my dresses."

"Colwyn, if your father finds out, I will be in serious trouble."

"I promise, I will never tell him! Please, Sir John, let me do this."

The knight heaved a huge sigh as he contemplated her request and his position. Personally, if he had a wife, he would be delighted to have her by his side. The world was changing, albeit very slowly. Perhaps sometime in the future, there would be female warriors. That thought he kept very much to himself. His peers and students would think him a madman for voicing such a thing. An eternity seemed to pass before he responded to her plea.

"Very well." He gave her a stern look to stop her from interrupting him. "We shall practice in secret, until you are up to the same level as these pages, then I shall let you join them. They will be sworn to secrecy. Now..." He leant down towards her. "...I need you to pretend that you are very upset," he whispered. "I will tell the pages I have told you off and sent you away. This will be our little secret until you are ready to join them. Understood?"

Colwyn nodded solemnly then, to John's amazement, changed her expression and began to cry, before turning from him and running away.

MacKenzie smiled to himself, then put on a stern expression and returned to his charges.

"Sir John! You must have really told her off!" one dared to say. "Did you see her expression?"

"She was crying," another broke in,

"Enough!" John snapped. "She has been told of her rightful place and none of you will speak of this ever again. It was a childish curiosity, nothing more. I simply indulged that curiosity and then told her she would never be able to wield a sword."

"Too right!" said another.

"Oh I don't know…I think she was better than you, Alun," a boy with rather unruly brown hair said grinning.

"Giles Dernley, that is quite enough!"

The youngster with the unruly hair, jumped and stood to attention, and Sir John cleared his throat. He was younger than the rest of the pages, and had started his training earlier due to his being the son of the Duke of Strathmere.

"Now…where were we?"

∛ ∧ ∛ ∧

Colwyn skidded to a halt, once she was out of sight, and smiled. She may have only been approaching five years of age, but she understood what Sir John had said to her. Her father would indeed be furious if he found out, and her mother probably wouldn't be far behind in her annoyance either.

She considered the knight's words about suitable clothing, and made her way to the stores, giving some story that she was helping Sir John, and had volunteered to deliver some hose, as he was busy, and a couple of the boys had damaged theirs and needed replacements whilst their originals were being repaired. She gave the store master her best, doe-eyed look and any thought of even questioning as to why she had volunteered for such a thing, went completely out of the storekeeper's head, and he handed her a couple of pairs.

Minding her manners, she gave thanks and then skipped off back to her rooms and hid the clothing at the bottom of one of the drawers in her wardrobe, before inspecting the clothes hanging in it. She needed something old, that she was planning on getting rid of.

She stumbled upon a dress she didn't particularly like and pulled it out. She could put slits in the front and back, rip the sleeves out, make more room around the arms, and shorten it. That would allow her more movement. Easy!

Colwyn had a fine talent in anything to do with a needle and thread, even at her tender years, so gathered her supplies together and set to work, converting the dress into a suitable surcoat she could wear. She had to do it in secret when her maid or her parents were not around, as she knew they would not approve.

Her red hair should have been a clear warning to anyone, that when she got a thought fixed in her brain, nothing could be done to change it, and anyone who tried, was likely to be on the receiving end of a tantrum. The ferocity of the resulting tantrum depended very much on her mood and how determined she was to see something through, and everyone was learning very quickly not to rile her too much.

She wasn't a spoilt or petulant child. Her normal disposition was one of kindness and generosity, but if anyone tried to take advantage of her, or treat her like a fool, they very soon realised their mistake.

Bronwyn hoped that she would learn to control her temper more as she got older, but being young, growing and developing, her daughter would often throw caution to the wind, do something outrageous, and fly off the handle. The Duchess realised this could be a problem when it came to finding her a husband, not that she was looking to marry her off in the near future. She wanted her daughter to be older before she was wed. Too many women died in childbirth because they were not mature enough to withstand the strain, stress and physical demands placed on the body during that time.

Colwyn managed to rip out the sleeves and prepare the dress for sewing of the new seams in the front and back, but suddenly realised that she had better stop and hide the garment. Having sneaked off earlier, Sarah would have been looking for her, and would probably be returning very shortly. She just managed to finish hiding it, when the door opened and Sarah came in, looking flustered.

"And just where have you been, young lady?" she demanded, puffing somewhat after the exercise she had just subjected herself to, looking for her charge.

"I went for a walk."

"Where?"

"Oh, here and there," Colwyn replied evasively.

Her maid had a very strong suspicion that meant she had been where she had no place to be going, but the destination of the Pell didn't even cross her mind! Not even Colwyn would be that foolish!

"Her Grace is expecting you. Something about lace making, if I remember correctly?"

"Oh yes! I'd forgotten. I'm learning Inver lace this afternoon. It's the most difficult of the laces in the Kingdom of Devonmere. Mama thinks I'm ready to learn it!" she exclaimed and ran out of the door before Sarah could say another word.

344

Inver lace was the most beautiful of laces, and extremely difficult to understand how the bobbins were worked, but Colwyn picked it up as if it were child's play. Bronwyn smiled at Mistress Betrys, the finest lacemaker in Inver, who was teaching her daughter.

The old woman got up from her seat and moved to where the Duchess was standing.

"Exceptional! I have never seen one so young, master the basic stitch so quickly. Your daughter is most gifted, Your Grace."

"Thank you, Mistress Betrys, but I think her teacher deserves a lot of the credit."

"You are most kind. Now, I will set her some exercises to create some small samplers which will need completing before I come again next week. Is that agreeable with you?"

"Yes, of course. Thank you."

"I will just check on my Lady's progress and, if all is well, I shall take my leave."

The old woman bobbed a small curtsey and moved back to her pupil to see how she was doing. Bronwyn saw her nod, and place a hand on her daughter's shoulder, before she turned, picked up the shawl draped on the back of the chair she had been sitting on, and left.

Bronwyn moved to sit in the now vacant chair.

"I think Inver lace is going to be my favourite. It is so beautiful," Colwyn told her mother. "I can't wait to get onto the more complicated stitches."

"Now, now, take your time. The basic stitch must be perfect before you can progress onto the next step. It is the foundation of all the others."

"Yes, Mama."

"You have done very well for your first lesson, Mistress Betrys is very pleased with you. Now tomorrow, I am holding court in place of your father. Will you attend me? You need to learn how to govern a duchy."

"I will attend. Will it be exciting?"

"Probably not," her mother confessed. "But you never know! Now come, it's nearly time for supper. Off you go."

Colwyn gave her mother a hug and skipped off to her rooms.

Bronwyn smiled to herself and stood up. She had just walked out into the corridor when she heard footsteps coming closer behind her.

"Your Grace!" It was Markus. He had obviously been running, as he was short of breath.

"Whatever's the matter?" Bronwyn asked, concerned.

"Your Grace, a messenger has arrived, he bears correspondence from the King!"

"Where is he?"

"I asked him to wait in the main hall."

"Very well. Let us see what news he brings!"

They swiftly made their way down a number of corridors and stairs and along to the main hall. A guard opened the door for them, and they went in. The messenger turned and approached them, bowing as he reached the Duchess.

"Your Grace, I bring a message from the King." He handed over the rolled and sealed parchment.

Bronwyn broke the seal and quickly unrolled it, reading the words carefully. A number of minutes passed before she sighed and nodded.

"Tell His Majesty, we shall be ready for when he arrives next month. Will you stay the night and rest before your return journey?"

"That would be most welcome, Your Grace."

"Very well. Markus, see that our guest is well cared for, and has a comfortable place to sleep for the night. Ensure his horse is also taken care of."

"At once, Your Grace. Sir, please follow me."

Bronwyn watched them leave and stood thinking for a little while. The King had written stating he had asked Richard to stay with him a little longer, and travel first with him to Rossmere for the investiture of Morgan as Duke, then they would all travel on to Inver. The Queen would also be accompanying them. This would mean a lot of preparation work, and no doubt, they would want to be entertained during their stay.

Her thoughts wandered to Morgan. It would be wonderful to see him after seven months, and she could not help wondering how much he might have changed during that short time, and soon he would officially be the Duke of Rossmere. Colwyn would be ecstatic about his return.

Bronwyn had two weeks to prepare for the arrival of the guests. Rooms were made ready, food menus agreed, entertainment arranged. Lookouts were posted on the towers to give advanced notice of the arrival of the King, so food would be ready on time, and pages and squires present to escort guests and take care of horses.

In between all that, she had held court in place of her husband, and Colwyn had sat by her side to learn how to be a good leader. As predicted, most of it was boring and some of it Colwyn was too young to understand. There were one or two interesting moments, but they were in the minority. The young girl did her best not to fidget, but her attention span was still short. Bronwyn just hoped some of what she had paid attention to, was starting to sink in.

Whilst all of this was going on, Colwyn had continued with her secret lessons in the use of the sword and starting to control her horse using her feet, legs and seat. She had also managed to complete the alterations on her dress. It was rather crude, but it served its purpose.

ભ્ઠ ભ્ઠ ભ્ઠ ભ્ઠ

Chapter Twenty-One

May had finally arrived with weather more suited to April. The pages and squires had still trained outside that morning and received a thorough soaking. It was now evening, and Morgan was studying in his rooms when there was a knock on the door.

"Enter," he called, his head still buried in a book on military strategy. It was heavy going, but he was determined to understand the layout of one particular battle, and was enlisting the use of various objects on the table to work out where everyone in the confrontation was situated.

"Morgan, are you free? I would like to talk to you." The voice was familiar, but he did not look up.

"Can you wait a couple of minutes, I'm trying to understand the layout of this battle," he mumbled, frowning.

He heard his visitor approaching, but still did not look up.

"Oh, you are studying the Battle of Dalesmere, just below the High Meres. That was a rather complex encounter. Is this stone meant to represent the King's army? If so, it needs to be further over, here."

The stone was moved, and the boy looked up in annoyance, straight into the face of Stuart. Horrified, he jumped to his feet and bowed.

"Sire, forgive my lack of manners, I—"

"Don't apologise, Morgan. I could see you were really trying to concentrate. It's not the easiest of battles to understand."

"Do you require assistance, my Liege?"

Stuart shook his head. "No. I want to talk to you. Come, sit down," he said, pulling up another chair and sitting astride it, arms resting on the back.

Morgan sat and waited patiently.

"These past three years I have watched you grow and mature faster than I anticipated. You have seen war, been by my side through thick and thin, in times of both joy and sorrow, and proved your loyalty. With all that I have observed, I have no qualms in granting you official possession of your title of Duke of Rossmere."

Morgan's eyes widened at this news. He knew he had reached the age where he could legally become Duke, but the final decree was the King's. It had been known to withhold a title for a number of years past the tenth birthday if that particular individual appeared to be lacking in maturity, knowledge and judgement, up until their eighteenth birthday.

"Sire, I...thank you."

"You show a maturity far beyond your years. In fact, at times I forget you are still only ten. I am making arrangements for us to travel to Rossmere within the next few days or so, to sanction your position with a brief ceremony in Belvoir Cathedral. I have already sent word to the noblemen of Rossmere to attend and confirm their support of you."

"Do you really think me ready for the responsibility, Sire?"

"I do. Now, I'm planning to leave in three days. Richard will be coming with us, as I thought after we have finished at Rossmere, you may want to travel on to visit Inver."

Morgan's face lit up. "Oh yes, I would like that very much!"

"I suspected you would. It means Richard will be away from home for a couple of weeks longer than he expected, but we can all travel together. Now, will you permit me to help you understand this battle?"

"I would be honoured, Sire."

Stuart gathered some ornaments, an ink well and a scribe and placed them on the table in set positions, explaining who or what they represented, then moved them according to how the battle had progressed.

"What do you think?" the King asked the youngster.

"The valley sides are quite steep from what I can gather..." He studied the layout before him. "Suppose the archers had been deployed on them, like at the battle on the Eastern Marches a couple of years ago; then a small group of militia consisting of knights could have charged along the valley floor in a feint to draw the enemy to attack. Then, as the knights performed their fake retreat, once they had dropped back far enough, the archers could have been let loose to initially take out a fair number..." He paused for a few moments. "Two further mounted militia could then have galloped along the sides of the valley to cover the back of the enemy to cut off their retreat, enclosing them and leaving them nowhere to go."

"You have obviously been doing a lot of studying and employing a variation to King Eurion's pincer attack by adding the archers to the valley sides. Very clever. I hope we never fall out with one another and finish up on opposite sides, that would likely result in a very bloody battle."

Stuart slapped Morgan good naturedly on the shoulder.

"You have the makings of a good strategist!"

"Thank you, Sire."

Ioan arrived on the scene, to assist his charge to get ready for bed, and Stuart took his leave.

It took Morgan a little while to settle down. His head was still spinning from the battle strategy he had discussed with the King and more importantly, of the news that he would shortly be officially invested as Duke of Rossmere.

The next few days seemed to flash by in a blur of non-stop activity. Somewhere during that time, he had been measured for clothing, and it had been delivered the morning he was due to depart. Ioan had taken charge of it and packed it carefully to minimise creasing.

Morgan had purchased gifts for Bronwyn and Colwyn and placed them in his saddlebags, along with some everyday clothing. Both bags were full to bursting, and he was fighting to secure the leather straps to keep everything safely inside.

Finally, he managed to fasten them, and Ioan took it from him to carry it down to the waiting horses.

Belvoir Castle, the ducal home of Rossmere. Morgan had never seen it. It was his rightful home, and he was about to journey to it, but it meant nothing to him. As far as he was concerned, Inver was his home; it was the only one he had ever known. When he was Duke, he would be expected to reside at Belvoir; that also meant stamping his mark on it. A huge responsibility: all his subjects, his advisors... he didn't know any of them. Could they be trusted? He would have to rely on Richard and the King. If they trusted them, then he knew he could too. He gave a huge sigh, took one last look around his rooms, then left and made his way down to the upper bailey, to mount his horse.

It was a relatively small party that left Ellesmere that morning, for Rossmere. It consisted of the King, Queen, the royal guard, Sir Trahaearn, Richard, Morgan, Ioan, Trystan, Aiden, Alys (Alexandra's personal maid) and a couple of servants.

The King had sent word north to Mereli and Rodric McLeod advising them of the forthcoming recognition, in case they wished to attend, and notice was given to the Rossmere Earls and Lords, who lived in the duchy, so they could also attend and swear allegiance to the new Duke.

The journey to Belvoir, the capital of the duchy of Rossmere, took four days, and for the first time, Morgan saw his ducal seat—Belvoir Castle—sitting atop a hill, as most castles did. It was not as grand as the castle at Ellesmere, but Belvoir possessed six towers and thick walls of dolomite limestone. The majority of city dwellings sat at the bottom of the hill, enclosed by a wide moat that encircled the entire hill. The mere of Rossmere stretched in a partial crescent shape a little distance away, fed by rivers born in the springs of higher ground, themselves fed by the rain that fell in the High Hills further to the east.

The sound of approaching horsemen caused those who were outside in the streets of Belvoir to stop what they were doing and look up. The King's banner was spotted at the head of the column and the towns people began to whisper and talk as the riders grew closer.

"God save the King!" was heard as the people lining the streets bowed and curtsied their respect, drinking in the sight of the King and Queen. Then they frowned as they spotted the fair-haired boy to the right of the King. *Who is that?* They whispered to each other, and then saw the rampant guardant gold dragon on the black surcoat and gasped.

"It's the Duke!" someone shouted. "The Duke has returned to us!"

None of them had seen him since he was a baby and had been presented by his father, Duke Idris Bodine, who had stood on the uppermost step leading to the keep and held the new born infant aloft for his people to see.

Word soon spread and the ever growing crowd scrutinised Morgan closely. The boy wore a serious expression, and his grey eyes were piercing, although he was not looking at anyone, but was staring straight ahead.

They watched as the King leant towards the young Duke and whispered something. The boy nodded and almost tentatively began to acknowledge his people with a nod of his head and the wave of a hand.

Those citizens that had been diligently working, lay down their tools and began to follow the horsemen towards the castle.

A herald proclaimed their arrival and, at the bottom of the steps of the keep, waiting to greet them were two men in Rossmere livery of black, trimmed with a gold trefoil counter flory and a small gold dragon emblazoned on the left side of their chests. Several pages in similar attire stood slightly behind.

They all bowed as the King and his party dismounted, then the pages stepped forward to take the reins of their horses and led them away.

The elder of the two men stepped forward and bowed again.

"Welcome to Belvoir, Your Majesty," he said.

"Justin, it is good to see you again," Stuart said warmly. "My Queen, Alexandra."

"Your Majesty," Justin said, bowing for a third time.

Stuart turned to Morgan, indicating for him to come forward. "Morgan, this is Justin, your chief steward. He has been responsible for running your duchy these past ten years."

"Justin, I am pleased to meet you, and thank you for looking after the duchy in my absence," Morgan said solemnly.

"Your Grace, welcome back to Belvoir. It is good to see you strong and well. With your permission, I would like to introduce my son, Edward, who I have been training to take my place, for I am old and feel I am no longer able to serve you as you deserve. I will present the records of the past ten years to you, so you may see that my son and I have been worthy servants."

"I thank you for your dedication and service these past years whilst I have been absent," Morgan said again. "If you feel able, I would like you to stay on, in an advisory capacity to your son, Edward, that he may make use of your vast knowledge, and to me."

"As you wish, Your Grace. Should Edward or you require advice, I will offer it freely."

Morgan nodded and motioned Edward forward.

"Edward, I look forward to our working together from this moment on."

The steward bowed.

"Your Grace, it will be my honour to serve you. I will have food and wine waiting in the main hall for you, but first, will escort you to your rooms so you may refresh yourselves after your long journey. Come."

He gestured for the party to precede him up the steps and enter the keep. Quarters had been prepared for Stuart, Alexandra and Richard, and pages escorted them, whilst Edward and Justin took Morgan to the Duke's rooms.

The boy felt like a stranger in what was his real home. None of it was familiar and he felt uneasy. Ioan picked up on his mood and did his best to put the boy at ease, but he knew it would be a while before the young Duke felt at home.

He quickly unpacked Morgan's saddlebags, then placed some water in a pan over the fire that had already been lit, to warm it, so the boy could freshen up before eating.

Whilst Morgan undressed and washed, Ioan lay out a clean set of clothes, then helped his master dress.

There was a discrete knock on the door. Ioan opened it to find a page, who escorted Morgan to the main hall, and then returned to his rooms to take Ioan to the kitchens.

Morgan was relieved to see Richard already present and went to join him at the table.

"This must all seem very strange to you," the Duke said to him.

"This is my home, but I feel like a stranger here."

"I understand. It must be very unnerving for you, but you will gradually feel at home here, and put your own mark on it."

"My home is at Inver. It's all I've ever known, until I went to Ellesmere."

"Bless you, child, but this is your rightful place of residence. However, know that you will always be welcome at Inver, whenever you wish to visit."

"Thank you, father," he replied, smiling tentatively.

At that moment, Stuart arrived, and the two of them hastily stood and bowed as their sovereign approached.

Stuart indicated for them to relax, telling them the Queen was tired and had decided to take her meal in her room, so they all sat and ate their fill. Edward had provided jugs of Rossmere's finest wine for the homecoming of the young Duke.

As they sat afterwards, having eaten well, Stuart outlined the plans for the next few days. Guests would be arriving from tomorrow, and a welcoming banquet would be held the evening before the investiture. The ceremony would take place the following day, in the early afternoon, followed by another banquet in the evening.

For a number of days after that, they would inspect the land immediately surrounding the castle and city, to enable the people of the duchy to see their Duke for the first time, since he had been taken from the castle all those years ago.

Sleep was a long time coming that night, as Morgan lay in a strange bed, in a strange castle. In a few days' time, the entire duchy would be his responsibility, and it frightened him. The decisions he made could mean life or death for his people. He hoped it wasn't wrong to rely on Edward and Justin, and their experience in running the duchy until he became more confident. Of course, there was also his council who had assisted in governing in his absence.

Sitting with Stuart whilst the King had held court had helped, and he had learnt a great deal from his sovereign as he had from Richard. He just hoped he would be a wise and just ruler of his duchy, and with that, he fell into a fitful sleep.

Ioan woke his lord the following morning. By the unruly state of the bedclothes, the steward surmised the boy had suffered a restless night.

"It can't be morning already," Morgan mumbled, as he tried to roll over and go back to sleep.

"Wake up My Lord, it is indeed morning."

"Just a little longer, Ioan, please."

"I've left you as long as possible, My Lord. Now it is time to rise."

Morgan moaned good naturedly but did as he was told.

"The majority of your earls and lords should be arriving today, Your Grace," Ioan reminded him. "I believe Edward has arranged a tour of the castle for you, so you may start to learn its layout. 'He will escort you himself, so it will give you the opportunity to get to know him."

"This doesn't feel like home, Ioan. I'm a stranger in my own castle."

"I'm sure it will pass, Your Grace."

Edward arrived after Morgan had finished his breakfast and escorted him around the entire castle, which took several hours. The young Duke was quiet but attentive.

"Your Grace, is everything all right? Have I displeased you in some way?" Edward asked.

"No, Edward. You have done nothing to displease me. I just...I am a stranger in my own castle."

"If I may be so bold, Your Grace, that will change, give it time. Come, we are nearly done. This is the final tower. After you, Your Grace."

They ascended the stairs and went up onto the battlements. This tower gave a distant view of the Rossmere coast, and the blue sea and

357

sky beyond it. Morgan surveyed the view, then peered out over the edge. It was a long way down to the ground from where he stood.

"What's this tower used for, Edward?" he asked.

"This one isn't used at all, Your Grace. A couple of rooms on the lower floors are used for storage but that's it."

Morgan went down to the room on the uppermost floor. The windows gave him views north-west to the coast and north-east inland. The door to the room was sturdy and had a heavy lock on it.

"Who has the keys to this room?" he asked.

"I have, Your Grace. There are two keys. One is kept locked away with all the other duplicates."

"I need a place of solitude, Edward. Somewhere I can relax."

"I understand, Your Grace. You are Kadeau, I know what that entails. My father is knowledgeable about such matters and taught me well. Kadeau cannot be expected to hold everything in, they need a place they can...release what they feel."

"Forgive me, Edward. I believe I have done you a great injustice. I assumed you would not know much about Kadeau as my mother died so young."

"You have not done me an injustice, Your Grace. When your father arranged to marry the Duchess Eirian, her parents came as well, and demanded a tour of the castle, looking for a suitable room. This was also the one they chose for their daughter to relax. My father, Justin, was educated, as he was trusted implicitly by your father, and has passed the knowledge onto me. Have no fear, I am a loyal supporter."

"So, I have grandparents somewhere?"

"Unfortunately not. I don't know what happened, but they are no longer alive."

"Oh."

"You must be feeling very strange at the moment."

"You are astute. I am. Edward... when I am more settled, do you think you or your father would tell me something of my parents? I can't really remember them."

"My father and I would be honoured to do so. But come, there is one other room I wish to show you, if I may."

Morgan nodded and followed his steward. The room was along from the Duke's chambers, and Edward motioned him inside.

"We didn't know where you would want to put this. So we have stored it here until you have decided where you would like it to go in the main gallery." Edward moved to the windows and opened the shutters and then gestured to the wall on Morgan's right.

On the wall, was a fairly large portrait of a very young woman with fair, almost white hair, grey eyes, with full lips, enclosed by an oval face. She was pretty, and as Morgan studied it he realised she was not fully a woman, but in transition.

"This is my mother," he finally said.

"Yes, it is. You have her eyes."

Morgan stared at the portrait for a long time as if trying to recognise her features or something that was familiar to him, but there was nothing.

"She is a stranger to me," he said sadly. "I consider the Duke and Duchess of Invermere my parents."

"Then, we shall leave her portrait here until you have decided where you want to hang it."

"Is there nothing of my father?"

"As far as I or my father know, a portrait was never done, but that doesn't mean there isn't one somewhere. You look very much like your father feature wise, but with your mother's colouring, although your hair is darker. Duke Idris was very handsome."

Morgan fell silent for a while, then finally spoke. "I've seen enough Edward, thank you. I suppose eventually this will feel like home."

"Both my father and I will do our very best to make it feel like home. Come, let me escort you back to your rooms so you may get ready for this evening. We've been gone several hours."

As he was home, Morgan was free to wear what he wanted, and thus chose black breeches and jacket trimmed with gold. The silk shirt was also black, along with the boots.

"How do I look, Ioan?" he asked.

"Imposing, Your Grace. When you are older, you will look positively intimidating." Ioan grinned at him, and the young Duke smiled.

"Right, I guess I'd better see if I can find my way down to the banqueting hall without getting lost. You have a few hours free now Ioan."

"Thank you, Your Grace."

Morgan successfully made his way down to the room behind the banqueting hall. This was where the guests for the table on the raised dais gathered before taking their places. The young Duke was the most nervous he had ever been and was relieved when Richard arrived. Stuart, Alexandra and Trahaearn turned up shortly after.

Further minutes passed, growing chatter filtered through from the double doors to the banqueting hall and then Edward slipped in discretely and approached the royal party. He bowed. "Your Majesties, Dukes Morgan and Richard, Sir Trahaearn, all guests have arrived."

The royal party acknowledged this piece of news. Stuart looked at Morgan.

"Are you ready, Morgan?" the King asked him.

The child swallowed and nodded.

"Carry on, Edward," Stuart ordered.

The head steward bowed and returned to the double doors. He threw them open, then picked up a long staff and walked through. The staff was struck on the dais three times to attract the attention of the waiting guests.

"All rise for His Majesty, King Stuart, Queen Consort Alexandra, the Duke of Invermere, the Duke of Rossmere and Sir Trahaearn."

The guests all rose.

"God save the King," Edward said firmly.

"God save the King!" the guests shouted as the royal party all came through.

The King and Queen took the centre chairs, Morgan was to the King's right, Richard to the Queen's left, Trahaearn to Morgan's right.

Stuart surveyed them all before speaking.

"Welcome to Belvoir castle. We have gathered here to witness the investiture of the new Duke of Rossmere, Morgan Bodine, son of Idris Bodine. Tonight, the Duke welcomes you to the castle." Stuart looked at Morgan and nodded.

Morgan stood up straighter and looked at the faces that were scrutinising him.

"I welcome you to Belvoir. Please, sit, eat and be merry." He nodded at some musicians along one side of the room, who began to play music.

The King sat, and everyone followed suit. Food and wine were served and gradually everyone began to relax as the evening went on.

Once the meal was finished, Morgan left the dais and went to the table immediately below, to say hello to his Uncle Rodric, Aunt Mereli, and he hugged his cousin, Colin.

"I'm so pleased you managed to come. Thank you."

"We could not miss this auspicious occasion," Rodric said. "My nephew being invested as Duke of Rossmere." He shook Morgan's hand formally, whilst his aunt hugged him.

"Morgan, you've grown! Are things progressing well?"

"Yes, I believe they are, but I suppose you'd better confirm that with Sir Trahaearn."

"I will have a word with him at some point in the next day or so, to see if I need to provide any additional support."

As usual, dancing followed the meal, but the wine still flowed. Trahaearn noted that a number of daughters of the various lower royals were attempting to attract Morgan's attention and gain his favour. Trahaearn mentally warned the young Duke of their intentions towards him to gain a higher title, and he raised his personal shields to protect himself. Trahaearn nodded in approval.

You would prove a good catch to a woman looking to improve her station, Morgan, Trahaearn sent through the link. *It would be ideal if you were able to marry for love, and not be tricked into it by the scheming of a woman. Not all are as pure and honest as the Duchess Bronwyn, so beware.*

Alexandra excused herself as soon as she was able. The rest of the party bowed as she was escorted out by a page and back to her rooms. She did not speak to Morgan at all, but pointedly ignored him.

Further time passed, it was almost midnight, and Richard decided it was time for Morgan to go to bed. He requested permission to remove the boy, and the King readily agreed.

"You have a long day tomorrow, Morgan, and a lot of words to remember," Richard whispered.

"Did you have to remind me?" the boy asked. He had been working on the words of the ceremony for a couple of weeks and although he knew them, he was worried about the investiture.

"Come on, lad. Off to bed. I'll escort you."

Morgan stood up, the musicians stopped playing and everyone turned to the raised table.

"Please continue to enjoy yourselves. The royal party will retire now."

Stuart rose also and led the way out.

Outside of the banqueting hall in the small ante chamber, the King turned to the two dukes. "It has gone well this evening. Make sure you all get some sleep now. It's a big day tomorrow." He smiled at Morgan, then turned and left for the guest quarters, accompanied by Richard.

Trahaearn escorted Morgan to his rooms and bid him goodnight.

In the King's appointed rooms, Stuart found his Queen was still awake.

"You left us early," he said to Alexandra.

"I don't see why I had to come in the first place," she replied.

"Because we are investing one of the loyal families to the House of Cantrell, and the boy who on his knighting will become my protector."

"Two Kadeau in your court, why?"

"Because the House of Cantrell has Kadeau in their court."

"But you know what they did!"

"That was hundreds of years ago, and these two particular Kadeau had nothing to do with what occurred back then. I suggest you remember that, and act with grace and dignity towards them. I command it."

He watched as her blue eyes flashed, then she remembered her station and said nothing. Stuart changed his tack.

"We are guests here, let us not argue and spoil the atmosphere." He stroked her cheek, then kissed her.

She tried not to respond, but his experience in the art of love drew it out of her, leaving her wanting more and she surrendered willingly to his advances.

଼ 8 ଼ 8

Chapter Twenty-Two

T he day dawned cloudy, with the threat of rain, and Morgan awoke with butterflies in his stomach. The forthcoming ceremony was all about him. He didn't like being the centre of attention and he was nervous. Suppose he forgot what he was supposed to say, or gave the wrong response, what would everyone think? He'd been rehearsing the required responses for the investiture and the speech for the evening banquet for weeks now, and knew it backwards, but that was no guarantee, nerves could make him forget.

Ioan had arranged a bath for him, and carefully laid out his finest clothes, which Morgan had scowled at because they were white with gold braid. He'd wanted to wear black but was told in no uncertain terms that wasn't going to happen. It would portray the wrong image to his people.

His personal steward helped him dress then stood back and nodded in satisfaction.

"How do you feel, Your Grace?" Ioan asked him.

"Queasy...and nervous."

"You will be fine, I have every confidence in you, Your Grace."

The Duke gave him a sickly smile.

"Now are you sure you don't want anything to eat? We don't want you fainting half way through the ceremony."

"If I eat anything I will be sick."

Ioan looked dubious but said nothing more.

A knock at the door made Morgan jump. It was Richard. He was dressed in royal blue with gold trim along the seams, a white silk shirt showing above the collar. The gold accentuated his broad shoulders and narrow hips. It was all finished off with a rich matching blue cloak that hung to just below the back of his knees, also trimmed with gold draped over one shoulder and under the opposite arm and fastened with a thick gold cord. At his waist was his dress sword in a matching scabbard that was also trimmed with gold. The pommel of the sword was decorated with the Inver coat of arms of the salient sable Pegasus on gules chevronels with an argent tincture.

"Good morning Your Grace," Ioan said, inviting him in.

"Good morning Ioan. Good morning Morgan, how are you feeling this morning?"

"Good morning, father, I am feeling nervous."

"You will be fine." He approached the boy and placed a hand on his shoulder. "Know that both Bronwyn and I are very proud of you. Stuart has great faith in you, formally recognising you as Duke of Rossmere at your age. Well done."

"Thank you, father."

"It's time to go. Are you ready?"

"As ready as I'll ever be." He looked at Ioan, who placed a white cloak trimmed with white fur and gold, that was fastened in the same way as Richard's with its own thick gold cord.

"Come then."

The horses were waiting for them at the keep, along with the Elite Rossmere Guard, resplendent in their dress uniforms, who were to escort Morgan and his supporters to the cathedral.

The visiting gentry were already present at the cathedral, which included the Queen consort. Stuart rode as part of the escort for

Morgan. This was the young Duke's day, and nothing was to detract from that.

They mounted up and left the castle, heading out and down the hillside road, across the moat and ditches to the city and the cathedral. people lined the streets, and as it was too early in the year for roses, threw spring flowers instead and cheered. Morgan acknowledged them as he rode past, and all too soon they had arrived at their destination.

Bishop of Rossmere, Oliver Treherne, was waiting at the entrance. As instructed during rehearsals back at Ellesmere, Morgan led the way up the steps. Behind him came Stuart, Richard, Rodric, Trahaearn, then Martyn, and officers of the Elite Guard.

The bishop bowed, then turned round, and entered the cathedral. The procession walked slowly down the aisle. Oliver went up the few steps to the altar and the rest stayed at the bottom. On the altar lay the Duke's coronet.

"Welcome to this special day, when we invest Morgan Rhys Geraint Bodine as Duke of Rossmere. Let us pray."

Following the prayer, a lesson was read, then another prayer. Morgan was invited to kneel. *Here we go*, he thought.

"Morgan Rhys Geraint Bodine, do you consider yourself worthy to be invested as Duke of Rossmere?"

"I do."

"Do you swear to serve your people in a just and fair manner, uphold God's holy law, protect the innocent, defend the weak, be truthful unto thyself?"

"I do so swear."

"Will you support King Stuart, abide by the governing rules of Devonmere to maintain peace, answer call to arms when requested, protect all women, defend the weak and rid the kingdom of evil doers?"

"I will."

"Who are the supporters for the investiture of the Duke of Rossmere?"

"We are, Your Grace," answered the supporters.

"State your names and roles for the register."

"King Stuart Cantrell, ruler of Devonmere."

"Richard Coltrane, Duke of Invermere."

"Rodric McLeod, Duke of the High Meres."

"Do you affirm the investiture of Morgan Bodine?"

"We do."

The bishop addressed Morgan again. "Morgan Rhys Geraint Bodine, your supporters have affirmed your right to the title of Duke of Rossmere. What is your statement?"

Morgan cleared his throat nervously. "I, Morgan Rhys Geraint Bodine, do solemnly swear that I will devote my life in protection of the citizens of the duchy of Rossmere, that I will be fair, just and loyal, follow the teachings of God, give protection to those deserving, defend the weak and protect all women. I will serve my King to the best of my ability and answer his call to arms. I will do everything in my power to defeat evil, uphold good, and serve Devonmere faithfully so long as I live."

"You have spoken your statement before your supporters, your people and God. Therefore..." he turned and picked up the Duke's coronet. "...as witnessed by your supporters, those present here and before God, I pronounce you Duke of Rossmere." He lowered the coronet onto Morgan's head. Arise, Duke Morgan."

Morgan stood. Another reading was said, followed by a final prayer, and then the congregation cheered as the Duke turned to face them. He stood there rather self-consciously as he waited for the cheering to stop, then the earls, barons and other gentry came forward to pledge their allegiance to the new Duke and reaffirm it to the King. This took some time, and once they had all done this, Morgan walked slowly back down the aisle, his supporters behind him.

He paused at the top of the steps as he saw a sea of bodies and eager faces before him, all trying to get a closer glimpse of the young Duke, and he swallowed convulsively.

"Smile," Stuart whispered in his ear. "And wave."

Morgan did as he was instructed, forced a smile and waved. The awaiting crowd cheered.

The little group walked down the steps of the cathedral, mounted their horses and were escorted back to the castle.

The banquet was to follow three hours later, so the guests and the Duke had a chance to refresh themselves and even relax a little before the event.

Morgan moved as fast as he could without appearing to rush towards his rooms. Safely inside Ioan looked at him.

"Get me out of these clothes!" he pleaded. "I feel so self-conscious in them."

Ioan smiled kindly and did as he was told, finally assisting the new Duke into a dressing gown. He then handed him a small goblet of wine, which Morgan took through into his bedchamber.

The simple service had exhausted him. He took a sip of his wine, placed it on the bedside table and threw himself down onto the bed. Ioan appeared in the doorway.

"I can leave you to rest for a couple of hours, Your Grace. What will you wear for this evening's banquet?"

"Black, Ioan. Black." Morgan rolled over onto his side and closed his eyes.

Ioan smiled kindly and covered him with a blanket.

C8 80 CB 80

The Duke of Rossmere was feeling nervous again. He had a speech to make at the banquet that evening. When Ioan had woken his master to help him prepare for the festivities, he had tried to make him eat a little something, as he hadn't eaten a thing the whole day, but the boy still refused.

When everyone was seated at their tables in the main banqueting hall, Morgan stood up again, cleared his throat, and gave his rehearsed speech, saying that as Duke of Rossmere, he hoped he would be fair and just, provide protection and support when required, defend the weak, support the King and the church and carry out God's will to the best of his ability. It was quite a long speech, and he spoke it perfectly. Finally, he invited everyone to eat, drink and enjoy the evening.

"God save the Duke of Rossmere!" Edward shouted, and the cry was taken up by all those present before they began to celebrate in earnest.

Morgan sat down thankfully. He had managed it.

"Well done Morgan," Stuart whispered to him. "Excellently spoken."

Suddenly, the boy's appetite was back, and he tucked in heartedly to the food.

Following taking their fill, Trahaearn spent some time speaking at length with Mereli McLeod. Morgan could literally feel his ears burning, knowing full well they were discussing his progress—or perhaps lack of it!

Mereli glanced up at him, smiled warmly and nodded.

The musicians were playing, guests were dancing, and once again, various daughters of the earls and barons were doing their best to gain the Duke's attentions without success.

The celebrating continued well into the night, but the royal party retired relatively early. Once the guests had left, Morgan was to embark on a tour of his duchy to meet the people, before travelling onto Inver to stay a day or so with his guardians before returning to Ellesmere to continue his studies.

The following day, he bid goodbye to his guests. The McLeods stayed on for a further day and would accompany Morgan on his visit to the northern villages as they travelled home, which also gave him a chance to talk and play with his cousin once more. It was probably his last chance to be a child before his responsibilities robbed him of that innocence.

That evening, Richard came to his chambers. "Morgan, please sit, I need to speak with you."

Frowning, the child did as he was told and watched as the Duke sat, looking at his hands as he contemplated how to begin the conversation. Finally he looked up at Morgan.

"You're ten now, and I told you, you would be informed as to what had happened to your parents when you reached that age."

"You needn't bother, father, I know what happened to them. My father was killed in battle, and my mother was poisoned by my wet nurse."

Richard could not hide his surprise. "How long have you known?" he finally asked.

"Since my first night at Ellesmere."

"You never said anything."

"There was no point." He looked up at his father. "But I thank you for keeping your word to tell me when I reached this age."

"And how do you feel about it?"

"I was angry at first, and bitter, but I have gotten over it, I swear. It was...easier... because I never really knew them."

Richard nodded; there was no more that he could say to that.

"Know that both Bronwyn and I are so very proud of you. We know you will be a just and fine leader of your duchy. Your people are in the best of hands and we are proud to have been a part of that."

"You both mean everything to me. I can't thank you enough for the love you have shown, and continue to show to me. It is you who have made me who I am."

Richard nodded, feeling rather emotional, so he simply nodded, hugged him and wished him a good night.

ഗ ഓ ഗ ഓ

Chapter Twenty-Three

A small detachment of the Rossmere guard accompanied Morgan and Stuart on the tour of the villages immediately surrounding the area of the castle and the city of Belvoir. They headed north from Belvoir, accompanied by Rodric, Mereli, Colin and their guard, who then carried on northwards towards their home in the High Meres.

The King introduced the people to their new Duke, and Morgan then addressed them with his prepared speech, growing in confidence as the day progressed.

Their final visit was to a small village called Halton, just a few miles from Belvoir, where they were welcomed and offered food and wine.

More relaxed now, Morgan had let his guard slip a little, warmed by the reception he had received. Sir Trahaearn became aware of this transgression and attempted to warn him not to let this happen but was unable to attract the young Duke's attention and was about to send him a mental instruction, when a feeling of dread came over him.

Automatically, his right hand moved to the hilt of his sword and his eyes began scanning the crowd, looking for the one who bore ill towards the young Duke.

Morgan! Trahaearn sent forcefully.

The boy physically jumped at the strength of the mental call and looked up towards his mentor. He frowned in confusion, wondering what he had done wrong, when the feeling of hate reached his mind. Startled, he also began scanning the crowd and, as he turned, continuing to search for the one who appeared to hate him so much, he felt something strike the right upper part of his chest, causing him to stagger back a couple of steps. Turning when he had, saved his life.

Suddenly, a woman screamed. Morgan looked down and saw an arrow protruding from just below his right collar bone. His eyes widened and the crowd turned as a cry was heard.

"Die, you filthy half-breed! Die!"

His eyes locked on those of a man he hadn't seen in five, or was it six years, back at Inver. Cadoc of the Mere, was running towards him, bow and arrow in his hand.

The boy stood, frozen in shock. Everything seemed to move into slow motion. Vaguely he heard the King shouting orders, the sound of swords being drawn from their sheaths, and the sight of a young man throwing himself at Cadoc, knocking him to the ground before he could get a closer shot at the young Duke, as the Rossmere guard descended on the attacker.

Only a few seconds had passed, but it felt like an eternity to Morgan as he became aware of Trahaearn appearing at his side. He was talking, but the youth didn't seem to hear him.

Morgan was feeling rather strange, he wasn't in pain, but he felt himself losing his grip on reality. He tried to speak to Trahaearn, but no words were forthcoming. He blinked several times, gave a little sigh, and collapsed. Somewhere, a long way away, a woman screamed again.

Trahaearn caught him, and gently lowered him to the ground.

"Morgan!" Stuart cried, and seeing Trahaearn had the boy cradled in his arms, turned back, his eyes blazing as the Rossmere guard dragged Cadoc towards him, with the young man who had thwarted the second attack, following behind.

Reaching the King, Cadoc was forced down on his knees, but the man was smiling at having inflicted a wound on the Kadeau he hated, and who was the cause of him losing his farm.

"Hold him!" Stuart ordered and turned back to Trahaearn and Morgan.

"Your Majesty!"

Stuart turned back once more and saw the young man approach him and bow deeply.

"I am a surgeon. Please, let me treat the young Duke."

"And you are?"

"Master Andrew. Please, I can help him. I do not see your battle surgeon here, let me help him."

Stuart looked back at his young protector, whose face was now white and creased in pain. He turned back to Andrew. The surgeon was relatively tall, with brown hair, light brown eyes, and square jawed. He was pretty non-descript to look at, but his eyes were kind. Stuart couldn't decide how old he was, as he possessed a somewhat ageless face. Andrew could have been anything between twenty and thirty-five as far as the King could see.

"The guards will be watching you," he whispered menacingly.

Andrew nodded and stepped forward, lifting the pouch containing his supplies that had been slung over his shoulder.

Trahaearn went to pull the arrow out, but Andrew stopped him.

"No! Wait!" He turned to Cadoc and pulled an arrow from his quiver. The arrow head had a vicious barb on it. He faced Trahaearn again. "We can't pull it out, look!" He held up the arrow. "We need to move him, to somewhere more suitable, it will have to be cut out." He moved to the Duke and looked down at him. "Your Grace, I am Master Andrew, and I am going to take care of you."

"I will carry him," Trahaearn said.

"Try not to jar that wound, I will assist you."

As they carefully lifted Morgan, a woman dared to approach.

"Please, my house is just over here, I have a table you can use."

"Thank you. Lead the way."

Stuart watched them carry Morgan away and turned back to face Cadoc.

"An attack on me I can understand," Stuart said to Cadoc, "but on an innocent child, that is—"

"He's a half breed Kadeau, no Kadeau is innocent!" Cadoc spat.

Stuart addressed the crowd.

"I will not tolerate attacks on my dukes or subjects, especially when they are so young. There is only one fitting punishment for this cowardly act, take heed, for the same fate will be applied to anyone who harms an innocent party."

The guards instinctively knew what was going to happen. They held Cadoc down, being careful to make sure they were standing behind his shoulders, and ensured his body was horizontal to the ground. If Stuart's subjects had thought him soft, they were in for a rude awakening, as the King unsheathed his sword, swung it and beheaded the attempted murderer with one blow before he could even struggle and try to escape.

There was a gasp from the crowd as Cadoc's body fell one way, and his head the opposite way to the ground and rolled towards the shocked spectators. Stuart cleaned his sword and returned it to its scabbard. He gave the onlookers a frighteningly cold stare before turning and heading towards the house where Morgan had been taken.

Inside, the boy had been laid on a table, and with Trahaearn's assistance Andrew had carefully removed Morgan's jacket and shirt so he had clear and unhindered access to the wound. He was aware the boy was watching him closely, a frown etched deeply into his youthful features as he bravely fought the urge to make a sound.

Andrew turned to the woman.

"Madam, do you have any hot water?"

She nodded, went to the fire and ladled some hot water heating in a pot, into a small bowl.

"Thank you," Andrew said as she put it on the table near to where he was standing.

He rummaged around in his bag, looking for a particular small cloth container, pulled it out and emptied some of the contents into the bowl and let it steep.

"The arrow needs to be removed carefully, so we do not do any more damage. This is his sword arm, I take it." Andrew didn't need to say anymore, Trahaearn understood. One wrong move, and Morgan could suffer permanent damage to his arm. "I need you to follow my instructions precisely."

Trahaearn nodded.

Andrew addressed the boy. "Your Grace, I need you to remain still and be very brave. It will soon be over. I will prepare a powder to lessen the pain."

Trahaearn stroked Morgan's head. "Morgan, remember what I have taught you about mental discipline, you need to concentrate, find that place in your mind, and go there. Take my hand, I will help you."

At that moment, Stuart entered. Andrew looked up and inclined his head in respect. He was too busy preparing the powder in some unwatered wine that he always carried in his pouch, to bow. When it was ready, he carefully lifted the boy's head and placed the goblet to his lips.

"Drink all of it, Your Grace."

The wine was quite bitter, and very strong, and Morgan slowly felt the warmth flow through his body, and his grip on reality slipping.

"Bite down on this," Andrew said softly, placing a cylindrical piece of wood in his mouth.

Morgan did as he was told, as the surgeon prepared a poultice for the dressing he was going to use once the arrow had been removed.

"May I be of assistance?" the King asked quietly.

"If you would assist to hold the boy down, Sire."

The King moved round to Morgan's head and gripped his shoulders firmly.

"I know you are brave, young Morgan, now you must show Master Andrew. Are you ready?" Stuart asked him.

Still just about conscious, Morgan swallowed slowly and nodded.

Andrew dropped some small squares of cloth to soak in the liquid, then picked up a small knife, dipped it into the liquid and leant over Morgan. He carefully probed the entry point of the arrow causing the Duke to moan as he bit down on the wood, took a deep breath and extended the wound beyond the barb. The boy screwed his eyes shut at the movement and bit harder on the wood desperately trying not to cry out or move but couldn't help it.

Stuart tightened his grip on Morgan's shoulders as tears appeared in his eyes at the pain.

"It will soon be over," Andrew said as he carefully manoeuvred one side of the arrow out of the wound, rotated it slightly and the other side came out easily.

Blood flowed from the extended wound, and Andrew calmly used the soaked cloths to clean it. Morgan tried his best not to move, but the liquid stung, and another groan forced its way past his lips.

Satisfied the liquid had done its work, Andrew placed the dressing he had prepared on the wound and held it firmly in place for a few minutes.

"Your Majesty, would you be so kind as to retrieve a bandage from my bag, please?"

Stuart did as he asked and handed it to the surgeon.

"Your Grace, we need to sit you up so I can bandage you."

Morgan was assisted up and went grey as they moved him. Holding the dressing firmly against the boy's wound, Andrew quickly bandaged the shoulder and indicated for his companions to lay him back down.

"There, all done. You've been very brave, Your Grace. Just rest." Andrew turned and addressed the woman again. "Madam, do you have a blanket we may borrow for His Grace?"

She nodded and went to fetch one. Andrew placed it over the boy's prone form.

"We need to keep you warm for a while. You were extremely lucky, Your Grace, it appears the arrow has missed your lung. Now rest awhile. The potion you have taken will make you drowsy, ease your pain and prepare you for the journey back to the castle." He removed the piece of wood from the Duke's mouth.

"Th – thank you Master Andrew," Morgan whispered quietly. His eyes closed.

Stuart released his hold on the boy and indicated for Andrew to follow him a little distance away.

"I offer you my thanks also, Master Andrew. How soon will we be able to move the Duke?"

"I would give him a couple of hours, then as long as the journey back is taken smoothly without too much jolting, he should be able to travel."

Stuart nodded. "Pray tell me, what are you doing here in this village?"

"I was journeying to Belvoir, hoping to find a position."

"The decision is not mine, but the Duke of Rossmere will be in need of a battle surgeon going forward. Your work today should put you in good stead."

"I would be honoured to be in service to His Grace."

"Excellent." Stuart turned to Trahaearn. "Trahaearn, there is some wine in my saddlebags, would you get it, please?"

"At once, sire." Trahaearn exited and returned a couple of minutes later with the wine.

The woman provided some goblets and Stuart poured three good measures. "I think we could all do with some wine," Stuart said, handing Trahaearn and Andrew a goblet each before picking up his own. He saluted the surgeon. "My thanks to you, Master Andrew for your quick thinking and for assisting Duke Morgan."

"Thank you, your Majesty, and may I also wish the Duke of Rossmere a long, prosperous, and happy life."

The three men drank again, then Andrew looked down at the boy, and saw that he had fallen asleep, a slight frown still etched on his features.

Stuart gently touched the boy's head, then turned to the woman of the house.

"Madam, thank you for the use of your home. We will be here for a couple of hours." He reached into a pocket and drew out a gold coin. "Please accept this token in payment for the inconvenience we have caused."

The woman curtsied as she accepted the coin.

"Your majesty, 'twas no trouble. I am pleased my humble abode was sufficient for your needs. May I offer you bread whilst you wait?"

"Thank you for your kindness, madam, but we will decline, we have put you to enough trouble."

The woman curtseyed again and withdrew.

Stuart went outside and spoke to the guard, explaining they would be staying for a couple of hours before they returned to the castle. One of the knights volunteered to go and get a carriage so Morgan would not have to ride, but Stuart shook his head. He didn't want to lose any of the guard, just in case.

Approximately two hours later, Andrew made one final check on his patient. He placed a hand on the child's forehead and nodded in satisfaction.

"No fever so far, that is good. Now we need to support that arm in preparation for the journey."

With Trahaearn's assistance, he constructed a sling for Morgan's right arm, so that it was not placed under any strain and deemed him ready for the journey back. The drug Andrew had administered had been a strong dose, and Morgan did not stir. Trahaearn stated he would ride with the child and support him.

Andrew carefully picked Morgan up and went outside. Trahaearn followed him, then mounted his charger and leant down to take the boy from the surgeon's arms, and carefully seated him on the front of the saddle, wrapping his cloak around him to keep him warm.

Although they were only a few miles outside of Belvoir, it took them well over an hour to get back to the castle, as they travelled slowly to prevent any jarring of Morgan's injury.

Finally, reaching the safety of the castle walls, they halted in front of the keep. Andrew, who had been given a ride by one of the Rossmere guard, slid off the saddle and went up to Trahaearn to take the boy from his arms.

Stuart suddenly appeared at his side.

"I will lead you to the Duke's rooms," he told Andrew.

"Thank you, your majesty."

He followed the King up the stairs, along a number of corridors, up more stairs and finally to the Duke's rooms. Ioan went white and stood frozen for a number of seconds as they entered, then pulled himself together and ran through to the bedchamber to pull back the bedclothes.

Between them, they removed the remainder of the boy's clothes, then Andrew prepared to re-examine the wound. Removing the sling and the bandage caused Morgan to stir, and he moaned as he became aware of a throbbing pain that seemed to match the beat of his heart.

"Steady, Your Grace, do not move. I will provide you with a further potion shortly. I just need to make sure no further damage has been done during the journey back to Belvoir."

The surgeon prepared a fresh dressing that he again coated with a special poultice to help keep infection out and aid in healing. Gently he removed the old dressing, inspected the wound, nodded in satisfaction and placed the new dressing on it, re-tightening the bandage and the sling.

"Now, you are not to move that arm. You need to allow the wound to start healing. However, I want you to try moving your fingers regularly. It will no doubt hurt, but it is important you do this. Also, you must clench and unclench your hand to make a fist." He turned to Ioan. "You are the boy's steward?"

"Yes. I am Ioan."

"Ioan, I am Master Andrew, a battle surgeon. Please would you get some more pillows, His Grace needs to be elevated slightly."

Ioan immediately went to get the requested items and returned within a few seconds. Andrew carefully lifted Morgan whilst Ioan placed the pillows as directed, with one providing extra support for the right arm, then the surgeon lay the boy back against them.

"Ioan, you must make sure that His Grace does the exercises I have set at regular intervals."

"I will, Master Andrew."

"Good. I will now prepare another potion for the Duke," he said rising from the bed.

"I will leave Morgan in your capable hands," Stuart said. "I must inform the Duke of Invermere of what has happened."

Everyone bowed as the King left.

Andrew prepared the potion, but just as he was about to return to the bed and administer it, the door burst open and Richard came striding across the room, worry etched in his features.

The Duke sat down on the bed. With one hand he took the boy's left, and with his right, stroked his head.

"Morgan, my son," Richard said, not realising he had uttered those two last words with such emotion in front of everyone.

But Morgan had. His eyes widened as the conviction and feeling in Richard's voice registered in his mind. The Duke had been like a father to him; it was no wonder that he thought of the boy as such.

"F—father," he mumbled in return, and Richard's resolve almost disintegrated at hearing that word.

Making a remarkable recovery, the Duke turned his attention to Andrew.

"The King has told me you saved the boy's life," he stated. "Thank you."

"It was my honour," Andrew said, still holding the goblet.

"Is that for Morgan?" Richard asked.

Andrew nodded. The Duke held out his right hand, indicating for the surgeon to give it to him. Richard turned his attention back to Morgan.

"This will enable you to rest easy," he said to the child. "Drink."

Morgan did as he was told, and Richard watched as the drug took hold, and the boy slipped from reality.

"He should sleep through the night," Andrew said. "I made it strong, so he would rest, and his body can start the healing process."

Satisfied that Morgan was sleeping, Richard stood up carefully and studied the surgeon.

"It will be the Duke's final decision, but for the moment, I would like you to stay at Belvoir, look after him until he is better. If you will accompany me, I will show you where the previous surgeon used to stay."

"Thank you, Your Grace." Andrew gathered his possessions.

"Ioan, watch over my son," Richard instructed and reluctantly left Morgan's rooms to guide the surgeon to his new 'home'.

෪ ෪ ෪ ෪

Andrew looked around in surprise. He had a bedchamber, day room, storeroom and a room where he could see patients. He had never had so much in his entire life. Like a boy who had received the best gift he could ever think of, he examined the storeroom.

"Your Grace," he said to Richard, "This is so much more than I expected."

"No doubt, some of the supplies in this room will need to be replaced. They will not have been touched since Morgan left here over nine years ago."

Andrew nodded.

"I will check everything and replace it where necessary."

"And I will arrange for Edward, the Rossmere steward, to provide you with funds to replenish your stores."

"That is most generous, Your Grace."

"A battle surgeon must have suitable supplies. There are also some books that you may find useful."

Andrew nodded. "I also have others that I will arrange to be delivered and notes I have made on my travels afar."

"Very well. Let me be your guide for the next hour, so you may orientate yourself within the castle."

"Your Grace, that is below your station."

"It is the least I can do, for the man who saved my so.... for saving Duke Morgan. The boy has been like a son to me, for I have raised him as my own since he was nine months old."

Now Andrew understood the heightened emotions of the Duke of Invermere. To all intents and purposes, Morgan Bodine was Richard's son in all but blood.

Richard was as good as his word and gave the surgeon a tour of the immediate parts of the castle that the Duke of Rossmere was likely to frequent when he was in residence, before returning to Morgan's chambers to sit by his bedside. The Duke had felt sheer panic when Stuart had told him the news, and he wished now he had executed Cadoc all those years ago, despite what Morgan had requested. To have lost his son, and then to hear of Morgan's wounding had almost been too much to bear.

Stuart had been surprised at Richard's reaction, until the Duke had confessed the reason, and told the King that had he lost Morgan, it would be as if he had lost another son. The King had been extremely sympathetic, asked if Bronwyn had recovered now, and then urged Richard to go to Morgan, to see for himself that the boy was alive.

"Your Grace, may I get you anything? Food, wine?" Ioan asked softly from the doorway.

"Thank you. Food and wine would be most welcome, Ioan."

The steward smiled, bowed and went to get the required nourishment. He was gone some minutes, but when he returned, asked if the Duke wished to eat in the outer chamber, or where he was currently sitting.

Richard didn't want to leave Morgan's side and stated he would stay where he was, so Ioan put the wine and the plate of food on the bedside table, bowed and exited.

The Duke drank the wine, but only picked at the food, having suddenly lost his appetite. He finally fell asleep in the chair, holding Morgan's hand. Ioan peered in, and carefully covered the Duke with a blanket before retiring to the outer chamber and making himself comfortable on the couch, staying close in case he was needed.

ᘓ ᘔ ᘓ ᘔ

"The news is all over the castle," Alexandra said as Stuart entered her chambers. "Is it true?"

"That someone tried to murder the Duke of Rossmere?" he asked her. "Yes, it's true. Fortunately they failed."

"A shame. That would have been one less Kadeau in the kingdom," she replied spitefully.

"Did you also hear that I personally beheaded the attempted murderer," he snapped back at her and was pleased when he saw her go white. "Morgan is but ten, and you wish him dead? What kind of wife have I married that would see a child murdered? You treated him with the utmost respect and kindness until you found out about his heritage, and you continue to blame him for something he has no control over. Get over it Alexandra, Kadeau are a part of the Cantrell House, and you are currently in a Kadeau stronghold."

The Queen said nothing.

Stuart took a deep breath and lowered his voice. "I know you do not love me. I hope in time you will learn to, but I cannot see that happening as long as you hate my most trusted allies and protectors. Did you know that Bronwyn lost the son she was carrying a few months ago?"

"I – I am sorry to hear that news. I like Bronwyn very much; she must have been devastated."

"She was. It also affected Richard deeply as well, but you should have seen him earlier when I had to break the news about the attempt on Morgan's life. He considers the child as his son, and to think he had almost lost him as well... I have never seen such a reaction from him."

"Richard is a good and loyal supporter, I've seen that. You and he seem very close."

"My father considered him a good friend, as do I, and he has watched over me all my life, not directly, but he has always been there when I needed him. So I ask you once again, for Richard, Bronwyn, Morgan, Trahaearn and myself, please try."

Alexandra stared at him. "I cannot promise, but I will try."

"Thank you."

ℭ ℬ ℭ ℬ

When Stuart discovered that Richard had not been in his chambers the entire night, he headed to Morgan's. It was the only place he could think the Duke would be, and he was right.

Richard looked particularly uncomfortable, the King thought, propped up awkwardly in the chair, still holding Morgan's hand, so he went to him and gently shook him awake.

"Richard," Stuart whispered. "Wake up, go to your chambers and get some proper sleep."

The Duke sighed and opened his eyes, then winced as he moved his head and saw the King standing over him.

"Sire!" he tried to rise and pay respect, but Stuart held him in place.

"Go to your chambers, Richard," Stuart said again. "Get some proper sleep. I will sit awhile with Morgan. That is my decree."

"Very well, Sire." Richard reluctantly let go of Morgan's hand, stood up, stretched his spine, bowed and went to his quarters.

Stuart looked down at Morgan, who was still sleeping as Master Andrew came in.

"Good morning, Your Majesty. I've just seen the Duke of Invermere; he says His Grace had a peaceful night. I am here to redress the wound."

"Carry on."

Andrew sat on the edge of the bed and pulled the covers down to Morgan's waist. He loosened the sling, and with Stuart's assistance removed the dressing. Ioan came in with hot water and removed the goblet and plate of food to give Andrew some room on the table. The wound was still oozing blood, but nowhere near as badly as the day before. The surgeon cleaned it, placed a new poultice on it, rebandaged it and nodded in satisfaction.

Just as he finished, Morgan stirred, frowning at the throbbing sensation in his shoulder.

"Good morning Your Grace, are you in a lot of pain?" Andrew asked him.

"S – some," he replied honestly.

"I can give you some pain relief if you so wish."

"No, it makes me groggy. I can stand it."

"Very well. You are to stay in bed. The wound is starting to granulate, that means it is laying the foundation for healing, so we don't want to cause anything that will damage this part of the process. The sooner this completes the sooner the healing can start. If you follow my instructions, you will be up and about sooner. Disobey and it will delay your recovery. Do I make myself clear?"

"Yes, Master Andrew."

"Where your health is concerned, I give the orders, Your Grace." Andrew looked pointedly at Stuart and dared to hold his gaze until he nodded in support of the surgeon's words.

Andrew pronounced Morgan well enough to travel two days later. He wanted the boy to rest longer, but the child was impatient to get to Inver and see Bronwyn and Colwyn.

So it was early the next morning when Richard gave Morgan a leg up onto his pony, and the group set off for Inver.

During the day's ride, Morgan did the exercises that Andrew had given him, which were very painful, but he knew he had to persist, so as not to lose function in his sword arm. The day was uneventful, but it took its toll. The young Duke tired quickly and as they approached the time to stop and make camp for the night, Andrew noticed Morgan was losing colour and beginning to look rather pale.

The surgeon asked Richard how soon it would be before they made camp and explained his reason for asking. Richard glanced across at Morgan, then informed the King, so they stopped shortly after, near a spring of beautiful clear water.

Ioan placed a blanket on the ground under a tree whilst Trahaearn assisted Morgan from the saddle. He collapsed with exhaustion immediately his feet touched the ground. The knight lifted him into his arms and walked to the one lonely tree and placed him down on the blanket.

Andrew knelt down beside him and replaced the dressings, whilst Stuart and Richard observed.

"I – I'm sorry," the boy mumbled, wincing as Andrew worked.

"It's all right. Don't worry about it. There, all done. Rest awhile. We should have delayed another day," he told him. "How much pain are you in?"

"I'm all right," the boy replied.

"Morgan, your colour is almost white. Don't tell me what I want to hear, tell me the truth."

"S – some," he finally confessed, then took a sharp intake of breath as Andrew and Trahaearn helped him back into his shirt and jacket, and the surgeon put his arm back in the sling. "I – I can go on now."

"We are camping here for the night," Stuart told him, then turned in surprise as Alexandra joined him.

"You must rest," she told Morgan and he nodded.

"Thank you," Stuart whispered in her ear.

The escort had built a fire, and food was being prepared. Andrew administered a mild potion to Morgan to ease his discomfort and ordered him to rest. The boy's eyes immediately closed. Richard retrieved the blanket from Morgan's saddle and covered him with it.

"How is the Duke, really?" Stuart asked Andrew.

"He will be all right, Your Majesty. We may have left a little too early. He's still suffering from shock and loss of blood, but he is a strong boy. We just need to ensure he eats well this evening."

The King nodded and looked over at the sleeping boy. Ioan had made a pillow out of another blanket and placed it under Morgan's head.

When the food was ready it was dished out onto small plates. Ioan took one over to his Duke and sat down beside him. "Your Grace," he said softly. "Your Grace." He gently shook him, and the boy stirred. "I have some food for you."

Morgan shook his head. "You eat it, Ioan. I'm not hungry."

"Your Grace, the King has decreed you must eat, to help regain your strength. Come, eat."

Trahaearn, who had been watching, came over and assisted the boy into a sitting position. "Do you require me to force feed you like a babe in arms?" he asked him quietly. "Because I will do it if you refuse to eat."

Morgan looked at the expression on the knight's face. "I will eat," he said.

"Good, because we have a further three days travel, and you need to look like you are recovering by the time we reach Inver."

CB „ CB „

Chapter Twenty-Four

————•————

It was a couple of days later than expected when the lookouts spotted a column of horsemen off in the distance. They were too far away to identify, but they were coming from the direction of Belvoir. Currently it would be another day before they reached Inver; plenty of time for final checks and to prepare food and wine.

Bronwyn was standing in her usual place in front of the keep when the horsemen arrived. She smiled warmly in welcome, curtseying as the King and Queen came up to her, blocking her view of the riders behind.

"Your majesties, welcome to Inver," she said.

"Bronwyn." Stuart took her hand, kissed it, then kissed her cheek and straightened up.

"Is anything wrong?" she asked, picking up on the charged atmosphere surrounding them.

Stuart stepped aside so she had a clear view behind him, and her smile faded as she saw Richard assisting Morgan to dismount and she started to walk forward as she spied his right arm in a sling and his pale colour.

"What's happened?" she asked, a hand going to her throat, as she saw him falter, and Richard pick him up. "Morgan!"

Richard instructed the pages and Markus to escort the guests to their chambers and then looked at his wife. "Come," he said to her

393

as he carried the boy to his chambers, closely followed by Ioan and Master Andrew.

The Duke placed the boy on his bed and stood back to allow Andrew to work.

"What's happened?" Bronwyn asked again. "And who is this?"

"Remember six years ago, the threat to Morgan by that tenant farmer?" He paused as Bronwyn nodded. "He turned up in a village just outside Belvoir and attempted to kill him. Morgan has been wounded, but I promise you, he is recovering."

"And where is the attempted murderer now?"

"Stuart beheaded him."

"Good." Bronwyn was usually a gentle soul, but on this occasion she let her feelings be known about the man who had attempted to murder her adopted son.

"This is Master Andrew. He is now Morgan's battle surgeon and saved his life."

"Master Andrew, I thank you for saving our son's life."

"It was my honour to do so, Your Grace," Andrew replied, looking up at her. He turned his attention back to Morgan. "How are you feeling now?"

"I'm all right, just tired," the boy replied.

"Very well. Some food, and then sleep," Andrew ordered. He stood up, bowed to Morgan, Bronwyn and Richard and stepped out of the way.

"Morgan, my darling," Bronwyn said sitting down by his side and kissing his cheek. She saw his bottom lip tremble and turned to the three men. Please, leave us, now," she ordered. She watched them exit the room, closing the door behind them and turned back to Morgan. "My son," she whispered, and that was the cue for him to offer himself into her arms and start crying, releasing all the stress and strain of the event. "It's all right," Bronwyn said softly, stroking his hair. "I've got you. Let it all out, it will make you feel better."

"W - why does everyone h - hate me?" he asked, his voice muffled as he hid his head in her shoulder.

"Oh, my darling, not everyone hates you. You must make the most of the love you do receive. For some, the hatred does run deep, but not all. Remember that. You have genuine friends, surround yourself with these people, they will help shield you and support you when the going is tough. When you feel in need, you will always find love here, with your family."

"I love you...mother."

Bronwyn kissed the top of his head at hearing those words and shed a few tears of her own. "How are you really feeling?" she finally asked him.

"I feel better now I..." he just couldn't admit to the fact he had shown weakness.

"Are you in any pain? Tell me the truth now."

"It aches more than hurts," he replied. "But I find it draining."

"That's to be expected. If you do as you're told, you'll heal faster. Remember that."

There was a discrete knock at the door.

"Are you all right for someone to come in now?"

Morgan wiped his eyes with his left hand and nodded.

"Enter," Bronwyn commanded, and Ioan came in with a tray containing a plate of food and some wine.

He bowed, then approached the bed. "Food and wine, Your Grace." He placed the tray on Morgan's lap after Bronwyn had fluffed up the pillows to make the boy more comfortable.

"Eat," Bronwyn ordered. "I'm not leaving until you've made a good attempt at emptying that plate."

Morgan managed to eat three quarters of it before he gave up. Bronwyn was pleased.

"Well done, darling. Now…" she said indicating for Ioan to remove the tray, "lie back and get some sleep and I shall see you in the morning." Bronwyn kissed his forehead and rose from the bed.

Morgan grabbed her hand and kissed it. "Thank you, mother," he whispered.

Bronwyn smiled at him, pulled the covers up over his shoulders, kissed him once more and left the room.

Richard and Andrew were waiting in the day room.

"Morgan should be asleep shortly. He has eaten and is now resting," Bronwyn told them.

"Then I shall change, and we will entertain our guests in the hall," Richard said. "Will you accompany me?" he asked of his wife, offering his arm, which she took, and they walked to his chambers.

Trystan looked up as they entered and went to the fire to retrieve hot water for his master to wash.

"I apologise, Richard," Bronwyn said to her husband, "seeing Morgan injured made me forget my manners. Welcome home."

He smiled at her, pulled her into his arms and kissed her deeply. "It's good to be home, despite the circumstances," he responded as they parted. "As always, I have missed you. How are you feeling?"

Tears filled her eyes, but she fought them back. "I'm all right."

"You're sure? Is there anything I can do for you?"

"No, I am fine. But what about you? How do you fare?"

"I will admit, I panicked when Stuart told me of the attack on Morgan. He…knows. I had to tell him, to explain why I lost control."

"Probably best he know," Bronwyn said quietly.

Richard held her at arm's length. "Let me freshen up, then I must see my little angel," he said.

"Oh grief! She must be wondering what's going on!" Bronwyn said. "I'd better go to her—"

"Wait for me, I'll be but a moment." He turned and motioned to Trystan, who helped him out of his armour so the Duke could wash. His steward lay out some fresh clothes which Richard quickly changed into, then released Trystan for the evening as he left with Bronwyn to go to Colwyn's chambers.

"Papa!" Colwyn squealed as the Duke and Duchess came through the door. She ran to him, and he leant over and picked her up. She threw her arms round his neck and kissed his cheek. Her welcome warmed his heart.

"Colwyn, my love. How are you?"

"I'm well Papa, thank you. I'm so glad you're home." She drew back and looked around. "Where's Morgan? Isn't he here?"

Richard sighed. "Yes, my love, he's here, but he's not very well."

"Is he going to be all right?"

"Yes, he's going to be fine. He's currently sleeping, so you must be patient. Let's see how he's feeling tomorrow morning. I know he wants to see you too."

"I will pray for him before I go to bed. Do you think that would help?"

"Yes my darling. That will help a great deal. Now, are you ready? It's supper time, and the King and Queen are here too. You remember how you must address them?"

"Of course I do, Papa!"

The three of them went down to the banqueting hall, where the King, Queen and Trahaearn were already seated. They stood up as they approached.

"Apologies for our lateness, Your Majesties," Bronwyn said.

"No need to apologise, Bronwyn. I understand. Is Morgan resting?"

"Yes, Sire."

"I am sorry this happened to him," Alexandra said quietly. "To attack a child is unforgiveable."

"Thank you, Your Majesty. Your words mean a great deal."

"And my goodness, Colwyn has grown these past months," Stuart said holding out his arms to take her from Richard.

"Your Majesty," Colwyn said.

"Aha, you have finally learnt some court etiquette," Stuart laughed remembering their first meeting, when she had simply called him by his first name. "Come, let us all eat."

Over their meal, Bronwyn asked how their majesties wished to be entertained. She had made outline plans, but it could be the royal party had something totally different in mind.

It turned out to be the latter.

"That is very kind of you Bronwyn, but do you know, I think we've all had more than enough excitement recently. What I would really like is to relax, enjoy the gardens, the scenery. Would that be acceptable?"

"Why of course, Sire. Your wish is our command."

Everyone retired early that evening and woke refreshed the following morning. After breakfast, Stuart and Alexandra took a walk in the gardens, and Colwyn crept off to Morgan's rooms to see her brother.

He had eaten and was resting quietly when Colwyn crept into his bed chamber. She climbed up onto his bed, which woke him.

"Colwyn!" he exclaimed.

"Morgan. Mama said you are not very well. I came to see you... oh your arm!" she exclaimed and hugged him carefully, kissing his cheek.

He kissed her back, then wrapped his good arm around her shoulders and she snuggled against him.

"So, what have you been doing since I last saw you?" Morgan asked.

Colwyn spent the next half an hour telling him of her exploits, apart from the sword training, but did inform him that she was learning to control her pony using feet, legs and seat. They chatted a while longer, then dozed off, and that was how Andrew found them when he came to check on his patient.

Ioan returned from completing various duties and some free time Morgan had given him, and Andrew asked if he would inform either the Duke or Duchess that the Lady Colwyn was here in Morgan's rooms, just in case they were looking for her.

Bronwyn and Richard arrived shortly after, ready to tell their daughter off for disturbing Morgan, but the words died on their lips as they surveyed the two of them asleep. Richard attempted to extract Colwyn without disturbing Morgan, but her left arm was laying across his waist and he woke up as the Duke lifted her from his side, as did she.

"I'm sorry, Morgan, I didn't mean to disturb you," Richard said.

"It's all right, father. All I've done is sleep."

"It's good for you," Andrew said from the doorway. "How are you feeling this morning?"

"Please, may I rise? I promise I will not go running around the castle."

"Very well. No running, and no exercise, apart from those I've given you. How does your shoulder feel this morning?"

"It aches."

Andrew checked the wound and redressed it. "It's healing well. Another couple of days and I think we may be able to let you do a little more. Not much, though, the arrow penetrated deep."

Everyone left apart from Ioan who assisted Morgan to wash and get dressed.

"It's so boring, Ioan, not being able to do anything, except read."

"Are you not able to practice some of your magic?" Ioan asked him quietly.

"Ioan, forgive me, I keep forgetting you know so much about me. Yes, I have been doing some, but at the moment it tires me so quickly." He looked wistfully at his sword, hanging behind the door and went to it, unsheathing it from its scabbard with his left hand.

"Your Grace! Master Andrew said no exercise!"

"That was for my right hand. I should be able to practice with my left, if only for a little while."

Practicing the various movements with his left hand still pulled on his right shoulder, and his movements were clumsy and jerky as he forced himself to continue. He found it extremely frustrating, and after fifteen minutes, threw the sword down in exasperation, swearing, tears forming in his eyes.

"Your Grace, what's wrong?"

Morgan didn't answer him, but left his chambers, slamming the door behind him and ran down the corridor, ignoring the discomfort in his shoulder as he did so. He kept running until he was out of the keep and had found his hiding place in the rose garden, away from prying eyes where he just about remembered to raise his mental barriers so Trahaearn would not be able to locate him before he collapsed onto the ground and sobbed quietly.

Back in his chambers, Ioan panicked. By the time he had opened the door and looked in both directions down the corridor, Morgan had disappeared. Ioan ran down to the banqueting hall. It was empty, he went to the main hall; it was also empty, so he ran back to the private chambers of the Duke of Invermere, hoping he was there.

Trystan looked up in surprise as Ioan knocked on the door and didn't wait for a reply before entering.

"May I be of assistance?"

"The Duke! Where is he?" Ioan gasped.

"He should be with the Duchess in her chambers, why, what's wrong?"

"Are you sure?" Ioan realised he sounded desperate, because he was. "It's the Duke of Rossmere, I fear he may do something...unwise."

"Come, I will guide you," Trystan said, leading the way.

They ran to the other side of the keep and knocked desperately on the Duchess's chamber door. Dilys opened it.

"Is the Duke or Duchess here?" Ioan asked urgently.

"No, they are in Lady Colwyn's chambers. Down the hall on the right."

The two stewards ran in the direction she pointed.

"Your Grace! Your Grace!"

The desperate shouting obtained the desired result and Richard appeared from a chamber.

"What on earth is going on?" he demanded, then realised it was Ioan.

The stewards both did a very quick bow. "Y – Your Grace," Ioan panted. "It's the Duke of Rossmere..." He paused as Richard went pale.

"What's happened?"

"He was trying to practice the sword with his left hand, it wasn't going very well, and he threw it down in frustration and ran off. I have no idea where he may have gone, and he seemed distraught."

Bronwyn appeared, hearing the final sentence. "We must find him," she said.

"Find who?" Colwyn asked joining them.

"Return to your rooms," her mother said.

"Find who!" Colwyn demanded.

"Your brother," Richard answered.

"Morgan's missing?" she asked. "But he's not well."

401

"Exactly."

Richard instigated a search of the entire castle. Colwyn listened quietly; she had a suspicion she knew where he might be but didn't want to tell anyone. If Morgan had run off to hide, that meant he didn't want to be found.

Once everyone had embarked on their search, Colwyn followed at a discrete distance, and went to the rose garden. She knew Morgan had a favourite spot in there, well-hidden out of view. She checked to make sure no one was in sight, ducked in behind a hedge, crawled a little way along until she came to a small break in another hedge and crawled through that. Sure enough, Morgan was in the corner, hunched up, sobbing quietly.

Concerned, she crawled over to him and hugged him tightly. "Don't cry, Morgan," she said softly.

He froze. She had managed to creep up on him without him hearing her. "Go away," he mumbled.

"I'm not leaving you," she said, still hugging him. "What's wrong? Why are you crying? You've always been so strong."

"But that's it. Everyone expects me to be strong! I'm ten years old! I'm a child still. Everyone thinks I'm something special, that I'm destined for great things. I'm constantly being pushed, I want to be me, but I don't know who I am!"

"You're my brother and I love you with all my heart. Let me help you, Morgan, I don't like it when you hurt."

"Oh Colwyn!" he hugged her back with his good arm and buried his head in her shoulder. "I want to run away. I don't want to be what they want me to be."

"I will help you, Morgan. Let me help you, I don't like to see you so upset."

"Bless you, Colwyn. I love you too."

"I want you to get better, Morgan. We can stay here as long as you want."

In the distance, they heard his name being called. They couldn't quite make out who was shouting, so kept quiet, but then they heard Bronwyn's voice, and it sounded desperately anxious.

"Mama sounds worried," Colwyn said.

"She does, doesn't she," he agreed.

"That means she loves you, like I do, Morgan."

"I know, but I'm not ready to go back. Not yet."

"I could go and tell them, but I don't want to leave you."

"I'll be all right, Colwyn. Tell them I'll return in a while; I just need some time to myself."

"You're sure?"

"Yes, I'm sure." He pulled back and kissed her. "I do love you," he said.

She smiled at him and crawled back the way she had come, keeping low so she didn't give his position away, then ran towards the voices.

Morgan watched her go and realised he was feeling lonely now that she was no longer there. He felt the tears welling again and cursed himself for his weakness, not knowing that he may have successfully blocked Trahaearn from finding him, but unconsciously had called for help from his cousin.

Morgan? Colin tentatively asked. *What's wrong?*

The Duke tried to pull himself together, but was failing miserably.

Morgan, you're frightening me! What's wrong? Colin asked again. *Talk to me!*

I – I'm sorry, Colin. I did – didn't mean to disturb you, Morgan finally responded.

I can feel your anguish...it's so great! What's wrong? Tell me!

403

I – I can't do it! I can't be what they want me to be. I don't want to be what they want me to be, but I don't know what I want to be! I don't know who I am! Everyone hates me!

Now you know that isn't true. Everyone doesn't hate you. You know you are loved. I love you too. Tell me what's happened.

Morgan attempted to get control of his emotions, but it all came pouring out. The doubt, the pressure, the fact that the Queen hated him, the attempt on his life. The intensity almost overwhelmed his cousin, but he rode it, absorbed it, let Morgan empty himself until he was exhausted.

It's all right, go on, let it all come out, Colin soothed.

Finally, there was silence.

Morgan? Are you still there?

Y- yes. There was another long period of silence before the Duke contacted him again. *I'm sorry. That was unforgivable. I have disgraced myself.* He felt the tears forming again.

No! No you haven't! That was a release. The pressure had become too much and you had to release it before you exploded. You know I will always help you, as I know you would always help me. Now, do you feel any better?

I – I think I do.

Then I have served my purpose. Where are you?

Hiding in the rose garden where no one can find me, except Colwyn. She's just left me to tell everyone to stop looking for me.

Good. Stay there as long as you need to. She loves you very much, Morgan.

I know. I love her too.

Are you going to be all right? I shall stay with you as long as you need me.

I'll be all right now. That outpouring seems to have made me feel a lot better. Thank you, Colin. I don't know what I would do without you. I love you, cousin.

Then my work is done. Take care, for I love you too, cousin.

Morgan felt Colin slowly withdraw, leaving a feeling of comfort and support behind and the youngster closed his eyes, lay his head on his good arm, and just let the emotion flow out of his body.

ය ෨ ය ෨

"Mama! Mama!"

Bronwyn turned and saw her daughter running towards her. "What are you doing out here?"

"I was looking for Morgan too. Don't worry, he says he will return in a little while, he just needs some time to himself."

"You've found him? Where is he?"

Colwyn shook her head. "I can't tell you, but he's safe and he's all right."

"Tell me where he is!"

Colwyn said nothing and simply shook her head.

"Colwyn, he's hurt! Tell me!"

It was at that point that Richard, Andrew, Stuart and Trahaearn arrived.

"What news?" Richard asked.

"Colwyn knows where he is but won't tell me."

"Daughter, tell us, now!"

"No!"

Stuart stepped forward. "Colwyn, as your King, I order you to tell us where Morgan is."

She looked at him, his eyes were kind, she knew he was worried, but Morgan meant more to her.

"No." There was a long pause before she added, "Your Majesty."

"Colwyn!"

"Morgan says he will return when he's ready. You're all pulling him in every direction, he doesn't know who he is. Why are you trying to break him?"

Their faces showed that her words had gotten through to them.

"Is that what he said?" Bronwyn asked, rather tearfully.

"He wants to be himself. Why won't you let him?"

None of them could answer her question.

"He's ten years old!"

"We're not trying to break him, Colwyn, we're trying to prepare him for his future. He is destined for great things," Stuart told her.

"Well, you've broken him," she told them. "I hope you're pleased!"

She turned and ran away back to the keep, ignoring the calls for her to come back and tell them where Morgan was hiding. They could have caught her very easily, but her words had hit a nerve and they looked uneasily at one another.

"Have we pushed him too hard?" Stuart asked.

"It was necessary," Trahaearn answered simply.

ଔ ଓ ଔ ଓ

Chapter Twenty-Five

It was the cold that finally forced Morgan to move from his hiding place, plus the fact it was getting dark, and he was feeling hungry. He managed to get back into the keep and to his room without being seen but hadn't expected a reception committee waiting for him in there.

It was Bronwyn who saw him first. "Morgan!" she exclaimed, running to him and hugging him tightly, making him wince. "Morgan, we've been so worried!"

He looked round at all of them. "I – I'm sorry," he whispered.

"Why did you hide, my darling?"

"I just wanted to try and find myself."

"Colwyn said you don't know who you are."

"It's true. I don't. I've spent my entire life being who you want me to be, but who am I, really?"

"You're our son, and we love you very much."

"But I'm not really your son, am I?" He immediately regretted saying it as he saw the pain cross Bronwyn's face and her eyes fill with tears.

"You are to me," she said, her voice wavering as she hugged him again.

Colwyn went up to him. "I didn't tell them where you were."

"I know you didn't. Thank you, Colwyn." He turned and hugged her. "You are a wonderful sister."

She beamed at him. "Are you feeling better yet?"

"A little, thank you."

"Morgan," Richard said approaching him. "I'm sorry if we have been too hard on you, but we need to make sure you are prepared for your future. With the King's permission, until you are recovered, we will let you be a ten year old boy." He looked at Stuart, who nodded in agreement.

"Thank you."

"As that is settled, I believe we need to feed our young charge and get him to bed. He has some play time to catch up on," Stuart said kindly. "Good night, young Morgan."

Everyone left and Ioan returned with some food which Morgan made short work of, then Ioan helped him prepare for bed.

"Your Grace, are you truly feeling better? I was really worried about you."

"Thank you, Ioan. I'm sorry if I caused you any concern. I'm worried about my sword arm. I can hardly move it. If I can't fight, what use am I?"

"It's early days, Your Grace. Master Andrew seems very knowledgeable, I believe he thinks everything will turn out all right, but you must be patient. It won't get better overnight. Healing takes time, and the best way you can help that along is to do what he tells you. Now come, into bed."

"Thank you, Ioan," he said again. "You—"

Andrew appeared in the doorway of the bed chamber. "I'm here to check you over before you go to sleep," he said, and sat down on the bed. He removed the bandages and the poultice dressing and inspected the wound. "I think we'll leave it uncovered for tonight and see what it's like in the morning. The poultice has done its work. I will help you with your recovery, Your Grace. Now get some sleep."

ω ɔ ω ɔ

Stuart decided to leave for Ellesmere the following day, but ordered that Morgan should stay at Inver, until he was fit enough to make the journey. Andrew would supervise his recovery. The King left some knights behind to escort him back when the battle surgeon was happy he could make the journey.

Trahaearn went to see the boy before they left and told him to only do what Andrew told him to do. They would pick up where they left off when he finally returned to Ellesmere. Morgan had hugged him goodbye and the Coltranes had waved them off as the King, Queen, Trahaearn and the escort left.

Colwyn was ecstatic at having Morgan at home for longer than had first been thought. When the boy wasn't carrying out the exercises Andrew had given him, or receiving massages to help loosen the muscles, he was allowed to be a normal ten year old child. However, he was surprised to find that after only a few days, he became fed up with this way of life, and returned to what training he was able to do.

Sir John took him under his wing again and helped him work on his sword skills with his left hand, as the boy was unable to even hold a sword in his right, it was just too heavy, so Andrew started him off with a small weight, and gradually increased it until he was again able to hold his sword again.

They stayed a month at Inver and by the time they departed for Ellesmere, Morgan was able to use his right arm fully, albeit not for the period of time as he had before the attack, but Andrew assured him that he would recover his stamina and reminded him how far he had come in the month.

So, towards the end of May, they departed for Ellesmere following a tearful farewell from Bronwyn and Colwyn. Richard had shaken his hand and hugged him and told him he would see him in a couple of weeks, as he would be taking some squires to Ellesmere for the knighting ceremony.

Morgan was welcomed back by Stuart and Trahaearn, along with Cuthbert and the rest of his friends, and the young Duke began to realise that what Bronwyn had said had been true. Not everyone hated him, and he had genuine friends that supported him and lifted his spirits.

ॐ ॐ ॐ ॐ

Chapter Twenty-Six

—•—

Almost two years had passed since Morgan had left for Ellesmere following the attempt on his life, and normal routine carried on at Inver apart from a daily confidential rendezvous that had taken place in a private and hidden location. Now Sir John deemed his secret pupil ready for the next step in their training.

"Giles, I have a special task for you; would you help me?"

"Really?" the boy answered, glowing with pride that Sir John had asked him to assist, rather than any of the other pages.

"You haven't answered my question," the knight added.

"Oh yes, I would be honoured, Sir John."

John smiled, nodded and addressed his other pupils.

"The rest of you are dismissed. Off you go now, I believe Father Jocelyn has something lined up for you."

The other boys groaned. Father Jocelyn taught religious studies. He was very old, very boring and took great pleasure in beating them if they were not paying avid attention to what he was saying.

"You don't want to be late now boys, do you?" John hinted, then smiled to himself as looks of horror appeared on their faces, and they ran as if the devil was after them, to be on time.

Once John was certain there was no one else about, he raised a hand and made a beckoning signal. Giles frowned, wondering what all the mystery was about. He soon found out, as Colwyn approached, appropriately dressed in chainmail and surcoat, carrying a shield

411

and helm; a sword sheathed and buckled around her waist. Her long chestnut hair was tightly plaited, and it was this that the young page had spotted as she confidently walked towards them. Seeing the way she was dressed he immediately had a suspicion of what was about to occur.

"Awww, Sir John, you're not really expecting me to practice with a girl, are you?" he exclaimed in utter disdain and horror, as Colwyn reached them. Giles was the son of the Duke of Strathmere and rather sure of himself and his position. He glared at Colwyn. "Shouldn't you be doing some needlework or something more suited to a girl?"

John MacKenzie turned to him and was just about to make a suitably crushing remark, when there was a dull clanking sound of metal hitting the ground, a blur of colour flashed past him and, before he could intervene, Colwyn had pulled off a leather glove, slapped the young page across the face with it and then dropped it on the ground at his feet.

"Pick it up, if you dare!" she threw back at him, her green eyes aflame with anger at his remarks.

Giles raised a hand to his cheek and gingerly rubbed it.

"Colwyn!" John snapped.

She whirled to face her tutor, her green eyes now displaying pure challenge.

"He insulted me!" she snapped back. "No one insults me and gets away with it!" She turned to Giles once more. "Pick it up...or are you a coward?"

The accusation hurt more than his stinging cheek and red faced, he bent down, retrieved it from the ground and threw it back at her.

"I'm no coward!" he retorted, standing straight backed as he stared down at her. "I accept your challenge!" But he swallowed a little nervously, as he saw her eyes glitter dangerously.

Placing the glove back on her hand, she stepped back to prepare herself for the forthcoming battle.

"Now wait a moment," John interjected. "We will lay down some ground rules! You will both conduct yourselves in a knightly manner. There will be no kicking, no foul moves, and no tricks, or you will forfeit the match. Do I make myself clear?" He glared at both of them for effect.

"Yes, Sir John," Giles answered.

"But of course, Sir John," Colwyn answered in a tone that intimated she did not believe her opponent.

Giles scowled at her as she raised her head and somehow gave the impression she was looking down her nose at him, even though he was several inches taller.

"Put on your helms and stand ready," John ordered.

He watched both of them carefully as they did as they were told. Colwyn then adjusted her shield, whilst Giles picked his up, then both drew their swords and stood ready.

"Salute!" John ordered.

The two youngsters held their swords vertically against their bodies in respect, then lowered them again.

"Begin."

The young page made his first mistake by assuming he would defeat his opponent after just a few strikes. As John indicated for them to start, Giles lunged, only to find that Colwyn was faster on her feet, side-stepped so he missed his target completely and was rewarded with a blow of surprising strength that made him lose his balance and land up in an undignified heap on the ground.

John sighed.

"Giles! Remember the first rule of combat!" he shouted.

The youngster got to his feet and adjusted his shield.

"Never make an assumption about your adversary," he mumbled back, embarrassed about his failure to land the first strike.

"Ah, so you do remember," John replied. "Continue."

Giles tried again, and missed, but on the third attempt, anticipated Colwyn's side-step to the right and made contact with her shield.

They exchanged several strikes before drawing back and circled one another warily.

Colwyn was finding the whole experience both exhilarating and a little frightening. She knew her opponent was taller, heavier and more experienced, but she had speed and suppleness on her side that resulted in Giles not landing as many strikes as he expected to. He wasn't used to her speed; the other boys were slower, and he began to feel exasperation building.

"Stop moving so much!" he shouted at her.

"Why don't you just move faster?" she teased him back.

He tried and managed to land a strike across her back.

Under her helm, Colwyn winced and pulled a face. That had hurt!

Pausing a couple of seconds to calm herself, she launched another attack, pushing Giles back towards the fence.

Up until that point, he had remained conscious of the fact that he was fighting a girl, but with this almost frenzied attack, that thought flew out of the window and he began to fight back.

Sir John let it continue for several minutes before intervening.

"Hold!" he shouted firmly; then seeing that neither of them had either not heard, or were ignoring him, used his own sword to stop them. "I said hold!"

The strength of his intervention forced the pair back in opposite directions, but they did as they were told and stood, breathing heavily, trying to get their breath back.

"Colwyn, are you all right?" John asked her with concern.

"I'm fine!" she gasped back.

"Giles?"

"I'm ready," he replied, his voice sounding strained.

"Very well, continue."

John stepped back out of the way and watched the two parry and counter attack as they moved around the arena. He was pleased to see that Colwyn was giving as good as she got, but she did not yet possess the stamina that Giles did and saw she was beginning to tire. Her opponent also spotted this and started to use this against her.

John finally called a halt to the proceedings, calling the match a draw.

"Well done both of you," he said, as they pulled off their helms so they could breathe more easily. "Now, salute and sheathe your swords."

They both straightened up with difficulty, held their swords vertically against their chests again and then sheathed them.

"Shake hands," John ordered.

Giles paused a fraction of a second before doing as he was told. Colwyn looked down at his outstretched hand, up into his brown eyes, then offered hers and they shook, firmly.

"Colwyn, I will come and check on you later, but for now, it's time for you to return to your rooms."

"Yes, Sir John." She went to curtsey, then caught herself and bowed instead. Turning to Giles, she bowed to him as well. "Thank you for the sword practice," she said softly and gave him a slight smile.

Giles's eyes widened at seeing her expression, but he minded his manners and bowed in return.

"My Lady Colwyn," he replied and straightened up to watch her leave the Pell and head back to her rooms.

"So, young Giles," John said, bringing him out of his stupor. "What have you learnt?"

The young page dragged his eyes from Colwyn's retreating figure and stared up at his mentor.

"I made an assumption that Colwyn was just a silly little girl and would be easily defeated." He paused. "I was wrong," he added quietly. "Sir John, I had no idea that girls could do such things. I thought they were weak, and not capable of such actions."

"And that was nearly your undoing. You may have been taller, stronger and heavier, but she had speed and suppleness that many boys and men do not. Never, ever, underestimate your opponent; it could mean the difference between victory or defeat; life or death. You were quick to notice she favoured a move to the right, and you successfully anticipated that. Observation in battle is vital if you wish to take advantage and win the fight."

Giles nodded. Although to all intent and purposes a training session, Sir John had almost treated the encounter as an actual duel and, as a result, it had felt like a real battle.

"If you ever get the opportunity, you should watch the young Duke of Rossmere. He is an exceptional swordsman, even though he is only twelve, and is as lithe and supple as Colwyn. He will be unbeatable if he continues to improve."

"If I can, I will most certainly try to observe him. Thank you, Sir John...and if you see Colwyn later, would you ask after her, please? I would never intentionally want to hurt her."

"I will do as you ask. Tell me, young Giles, are you smitten with the duchess-in-waiting?"

Giles coloured fiercely.

"No! Of course not!" he replied far too vehemently.

John smiled kindly.

"My mistake, please accept my most sincere apologies," he said laying a hand on the boy's shoulder. "Go on, off you go. By the time you've cleaned your armour and put it away, it will be time to eat. And Giles...not a word to the other boys, do I make myself clear?"

"I give you my word." Giles bowed respectfully, before turning and walking away, his shield on his left arm and his helm tucked under his right.

John shook his head, smiled, and pondered. The lesson had gone better than he had anticipated, and Colwyn had even managed to get her temper under control. That in itself was an achievement, knowing how practically anything could spark it.

She couldn't help it; it was just her make-up. Ever since she had been born, her parents and nursemaid had done their best to help her curb it. Morgan had seemed to have the most influence in that respect and, for a while, after he had left for Ellesmere, it seemed to run amuck, but gradually, she had begun to calm down, and John firmly believed the training and discipline she was undergoing was the key to the control she now had.

He took one last look around and headed for the keep to check on his secret pupil.

A few minutes later, Sarah opened the door, having heard the firm knock.

"Sir John?"

"I came to see how my little princess is," he replied.

"Please, enter. Do you know if she had a fall today? She seems rather tender around the right shoulder."

John thought quickly about how he could reply.

"That's why I came," he finally answered. "She did indeed have a fall. I failed to reach her in time, to prevent it."

"She's been running again, hasn't she," Sarah said more to herself than the knight. "A lady of her standing has no business running anywhere!"

"Don't be too harsh on her, she is but a child with a lot of energy. She was just attempting to release some of it. You and I both know what she's like if…"

"Yes, you are right. Please come in and sit down. I will fetch her."

"Thank you."

The knight sat down on a chair, next to a small table and waited. A few moments passed, then Colwyn appeared.

"Sir John!" She smiled warmly and ran to him to give him a hug. "Thank you for today. I learnt such a lot!"

"Did you now? Give me some examples."

"Well, I know Giles did not take me seriously; so that enabled me to land the first strike. I also noticed he was not as quick as me, but towards the end, when I began to tire, he started to use that to his advantage."

John nodded in satisfaction.

"You did very well today for your first proper encounter. Now, regarding your side-steps, you must practice moving to the left more. I know it's more awkward for you, but I will show you some additional moves you can make to reduce that feeling. I have sworn Giles to secrecy, now what about Sarah?"

Colwyn glanced back towards her bed chamber to make sure her maid was still in there, before answering.

"She still does not know. I managed to get out of my armour and put it all away before she came to my rooms."

"Are you hurt? Giles was most concerned that he may have injured you and asks after you."

"I thank him for his concern, I think I shall have a bruise across my back, and my right arm is rather sore. I haven't fought for that length of time before."

"Mmmm, we must be careful. Should the Duke or Duchess find out, there will be hell to pay!"

"We've managed to keep it a secret for two years now. I still don't understand why girls can't fight, but I thank you for teaching me."

"Ladies of any description are known as the fairer sex, and thus are to be protected by men, for they are gentle, and should do women's work, be married and bear children. That is their role in life."

"But it's not fair!"

"Life is seldom fair, dear Colwyn."

"Would you...would you be ashamed to have me fighting at your side, Sir John?"

"I pray it never comes to that," he began, then hastily carried on as he saw her expression of disappointment, "but, if it were to occur, I would be both honoured and proud to have you by my side. War is not glorious, Colwyn. Remember that. It is a horror that someone of your gentle breeding should never be subjected to. It requires the taking of another life and I have purposely not given you that test."

"What test?"

"To take a life. The boys will practice on chickens and rabbits."

"But they are innocent!"

"True, but they are also food and part of our staple diet, that is why they are chosen as targets, for they can be eaten afterwards. To that extent and purpose, it is not a needless death."

Colwyn's face fell as she contemplated the killing of a large-eyed, fluffy, cute rabbit, or even a chicken.

"I must pass the test," she said sorrowfully.

"Perhaps eventually, but we need to work on your stamina and your horsemanship. I think we also need to discuss your current pony. You require a new mount, something that will be able to serve you for a few years."

"Romaine has given me loyal service."

"I know. He was also Morgan's mount before becoming yours, but he is getting rather old now, to be carrying you and your armour."

"Then I will put him out to pasture to live out his final years. He would like that."

"I'm sure he will. I will speak to His Grace about a new mount for you."

"May I come with you to choose it?"

"If the Duke allows it, then yes."

"I will mention it at dinner tonight." Colwyn was about to say something else, when Sarah returned from the bed chamber.

"My Lady, it is time for you to change for dinner," she said.

Colwyn sighed and nodded, then faced John again.

"Thank you for coming to see me, Sir John."

"My pleasure as always, and Colwyn, ladies are not supposed to run and trip over, remember that."

For a fraction of a second she started to frown, then the penny dropped, and again she gave a fine acting performance and looked shame faced.

"I apologise for my un-ladylike behaviour, but I was in a hurry!"

John smiled at her and patted her hand.

"Until tomorrow," he whispered, then stood up, bowed, and left the room.

That night, dinner was served in the Duke's private chambers. After they had eaten, Colwyn decided to broach the subject of a new pony.

"Papa, you know Sir John is helping me with my riding, well...he thinks Romaine is too small for me now, and that I need something taller."

Richard looked at her and breathed deeply.

"Let us see what August brings us," he replied.

"August! But that's two months away! I can't wait that long!"

"You can, young lady, and you will. You need to learn patience. You cannot have everything you want immediately. I think we have over indulged you."

"But how can I learn, when I don't have the proper equipment?"

"Romaine is quite capable of serving you another couple of months. You are not going to grow that much in so short a time."

Colwyn pouted and folded her arms, indicating her displeasure.

"It's not fair! How can I improve when—"

"Life isn't fair. Remember, you are in a privileged position, but you should never, ever, take anything for granted. You should be grateful for what you have, for the majority have very little, or nothing at all."

"Mama…" she turned to Bronwyn, hoping to obtain support.

"Your father has spoken, Colwyn. As he has said, August is not that far away. Besides…" she carried on quickly, recognising the signs of an approaching temper tantrum, "…your father has some other news."

The impending tirade ebbed immediately as Colwyn turned to face the Duke, her expression displaying curiosity.

"Papa?" she prompted.

"We have received news from the King. He is paying us a visit, along with the Queen and your brother."

"Morgan! When? When?"

"The end of July or beginning of August."

Colwyn's eyes lit up and she clapped her hands with glee at the thought of seeing him again after two years.

"I will need you to conduct yourself accordingly when Morgan and our guests are here. I expect that temper to be under control, and you to act in a disciplined fashion, as befitting your station. Failure to conduct yourself in the appropriate manner will result in no new horse, until you can convince me that you can control that temper of yours. Do you understand me?"

"Yes, Papa."

"Good, because I will not have you embarrass this house, or Morgan, with your tantrums."

"Yes, Papa," Colwyn repeated meekly. "I understand."

She looked at him from under her long lashes, her green eyes huge and mournful.

Richard managed to hold his stern expression for longer than he thought capable when she looked at him in that way, and after five seconds, he felt the sternness start to leave his face.

Colwyn smiled tentatively, then looked at her mother again.

"I would like to make something for Morgan...and the King and Queen, if I may?"

"I think an embroidered or lace-edged handkerchief for each of them will suffice," Bronwyn said kindly.

Colwyn nodded in agreement, just as a respectful knock on the door sounded.

"Ah, that will be Sarah," Bronwyn almost said to herself. "Enter."

She was right. Sarah entered and curtseyed.

"Time for bed, Colwyn," Bronwyn confirmed.

The child rose from her chair in a dignified manner, kissed her mother's cheek, then moved to the other side of the table and kissed her father.

"Goodnight, Mama, Papa."

"Goodnight, Colwyn," Bronwyn said.

"Goodnight, my dear," Richard replied, and they both watched as she left the room. "Tantrum averted," Richard added, pouring himself another goblet of wine.

"She is getting better at controlling her temper," Bronwyn countered, "but I still don't understand where it came from."

"It must be on your side of the family," Richard teased once more, refilling her goblet, and smiling broadly as her hazel eyes flashed a warning.

 C3 80 C3 80

"So, what did Sir John want you for?" a boy named Lewis asked Giles as they sat at the table to eat their evening meal.

"Extra training," Giles was able to answer truthfully.

"But you're better than I am! Why should you need more training?"

"I think it's because I'm a future Duke. I have to lead by example," he replied. He'd been thinking about excuses he could make should his friends ask him, since John had dismissed him.

"I guess that makes sense. How did it go?"

"Not as well as it should have," Giles replied, thinking back on the episode. He had really expected Colwyn to be easily defeated, but she had given him the battle of his life, so far. On one hand he was ashamed that he had not managed to win easily, but on the other hand, he found he was developing a rather warm feeling for the girl, and hoped he would be able to see her again soon.

"Giles!" Lewis almost shouted at him, bringing him out of his reverie and making him jump. "You were miles away! I said, in what way?"

"Pardon?"

"You said it didn't go as well as it should have. In what way?"

"I assumed I would win very easily, and it wasn't so."

"Was it anyone we know?"

"No; but I won't make the same mistake again. How did the lesson with Father Jocelyn go?" Giles said, abruptly changing the subject.

"He nearly fell asleep. Conor wanted to throw something at him and wake him up."

"I did not!" a light brown haired boy with brown eyes shouted back from further down the table. "It was tempting though."

Everyone giggled, but Giles stopped laughing first. He was still thinking about his chestnut haired opponent, and he dreamed of her that night when he went to sleep.

Giles was given the duty of training with Colwyn for the foreseeable future, until she was good enough to hold her own against the other pages. John had personally taken charge of teaching her to ride, as he had done with Morgan all those years previously. When she had managed to learn the skills necessary to control her horse without the use of reins, he had then begun training with the lance. Currently though she had reached her limit with Romaine. The pony was getting older, and he simply was not up to performing as was required. Colwyn was quickly outgrowing him, and she needed something taller and faster to master the rings. That itself would be a challenge, she was collecting the rings with ease on Romaine, but her new pony would present her with fresh obstacles. It would be interesting to see how she would adapt.

He had spoken with the Duke regarding a new pony and Richard had told him a new one would be provided for her on her birthday. John did not press the matter; the Duke was no fool and would be suspicious if he pushed to obtain one earlier. So he decided to borrow a larger pony from the stables and get Colwyn to train it. It would be excellent practice for when she got her new one.

ℭ ℬ ℭ ℬ

The King and Queen had been touring Devonmere for the past couple of months, visiting a number of duchies, and their final stop was Invermere. Morgan had not accompanied them but had returned to Rossmere as part of his ducal duties for an update from his steward, but they rendezvoused at Inver for the return journey to Ellesmere. They spent a couple of days relaxing before returning to the capital to resume their duties. Colwyn was disappointed that Morgan could not stay longer, but even just a very short visit was better than none at all.

She had presented the three guests with the Inver laced handkerchiefs she had made and in return, Alexandra had given Colwyn a necklace, as she had taken a great liking to the young child. She still did not like the fact that she and Morgan seemed inseparable when they were together, but wisely kept silent, and wondered what Bronwyn would think if she suggested that the child join the court at Ellesmere in a couple of years, to start seeking out a suitable husband for her. Hopefully by then, she too would have a child of her own to dote on.

Colwyn spent some time thinking a great deal about Morgan after the royal party had left. She had become aware of the Queen's dislike of her brother and went to the library to do some research. It was then she found out about the Kadeau Reign of Terror, and that the Ulrich family had been hit particularly hard and had had to flee Devonmere for their lives.

Having discovered that, she then started to read about the Kadeau, very much like her mother had done all those years previously and about the magic they had performed. Following Morgan's near breakdown, she was determined to find out all she could, so that she would be able to support him better in the future should he need it.

The entire tour and journey back to Ellesmere had been uneventful, for which Stuart was thankful, but it had been tiring, so the couple of days of total relaxation at Inver had been a much welcome break before returning to courtly duties, and all the pressures that came with running a kingdom.

CR & CR &

Bishop Douglas was nagging Stuart again about an heir to Devonmere. He did it on a regular basis, but the period between these gentle reminders seemed to be getting shorter and shorter. The King had continually fobbed him off with one excuse or another, but it was getting to the stage where James would not back down about it.

"Sire, you must have an heir! This current situation cannot continue. The line still rests with Prince Michael should the unexpected occur and something happen to you. You must address this situation as soon as possible."

Somehow, Stuart managed to keep his temper in check, and came up with yet another delaying tactic.

"After the knighting ceremony at the end of June, I will give it my full attention. Will that be acceptable?" Stuart had finally snapped. "I've got too much on my mind at the moment."

The bishop sighed. He was not happy at this piece of news, but finally nodded in agreement. At least he had managed to get an approximate date out of his King! "That will be acceptable, Your Majesty," he replied.

Stuart then thought he would stop pestering him about it, but he was wrong. The bishop switched to giving him polite reminders about the agreed date to work on the issue of providing the heir.

Finally midsummer arrived, Richard returned to Ellesmere with the news that Bronwyn was carrying another child, and he hoped the King would forgive him, but he planned to return to Inver straight after the tournament to be with his wife to support her, having lost their first son at six months through the term. Stuart understood and said he would pray for the safe delivery of their child.

The knighting ceremony and tournament completed successfully. Colin McLeod was knighted that year, much to the delight of his parents, and his cousin. Shortly after, his proposed marriage to the Lady Eilidh was announced. Colin seemed very happy about it and told Morgan that he loved her very much. Richard left Ellesmere to return to Inver and Stuart did indeed pray that Bronwyn would successfully carry a child to full term and safely give birth.

Following yet another reminder from his bishop that the knighting ceremony was now over, and he had promised to do something about providing an heir, Stuart visited his queen in her chambers that night. He'd been thinking of the issues the Coltranes were having, and finally decided that he ought to keep his promise and do something about his own, just in case Alexandra also had issues carrying a child to term. Up until that point, he had been extremely careful with regard to his visits to his wife, not wanting her to fall, but that time was now over. Devonmere needed an heir, and he would now fulfil his duty.

"Sire," Alexandra said curtseying as he came into her chambers.

"My Queen," he responded. He dismissed her maid. They were alone.

Even now, after all this time, she was still shy in his presence. He had never forced himself upon her, and she now found herself looking forward to his visits, for he awakened feelings and desires in her that she had not believed possible. Was he now the man of her dreams? More importantly, did she now love him? She believed she did.

Stuart asked a lot of her that night, as he possessed her body time and time again, on each occasion bringing her to complete fulfilment until she thought she might die from the pleasure, but it resulted in the required outcome.

A few months later, it was confirmed that the Queen was with child, and James Douglas fell silent, and instead prayed for the safe deliverance of a young prince to continue the Cantrell line.

The pregnancy continued, and by February, there was just a month left to go, but sad news had reached them, due to the mildness of the weather enabling a messenger to reach Ellesmere, that Bronwyn had again lost her baby, and both the Duke and Duchess were distraught with the loss of yet another son.

છ ૪ છ ૪

Chapter Twenty-Seven

——◆——

The changes began the winter before Morgan's fourteenth birthday. The first one affected his voice, he found on occasion it suddenly started dropping in pitch, then returned to its normal higher tone. The periods of this drop in pitch gradually became more frequent and Trahaearn had great delight in informing him that his body was changing, and he was becoming a man.

Following on from this, he underwent a substantial spurt of growth that actually made his joints ache and was rather painful. Andrew spent a great deal of time massaging his limbs to help ease his discomfort.

By Christmas, his voice had broken and was developing into a rich, deep sound. The inflections within it were expressive and on occasions, almost hypnotising. But he wasn't worried about his voice anymore, he was able to hold a tune again, and could once again sing in church. When he had been younger, he had often sung to Colwyn; it seemed to help calm her down when she was beginning to get agitated about something.

It was his wild mood swings that were beginning to concern him. Normally even tempered, he was finding that the most trivial of things could trigger an overreaction, far above what was necessary, and it unnerved him.

So far he had managed to regain control of himself before losing his calm completely and no damage had been done, but he was a Kadeau.

It was vital he remain composed, not only for his own safety, but for all those around him.

Both Trahaearn and Aunt Mereli had emphasised the importance of control. The knight had been especially hard on him, because of his future position. He had also set him a task to read a book that detailed examples of Kadeau who had over-stepped the line and carried out terrible things which resulted in the majority of them being hunted down, murdered, or burnt at the stake. There was one individual who had been hung, had his private parts cut off, drawn and then burnt whilst still alive.

That particular example had made Morgan shudder and he fought hard to master his feelings, as he didn't want that to happen to him; not that any of the Cantrells had ever burnt, hung or drawn anyone. Beheaded, but not the others.

Trahaearn had increased his training in an effort to help release any pent up emotions that lurked within the boy's body, but his current training companions were no longer suitable opponents, as his skill was far advanced above what they possessed. Training with Stuart and the knight had been more of a challenge, and with his increase in height, he was at last beginning to hold his own against the two of them, which gave him the incentive to work harder.

Reaching his fourteenth birthday meant he was promoted from page to squire. His studies in reading, writing, strategy continued, along with court etiquette and he had also had to learn how to dance, much to his dismay. In Morgan's case, being of royal blood, also meant he assisted Stuart when the King held court, and more lowly duties as ensuring Stuart's armour and his horse were taken care of by his steward and the pages. His duties were not the same as other squires because of his standing, but he did still run errands and assist Stuart when required.

Due to his improvements with the sword, Stuart had also increased his training, despite the awful weather. It was a very chilly February morning; the ground was frozen and rather slippery. Morgan was undergoing a heavy training session with Stuart when it hit him. The excruciating pain in his head stopped him cold, allowing the King to land a significantly heavy blow that knocked the young squire to his knees. Morgan dropped his sword, clutched his head and groaned loudly.

"Morgan!" Stuart sheathed his sword and ran to his side, kneeling by the now collapsed Duke who was writhing in agony on the frozen ground. "Morgan!" the King said anxiously. He attempted to cradle the youngster in his arms, but the boy was thrashing around, almost screaming.

Trahaearn appeared and ran over to assist Stuart in stopping Morgan from writhing and possibly hurting himself.

"What's happened, Sire?" the knight asked.

"I don't know. One minute we were training, then he suddenly froze as I was delivering a blow... he's in agony! But I didn't strike his head."

Trahaearn pulled Morgan's helm off and clasped his head, desperately trying to position his fingers for initiating a meld, but the youth was continuing to roll in pain.

"Morgan!" Trahaearn shouted. "Let me help you...hold still!"

The knight finally managed to position his fingers on the Duke's face and started to gently probe his mind. Trahaearn suddenly gasped and almost broke contact, but hung on, gritting his teeth to gain control, as tears sprung from Morgan's eyes.

Stuart was now extremely alarmed. He spied a nearby page and shouted at him to find Master Andrew, quickly.

Trahaearn grunted with the effort, and suddenly, Morgan stopped moving, but his chest was heaving, and he was trembling violently. A number of minutes passed before Trahaearn relaxed a fraction, but maintained his link with the Duke, then Andrew arrived and knelt by them. By now, there was also a small trickle of blood coming from Morgan's nose.

"A seizure?" Andrew questioned, as he searched through his ever present medical bag.

"N – no," Trahaearn managed to gasp. "I – I nearly have control... wait..."

Another couple of minutes passed, then Morgan's eyelids flickered a number of times and opened. He was still breathing hard, gasping for breath, but he was no longer trembling.

Trahaearn looked into his eyes. *Are you all right now?* he mentally asked the boy. *Have you regained control?*

Y – yes...thank you Trahaearn, he sent back.

The knight carefully removed his fingers from Morgan's face and nodded at him.

The Duke was suddenly aware of two other extremely worried faces looking at him, and he swallowed a number of times.

"Your Grace, how do you feel? Can you explain what happened?" Andrew asked.

Carefully, Stuart attempted to raise Morgan into a sitting position. The movement made his stomach churn and he retched, but nothing came up.

"Steady, don't move him anymore, Sire," Andrew instructed.

A number of other squires had started to gather, and Stuart glared at them. "Return to your duties!" he barked, and they all fled.

"I – I'm s – sorry," Morgan whispered. He wiped his eyes with a sleeve, then aware of an odd feeling under his nose, touched his skin there and his eyes widened at the sight of blood on his fingers.

"Do you feel up to telling us what happened?" Stuart asked gently.

"W - we were training when...when my mind was hit by an overpowering feeling of loss and...grief that kept breaking over me like waves on the shore. I - I've never felt anything like it before, it was totally overwhelming and I couldn't stop it...it's still there, but Trahaearn has helped me gain control...It's from my cousin, Colin... his intended is...is dead..." Morgan stopped, unable to go on.

Trahaearn continued. "We don't know the facts," he said, "But the Lady Eilidh is dead. Colin must have loved her very much for such an intense reaction to have struck Morgan that hard. The cousins are close, I know, but they appear to have forged an almost brotherly connection. I can sense Duchess Mereli, she has stepped in to assist Colin."

"How do you feel now, Your Grace?" Andrew asked.

"I - I have control now. The grief is overwhelming, but it is diminishing. Aunt Mereli is gaining control of Colin." He took a deep breath to steady himself.

"We will need to do more training on shielding," Trahaearn said softly. "I will admit, the strength of that 'attack' for want of a better word, took me by surprise also. Your cousin thinks a great deal of you Morgan, it was a plea for help."

"And I - I failed him."

"No, you didn't. You absorbed some of his grief, so you did help him even though he incapacitated you."

"If this is what grief feels like on the loss of a loved one, than I shall shield myself from all feeling," Morgan mumbled.

"That is not healthy," Trahaearn countered. "You must feel; happy, sad, angry. You cannot and must not block them out completely. It will drive you to madness."

"I think you should take it easy for the rest of today," Andrew said.

"Agreed," Stuart added. "We will take you to your chambers, then Master Andrew will give you something to relax you. We can train tomorrow."

"Are you able to stand?" Andrew asked.

Trahaearn and Stuart assisted Morgan slowly to his feet. He was very unsteady, so Trahaearn placed Morgan's arm around his shoulders and his own arm around the Duke's waist. Andrew picked up Morgan's sword and helm, and they all walked slowly back to the Duke's chambers.

Ioan wasn't there, so Trahaearn and Andrew helped Morgan out of his armour, then assisted him down onto his bed. The battle surgeon mixed up a concoction of herbs in wine and made the Duke drink it. They all stayed until sleep overtook him, then Stuart and Trahaearn left. Andrew remained until Ioan returned and explained the situation to him.

"I will keep watch, Master Andrew and send for you should things take a turn for the worse."

"I will return this evening to confirm that His Grace has completely recovered.

"Thank you, Master Andrew."

Ioan waited until the battle surgeon had left, then went through to the bed chamber. Morgan was dead to the world, his features totally relaxed thanks to the potion Andrew had given him. The steward pulled off his master's boots, then covered him with a blanket, before leaving him to sleep undisturbed.

ം⁊ ⁊ ⁊ ⁊

"Trahaearn, you've really never come across that before?" the King asked his protector as they walked back to the Pell.

"Not that strong, My Liege. It appears Colin is a powerful Kadeau also, but that is to be expected as his mother is Mereli McLeod."

"I wonder what happened to the Lady Eilidh," Stuart mused.

"Whatever it was, it is tragic. Colin loved her very much."

"Love and relationships seem to weaken us...have you ever loved, Trahaearn?"

There was a period of silence whilst the knight contemplated what to say.

"Once Sire," he finally replied, "but I realised that my position would keep me away from home for long periods."

"Your intended could have come to Ellesmere, Trahaearn."

"I did not think it would be fair on her, Sire."

"Do you still keep in touch? Do you know where she is?"

"She still lives in a small village on the borders of Ellesmere and Strathmere."

"Did she marry someone else?"

There was another long pause.

"I apologise, it's none of my business, but you have been of great service to both my father and me. I would like...like to see you have some happiness in your life."

Trahaearn sighed. "As far as I know she has never married."

Stuart stopped and turned to face his protector. "Send for her, Trahaearn. We will make her welcome here. Your position as my protector will be ending in a couple of years, when Morgan takes over. I would like you to stay here though, as a trainer, but if you wish to go elsewhere I would understand. Please, write to her, ask your lady to come."

"I...I will think on it Sire."

Stuart nodded, accepting the knight's response for the moment, but was determined that his protector should have some happiness in his later years; someone to share his life with.

છ ૪ છ ૪

Morgan was just beginning to stir when Master Andrew returned to check on him. The surgeon pushed him firmly back to lie flat on the bed.

"You're not moving from this bed until I'm satisfied that you have recovered," Andrew said sharply. "Some kind of mental interaction that results in you collapsing in agony and causing a nosebleed must be taken seriously."

"I feel all right now," Morgan protested.

"Headache?"

"No."

"Blurred vision?"

"No."

"Any more bleeding?"

"No!"

Andrew looked in his eyes and decided they looked normal enough. "Very well, you may get up, but no strenuous exercise for the rest of the day, and gradually work up to it tomorrow." He paused before speaking in a whisper. "You frightened all of us. We thought we were losing you."

"I'm tougher than I look," Morgan responded, sitting up and swinging his legs over the edge of the bed. "Where are my boots?"

"Here," Andrew replied bending over to pick them up from the other side of the bed and handing them to him.

Morgan pulled them on and went through to his day room. Ioan was just setting his supper on the table.

"Your Grace, I'm pleased to see you up and about."

"Thank you Ioan." He turned to Andrew. "Will you both join me?"

The two men gave a start.

"Your Grace..." Ioan began nervously.

"Come, sit with me. I insist."

"Thank you, Your Grace," Andrew said.

They waited for Morgan to sit, then did so themselves.

"I want to thank you both for your support," he said.

"We serve with pleasure, Your Grace," Ioan said softly.

"I have something to say, so please hear me out before responding." He paused as the two men frowned at him. "I am...becoming a man. My voice has broken, my body is undergoing changes that I do not wholly understand, and I am finding I am having issues controlling my emotions, so I want to apologise in advance if I seem short tempered—"

"—Never apologise, Your Grace," Ioan broke in.

"Thank you, Ioan, but you have been with me seven years now and I wouldn't want to lose you—either of you. I need...grounding. I know this is unheard of, but when we are alone, would you call me Morgan?"

"Your Grace!" Andrew exclaimed. "We cannot do that; we are not your equals."

"Please. It will help me. I need you both to help me get through this...transition. This is the only way I know that may help."

"If it will help you, then it would be my honour, Your...Morgan," Ioan said correcting himself.

"I too would be honoured...Morgan."

The young Duke gave them one of his rare smiles. "Thank you. Come, let's enjoy our meal."

"Methinks I should have brought more food back with me," Ioan said as he retrieved two further goblets and filled them with wine.

"I'm not overly hungry," Morgan replied.

"As your battle surgeon, I must insist you eat something," Andrew stated firmly.

Morgan laughed then, and his two companions looked at him in shock. They had never heard him laugh. Andrew looked hard at him.

"What?" Morgan questioned.

"Are you sure you're not an imposter? In my four years in your service I have never heard you laugh!"

"Yes I have."

"No Morgan, you haven't," Ioan came back with. "You may have given us a smile now and again, but you are the most serious person I have ever met. I assume it is to fuel the persona you are trying to portray? If I may speak frankly." He paused until Morgan nodded. "If you are attempting to instil fear over those you meet, you are succeeding. It doesn't affect those you have known a long time, like your family, the King, Andrew and me, but to others, your ruse is working."

Morgan considered his words. "You are correct," he finally confessed. "I thought as the Kadeau are feared anyway, and as I am to be the King's protector it might help keep him safe."

"Then I too confirm it's working," Andrew said. "We will keep you grounded."

Morgan reached out and took their hands. "Thank you, my friends."

They finished their meal in silence, thinking their own thoughts and were suddenly brought back to the present by a sharp knock at the door. Andrew and Ioan jumped to their feet, and the latter moved to open the door. It was the King. Ioan bowed.

"Your Majesty, please come in."

Morgan got to his feet and bowed, along with Andrew.

"Sire," the Duke said.

"I wanted to check that you have recovered after this afternoon's incident."

"I can confirm that His Grace is fit and well, Your Majesty," Andrew replied. "I have recently checked him over."

"That is good news." He spied the three goblets on the table but made no mention of it. "In which case, I will bid you good evening. Morgan, you will attend me at the council session in the morning. I will see you there an hour after sunrise."

"As you command, Sire." Morgan bowed again.

"It will afford you the experience of dealing with politicians!" Stuart gave them all a rueful smile and left.

"Morgan, the King is very astute. I think he spied the three goblets," Ioan said.

The Duke looked at him. I don't care," he said. "What happens in my chambers is my affair, what goes on in here, stays in here."

With the meal finished, Morgan dismissed his two companions. He needed to try and contact his cousin, if only to offer moral support and let him know he was not alone, and he didn't want anyone else around when he attempted it. Carefully he sent a tenuous request.

Colin...I am here. If you need support, or to talk, or to release your grief, then I offer my support. Know that you are not alone.

He didn't really expect a response due to Colin's overwhelming grief. He just hoped his cousin would hear the support that was being offered and draw some comfort from it.

Morgan. It was a tightly controlled reply. The Duke heaved a sigh of relief. *I apologise cousin, I believe I caused you great pain earlier.*

Colin, there is nothing to apologise for. You received shocking news...news you never expected to hear. Just know I am willing to help in any way I am able.

Just knowing you are here is sufficient. Mother is helping me. I confess I am beyond heartbroken... Eilidh and I were to be wed shortly now that I have been knighted. But I feel my life is over.

Colin, I know it hurts, Eilidh will always be in your heart and will never be forgotten as long as we remember her. The pain will fade with time; it may never disappear, but eventually it becomes bearable.

As always cousin, you offer wise words of comfort. It warms my heart. It is early days. I don't know what I am going to do yet.

Do?

I will never find another such as her, I may go into the church.

Please don't make hasty decisions. Give yourself time, please.

I will heed your words. Do not worry about me, mother is by my side...I have to go now.

Please keep me appraised. Don't be a stranger. Take care, Colin.

And you, Morgan.

The link was broken, which immediately lifted the grief that Colin allowed to trickle through the bond, although a little of it still lingered, leaving Morgan feeling sad as he prepared for bed that night.

Morgan still knew nothing of the tragic circumstances of Eilidh's death. He hoped it had been an accident and that Colin would have no one to seek vengeance on.

CB & CB &

The next morning, Morgan sat as an observer at Stuart's side in the council chamber. Compared to where the King held his daily court, this room was much smaller and consisted of a long table that was able to seat eight people comfortably. In addition to the King, council meetings were attended by the bishop, head steward, captain of the guard, the officer of finance and three other officers of station within the castle, who all provided advice and guidance to him. Stuart was not obliged to follow that advice, but he did listen and consider it.

There were a couple of heated discussions between his advisors and Stuart let them argue as he listened to both sides, then intervened and made his decision. Morgan hoped his advisors at Rossmere would be less argumentative but then thought they might try to rule him rather than the other way around because of his age. He had to be firm and decisive when holding council.

Finally Stuart dismissed them and once his advisors had left the room stretched and rubbed the back of his neck.

"Are you all right, Sire?" Morgan asked.

The King nodded his head from side to side, heard a couple of clicks in the bones of his neck and looked at the Duke.

"I don't know why, but these meetings always make me tense. I think it's because I expect some form of disagreement or battle every time. I'm just trying to relieve the tightness. But tell me, how are you feeling this morning?"

"I am well, thank you, Sire. I managed to talk with Colin last night. He says he will never find another like Eilidh and is thinking of joining the church."

"That will be a shame, he was only knighted last June and showed a great deal of promise."

"I asked him not to be hasty and take his time."

"That's all you can do, Morgan. At the end of the day, it is his decision what he wishes to do with his life."

The boy nodded thoughtfully.

"I believe Trahaearn wants you at the Pell as soon as you are able."

"At the Pell? But at this time of day, he is with the senior squires."

"He thinks you are ready to take on some more experienced opponents and frankly, I do too. You've grown considerably in height;

your skills can easily compete with them. You'd best suit up and get there as soon as you are able."

"At once, Sire." Morgan ran to his rooms and donned his armour. Ioan handed him his sword, shield and helm, and the youngster left for the Pell.

Trahaearn had decided to give Morgan more of a challenge and invited him to join the older squires, because the boy was now equal in height to many of them, but still shorter than those that were due to be knighted in June.

Morgan was immediately aware of the mixed reception as he arrived at the Pell. A couple of the boys welcomed him, most were indifferent, and a few were downright hostile.

For the first few visits, Morgan trained with boys who were up to a year older. The majority he defeated with ease; with a couple he had to work harder, but still won. Trahaearn smiled, decided he would let him battle with the older squires and pulled the boy aside.

"Morgan, tomorrow I am going to assign you to the oldest group. You now need opponents that will challenge you to your limit, to develop your skills further. Obviously, these boys are taller, more experienced and stronger, but you have the ability, the suppleness and the skills to defeat them. I have every confidence in you."

"Thank you, Trahaearn. The prospect both excites and concerns me. I know I've reached a turning point in my swordsmanship. I have been unbeaten now for just over a month against my peers and it's a record I would like to keep, so I am nervous."

"There is one squire you need to be especially aware of. Taliesan Prescott, the Duke of the Eastern Marches second son."

"Is he not the Duke?" Morgan queried.

"The King has so far withheld the title, until he is sure that Taliesan is worthy and capable of holding the title."

Hearing this piece of news Morgan realised that could result in resentment against him. After all, he had been a Duke since he was ten and Taliesan still had not been acknowledged.

"He is the top swordsman of his year, but he is arrogant, and that is his weakness. He also has a reputation to uphold, for he too has been unbeaten since he became a squire. He will be your toughest opponent, but you can defeat him, providing you stay calm and use your head and the knowledge that has been imparted to you. We will begin tomorrow, but Morgan, you should be aware, that Taliesan may hold a grudge, because you were the cause of Owain Prescott's death."

Morgan swallowed and nodded. "And I was made Duke at ten." He was pleased he had been practicing hard and that he had finally mastered the intricate moves that both Richard and Stuart had taught him, much to Trahaearn's intense displeasure, but more than that, the young Duke could perform the manoeuvre with either his left or right hand and was currently learning to do it with both hands at the same time.

☙ ❧ ☙ ❧

March arrived along with some harsh weather. Snow fell, the winds blew, and the temperature dropped well below freezing. The court fell silent as no one ventured far to put their pleas to the King. It was impossible to train outside, so small groups practiced in the banquet hall and any spare space they could find.

Alexandra had finally been moved into the birthing chamber in preparation for the birth of her child, and on a freezing March morning, she went into labour.

Stuart had paced up and down the corridor, hearing her cries and screams. After seven hours he had gone down to the private chapel to pray for the safe delivery of the child and that Alexandra come through the ordeal safely. Morgan, Trahaearn and the bishop had joined him until he returned to his pacing along the corridor and finally, another three hours later, and one final scream, the child was delivered.

It went deathly quiet, and Stuart found himself holding his breath. No sound. He felt panic rising and was just about to start banging on the chamber door when a baby's cry was heard. The relief was almost overwhelming. Now all he needed to know was...son or daughter?

Another thirty minutes passed and then the door opened, and a midwife jumped back surprised at seeing the King already standing so close.

"Your Majesty!" the midwife almost shrieked. She recovered herself quickly. "Please come in." She stood back and he walked in.

Alexandra was sitting up in bed, holding a bundle wrapped in blankets in her arms. She looked exhausted but smiled tentatively at him as he approached.

"Sire," she said as he sat down by her side on the bed. "You have a son." She handed him over and Stuart found himself looking down at a sleeping baby.

"He is...well?"

"He is perfect, Your Majesty," another midwife said.

"And how fare you, Alexandra."

"Tired, very tired and in some discomfort."

"I am proud of you, my love." He leant forward and kissed her. "As you are tired, I will leave you to rest. I must just take the baby for a short while, but I will return him."

Word was sent and the cathedral bells were rung announcing the birth. As a result of this, despite the weather, a crowd gathered in the upper bailey and Stuart took his son, and presented him to the people, holding him aloft as he stood at the top of the steps to the keep.

"I present to you my son. Llewellyn Rhisart Gruffydd Richard Cantrell."

The crowd cheered, then Stuart took the baby back into the warmth of the keep and returned him to his mother. He then ordered anyone within the castle who was available to report to the banqueting hall, and a lot of celebratory drinking was done.

For a moment, Stuart was sad, as he thought of Richard and Bronwyn. Would it feel as if salt was being spread on the wound to hear that he had a son, the first time of asking, and they had lost two? Stuart prayed extra hard that night in the chapel that God would see fit to grant them their wish of a son.

The christening took place a couple of days before the next midsummer's eve. Richard came, but Bronwyn refused. Her despair continued and hearing that the King had his son, seemed to make it worse. Stuart named them as God parents, along with Morgan, and Prince Michael. Alexandra was not happy that Morgan had been named at the christening. He promised along with the others present to protect and cherish the child, but the Queen resented it, although she said nothing.

The ceremony was difficult for Richard, as his mind kept drifting to the two sons he had lost, but he had been deeply moved that Stuart had included his name within the future King's names.

With the christening complete, life returned to as normal as it could within the confines of the castle.

埃 ꙮ ꙮ ꙮ

Morgan found that training turned out to be a lot harder against the older squires, but that made it all the more rewarding. He did his best to keep Trahaearn's mental teachings to the fore, which helped him remain relatively calm during the more difficult sessions. He observed, he learnt, he stored the knowledge, calling upon it when required.

He started his training with the worst member of that particular class and slowly worked his way up to the best. There were twenty-eight squires in their final year. If he could manage to defeat all of them, he would be deemed the best squire with two years still to go. Then, only the knights, Trahaearn and the King would be between him and the title of best swordsman in the kingdom.

Morgan also grew excited at the prospect of a real training session with Trahaearn, Stuart, and even Richard, when he was next at Ellesmere.

Over the next few weeks, Morgan worked his way through the squires. The first few he beat with ease, but it gradually became harder and more difficult, and he had to call on all his skill, but so far he was managing to hold his own and defeat his opponents.

With only the last six squires left, it became exceedingly tough, and Morgan was finishing the days with bruises, aches and pains as he continued to fight his way to the top.

Finally, only Taliesan Prescott was left, and he was concerned. His title was under threat by the young Kadeau but he wasn't going to let the brat win. Taliesan had his followers; it was his plan to put a stop to Morgan gaining the coveted title.

Morgan was alone in a quieter corner of the Pell waiting for Stuart to arrive when Taliesan and his two closest supporters found him, practicing with two swords. He wasn't wearing any armour, so he had full and free movement and was at last beginning to get the hang of handling them, which was just as well, as he was about to face the three top swordsmen of the class.

"So...what do we have here?" Taliesan asked his two supporters conversationally. "Looks like our Kadeau brat is trying to impress us."

Morgan stopped what he was doing and faced the three of them.

"You were responsible for the death of my brother. I am going to repay that debt now."

"Your brother attacked King Rhisart. He committed treason."

Those words seemed to infuriate Taliesan, who drew his sword. His companions did the same. Morgan swallowed and backed off slightly to give himself some space.

"Running away, are we?" came the sarcastic comment.

Morgan felt himself bristle with indignation and assumed a defensive pose, but he now had enough room to move.

His three opponents laughed and moved in.

"I'm going to have your head, Kadeau!"

They attacked, and Morgan used his newly honed skills to fend them off. He parried, lunged, his two swords moving as a blur as he fought them off. The one thing he had to do was stop them from encircling him. As long as he kept them in front of him, he stood a chance, but they were beginning to spread out and encircle him, so be backed off some more, and then put a desperate and fast riposte and knocked one of them out, leaving just the two.

Taliesan made a frantic slash and caught Morgan's thigh. The young Duke gave a cry and staggered back, giving himself a little more room to gather himself. Taliesan's remaining companion moved round to the side and attempted to attack, but Morgan was ready for him, and managed to disable him with a blow to his helm that caused the squire to drop.

"Now it's just you and me, Taliesan," Morgan said, breathing heavily.

The older squire resorted to insults about Morgan's parentage, and the Coltrane's, and the youngster began to lose his temper. After another five minutes of fierce fighting, and neither of them gaining an advantage, Taliesan began to use some more unknightly moves. Morgan was now tiring and knew this had to stop, and then his opponent uttered one insult too many, and Morgan snapped.

Breathing hard, his eyes narrowed, and he threw his swords to the ground. Taliesan foolishly thought he had won the battle at this point as he too dropped his sword and drew out a dagger.

"I'm going to cut out your heart Kadeau!" he spat as he stepped forward.

Morgan closed his eyes and breathed deeply for a couple of seconds as Taliesan closed in, then opened them. The squire stopped as he saw the almost hypnotic gaze in them, and Morgan fixed him with a stare that made his blood run cold. He took another step forward.

The young Duke began to mutter something under his breath and Taliesan found he was unable to move. Morgan was still staring at him, his eyes changed, going transparent; not blinking as he continued to utter unknown words and Taliesan found himself moving the dagger towards his own throat.

The squire desperately tried to stop his hand from moving. It shook with the effort, but slowly continued to move closer.

"M – Morgan!" he said desperately. "Morgan, stop!"

"I am waiting for an apology," Morgan hissed, as the dagger pressed its tip just under Taliesan's left ear.

"Morgan!" It was Trahaearn's voice. He was walking towards him with the King when he realised what was going on. "Morgan, hold!"

But the young Duke either didn't or couldn't hear him as he continued delivering the punishment to Taliesan.

The knife pierced the skin by Taliesan's ear.

"*Prohibere!*" Trahaearn said forcefully, preventing the knife from moving further.

Wild eyed, Morgan turned his head and glared at Trahaearn.

"Morgan! Stop!" Stuart said desperately running towards him as the boy returned his concentration on slitting Taliesan's throat.

"Help me!" Taliesan screamed as the knife moved a fraction. He felt something trickling down his neck.

"Morgan!" The King's shout was forceful, but it was ignored, so Stuart did the only thing he could think of and struck him.

The blow broke Morgan's concentration for a moment. Furious, the youth glared at his King, then returned his attention to Taliesan. The knife returned to the squire's neck. Stuart struck him again, knocking him to the ground, and the transparent stare switched to his sovereign but before he could do anything else, Trahaearn was there, holding him down and forced himself into his mind.

Morgan! Stop! Listen to me! Trahaearn blazed into his mind making him cry out in pain. Control! Control!

"No!"

The two of them had a mental battle for domination and it took every ounce of Trahaearn's strength and skill to gain control of his mind.

"I said, control!" the knight literally screamed into his mind, almost causing the Duke to black out by the force of the command, and he suddenly stopped struggling. His eyes flickered open, changed colour back to grey and they closed again as he fought to obey the knight's order.

Stuart looked over at Taliesan, who had collapsed to the ground, thoroughly shaken, then at the other two fallen squires, and was quietly impressed with his future protector. To have taken on three older squires and despatched two of them was impressive, but he wondered what had happened to make Morgan resort to magic. He would ensure he found out.

He got to his feet and walked over to the older squire who was still sitting, numb. A trickle of blood on his neck.

Trahaearn stared hard at Morgan.

"What were you thinking!" he said harshly. "Do you realise what would have happened had you succeeded in slitting Taliesan's throat? I thought I'd taught you better than that!" The knight was so angry, he shook him until his teeth rattled.

Morgan heard the hurt in his mentor's voice and suddenly felt ashamed. "I – I'm sorry," he mumbled. "But – but he... he insulted..."

"That's no excuse! What have I been telling you since you arrived here? Kadeau must maintain control no matter what! I will try and repair the damage... make Taliesan forget what has happened today. But you must promise me, you will exercise further control going forward. This cannot happen again. Do I make myself clear?"

Morgan nodded. "Yes, Trahaearn. I really am sorry, but I just couldn't let the insult go, I was tiring, and I wanted to shut him up."

Trahaearn's expression softened as he released his hold on his pupil. "As long as you understand the possible consequences of your actions... That was exceptional, fending off three opponents. You're far better than I gave you credit for. How long have you been practicing Florentine?"

"Since Richard first showed me the move with one sword. He told me a couple of knights could manage to use two swords, so I made a vow to be one that could as well."

Trahaearn nodded. "Stay here, my work is not yet done." The knight got to his feet and went over to join Stuart. He knelt by the still stunned Taliesan, placed his fingers on his face, closed his eyes and sent out the instructions for the squire to forget all about what had happened after his companions had been knocked unconscious by Morgan, and that the fight had been stopped by the King. He then instructed the squire to return to his chamber and clean himself up.

In a trance, Taliesan got to his feet and walked almost zombie-like back towards the keep. King and knight then checked on the other two squires who were just returning to consciousness. Seeing they were all right, they too were ordered back to their rooms, then they returned to Morgan.

"Morgan?" Stuart questioned, as the boy knelt before him, head bowed.

"I beg forgiveness, Sire," he said quietly. "I have shamed myself and all Kadeau by my actions. I – I will leave if you so desire."

Stuart shook his head. "That will not be necessary, but be warned, Morgan Bodine, Duke of Rossmere, you are training for knighthood, and you will conduct yourself accordingly from now on."

"I pledge my allegiance to the house Cantrell, and that I will behave as befitting a knight going forward. I don't know why I lost control like that, I – I've been having some problems with moods; how I feel. I have lost some semblance of control, and I don't know why."

"You are becoming a man, young Morgan, your body is changing, maturing, it affects your thinking for a while, until your body has completed undergoing its transformation. Believe me, I know, it's something that happens to all men. Therefore it takes more effort to control your feelings. Now you know this, you can understand the extra effort that is required at this time."

"Yes, my Liege."

Stuart held out his hand. "Come then. That was most impressive, and with no armour," the King said jovially, then frowned as Morgan struggled to get up, and it was then he saw the blood on the youth's thigh. "You're hurt!"

"'Tis nothing, sire. I was clumsy."

"You fought three, with no armour! Come, let your Master Andrew take a look at that wound."

"Yes Sire." Morgan limped towards his armour, but Trahaearn stopped him.

"I'll get it," the knight said.

They followed the limping Morgan back to the keep and up to his chambers. A page was sent to find Master Andrew and send him to the Duke's rooms.

A few minutes passed before the battle surgeon arrived. He ordered Morgan to strip. His chest and arms were already beginning to exhibit some bruising, which he treated with witch hazel. His left cheek was slightly puffy where Stuart had hit him and received the same treatment. The wound on his thigh was superficial and just needed cleaning up.

"How did you get this through the armour?" Andrew asked, frowning.

"He wasn't wearing any," Trahaearn told him.

"What!"

"He was ambushed."

Andrew looked shocked, but he could see by the expression on Trahaearn's face that he wasn't going to get an explanation.

Trahaearn returned to the King.

"We were fortunate there were no witnesses to today's events, Sire," he said.

"Yes." Stuart watched his trainee protector get dressed again and nodded in satisfaction. "No serious harm done, this time." He lowered his voice. "Will you have him under control going forward?"

"Yes Sire," Trahaearn whispered. "I believe he now realises what almost happened. I doubt it will happen again."

"Very well." Stuart rose from his chair and waved a hand indicating for Morgan and Andrew to stay where they were. "Training will resume tomorrow," he said. "Trahaearn." They both left Morgan's chambers.

Andrew turned to his Duke. "What happened, Morgan?"

"I lost my temper."

"With the King?"

"No, three squires."

"What!"

"Trahaearn took care of everything. Andrew, I almost ruined it all. Kadeau reputation, my future...I lost control of myself, and I am ashamed. But... am I wicked, Andrew? I felt intense pleasure seeing the fear in that squire's eyes, and hearing him beg for mercy and I had every intention of killing him."

"You are not a spiteful person, Morgan, I firmly believe you must have had a valid reason for doing this. However, will you let it happen again?"

"No."

"Then it has been a valuable learning experience. Remember it."

ল ৪০ ল ৪০

Chapter Twenty-Eight

———◆———

Stuart had ordered that Taliesan and Morgan should not compete against one another, much to Morgan's disappointment. He had wanted to see if he could defeat him, but that would now be out of the question, unless they met on opposing sides on the battlefield, which knowing how the younger Prescott felt about the Cantrells, was more likely than not. Taliesan was also unlikely to take part in any future tournaments at Ellesmere either.

The peace between the two squires had to be maintained for a further month until knighting took place, then Taliesan would return home to the Eastern Marches. This would result in both remaining unbeaten in their training and perhaps pacify Taliesan somewhat. Once knighted, Stuart could see no reason why the young man could not take possession of his title as Duke of the Eastern Marches.

Fortunately, the peace was maintained, and the knighting ceremony passed without too much unrest. Still being a squire meant Morgan did not take part in any tournament, but just in a demonstration of the growing skills of the pages and squires, but his turn would soon come. His knighthood was now two years away.

Stuart was in a jovial mood after the tournament, Alexandra had been relatively pleasant to both Morgan and Trahaearn, and Richard appeared to have recovered from the loss of his second son, but Bronwyn was still grieving, so he begged Stuart's forgiveness, saying he would be leaving directly after the tournament had finished again to give her the support and love to try and bring her out of her dark mood.

"But how are you, Richard, truly?"

"I admit, it has been a difficult time, Sire. We are trying to understand why God is testing us to this extent. I know we should not question His word, but Bronwyn is a good and gentle soul. She doesn't deserve this heartache."

"Neither of you deserve it," Stuart replied. "I will continue to pray that you are blessed with a son."

"That means a great deal to me, Sire and, thank you for the honour within your son's name."

"I thought it was the best way to show you what your loyalty means to me. Now, I wish you a safe journey back to Inver. May God go with you."

Richard had departed, taking a very long letter from Morgan back with him. The youngster updated Bronwyn on what had been happening recently, although he left out the part about the ambush, and instead filled his letter with amusing stories that he hoped would make her laugh and improve her condition.

February was once again Morgan's birthday. He had reached fifteen years of age, but it had been a day like any other. He'd risen, washed, dressed, trained, practiced shielding with Trahaearn until he had developed a headache, then accompanied Stuart; standing guard in the throne room as the King conducted business; walked with him around the castle; carried out further training with his King. A couple of squires had wished him a happy birthday, Cuthbert had given him a small gift, but that was it.

Towards the end of the day, he thought Stuart was going to dismiss him as he usually did, but on this occasion he did not. Instead, he found himself at the stables. Once there, he followed Stuart along the stalls, past where his own horse stood, munching contentedly on some hay, to one at the far end.

The King indicated for the stable boy to enter this particular stall, which he did, and led a young black stallion out. The horse was about two or three years old, tall, short backed, but as yet, very raw and underdeveloped.

"What do you think?" Stuart asked Morgan.

The youngster put a hand out, allowing the horse to absorb his scent, before he began to stroke him, and check him over. There was not a white mark on him anywhere.

"He's beautiful!" Morgan exclaimed. "I assume, as he is so raw, he needs to start his training?"

"Yes."

"Who does he belong to?" the young Duke asked wistfully, wishing the horse belonged to him.

"You, Morgan. Happy birthday."

Stuart was grinning from ear-to-ear as Morgan's mouth dropped open and he stared at his king in disbelief.

"Sire...I...I don't know what to say...'thank you' seems so inadequate."

"You deserve him, Morgan. He took some finding, there were plenty with white markings, but totally black, very few of good enough quality. He will need a lot of work, but I wanted to get you a young horse, so you could stamp your own mark on how he is trained and handled." He indicated for the stable lad to put the horse back in his stall, and walked towards where his own horse stood waiting, all saddled and ready. "Now go get your present horse. I have one more surprise for you."

Morgan did as he was told, and the two of them left the castle and the city, and headed east, over the river to the wood in the distance.

The youngster frowned; unsure that it was wise for the King to be outside the safety of the castle without a full escort.

Sensing his concern, Stuart said, "I have the best swordsman in Devonmere with me, do I not? What more could a King ask for? Besides, we're not going far."

It was a cold clear night, and the stars were shining brightly. The nights still drew in early in February, but the rising moon provided plenty of light to see the trail.

After approximately half an hour's journey at a gentle canter; they reached their destination—the Royal Hunting Lodge. Morgan found himself frowning again as they dismounted; there were two horses already in the stable as they made their own beasts comfortable, before walking to the lodge.

The light flickering from the lamps inside, intimated that someone else was there, and Morgan wondered who it could be.

Opening the door, he motioned for his Liege to precede him, but Stuart shook his head and indicated for Morgan to go first. Inside, two women were waiting.

"Your Majesty," the older of the two women said, as they both curtsied.

"Cassandra," Stuart replied, taking her hand and placing it to his lips. "How lovely to see you again."

"Sire, this is Raven." She indicated for the younger woman to step forward.

Stuart eyed her critically, appraising her long, wavy black hair, the delicate features and the slender, shapely figure.

"Raven," Stuart said, kissing her hand.

"And this must be Morgan," Cassandra said looking at the young Duke. "A very handsome young man indeed, just as you described him, Sire." She flashed the perplexed youth a charming smile.

"Raven is Kadeau?" Stuart asked.

"Yes, Sire, just as you requested."

"Excellent." He turned to his young squire. "Morgan, today is your fifteenth birthday, and today is the day you will become a man in the true sense of the word."

Morgan blushed fiercely and gulped with embarrassment. Raven stared intently at him, admiring his colouring and build.

"My Lord," she said softly, her long lashes shielding sapphire eyes for a moment as she blinked slowly. "Come."

She held her hand out to him. Morgan looked down at it and swallowed again, this time with nervousness, before looking at Stuart, who nodded slightly; realising his young companion was acutely embarrassed about the whole situation.

Raven took his hand, and immediately her thoughts delicately touched his mind. *Come, my Lord, you have nothing to fear from me, I am here to teach you the art of love. The night awaits us.* Gently, she pulled at his hand and Morgan found himself following her up the stairs to one of the bedchambers.

Cassandra turned to Stuart. "'Tis a generous thing you do for him, my Lord," she said.

"I think a great deal of him. He will be my protector and champion shortly, and in a couple of years' time, General of my Armies; but his Kadeau heritage means his options for love are somewhat limited. If he is skilled in its art, I hope he will eventually find a woman who will complete him. He has had much sadness in his life. If Raven can teach him what his Kadeau heritage can do for a relationship, I shall be pleased."

She nodded at him and moved to a table to pour two goblets of wine. "Let us at least be comfortable; it is likely to be a long night, now that you are a faithful husband."

Stuart smiled at her, as he took the offered goblet.

Upstairs, inside the bedchamber, a single lamp was already burning. Morgan stood, just inside the room as Raven closed the door, and moved to a small table to pour them both a generous goblet of wine. She turned and handed him one of them.

"You have never—" she began.

"No," he interrupted, not wanting to hear her utter the words about his lack of experience. He had overheard some of his fellow squires boasting of their conquests and their conversations had unnerved him somewhat.

"Then, my Lord, you will know of a wondrous joy this night. The joining of two bodies—especially Kadeau—is something that has to be experienced. It is beyond verbal description." She smiled kindly at him. "Your King has requested I teach you about the act and art of love."

Morgan took a large gulp of his wine. Up until now, the only interaction with women he'd had was with his sister, and Bronwyn. A few girls had fluttered their eyelashes at him; a couple on the island of Isatiri had wanted much more, but he had been too young. Most during his time at Ellesmere had avoided him because of his Kadeau pedigree.

Raven took the goblet from him and placed it back on the table, then turned to gaze into the grey, rather apprehensive eyes.

"I had heard that you were handsome," she said softly, "but they have done you an injustice." She ran her fingers through his hair, examining its texture, then pulled his head down to hers and placed a gentle kiss on his lips; feeling him tremble slightly. Drawing back, she saw his eyes had changed colour—a hint of blue had appeared.

Turning from him, she walked to the bed and pulled down the covers in readiness, and Morgan swallowed nervously yet again. A part of him wanted to run—something he had never done in his life—

another part was aware of something stirring in his groin; a strange feeling; something he wanted to find out more about.

"Making love is akin to baking," Raven said looking back at him.

"What!" Morgan exclaimed.

"Yes. First you must gather your ingredients; mix them, heat them, so they rise to finally result in the finished article."

There was no way he could miss the implied sexual undertones in her sentence.

"To get the most out of the experience, you must explore, take your time, go on a journey of discovery." She paused and then said, "Are you ready to begin your journey of exploration, my Lord?"

"C-call me Morgan," he almost stuttered, suddenly aware of his heart thudding painfully in his chest.

Raven walked back and stood in front of him. "Morgan," she whispered, her voice seeming to caress his name.

She ran her hands up his arms, along his shoulders and down his chest, before slowly unbuttoning his jacket. Every move was sensuous, and she kept glancing up at him to gauge his reaction. He seemed frozen, like a statue, but his eyes were fixed unblinkingly on her face, as she completed her first task and eased the jacket off, allowing it to fall to the floor.

Repeating her move, she again ran her hands up his arms. Her touch this time, was firmer, but still incredibly sensuous as she undid the fastenings of his gillet, which joined his jacket.

She stood up on tiptoes to kiss him again, this time teasing, and encouraging him to respond, which he did, slowly, and Raven smiled inwardly. She teased him with her body, moving slowly against him, causing him to gasp, as heat suddenly engulfed him, and without even thinking about what he was doing, he kissed her eagerly.

Coming up for air, she said, "You learn fast, Morgan," as she started on the lacings of his silk shirt and divested him of it. He saw the satisfaction in her eyes as she surveyed and touched his bare chest; the firmness of skin over muscles, the scar on the front of his right shoulder. She could see he had not yet matured; his shoulders still needed to broaden, and he was probably still growing. He would be over six feet tall, she surmised, hoping that she would get to be with him at that time. Gently she touched the scar on his right shoulder and realised he had been but a child when he had received it. "May I remove this?" she asked fingering the locket around his neck. All Morgan could do was nod. Carefully she removed it and placed it on the bedside table.

Boldly she caressed his nipples, noting his response to her touch; including the fact that his eyes were taking on a deeper shade of blue, and his breathing altered, as he became aroused.

Taking her time, she continued her advances. A hand slid slowly down his chest, over his stomach and came to rest on his groin, forcing a gasp from his lips as a new sensation hit him, and he found himself moving his body against her hand; he just couldn't stop himself, as he succumbed to the sensations.

Raven stepped back, took hold of one of his hands and placed it on a breast; encouraging him to gently squeeze and massage it through her clothing. He felt the nipple respond to his touch as it hardened, whilst she leant forward, kissed his chest and used her tongue to invoke a response from him.

Satisfied, she drew back again and led him towards the bed, where she playfully gave him a firm shove, causing him to lose his balance and sit down suddenly. She bent down and pulled his boots off, before grabbing his hands and pulling him back to his feet.

Provocatively, she started loosening the laces of her dress, and after what seemed like an absolute age to Morgan, let it slip from her shoulders and land in a heap at her feet. Morgan's eyes widened as he took in the sight of her body through the almost sheer material of her shift and felt his breeches getting uncomfortably tight.

Raven took pity on him and reached out loosening the laces on them. Briefly, she reached round to caress his buttocks, then hooked her thumbs in the top of his breeches and slowly drew them down, releasing his manhood from the confined space. She helped him step out of them, stood back to admire his youthful body, then removed her shift.

They stood staring at each other for a few moments, then Raven stepped forward and gave him another shove, so he fell back onto the bed.

"Make yourself comfortable," Raven ordered, and watched as Morgan pulled himself up, so his head was resting on the pillows.

Satisfied, she climbed onto the bed and straddled his hips before leaning forward to kiss him once again, allowing her body to press against his, and Morgan was lost. Embers of a fire in his groin burst into flame at the feel of her breasts against his chest.

Knowing he was likely to have little control over his responses this first time, she went straight into the attack, assaulting his body with kisses, soft bites and caresses. She nipped his ear, and trailed kisses down his throat and chest, whilst all the while moving against him.

A groan was wrenched from his lips at the continued onslaught, and his back arched as he became painfully aroused. Knowing he was nearing his climax, Raven rolled onto her side, and then onto her back pulling him with her.

Vaguely, Morgan heard her gasping, as he continued to move against her; and her fingernails dug into his shoulders as the passion took over.

Reaching down between their bodies, she grasped his manhood and guided him and suddenly, he was thrusting strongly, firmly, tirelessly, and he quickly climaxed, giving a low guttural groan as she cried out in orgasm, grasping his buttocks to hold him tightly against her.

He had never experienced anything like it in his entire life; the total loss of control; the mindless need to relieve himself of the urges that possessed his body. Part of him had revelled in the sensations, but the reserved, calculated part of him was shocked and somewhat ashamed at his lack of control; and yet, deep down, he knew he had enjoyed it very much, and wanted to experience those feelings again.

"Do not be ashamed of what you felt, Morgan," Raven whispered in his ear, as she absorbed the final sensations of orgasm, and sighed deeply.

"But to lose control like that..."

"It was your first time. Now I will teach you about control; about the power you possess; how to please a woman and leave her begging for more."

She released him then and felt him slip from her body.

"By the time I am finished, you will wish the night to never end," she added, and thus began his education.

First, she taught him about his own body, discovering what he liked, what aroused him; about control; using his mind to dampen his ardour to hold back until his partner was truly ready for him, and as a reward, she again brought him to the brink and threw him mercilessly over the edge.

Next, she taught him about a woman's body; how to use his lips, his tongue, his fingers and his body to arouse her; where to touch her, and he was an incredibly fast learner she discovered, as she ordered him to bring her to fulfilment without entering her body.

Morgan watched, fascinated as she responded to his touch. Her cries excited him, but he practiced control, and instead absorbed the knowledge of the sounds she made, her movement against his fingers, what to look out for to know she was nearing the precipice.

Finally, she taught him several positions. He was young and extremely fit, so he was able to possess her time and time again until she could take no more, and for their final time together that night, she initiated a link to one another's minds, so they could share what each other was feeling, and Morgan felt he was going to die from the sheer intensity of the emotions that assaulted him; erotic thoughts, a kaleidoscope of colour, swirling, twisting around them, like a tornado, that lifted them to new heights of unparalleled passion. They finally succumbed to sleep an hour or so before the dawn, with her wrapped securely in his arms.

As the sun rose, Raven awoke, carefully disentangled herself from his body, eased herself to the edge of the bed, and stood up. She stared down at him for a few minutes, a soft smile on her face as she remembered the night they had spent together. It was not something she was going to forget for a long time, for nothing could match the passion of two Kadeau lovers.

Morgan gave a soft moan of contentment as he rolled onto his back and Raven felt her heart give a slight flutter. His burnished gold hair had fallen over his right eye, and his slightly parted lips were a pure invite, so she succumbed and leant over to kiss him softly.

"Thank you, for a wonderful night, my Lord," she whispered quietly, before dressing and slipping out of the room.

Cassandra and the King rose from their comfortable chairs as the dark-haired beauty came down the stairs.

The King approached and held his hand out to her as she reached the bottom.

"Thank you, Raven," he said softly, appraising her, and seeing her glowing skin.

"Sire," she replied just as quietly, a smile on her lips.

He handed her a small bag of gold, and then turned and handed another to Cassandra.

"Cassandra, thank you for arranging this. It has been most appreciated."

Both women curtseyed, and Stuart escorted them to the stables, where their horses were resting, helped to saddle them, then assisted them to mount.

"Until next time, Your Majesty," Cassandra said, and then they left.

Stuart returned to the lodge, and went up the stairs to the bedroom, where Morgan was still asleep.

"Morgan," he called softly. "Morgan, wake up."

The Duke gave a sharp intake of breath, and awoke with a start, to see his Liege standing in the doorway.

Seeing he was about to grab some bedding to get out of bed and show respect, Stuart quickly raised a hand as he entered the room and sat down by his side.

"Good night?" the King asked, a broad smile on his face, noting the untidy hair framing the handsome features.

Morgan coloured fiercely and swept the infamous unruly lock back from over his eye.

"Sire, I..." He gulped and swallowed. "I have no words," he finally replied. "But it concerns me. I have never been so out of control, not even during that incident last year. I lost all sense of discipline; my body ruled my mind."

"But did you enjoy it?"

Silence reigned for an aeon, or so it seemed.

"Yes," he confessed.

"Good. Being...skilful in that area is one of the keys to a successful marriage; especially if it has been an arranged one, where you are almost strangers to each other. To have a woman writhing beneath you, begging for release proves your prowess in the bedchamber. One warning though, if you decide to continue to explore this new experience; be very careful. We do not want any...accidents and claims made against you regarding the parentage of any children that could result from carelessness."

Morgan gulped, suddenly realising that an unscrupulous woman, looking to have a title bestowed upon her, could trick him into marriage by claiming she was carrying his child.

"Remember, your title means you are royalty, and actually a prince, even though you are not in direct line to the throne. You would be an exceedingly good catch, so be extremely careful."

"I think then, it would be better for me to practice more stern mental discipline going forward," Morgan said.

"My friend, all work and no play...I'm not saying not to indulge, I'm just saying if you do, be careful. I'm sure Raven would be most accommodating, going by the demure expression on her face this morning. I can advise how to get word to Cassandra, and you may use the hunting lodge so it is private. Now, permit your King to make you some breakfast."

"Sire, no!"

"Sire, yes! Make the most of it, it's back to normal afterwards!" Stuart stood up laughing and went to the door. "See you downstairs shortly." With that he left, shutting the door behind him, leaving Morgan thinking furiously about the conversation they had just had.

He had enjoyed the sexual experience, there was no denying that fact, but he could not afford to be so out of control. Life was so much more difficult for him as a Kadeau, and what he was working towards;

to be the King's Champion and protector. He was under constant scrutiny, everywhere he went, what he did, how he conducted himself. Many viewed him with suspicion, for the hate of his magical race was still very close to the surface in certain areas of Devonmere, despite the fact that no Kadeau had committed an atrocity for over two hundred years.

But he was still a man; with a man's needs. He had tasted what that had felt like and enjoyed it. Perhaps he could visit Raven every now and again, to enhance his skills in that area and learn further control. He sighed forcefully.

The responsibility of what he was and what he was to become, weighed very heavily on his young shoulders. He had been giving his situation a lot of thought recently, especially as he had a little over a year to go until he was knighted. He had decided he needed a place he could go; somewhere he could be alone, relax, unwind, regather his thoughts, calm his mind, even let off some steam, without anyone else being around to know what he was doing, or spying on him.

When he next returned to Rossmere, he would do some investigating. He had the room high in one of the towers, but he felt he needed something like Trahaearn had; something out of human sight and ears. There had to be somewhere that would be suitable, somewhere he could go and be himself but...what did that even mean? Who was he, really? All his life he had strived to be what everyone else wanted him to be, but what about what he wanted? He was sure he was a good person, but he'd spent so long holding emotions in check, being reserved, he wondered what he'd be like if he ever really just threw caution to the wind to be himself—whatever that was.

He sighed heavily again. All he was doing was giving himself a headache, so he got up to get washed and dressed, but he did notice there did seem to be a different expression in his eyes.

A little while later, both men were sitting at the table eating bread, with meat, drinking wine.

"So, Morgan, was it a good birthday?" Stuart asked him.

"The best, thank you, my Liege."

"I am pleased you enjoyed it. I was thinking, we can either train here this morning, or we can return to Ellesmere, what do you think?"

"It would be pleasant to train somewhere else for a change," Morgan admitted.

"I think so too. We do seem to think very much alike. I think that's why we get on so well. Once we finish breakfast, we'll go outside. It's pretty cold, but it should be an invigorating session."

"I look forward to it, my Liege."

Half an hour later, they were outside the hunting lodge, no armour, just their swords. Morgan was used to this by now, they were both skilled enough not to inflict any serious damage on each other but fight fiercely enough to get their hearts beating fast and test their expertise.

Stuart had brought a couple of extra swords and threw one of them to Morgan. "I saw you practicing with two swords the other day. Do you want to try an exercise with them?"

"I've only practiced on my own, Sire, but I would very much like to practice with an opponent."

"Excellent. Let's go." He picked up a second sword, and they started slowly, getting used to each other's moves before gradually increasing the pace. Sparks flew as their swords clashed against each other. Stuart felt invigorated with the challenge Morgan presented him with. He too didn't get much of a chance to practice Florentine against an opponent, and he realised that the Duke was almost his equal with regard to sword play. By the time he was knighted, the King expected to start losing his matches against him. Currently, they were just about even.

Their training session went on for an hour or so before Stuart called a halt and they returned to the castle.

Morgan was pleased to be back, as he wanted to start training his charger as soon as possible. However, before he could start, he had his studies and duties to the King to complete.

ผ ผ ผ ผ

Chapter Twenty-Nine

——•——

At last free of his duties for the day, Morgan made his way to the stables to spend some time with his new horse. Stuart had been generous, and only requested his presence until midday, so he had a few hours he could dedicate to starting to build a relationship with his future charger. He had gone via the kitchens and stolen some carrots to help him in his quest.

The stables were practically deserted, as almost everyone was out training, either in the Pell or in the arena, which was what he wanted, for he was going to start forming a bond that horse and rider would share all their lives when they were near each other.

The young horse looked up curiously as Morgan entered the stall, hand outstretched with half a carrot in his hand. The ears flicked forward, and Morgan saw his nostrils twitch as he picked up the scent of the vegetable. The horse took a tentative step forward and stretched out his neck. Realising he wasn't quite close enough, he took another, that enabled him to take the offered carrot which he quite happily munched on.

Morgan carefully retrieved the other half of the carrot, which he again offered, but did not extend his arm as far, so the horse had to come closer. Two carrots later, the horse was sniffing at his hand, then licked it, and Morgan gently placed his other hand on the horse's cheek. They both stood motionless for a few minutes before the Duke started talking quietly, so the horse could get used to, and become familiar with his voice.

"You need a name, lad. What shall I call you?" Morgan stood thinking, idly stroking the horse's cheek, when a name just suddenly popped into his head. "Banner. I shall call you Banner."

He stroked the horse's neck, back and sides, then returned to his head and placed a hand on his forehead and sent out the most gentle of thoughts. Initially, nothing happened, then Banner snorted, stamped a hoof and gave a little jerk of his head. Morgan continued to talk in a soft tone, telling him what a good boy and how handsome he was, and that they would be companions for many years to come, as he carefully made contact with his mind.

Connection made, he gently began to speak the same phrases, this time with his mind, and felt Banner tremble slightly. Sending calm thoughts, the horse finally relaxed, and even appeared to doze, feeling totally at ease with his new owner.

Morgan patted his neck softly. "We both have a lot to learn, lad," he said quietly, "and we will start tomorrow. Our lives are now entwined with each other's. I will always do my very best to look after you; but there will be times when I ask more of you than I ought, and for that, I ask your forgiveness in advance."

The education of his horse would start the following day, but for now, Morgan decided to take Banner out for a walk around the castle grounds. He might as well see how the horse reacted to his new surroundings.

He fastened a leading rein onto Banner's halter and led him from his stall and outside into the bailey where he paused to let the horse look around. There was a lot of ear flicking and head turning as the horse took in the sights and sounds. Morgan simply stood quietly, stroking his neck and sending calming thoughts for a few minutes, before leading him on under the barbican, over the drawbridge and down the hillside towards the town.

There were all sorts of noises, smells and objects for the horse to get used to. Banner almost jerked the leading rein out of the Duke's hand when a door was opened and some water was thrown out into the street, just ahead of him, and Morgan had to quickly tighten his grip, but continued to talk quietly to him.

When they returned to the stables, Morgan spent time grooming his horse, brushing his mane and tail and just generally building a relationship with him. He always carried a carrot or two in his pocket for Banner and the horse very quickly learnt which one it was carried in, and nuzzled at it every time Morgan came to the stable.

Banner was taught commands so that when the Duke finally started riding him, he would know what was asked of him. For the moment, he used his hands to simulate future foot movements. Morgan took his time breaking his horse and finally sat on his back six months later. The horse was too young to take a knight in full armour, so Morgan initially rode him bare backed, then introduced him to the saddle and gradually worked up the weight with his armour.

They practiced with the lance, Morgan taught Banner to run straight and true, and the Duke collected the tiny rings successfully as he practiced, and then against fellow squires on the run where the tournaments were held, to let the horse get used to the sound of the lances hitting shields and disintegrating.

Different sounds, smells, ground, and situations were explored. Morgan needed his charger to be solid and sound, especially in battle.

In the months leading up to the knighting ceremony he had continued to train the horse, increasing Banner's stamina and strength, subjecting him to mock battles with both sword and lance. As far as Morgan was concerned, his horse was steady, and hardly spooked at anything. He still had a lot to learn but had come on in leaps and bounds since the King had presented him to the Duke on his fifteenth birthday.

Thinking about his image, Morgan treated Banner to some new livery; it was all black, as was the saddle. Everything was black, and the horse now looked every bit as menacing as Morgan knew he was going to be, once he was knighted and allowed to wear his own clothes again.

Now he was happy with his charger's progress, he released his previous horse, Flint, from his control, once again thanking the horse for his service. He would take him back to Inver when he next visited, perhaps to be passed onto the next person who could make use of him or release him into the pastures to run free for a while.

Time flew by. His sixteenth birthday passed, and then suddenly, mid-summer's eve and the knighting ceremony was upon them.

C3 80 C3 80

Chapter Thirty

I t was mid-summer's eve and the start of the knighting ritual. It began with a ceremonial bath. All the squires that were to be knighted the following day, sat in wooden bath tubs and thoroughly cleansed themselves in preparation for a visit from Bishop Douglas. He went to each of them in turn and asked them if they were ready for the water to wash away their former life, so they could begin anew.

Each squire answered that they were ready, and the bishop poured a large pitcher of water over their heads which completed the act of purification.

Once they had all been purified, they got out of the tubs, dried themselves and put on simple robes to have a symbolic lock of hair cut from their heads, for which Morgan was grateful. Originally, in days of old, the entire head would have been shaved, but this was now deemed too extreme a sacrifice, so it had been reduced to one lock.

Over the years, his hair had darkened to a burnished gold that was currently gaining its light summer streaks. He had let it grow so it hung almost halfway down his shoulders, and that was another reason he was thankful to lose only one lock.

Page boys then assisted the squires to dress. It began with black hose which reminded the squires of death. Next came a new white tunic to symbolise their purity. A magnificent red cloak that denoted nobility and the willingness to shed blood for God, the church and his King was next, and the final item of clothing was a white belt, to denote their chastity.

Now dressed they made their way to the cathedral, carrying their armour. There were thirty of them that were going to be knighted, and they were escorted in a procession out of the castle, down the hill and through the city to their destination. Although it was an annual event, people still stopped and cheered as the squires marched by.

Morgan's armour was neatly piled, like the rest of the squires', as he stood in vigil over it, mentally preparing himself for the forthcoming ceremony the following morning. Again, he quietly repeated the prayer of initiation.

"Harken, we beseech Thee O Lord to hear our prayers,

"And deign to bless with the right hand of Thy Majesty,

"That this sword with which Thy servant desires to be girded,

"That it may be a defence of the faith, widows, orphans, the weak, the righteous,

"And all thy servants against the scourge of pagans, enemies of Thy church and the Kingdom,

"That it may be the terror and dread of all vile doers,

"And that it may be just in both attack and defence, and carry out Thy work,

"Amen."

Although it was the shortest night of the year, time seemed to drag, even though he also contemplated his future duties. With the knighting completed, he would then officially become the King's protector. Morgan knew he was more than capable of performing that duty, he had already proven his worthiness, having remained undefeated with the sword since the age of fourteen. However, he still had a lot to learn, but Richard had also helped a great deal, in preparing him to rule his own Duchy of Rossmere, and to be a good, honest and just leader.

Disguised in a hooded cloak, King Stuart visited the cathedral to offer his support to the young Duke. If he had been able, he would also have liked to have stood as his sponsor, along with Richard, but he was to perform the knighting ceremony, and he realised in all honesty, that the young squire could not have had a better sponsor, who would dress the forthcoming knight in his armour in the morning and aid in the final preparations for the ceremony.

Stuart stood a few steps behind the young man, observing him as he stood, head bowed in prayer. The burnished gold hair was tied back with a leather thong and the simple clothes he wore seemed to accentuate his nobility, rather than diminish it. The rich red cloak fitted the broadening shoulders well. The King realised the youth was still growing, but in the last year or so, seemed to have gained a few more inches in height and Stuart surmised he would be over six feet, by the time he was seventeen or eighteen. Height and his aura would make him appear even more menacing to the King's enemies.

Morgan suddenly became aware of a presence behind him and brought himself back to the present.

"I hope I'm not disturbing you," the hooded figure whispered quietly, but Morgan immediately recognised the voice.

"Sire." He went to take a knee in respect, but Stuart stopped him.

"No, Morgan. Tonight, I am not here as your King, but to offer support as a friend. You have been with me now, for nine years. Tomorrow, after you are knighted, you will officially become my protector. I wanted to come and see how you were doing in your vigil. If you will permit me, I would like to stay and pray with you for a while."

"I would be honoured, my Liege," Morgan whispered back.

The two men stood shoulder to shoulder, heads bowed and repeated the prayer of initiation together. Stuart may have been King, but he was also a knight and knew it would do no harm to repeat the prayer to remind him of his requirement to conduct himself in a knightly fashion. He stayed for a couple of hours, then lay a reassuring arm on his shoulder.

"Your sponsor is here," he whispered, then took his leave.

Richard, recognising it had been the King standing with Morgan in prayer, even though he had been in disguise, nodded his respect to Stuart, so he did not reveal the true identity of Morgan's visitor. The King smiled and nodded back before moving on.

"Morgan, my son, how are you?" Richard asked quietly.

The squire turned his gaze upon his guardian and sponsor and smiled warmly.

That gesture alone, gave Richard a sense of love; he knew his young charge rarely smiled, and to be on the receiving end of one, touched his heart.

"Father, thank you for coming and offering your support this night. I am feeling surprisingly calm."

Richard smiled back, the movement crinkling his eyes.

"I know it's the shortest night of the year, but time can seem to drag, believe me! I remember I grew very impatient at how slowly it passed. You only have a few more hours before the sun rises on this glorious day." He lowered his voice to a mere whisper. "I see Stuart paid you a visit."

"Yes, we prayed together, and he stayed a couple of hours. It was most generous of him."

"He favours you and wants you to know you have his full support. Had he not been the King, he would have offered his sponsorship as well."

Morgan was silent as he digested this piece of information.

"Tomorrow, after the ceremony, you will officially become his protector, releasing Trahaearn from the duty."

"I confess, I am nervous about it."

"That is good. You will be an excellent protector; I am sure of it. Now, will you permit me to stand and pray with you for a while?"

"I would be honoured, father."

They were joined by Trahaearn a little later and both stayed with him until dawn, before laying a hand on his shoulder and taking their leave. Both men went to refresh themselves and change for the actual knighting ceremony or accolade as it was more commonly known.

A couple of hours later, the cathedral was packed with family members, visitors and other dignitaries and Bishop Douglas conducted Mass and gave a blessing.

Once this had been completed the sponsors of the squires came forward to fit them with their armour. Richard removed the cloak and white belt around Morgan's waist, then assisted him into his hauberk, cuirass and gauntlets, before kneeling down to attach the golden spurs. The right one was fitted first, followed by the left. Gaining his feet once more, he refitted the white belt and girded his new sword, specially ordered by Richard for the occasion on Morgan's right side. It was beautifully decorated and had the Rossmere rampant guardant golden dragon emblazoned on one side of the blade and a miniature double trefoil on the other. The pommel was decorated with a miniature golden dragon. Finally, he placed the rich red cloak around his shoulders and stood back, nodding in satisfaction, a slight smile on his face as he surveyed his adopted son.

One by one the squires moved to kneel before their King to accept the accolade. Morgan was the last to be presented and knelt at Stuart's feet.

"Who is thy supporter this day?" Stuart asked in a firm voice.

Richard stepped forward. "I am the supporter, my Liege; Duke Richard Conall Lyall Coltrane of Invermere."

"Is thy candidate worthy and free to take the oath and the responsibility of knighthood and all it entails?"

"He is, my Liege."

The King nodded and said, "Duke Morgan Rhys Geraint Bodine, I dub thee in knighthood," as he lay the sword first on his right shoulder, then the left, and finally back to the right. "Your sponsor deems you ready for knighthood. Know that to wear the belt and arms of a knight is granting that you will hold the sacred trust of God, the Church and your King, and that you are bound to it for life. Arise."

Morgan obeyed his King and rose to his feet before bowing deeply. "I will serve thee with honour, my Liege," he said and returned to his place in the line of knights.

They all then recited the ten rules of chivalry:

"Thou shalt follow the dictates of moral conscience,

"Thou shalt be willing to defend your values,

"Thou shalt have respect and pity for all weakness and steadfastness in defending them,

"Thou shalt love thy country,

"Thou shall refuse to retreat before the enemy,

"Thou shalt wage unceasing and merciless war against all that is evil,

"Thou shalt obey the orders of those appointed above you, as long as those orders do not conflict with what you know to be just,

"Thou shalt show loyalty and truth and your pledged word,

"Thou shalt be generous and giving of ones' self,

"Thou shalt be champion of the right and good at all times, and at all times oppose the forces of evil."

King Stuart then walked along the line of new knights and delivered the colee, which involved him striking each knights' chest with the flat

480

of his sword. When he had completed this, he returned to his original position on the dais and spoke a final time.

"Let the colee remind you all, that knighthood can bring you pain as well as honour, in the service of the King. Welcome knights."

This concluded the ceremony. A final prayer was said by Bishop Douglas, followed by a herald, and it was all over, until the banquet in the evening.

Richard came forward to shake Morgan's hand. "Well done, son," he said.

Morgan smiled at him, and glanced up to see Stuart nod his head, then exit.

Richard continued. "I believe the King will announce your position as King's protector at some point during the celebrations. I'm not sure if he will do it tonight, or after the tournament, but it will be announced."

Morgan nodded. "Father, I just want to say, thank you to both you and Bronwyn for taking me in, caring for me, loving me all these years. It has been appreciated more than you can ever know, and..." He pulled his sword from its sheath. "...this sword is beautiful. I shall cherish it, always."

"It has a brother. I heard you had mastered the Florentine, so thought it wise to provide you with a pair that are perfectly matched weight and balance wise."

"I – I don't know what to say. 'Thank you' seems so inadequate for everything you have both done for me."

"It has been our pleasure and honour. We know you are not of our blood, but to us, you are and always will be our son."

Morgan saw Richard's eyes glisten slightly and knew immediately he was still in pain from the loss of his two sons. Instinctively, he threw his arms around his father and hugged him tightly, trying to draw the hurt from the Duke's body and take it upon himself, for as far as Morgan was concerned, Richard was the nicest, fairest and most knightly man in the kingdom. If anyone deserved a son, it was him, and Morgan was at a loss as to why God had chosen to test the Duke to this extreme.

Not one to admit to his feelings, Morgan knew this was one occasion where he needed to express them. "I love you, father," he whispered in Richard's ear as they parted.

For a few seconds, Richard was almost overcome, but dug deep within his soul to regain control of his emotions. Morgan never admitted that he felt anything. The last time had been when he was just ten years old, when they had all submitted him to too much pressure and a crack had formed in his armour, which had taken some time to repair.

"Son, I am so proud of you," the Duke finally managed to say. "And so is your mother. She offers her sincere apologies, but she is not ready to be seen at official functions."

"I understand. Even though she is absent, I feel her love here." He placed his hand on his heart. "And I am still carrying the locket."

They smiled at each other and left the cathedral side by side.

ॐ ॐ ॐ ॐ

The celebrations now followed. The first was that very evening, to commemorate the creation of the new knights.

Morgan decided he would follow Richard's advice and not overindulge in the celebrations, so he would be fit and able to perform to the best of his abilities in the two days of the tournament. It was likely to be very hard on him, as if he was fortunate enough to win the one for the newly knighted squires, he would then be eligible to enter the one for the experienced knights.

If Stuart was to name him King's protector, Morgan knew he had to at least win the squire's tournament. If he could possibly win the other tournament as well, then he would feel he justly deserved the position, and that it would also make him the King's champion, a title he really wanted to achieve.

That first evening, he dressed as he meant to go on, in black, from the boots to the leather breeches, silk shirt, and jacket. His regal expression, the grey fathomless eyes and the non-smiling face gave him the look of menace he was after.

Ioan stepped back and looked at his master.

"You're even making me feel uneasy, Morgan," he finally said.

"Really?" The Duke smiled at him.

"Don't smile, that's ruining your image."

Morgan's smile changed to a grin. "Excellent," he said, letting the grin fade and assuming his normal expression.

Ioan laughed and shook his head. "Go and enjoy yourself, Morgan!"

"I will, but not too much, I need to win. I'll look after myself when I get back, you go and enjoy yourself as well, Ioan."

"Thank you, Morgan." Ioan bowed and followed his master out of the room.

Morgan was seated on the top table with the King and Queen, Richard and Trahaearn. Stuart welcomed everyone to the celebration for the new knights and bid they eat, drink and be merry. Both Richard and Morgan were careful about how much they consumed, and afterwards, Richard danced with the Queen.

"Duke Richard, please, may I offer my sincere condolences to you and Duchess Bronwyn. How is your lovely wife?"

"She has...recovered, at least physically. Thank you for asking, Your Majesty."

"I will pray for you both. I know of no couple more deserving than yourselves. Tell me, how is your beautiful daughter?"

"She flourishes and is blossoming, but is still wilful, although she is beginning to control her temper more. I'm not sure what's she's doing to manage this, but whatever it is, it appears to be working."

"I'm pleased she is well. She will be a beautiful woman, I'm sure. A prize for whomever wins her hand in marriage."

"Bronwyn and I are determined that she will have a childhood, and not marry too soon. I saw what expecting too much almost did to the Duke of Rossmere. We expected far too much from him too soon and almost denied him his childhood."

Richard saw the hardening around her mouth at the mention of his adopted son.

"You still do not trust my son, Your Majesty?" he asked her.

"Forgive me Richard, but Morgan Bodine is not your son. You may have raised him, but he is not of your blood. He is a Kadeau, and therefore is not worthy of my trust."

"I wish I could make you see differently, Your Majesty. All his life we have put upon him to do what we wanted him to do, and he has strived to rise to that. He has made great sacrifices in his life to be what we want him to be, and not what he wants or needs to be. How can meeting our expectations be evil?"

"I am sorry, Richard, I have been raised with my hatred inbuilt. I am endeavouring to cast it aside, but I am finding it exceedingly difficult. I hope one day that I may be able to look on him without that feeling. He is a fine looking young man, who has been raised by the most loyal family to the House of Cantrell."

Richard did a small bow at that remark and kissed the Queen's hand before escorting her back to her chair and bowing again.

Stuart then made her dance with Trahaearn, and afterwards with Morgan. Alexandra found she could not relax as Morgan held her. She looked at him and found him unreadable. She had no idea what was going through his mind, or what he may have been thinking, and he actually frightened her a little, but she minded her manners and spoke to him, albeit briefly.

"Congratulations on your knighthood, Duke Morgan."

Morgan was surprised at her comment but hid it well. "Thank you, Your Majesty," he replied quietly.

"I assume you will be returning to Belvoir shortly?"

"Yes, once the King has released me. I have neglected the duchy for too long."

With the dance finished, he escorted her back to her seat, bowed slightly and kissed her hand. "Your Majesty," he said, and returned to his own chair.

Stuart leant towards his wife. "Thank you for agreeing to dance with the Duke of Rossmere. Did you talk about anything?"

"I congratulated him on his knighthood," she replied.

"That's all?"

"And asked him when he would be leaving for Belvoir."

Stuart sighed. At least she had said more than one word to his protector, it was better than nothing.

"He frightens me," Alexandra whispered to her husband. "He gives nothing away, and I have no idea what he's thinking."

"He does that on purpose," Stuart replied just as quietly. "He feels it fitting, as my protector, to instil fear in everyone. But I swear to you, he is completely trustworthy."

His attention was diverted as Morgan rose from his seat again, along with Richard.

"If you will forgive us, Sire, we are retiring, so we are rested for the start of the tournament tomorrow," Richard said as they both bowed.

"I understand and...good luck for tomorrow."

The two men took their leave and walked amicably to their chambers. They came to Richard's first. He stopped and turned to his son.

"Morgan, I want you to promise me you will give no quarter should we meet tomorrow. I would consider it an honour to lose to my son, and I think it would be fitting as well."

"Father, I..."

"You must promise me," Richard said again. "It would make your mother and me extremely proud."

Morgan sighed and finally nodded. "Very well. I promise I will give no quarter to you should we meet in combat."

"Thank you. I have something for you." Richard reached into his pocket and pulled out a delicate handkerchief. "This is from Colwyn, it is her favour to you and to bring you luck."

"Surely, it should be you who has the favour."

"I have my own, from Bronwyn. Take it."

Morgan took it and tucked it in his pocket. "I will carry this with me always, the other favour is falling apart I've had it so long!"

Richard smiled at him, his hazel eyes twinkling with love. Then he said, "Be warned, I will not make it easy for you tomorrow."

"I expect no less from the man who raised me. Sleep well, father."

☙ ❧ ☙ ❧

Chapter Thirty-One

The newly appointed knights were first in the arena the following day. The King, Queen, Richard and Trahaearn were up on the dais to watch the event.

Morgan was nervous. This was his first actual tournament, anything could happen, but on form and experience, in theory he should win, but there was always that element of uncertainty, as he had seen in the past.

On the dais, Stuart leant towards Richard, who was suited up ready to take part in the tournament for the more experienced knights. "So Richard, who do you think will win the squires' tournament?"

"Morgan," Richard said without hesitation.

Stuart grinned at him. "You know, you're right. You told him about the Florentine two sword combat, didn't you?"

"Yes, I did, why?"

"He's exceptional at it. I last trained with him doing that a year ago and was unable to defeat him. We had to call it a draw. A year has passed since then."

"I had two matching swords made for him in celebration of his knighthood, because he'd written to tell me he'd just about mastered it."

"So I assume, you're not willing to make a wager on the outcome?"

"Sire, why bet on a sure thing? The odds will not be worth it."

"You are that confident, then."

"I am."

"Then let us watch and see." Stuart indicated for the tournament to get underway.

It was as predicted; Morgan worked his way through easily to the final. And as there was no one in his year that could match him, he won effortlessly.

"That was hardly a competition," Richard remarked to the King as Morgan came up the steps to the dais to accept the gold band from Stuart.

Morgan took a knee before him and bowed as Stuart placed the band on his head and indicated for him to rise.

"My lords, ladies, gentlemen... Morgan Bodine, Duke of Rossmere, winner of the squire's tournament of the sword."

Clapping and cheering followed as Morgan acknowledged his audience.

"As winner of this tournament, and as per tradition, the Duke has automatically won entry to the major tournament that follows shortly." He looked at Morgan and whispered. "Well done. Now show me what you can really do."

Morgan bowed and left the dais with his father. As they walked to the warm up area, Richard repeated what he had said the night before.

"Remember, give no quarter to me today. I would be proud to see you win. It's never been done by a new knight before. You have the ability to do it, I have no doubt." He laid a hand on his shoulder. "Good luck today, son."

"And you too, father."

Neither of them were sure if Stuart had purposely arranged it, but father and son did not engage until the actual final. Morgan had had a reasonably difficult route through the various rounds. These were hardened battle experienced knights who had no intention of letting the new upstart win, but win he did.

Richard was inspired that day. He really wanted to reach the final and face his son. If he were to finally lose his title as tournament champion of Devonmere, then he wanted it to be facing Morgan.

He got his wish.

Up on the dais, Stuart leant forward, avid interest etched on his features, wondering how the final match would unfold.

Richard and Morgan entered the arena to cheering and clapping. The Duke of Invermere was exceedingly popular and had won the hearts of the people over the years. They saluted the King, then turned and saluted each other, made their final adjustments and the combat began.

It started relatively slowly, with both men measuring the gauge and skill of the other. Cautious ripostes and feints followed as they learnt more about each other's techniques. Blows landed against one another's shields as they moved around the arena.

As Richard had stated, he was determined to make Morgan work for the title, and stepped up the pace, using his experience from battles and previous tournaments, and suddenly Morgan realised he was going to have to seriously up his game.

A particularly heavy attack from Richard forced the youngster backwards as heavy blows landed on his shield, making Morgan wince at the force.

In the background they could hear the approval of the crowd as it cheered and clapped at the ongoing match.

Morgan was just about holding his own against his father and realised the Duke had been very serious about making him work for the title. He was forced to defend as he was driven back further towards the rails, sparks flying as swords connected with each other and the shields. Seeing his advantage, Richard attacked him with a barrage of heavy blows, and Morgan finished up on the floor as his father advanced on him.

Realising he was going to lose unless he really put in a supreme effort, he frantically rolled out of the way, and gained his feet in one smooth movement, giving him a little space to gather himself.

He looked into his father's brown eyes and found them unreadable as the Duke spun the sword using his wrist to refresh the grip and Morgan swallowed, took a very deep breath, renewed the grip on his own sword and circled round away from the railing.

They attacked each other at the same time in a double action, trading heavy blows, then got close enough for a corps-a-corps—physical contact—and Richard shouted at him.

"You can do better than this, Morgan! Come on, show me what you've got!"

"Fa – father, I don't want to hurt you," he gasped in response.

"Don't think of me as your father. I'm your enemy, and I want to win that band as much as you do! Now fight!"

Richard followed up his words with another vicious attack causing more sparks to fly. The audience were shouting and screaming their approval. Up on the dais, Stuart spotted Richard shouting at Morgan but couldn't hear what was being said because of the noise of the crowd, it was almost deafening.

It looked as if Richard was going to win, then the King noticed Morgan say something to his father. It almost looked like it was an apology.

"I'm sorry father, for what I am about to do," he shouted at him.

"Stop apologising!" Richard shouted.

Morgan paused for a fraction, making Stuart frown, wondering what he was playing at. Both King and Duke soon found out, as the youngster, called on all his reserves and fought back with everything he had, at last forcing Richard back. Morgan saw the approval in his father's eyes and with renewed vigour, pressed home his attack.

Richard parried, but from somewhere, Morgan found the strength he needed to rally against the attack by his father, forced him back against the rail and then with a complicated series of moves, disarmed him, finishing with the point of his sword against his father's neck.

"Do you yield?" Morgan asked him.

He saw Richard's eyes crinkle as he smiled and nodded. "I do," he said. "Well done, Morgan. I'm so proud of you."

The youngster lowered his sword, then saluted his father with it before sheathing it.

Richard retrieved his own sword, and did the same to Morgan, then the two of them removed their helms, shook hands and hugged. They were both breathing hard after their exertion and partly supported each other as their hearts gradually slowed.

The audience cheered and shouted at the love that was expressed by the two men towards each other and carried on cheering as they walked to the dais.

They faced the King, and with helms tucked under their left arms, unsheathed their swords, saluted the King, then one another again and sheathed them, before ascending the steps.

They both knelt before their King.

"That was exceedingly entertaining," Stuart told them both. "For a moment, I thought you were going to win, Richard."

"I was, until I gave my son some encouragement to do better, My Liege."

"I did see you shouting at Morgan but couldn't hear a word because of the noise of the crowd."

"My father was ordering me to reach my full potential, Sire," Morgan explained.

"You have both done well," Stuart said handing Richard a small bag of coin. He then picked up the band for the sword tournament winner, placed it upon Morgan's head and indicated for both men to rise. The King turned to the crowd. Morgan quickly transferred his helm to his right hand as Stuart grasped his left, Richard's right and raised them above their heads. "Our runner up, Duke Richard Coltrane, and our winner Duke Morgan Bodine!" He then stepped back and let the two dukes take the accolade the crowd were bestowing on them.

"Well done, my son, you have achieved what no other novice knight has done this day. Your mother will be as proud of you as I am." Richard winced as he lowered his arm.

"Father, have I hurt you?" Morgan asked, worried.

Richard shook his head. "No, just a little bruised."

Morgan smiled at him slightly. "That makes two of us," he replied, as they walked off the dais and headed for the keep. "Did you bring Master Gethin with you?"

"No, not this time."

"Then come with me to my chambers, I will get Andrew to treat your bruises."

"That's not necessary," Richard began.

"I insist, father. It is the jousting tomorrow. It won't be a fair match if I get treated and you don't."

Richard nodded acquiesce and they continued their journey in silence.

Both Andrew and Ioan were in Morgan's chambers when they arrived and assisted the two dukes out of their armour.

"Andrew, please treat my father first, I believe he has some bruising that needs tending to. I insist," he added as Richard went to protest.

Richard saw his look and nodded once more as he started to undo his aketon. Andrew assisted him out of that and his shirt and made him sit on a stool whilst he checked him over.

Ioan poured both dukes generous goblets of wine and handed them to them as Andrew started applying witch hazel to the red areas of Richard's chest, back and arms. The liquid was very cold and designed to bring out the bruising.

In between sips of his wine, Morgan couldn't help studying his father and noted the powerful build and firm muscles. He was still in excellent physical condition despite being almost forty years old and Morgan hoped he'd be in as good a shape as his father at the same age, providing he lived that long. He was just relieved that he hadn't inflicted any serious damage on him.

"Your Grace, give this a couple of hours, then get your steward to reapply this witch hazel. I have a small bottle here you can take. Now, let me take a look at your arms." Andrew felt the Duke's arms and applied some pressure in certain areas, making Richard pull a face, which the battle surgeon noticed, so he worked those particular areas harder to ease the tightness, then did some work on his shoulders. "I recommend a relaxing bath, then reapply the witch hazel and get a good night's sleep."

"Thank you, Master Andrew," Richard replied placing his now empty goblet on a side table, before easing his shirt back on.

"I'm pleased he didn't find anything serious," Morgan said to his father. "I will see you at supper tonight?"

"Yes. Right, bath, witch hazel, and a couple of hours rest before tonight's festivities," he smiled, his hazel eyes twinkling. "See you later." He picked up his armour and went to his own chambers.

"He's a very nice man," Andrew said as he started examining Morgan.

"The nicest," the Duke replied wincing as the battle surgeon found some tender spots on his body.

"Mmm, you were pretty hard on each other," Andrew said, applying more witch hazel.

"He made me," Morgan replied. "Ordered me. I didn't want to hurt him, he's my father and I love him, but he was determined to make me fight for the title and as I didn't really want to lose, I had no choice."

"Well, I'm giving you the same instructions, give the witch hazel a couple of hours, bath, more witch hazel and rest. Your shoulders feel tight..." Andrew dug his fingers into the muscles at the base of his neck causing the Duke to pull a face and grunt in discomfort. "Other than that, you're in pretty good shape. Just make sure you do as you're told. I'm your battle surgeon."

CB & CB &

At the banquet that night, Stuart made the formal announcement that Morgan was now his protector and released Trahaearn from the duty. The knight was staying on as an instructor and had finally done what the King had asked him to do; sent for the woman who at one time had been his intended. She would arrive in approximately a month.

Stuart thanked Trahaearn for his years of loyal service to both his father and him and wished him well in his new life and presented him with a considerable amount of gold coin as a reward for his sacrifice of a wife and children. He then shook the knight's hand.

Once again, food was washed down with copious amounts of wine, but like the previous evening, both Richard and Morgan were careful about what they ate and drank and retired relatively early.

The next morning was dull and cloudy with the threat of rain. Morgan was nervous again. This would be Banner's first proper tournament and his first test. With an untried horse, anything could happen. The mental link he had with the animal would help, as long as the Duke could also remain relatively calm. Any unease and the horse would pick up on it immediately.

As yesterday, the newly knighted squires would joust first, and the winner again invited to participate in the main tournament.

Morgan's route through to the final was a little more difficult and it hadn't been helped by Banner getting over excited and prancing impatiently, making it difficult for Ioan to hand the Duke his lances. A firm mental command was finally required, and the charger settled down before galloping along the run enabling Morgan to knock his opponent clear out of the saddle.

The Duke collected his third gold band, and again left the dais with his father at his side.

"I'm more nervous about this joust," Morgan confessed. "If we meet again in the final, I'm concerned about what could happen. The joust is more dangerous."

"Don't be nervous or scared. What God decrees will be. Hopefully we will both come through relatively unscathed. Again, give no quarter, Morgan. I want you to be the champion. I know my reign is at an end now, my age is against me, but I am content, I have won a number of tournaments, and now my son is ready to take over. However, I will not give up without a fight. Do what you must to secure victory, I have suffered worse on the battlefield."

In the warm up arena, Morgan hugged his father one last time. "No one could wish for a better father than you have been to me," he said.

"Morgan, are you going soft on me?" Richard teased.

"Never!" he replied as he mounted Banner, and Richard smiled and nodded at him before mounting his own charger.

The rounds against the experienced knights were a lot harder. Rodric nearly managed to unseat him on the first run, but somehow Morgan managed to stay in the saddle and fought his way back on the next two runs. After that unsteady start, he settled down, but as he battled on, round after round, the number of runs increased. Banner certainly had the stamina, but Morgan wasn't too sure about himself. In between the runs, he kept watch on how Richard was progressing. He could see his father was a better jouster, so he took the opportunity to watch his runs to see if he could learn anything, discover any flaw or weakness in his technique that might help him defeat him.

Richard didn't manage to unseat his opponent, but he knocked him sufficiently that the knight slipped sidewards, dropped his lance and got his boot caught in a stirrup. The knight's steward came to his rescue and stopped the horse before he slipped further and finished up under the hooves of his charger.

Now it was time for the semi-finals, and father and son had two stiff opponents to overcome. There were a few minutes before the first run and Richard stopped by Morgan's side.

"You're up against Eairdsidh Allbright," he said to his son. "Be careful, he stretches the rules to the limit. Watch how he alters the position of his lance at the last minute...he'll try for your helm."

"Thank you, father. How fare you so far?"

"I'm sore, but I'm still in the saddle. What about you?"

"Sore. I'm finding it hard."

"The measure of a man," Richard reminded him. "How he conducts himself. Be careful."

"And you." Morgan watched as his father entered the jousting arena to face a knight called Niall McDouglas who came from the far north of Devonmere. He was known to be cold and calculating, but Richard had made a point of taking a look at his rounds and had seen he had despatched most of his opponents with a single run, unseating them.

They lined up at either end, took their lances from their stewards and started their run. Richard adjusted his shield slightly, altered the height of his lance and they struck each other's shields firmly, the lances shattering into pieces at the force of the impact.

They returned to their own ends to collect new lances and ran at one another once more. Again the lances crashed against the shields, and they returned for a third. On the next run, Niall shifted his lance slightly to the left. It skidded off Richard's shield and caught his right shoulder, but Richard had also caught Niall and done some damage himself. Watching from the sidelines, Morgan unconsciously winced and studied his father as he cantered back down the run to retrieve another lance. Richard's face was expressionless as he rode past, and Morgan bit his lip. His father had received a hard blow. He noticed the Duke had issues taking the lance, but eventually he had it positioned as he wanted and set off down the run again.

As the lances crashed against their opponents, Richard lurched in the saddle, but somehow stayed in it. Niall was nearly unseated, recovered, but then as he reached out to take a new lance, toppled from the saddle. That immediately made Richard the winner. He saluted the King and Trystan ran up, grabbed the horses reins and led him out of the arena.

Morgan stopped them as they drew level. "Father?" he questioned.

"I – I'm all right. It's your – your turn now. Remember what I told you."

Morgan stepped back so they could continue onwards, went to his own horse and was given a leg up into the saddle. Ioan led Banner into the arena, they bowed to the King and Queen. Eairdsidh and his steward joined them and also bowed, then the two knights looked at each other without any expression and moved to either end of the run.

Ioan handed Morgan his helm. He put it on, adjusted it, then reached for his shield.

"Good luck Morgan," his steward whispered.

The Duke nodded at him and held his right hand out. Ioan handed him a lance and he positioned it in readiness. A flag was dropped, and the two riders urged their horses towards one another. Both lances shattered on impact and they returned for the second. Morgan adjusted the grip on his shield slightly, seeing that Eairdsidh was aiming higher than usual and suspected he may try going for his helm. It was possible for a knight to be blinded by a lance, so he took as many precautions as possible.

The second lance was higher still and Morgan instinctively closed his eyes as it shattered against his shield, throwing splinters in all directions. His own lance dropped a little lower and struck Eairdsidh's shield quite low, pushing him out of the saddle, but somehow he managed to stay on the horse.

The third run winded both riders and the fourth went horribly wrong and struck Morgan's left thigh. How he managed to stay in the saddle, he had no idea, but he did.

"Are you all right?" Ioan asked him as he came back for a fifth lance.

"I – I think so." He pulled a face. "I can hardly feel my leg. Come on, let's get this over with."

The fifth run started. Morgan adjusted his lance, it slid sidewards and upwards slightly hitting Eairdsidh in the right shoulder, he toppled, tried to recover, and then lost his balance and fell onto the barrier separating the two opponents which knocked the wind completely out of him. Morgan gritted his teeth as his leg started to throb as the initial numbness wore off. He saluted his sovereign and exited.

In a few minutes time it would be the final.

"Morgan, are you all right? That strike to your thigh...?"

"It's hurting like the devil," Morgan admitted.

"Do you need Master Andrew to take a look at it?"

"There isn't time." He glanced up and saw his father approaching on his bay stallion.

"Good luck Morgan," his father said.

"And to you too, father." They shook hands and Morgan saw his father do his best to hide a wince.

"Remember, give no ground to me."

"Yes, father."

They rode in together. The noise from the crowd was deafening as they stopped in front of the dais, bowed to the King and Queen and went to opposite ends of the run.

Final adjustments to armour were made, and then they took their lances from their stewards, adjusted their holds, then squeezed their legs against their horses flanks and took off towards one another.

The first lance was used to gauge each other, the second they tested each other's defences. Both times, the lances shattered. For the third run, they thought they had seen slight gaps in each other's defences and aimed for those spots. Both lances found their marks.

Up on the dais, Stuart was leaning forward again, paying close attention. He surmised it must be difficult to compete in a sport against someone you love, who you could seriously injure and his admiration for the two increased.

Down in the arena, the fourth lances were taken, minor adjustments made and they struck each other again. Morgan's lance hit Richard in almost the same place as Niall's had and a sharp pain shot through his right arm into his shoulder. Somehow he held onto what was left of his lance as he returned to Trystan.

Morgan was gasping as Richard's lance managed to hit him on the side of his ribs. They rode back past each other to collect their fourth lance and ran at one another again. The lances disintegrated and Richard screwed his eyes shut. His right hand had gone completely numb so when he went to take the fifth lance, he dropped it. He flexed his fingers, but that just made the pain worse.

"Your Grace," Trystan asked, his tone worried.

"I – I can't feel my fingers," he gasped trying to take hold of the offered lance again.

At the other end of the run, Morgan saw Richard drop the lance and that he was having difficulties gripping it. He suddenly felt he didn't want to do another run if his father was hurt, but the Duke seemed determined make a run somehow.

"Your Grace, you can't hold it!" Trystan exclaimed.

"I – I have to, I can't go out like this!" Richard said gritting his teeth. "Have you got any rope? Tie it to my arm."

"Your Grace, no!"

"Do as you're told, Trystan. I just won't go out of the tournament like this! Do it!" Richard clenched his teeth as his steward retrieved some rope and tied the lance to his arm. Although the lances used in tournaments were of a light wood, the weight of it pulled and the Duke felt the bile rising. He swallowed convulsively, took several deep breaths and lined the lance up how he wanted it and urged his horse forward.

At the other end, Morgan frowned with worry, but lined up his own lance and urged Banner on.

Again the lances splintered as they made contact with their targets. Morgan clutched at his ribs as he felt something give. Richard collapsed forward in the saddle. There was a red fog hovering in the corner of his eyes, but he fought it and made it back to Trystan, who undid the rope as fast as he could to release what was left of the lance. He then hurried round to the left side and managed to catch Richard as he slipped from the saddle and collapsed to his knees.

Morgan, dropped his shield and what was left of his lance, pulled off his helm and threw it at Ioan before galloping up to the other end of the run. Ignoring the pain in his ribs, he dismounted, staggering slightly as the pain from his thigh also hit him and limped the rest of the way to his father, who Trystan was helping to his feet.

"Father!" He went to take his right arm and assist him, but Trystan stopped him.

"No, Your Grace! I think it's dislocated."

"I'm – I'm sorry!"

Richard shook his head. "It - it's not your fault. I think most of the damage was done by McDouglas." He managed to straighten up. "Come, the King is waiting." He glanced in Stuart's direction and saw the frown on his face.

With Morgan supporting him on his left side, they walked up the steps, and knelt awkwardly before their King.

"Richard, are you all right?" Stuart asked in a whisper.

"I believe, I have...dislocated my shoulder, Sire," he replied.

"Then we will not linger. You must get that seen to."

The King acknowledged the two dukes, presented Richard with some more gold, and pronounced Morgan as tournament winner, the youngest ever to win, placed a more ornate band on his head, then dismissed them both and told them to report to a battle surgeon.

Master Andrew accompanied them to Richard's chambers. It took quite a while to remove the Duke's armour as he had little mobility on his right side. Finally stripped to the waist, Andrew examined him.

"Definitely a dislocation," he finally said as he gently probed the arm and shoulder. "Your Grace, would you lie on your bed, I can fix this."

"Won't you need the—"

"No, it's best done by manipulation. Something I learnt on my travels." He poured Richard a goblet of unwatered wine. "If you would drink this, Your Grace. It will help ease the discomfort."

Richard downed the wine in a few mouthfuls, then was helped to lie on the bed. Andrew removed the pillows, so he was laying completely flat.

The surgeon was just about to ask Morgan for his assistance when Richard's steward arrived. "Trystan," he said. "I could do with some assistance for this."

"What do you need me to do?"

Andrew showed him where to hold Richard and explained how he was going to manipulate the arm to get it back into the socket. It was quite a tough procedure but resulted in less damage than the traditional method of strapping the arm in a wooden device and cranking a wheel to put tension on. He nodded at them both, took a very firm hold on Richard's arm, put a foot against his upper ribs, just below the armpit, pulled and manipulated. The Duke screwed his eyes shut and grunted.

"Almost there," Andrew mumbled.

He gave a sharp pull did another twist and there was a loud click. Richard couldn't prevent a cry getting past his lips.

"There, done," the battle surgeon said. He made up a sling to support the newly relocated shoulder, then checked the rest of the Duke's chest, and applied some of his faithful witch hazel.

Trystan picked up a blanket and covered Richard with it.

"I recommend you lie there for a couple of hours after you take this." Andrew had made up a potion to help ease the pain. He looked at Trystan. "Make sure His Grace drinks all of it."

"Thank you," Richard said to Andrew, then looked at Trystan. "Is my horse all right?"

"He is still full of himself, Your Grace, and is fine."

Richard nodded and gingerly sat up to drink the potion Andrew had made up for him.

"I shall check on you in a couple of hours and before you retire for the night." He turned to Morgan. "Your turn, Your Grace," he said, indicating for him to head to his own chambers.

Arriving, Morgan immediately asked after his horse.

"Unharmed, Morgan, he was a bit of a handful, but he's settled in his stable now."

"That's good to hear."

Andrew interjected and got straight to the point. "And how are you, Morgan?"

"Bruised, and I think I've cracked a rib."

"Was that your father, or Eairdsidh Allbright?"

"Both, I think."

The Duke stripped off; Andrew looked at the bruising around Morgan's ribs, and gave them a slight prod and poke, making the Duke flinch. "Just cracked. We don't need to strap you up, but no strenuous exercise for a couple of days, give it a chance to start healing." He applied his ever faithful witch hazel. "Same orders as yesterday, Morgan. Anything else I should know about?"

"No."

"I want you to rest for a couple of hours. Bed. Do as your battle surgeon orders."

"What? Really?" Morgan stood up and limped a few steps before he managed to disguise it, but nothing got past Andrew.

"You're limping."

"It's nothing, just a twinge." Morgan saw the look on his surgeon's face and sighed. Not disguising the limp anymore, he went to his bedchamber, stripped and lay down on the bed. Andrew spied the heavy bruising on his left thigh.

"When did you get this?" he demanded.

"Tournament. Allbright did it to me in the joust."

"Why wasn't he disqualified? That was too low a strike! Let me use my infamous witch hazel on it." He stood up. "Ioan, bring my bag in here please!" he called.

Ioan appeared quickly and Andrew treated the large bruise.

"How much of that stuff do you get through?" the Duke asked out of curiosity.

"Bottles and bottles!" Andrew replied smiling. "Now do as you're told!"

ॐ ॐ ॐ ॐ

As it was the final night of celebrations, both Richard and Morgan had a little extra to drink in way of celebration. Stuart took great delight in proclaiming the young Duke as the new King's Champion, and a toast was made to him.

Stuart leant towards Richard. "At least you're keeping it in the family!" he joked, and Richard smiled.

"Indeed. I will now step down from tournaments, I'm getting too old anyway."

"Rubbish!" Stuart came back with. "You're what...coming up to forty?"

"Yes Sire."

"Plenty of life left in you yet!"

"Yes, but I would like to live and see it!"

Stuart laughed out loud, and everyone looked at him for a moment. They had not heard him laugh like that before.

"I suppose you're going to use that as an excuse not to dance?" the King asked indicating Richard's right arm that was still in a sling.

"I was, but if you insist..."

"No, you rest it. That's your sword arm, you need to look after it."

They all carried on drinking and staggered off to their chambers at a ridiculous time in the early hours, to collapse, fully clothed on their beds.

There were several sore heads the following morning. Richard couldn't believe he'd let himself succumb to his old bad habits, but it had enabled him to get a good night's sleep. It was Morgan's first hangover and he vowed never to drink as much again, as he held his head in his hands and tried to will the man with the anvil hammer in his head to go and pound it in someone else's. Even Stuart had over indulged and was currently suffering the consequences.

Personal stewards arrived and quickly disappeared to obtain various supposed hangover cures that worked to varying degrees. But apart from that, the castle was like a tomb for the day, where no one stirred as they recovered from their over indulgence of the past few days.

Visitors left later than intended as they travelled back to various parts of the kingdom. Richard took another letter from Morgan back with him to Inver in an effort to try and bring Bronwyn out of her depression. The young Duke suspected that only a visit might do the trick, but he was still stuck at Ellesmere for the time being.

ᘯ ᘒ ᘯ ᘒ

Chapter Thirty-Two

Now formally knighted, Morgan no longer had to wear the livery of the House of Cantrell, and chose instead, to wear dark, sombre colours; usually black. Following the incident almost two years ago, he had already instilled fear into many—they had heard about him defeating three squires without armour—and decided to cultivate it further by wearing black. His horse was as black as night; so, dressing in the same colours would almost complete the picture. Shame he didn't have black hair and dark eyes; but then he realised, the vision of the black would be in stark contrast to the burnished gold hair and grey eyes, and make all those around him much more wary.

In moments of self-doubt however, he found himself craving someone who was his equal, as a friend. Of course, Stuart Cantrell had told him to consider him a friend; but he was the King, so he felt he could never really be the one person who Morgan could truly be himself with. During these times of weakness, he tried to isolate himself in his rooms, or in a deserted part of the castle, or even ride out away from the castle, to gain control of his emotions again.

Ioan did his best to make the young Duke feel at ease, as did Master Andrew, but it just wasn't quite right, for they were not his equal.

Abruptly, his thoughts turned to Bronwyn, Richard and Colwyn, and a slight smile touched his mouth. He felt at ease with them, especially Colwyn. She exhibited no fear of him whatsoever, despite some of the 'stories' she may have heard. As far as she was concerned,

Morgan could do no wrong. He wondered if she knew what had almost happened a few months after his fourteenth birthday. Should he tell her when he next saw her, before she heard the wildly exaggerated tales from others? He could not bear to think of her becoming afraid of him.

The only person who truly understood, was his cousin, Colin. Their bond was as close as brotherhood. Colin had been there for him, offering wisdom and love, and he, in turn, had been there to support and console Colin, when his cousin's bride-to-be had been killed. They had both come so close to stepping over to the black arts and being banished from the Kingdom.

Colin, Morgan thought fondly, hoping he was doing all right in his studying for a life in the church. He hadn't wanted him to go, but had accepted his cousin's decision in the end, although he missed his company.

Morgan? The question resonated in his mind. *Is anything wrong?*

Forgive me, cousin, if I have disturbed you, Morgan sent back. *I apologise, I was feeling sorry for myself.*

Morgan, you could never disturb me. What troubles you? Perhaps I can help.

You are generous as always, Colin. I am missing the company of someone who is my equal, who I can be myself with. I am missing you.

Not for much longer. I am expecting to return soon. My studies are almost over, and I believe I am being assigned to Bishop Douglas at Ellesmere.

Really? Morgan's eyes lit up at this news. *It will be good to see you again!*

As soon as it is confirmed, I will let you know. Now, I must go, I am being summoned. Take care.

And you.

As always, his brief conversation with Colin had eased the ache in his heart and lifted his spirits. Colin here, at Ellesmere!

Morgan needed to return to Rossmere, he had several tasks that needed to be done; the most important to find a place of solitude like Trahaearn had, to unwind, relax and find himself. It would be difficult because he would have to leave the castle without anyone noticing. A Duke was always accompanied by his guard, but his place of seclusion had to be a secret from everyone, including those most close to him.

The Duke instructed Ioan to pack their saddlebags whilst he went in search of Stuart to tell him he was returning to Belvoir and to find out how much time he would be able to stay there before having to return to Ellesmere.

"Morgan, how are you feeling now?" Stuart asked him.

"Still a little sore, but on the whole, I'm fine, Sire. Thank you for asking. I need to return to Belvoir before everyone there thinks I've deserted them."

"Of course you must. I will be sorry to see you go, as always, but I completely understand. There may be a number of items that need your attention there. Currently, all is well in the kingdom, so take your time, get to know your home properly. I would like you to return next April. I was thinking I would like to go to Inver after the June knighting ceremony. Perhaps some outside company may cheer Bronwyn up. It's a sad business. Come and say your goodbyes when you are ready to leave."

"I will Sire. I am planning to depart in an hour or so, whilst there is still plenty of daylight."

With their saddlebags packed, Ioan carried them down to the waiting horses whilst Morgan bade his King goodbye.

"Take care of yourself. I will see you again in April," Stuart said.

"And you, Sire."

There seemed to be a bit of awkwardness in the air. Morgan was his own man now, a knight, a Duke. For a moment, Stuart remembered the first time he had set eyes on him, just over nine years ago, standing defiant, grey eyes not fearing to meet the King's gaze as he demanded explanations. The Duke had changed almost beyond recognition. Close to six feet tall, his hair had darkened to a burnished gold with almost white streaks in it caused by the sun. Piercing grey eyes looked at him out of a healthily tanned handsome face that possessed a dimple in the chin. Broad shouldered, slim hipped, accentuated by the surcoat belt and sword belt at his waist, he looked every part the regal Duke that he was.

"I was just remembering the first time I set eyes on you," Stuart finally said. "You certainly have changed these past nine years. You arrived a child, and now leave a man. I wish you a safe journey, my friend, and I will see you in April." The King made sure the two of them were alone, then stepped forward and gave the young Duke a hug, which the surprised Morgan returned. "I consider you a brother. I have been through more with you than I have with Michael."

"That is true." Morgan stepped back, out of the embrace. "Until April, Sire. Stay safe and well." He bowed and left his King watching him leave his presence.

 C3 80 C3 80

The journey to Belvoir was totally uneventful and on arrival, Morgan found several matters needed his attention. He only just about had time to wash and change before he was bombarded with questions, requests, queries. The Duke dealt with the most pressing ones first, then dismissed everyone else, apart from his head steward, Edward.

"It is good to have you back home, Your Grace," he said. "Apologies for that manic session, but they needed to be dealt with. How was your journey?"

"Uneventful. How are you Edward, and your father?"

"We are both well, thank you for asking, Your Grace. You will not be disturbed for the rest of the day; you must be tired after your journey. Did the knighting ceremony go well, and how was the tournament?"

"The knighting ceremony went off without a hitch. Father gave me two matching swords as a present. My horse behaved himself in the tournament, and in both sword and joust, I had to battle my father for the titles."

"So it is confirmed, you are now the King's protector, his champion and tournament champion."

"Yes."

"Congratulations, but what did your father think of you usurping him?"

"He ordered me to usurp him; to give no quarter and he was very proud."

Edward nodded.

"What is our itinerary tomorrow? I need some time to myself. I would like to explore my duchy."

"I can postpone everything, Your Grace. Go on your journey of exploration, get to know your duchy properly. Take as long as you need."

"Thank you, Edward. I'll leave in the morning."

Andrew and Ioan joined him that evening for supper. He was finding it rather lonely. No one was his equal, there was no one he could bear his soul to, no one to comfort him here. The pressure was building again, but he had to maintain control until he found the secret place where he could vent those emotions. He told them he would be away for a few days.

"But we've only just got back," Ioan said. "So where are we going?"

"'We', aren't going anywhere. I'm going...on my own."

"You can't!" Ioan protested. "You're taking a small guard at least?"

"No."

"But Morgan!" Andrew began.

"I need to go on my own."

"But you can't!" Ioan said again.

"I have to."

"Why?" Andrew demanded.

Morgan took a deep breath before speaking. "I – I need to find a haven, away from everyone before I lose myself again. Ioan, you know what happened at Inver...I can feel the pressure building again. If I don't do something about it, I might...I can't afford another incident like I had at Ellesmere two years ago."

"You never did tell us what really happened. Perhaps it would help if you shared that memory," Ioan said gently.

Morgan shook his head. "I can't."

"Can't...or won't?" Andrew asked.

The Duke looked at him sharply and the grey eyes flashed briefly before he looked away again and shook his head.

"You can trust us, Morgan, you know you can."

He took a deep breath.

"It may make you feel better," Andrew prompted.

The Duke looked at both of them, his eyes filled with a mixture of shame and regret. He swallowed and looked away.

"Taliesan Prescott made me lose my temper. He ambushed me with two of his comrades when I was alone, practicing my Florentine. I managed to knock his supporters unconscious eventually so it was one-on-one, and then he realised what he was up against, and started with the foul moves. I didn't have any armour on, and he did manage to inflict a slight injury on my thigh. Seeing he was not making any ground, he began to insult my family and when he uttered one insult too many against the Duke and Duchess of Invermere, I snapped.

"I almost killed him with magic," he said quietly. "And what's more, I was enjoying watching as I forced Taliesan to start cutting his own throat with his knife. I loved the look of fear in his eyes as he realised what I was doing to him. I could hear the panic in his voice as he begged me to stop, but that just made me want to continue. I wanted not only an apology, but to hear him sobbing for forgiveness." He got up from his chair and prowled the room. "Trahaearn and Stuart managed to prevent me from inflicting any serious damage back then, but I don't think they'd be able to stop me now, I'm too powerful."

He dared to look back at them and saw the shocked and wide-eyed expressions on their faces.

"You had a valid reason," Ioan finally managed to say. "You've never done anything without a reason."

"That's no excuse. I'm Kadeau, I have to maintain control, no matter what the cost. I let every Kadeau down, I failed my mentor, and my King."

"They forgave you."

"Yes. But that's not the point. I shouldn't have done it in the first place."

"You really are too hard on yourself, Morgan," Andrew said. "Remember, your body is still changing and with that comes the surge of emotions, until you have come through it."

"It still doesn't change the fact that I need to find a safe haven away from everyone. Ioan, pack my saddle bags with three days supplies. I will leave first thing in the morning."

Ioan and Andrew wisely kept quiet. The latter wished his master a good night shortly after. Ioan decided to pack the saddlebags straight away so he only had the food supplies to collect in the morning, helped prepare Morgan for bed, then said goodnight, pondering on his lord's decision to go off completely on his own.

The following morning, just after dawn, Morgan slipped out of the castle. He was dressed in black, but without any identifying crests, marks or other things that would give away who he was.

Banner was eager for a run, so once Morgan was sure he was warmed up, he let him have his head and gallop to the top of the next hill. They halted when they got there, and the Duke looked around him at the view. To the west was the coast, to the east, fertile fields with crops. To the north, rolling hills of pasture, that gave way to forest.

Ideally he needed to find somewhere that was relatively close to Belvoir, not the other end of the duchy. He sat contemplating what direction to go in, then decided to head towards the coast.

It took him a while to get there, and he found himself at the edge of a cliff that stretched both north and south for a number of miles but curved round to make a small cove. He walked for a little while, then thought he spied something, so he dismounted and went to investigate.

To his surprise, it was an overgrown path that zig-zagged its way down to the beach below. Morgan stood looking down at the beach, working out how far the tide came in and spied the seaweed that marked the extent of the sea's encroachment on the shore.

Cautiously he moved aside some of the overgrown vegetation. The path looked wide enough to take a horse, so he started down it, leading Banner. The horse did not seem phased by the perilous trail and followed obediently. Twenty minutes later they were at the bottom.

The tide was coming in, and the water was forming a natural barrier at both ends of the cove, so Morgan removed Banner's saddle and bridle and let him run free on the beach. He couldn't get out of the cove, so Morgan wasn't worried. The horse kicked up his rear legs, and with his tail high in the air, shot off down the beach at a full gallop. The Duke watched him go, then turned his attention to the cliffs.

A couple of hundred yards north, was a dark marking, which Morgan surmised could be a cave, so he went to investigate. Sure enough, it was a cave that went back into the mainland. Next to it a very small waterfall appeared part way up the cliff and fell into a pool that would provide Banner with fresh water. Conjuring up some fire-light, he went in and discovered three chambers, one on each side of the main one. Exploring them, they appeared relatively dry, although there was a small pool towards the back of the main one, fed by a trickle that ran down the wall. It then meandered its way out of the main cave towards the sea. There was grass growing on the sides of the cliff that the horse could feed on, as well as seaweed. He remembered a few of the species from his trip to Isatiri, as they'd eaten some with their meals. The smallest chamber he could make into a comfortable bed chamber, the other for storage and the main one for...whatever took his fancy.

He returned to the entrance and removed the saddlebags and blanket from where he had dropped the saddle and took them into the smallest chamber, then moved back out onto the beach and collected some driftwood to make a small fire.

Banner chose that moment to return and followed him into the cave.

"What do you think, lad?" Morgan asked him. "Our safe haven away from everyone." He patted him on the neck and the horse nuzzled into him.

Morgan spent the rest of the morning meditating, breathing in the fresh sea air, listening to the waves and the odd seagull. He finally managed to find that place within his mind that granted him peace and the surroundings helped a great deal.

515

By midday, the tide was fully in, so he stripped off his clothes and went for a swim. The exercise also helped to alleviate some of the stress he was feeling, and he was breathing hard when he finished. Banner had briefly come to investigate what he was doing before trotting off to the back of the cove.

The Duke put his breeches back on and had something to eat, which consisted of some simple bread and meat, washed down with some wine. Afterwards he removed his two swords from their scabbards and practiced the Florentine. His ribs protested but he persevered and kept going until the sweat ran down his face and chest.

He then took a break and practiced some magic. Some he did inside the cave, some he did outside. To finish, he blindfolded himself and practiced using his sixth sense. Hearing water dripping somewhere, the breeze wafting through the cave, the sound of something small walking near the cave entrance, and his horse munching. All in all it had been a good day, and Morgan was feeling reasonably relaxed. Having time away from his responsibilities, the castle and people was helping.

He made himself a hot meal that evening, and watched the stars appear as night descended. The only sound were the waves, the sound of nightlife and the wind rustling through the dry seaweed and grasses. He fed the fire, then retired for the night on his bed of seaweed and blankets.

Morgan spent another day and night in his safe haven and then returned to Belvoir. Ioan and Andrew were both pleased to see him safe and well.

"You look refreshed, Morgan," Ioan told him. "How do you feel?"

"Better," was the reply.

The next day, the Duke threw himself into his duties, dealing with disputes, pleas, checking finances. He then went to the Pell to inspect the pages and squires. Sir Derec, the chief trainer was putting them through their paces and frowned as he saw the black clothed figure striding towards him, a sword on either hip. He was just about to challenge the stranger, when Captain of the Guard Sir Martyn Welles spoke.

"Your Grace, good afternoon," he said bowing and Derec did a double take.

This is the Duke of Rossmere? he asked of himself.

"Martyn." Morgan held out his hand and they shook. "It is good to see you again."

"I almost didn't recognise you, but your hair gave you away. May I introduce you to Sir Derec, who has been responsible for training the pages and squires."

"Sir Derec," Morgan said.

"Your Grace." He gave a little bow, but his eyes appraised the youth. *This boy is the king's protector, champion and tournament champion?* It was hard for him to believe.

"May we be of assistance?"

"Who is the best swordsman here? I need someone to practice with. I would also like to see how the pages and squires are progressing."

"The best swordsman is myself, followed by Martyn here," Derec replied.

"Very well. Let's see a demonstration from the pages and squires."

Derec proceeded to put the novices through their paces whilst Morgan and Martyn watched from the sidelines.

Morgan nodded. They weren't exceptional, but they weren't the worst he'd seen either. He would change that. He praised them, then said, "I am in need of worthy adversaries. You will both make yourselves available when I have need. Carry on."

With that he turned on a heel and left, leaving Derec and Martyn staring at one another.

☙ ☙ ☙ ☙

The remainder of the year came and went, as did Morgan's seventeenth birthday the following February, and all too soon he was back at Ellesmere in April. He spent some time with young Prince Llewellyn who was now three and started him practicing with a small wooden sword, just like he had at the same age. Stuart had the child on a small pony teaching him to ride, and Alexandra seethed. It was bad enough that the Kadeau spent time with Colwyn Coltrane, now he was spending time with her son, and she did not like it one bit. Llewellyn on the other hand, loved it and loved Morgan, especially when he entertained him with little magic tricks, very much like he had also done with Colwyn.

His cousin, Colin, had arrived in Ellesmere just before winter had set in but had not let Morgan know. There was nothing the Duke could have done to get back due to the weather. They hugged fiercely, delighted to see one another again, but Morgan was sad that Colin had joined the church instead of staying a knight.

"Don't feel sad, Morgan, I am content."

"Really?"

"Yes. I have a year to stay here, then if you wish, I will attempt to get myself assigned to you if you are agreeable. I sense some unrest and despair in you. Let me help you."

"You always were sensitive to my feelings, Colin. I would like it very much if you could join me. I have no one at Belvoir to whom I can turn."

"Then I will do my utmost to make it happen. I am being kept very busy, so in case I don't get to see you beforehand, good luck in the tournament in June."

As expected, Morgan again won the tournament, and it was then they prepared for the journey to Inver. Stuart had advised the various duchies there would be a tournament at Inver in July for those who wished to attend, and that they were welcome to join the march there in the company of the King.

☙ ❧ ☙ ❧

Chapter Thirty-Three

———◆———

The journey to Inver was uneventful, as it was expected to be, with the combined forces of Ellesmere, Rossmere and lesser dignitaries who had joined them along the way, descending on the local capital of the duchy. It was an extremely colourful procession that made its way along the main street of the city towards Inver Castle. Pennants and banners had been uncovered and were fluttering gaily in the gentle breeze. Leading them all was the King's rampant red (gules) lion set on a tincture of gold (or), with a saltire of green (vert) followed just behind by the black (Sable) tincture bordered with a gold double tressle trefoil which framed the gold rampant guardant dragon of Rossmere. A trail of banners belonging to the other dukes and other gentry were mingled in the huge column as it made its way towards the castle, set high on a cliff, overlooking the bay.

People lined the streets, watching as the procession walked by. Many cheered and shouted, "God save the King!" as Stuart rode by, and he acknowledged their welcome with a wave of his hand.

Inver Castle was built of the same rock as it stood upon, a green and red speckled serpentine with narrow veins of white quartz, that shone in the sunlight due to having had the sea polish it before it was cut and used to build the great bastille. On certain days it almost resembled the skin of a snake or lizard. There were six towers between its high, solid walls. One looked over the bay, another beyond that to the sea, one kept watch over the town, and the other three surveyed the surrounding countryside. Although much smaller than Ellesmere Castle, Inver still looked magnificent because of its unusual colouring.

Stuart glanced at Morgan, who was riding beside him and smiled. The young Duke had certainly taken his new role of King's Champion and General of the Armies whilst Dafydd was recovering from illness, very seriously, and, dressed all in black, riding his black stallion, Banner, looked every bit as menacing as the image he had tried to cultivate. The only splash of colour was the golden dragon on his surcoat and the gold of his hair, bleached even lighter in places by the sun. He had also decided to cultivate a beard, which was gradually taking form, but had a little way to go before it was fully developed.

Morgan just caught the smile Stuart gave him out of the corner of his eyes, and returned it, nodding his head.

Stuart leant towards him slightly.

"Do you think the Duchess and Colwyn will recognise you?" he teased. "After all, it's been around five years since you saw them last, you have grown, and matured almost beyond recognition."

"Fortunately, my Liege, I am wearing my surcoat, so if they don't immediately recognise my face, they will recognise the coat of arms, I hope!"

Stuart laughed then. He was feeling relaxed and glad to be away from the pressures of rule, just for a little while. The Coltranes were to be their hosts for the next week, and all the arrangements had been left to them to sort out. He wondered what had been laid on in the form of entertainment in addition to the tournament, and assumed there would be some hunting, banqueting and dancing as well.

As they crossed the drawbridge over the moat and under the barbican, the ground changed to stone within the lower bailey. The majority of the knights stayed back, whilst the rest of the gentry carried on through the gatehouse and into the main bailey, towards the keep.

The Duke and Duchess of Invermere were standing at the bottom of the steps to the main keep, waiting patiently for their visitors to reach them. Lined up on either side were a number of squires and pages, ready to escort their guests to their rooms and take their mounts to the stables.

The King halted his charger at the base of the steps, and the carriage carrying the Queen and young Prince Llewellyn halted behind. Immediately a couple of pages ran forward. One to hold the King's mount, and the other to open the door to the carriage and assist the Queen and her son to descend its steps to the ground.

Morgan dismounted, idly patted Banner's neck and handed his reins to another page, then waited patiently for Stuart and Alexandra to address the Duke and Duchess before he moved from his position behind them.

"Your Majesties, welcome to Inver Castle," Richard said bowing deeply and kissing the ring on the sovereign hand of the King. He bowed again and kissed Alexandra's hand, then bowed to the young Prince. "We hope you had a pleasant journey here."

"Yes, thank you, Richard."

"The young Prince is growing fast," he added, smiling at the three-year-old. It was his first trip away from home and he was clutching his nurse's hand tightly. The boy had black hair like his father, but blue eyes, like his mother. "And he is a fine-looking boy."

"He is indeed," Stuart agreed. "Not that I'm biased or anything you understand!"

"Your Majesties," Bronwyn said, curtsying and straightening up. Her eyes strayed to the right slightly, and she smiled warmly as her hazel eyes locked with those of grey.

The King and Queen slowly ascended the steps, escorted by a trusted squire, as the Duke of Rossmere drew level with his guardians.

"Morgan, my son," Richard said warmly, clasping his hand tightly, and then giving him a hug. "You're looking well."

"Thank you, father, it's good to see you again," the young Duke responded. "How is your shoulder?"

Richard smiled. "Back to normal, thanks to your Master Andrew."

"Morgan!" Bronwyn breathed, giving him a hug and reaching up on tiptoe to kiss his cheek. "My, how you've changed since I last saw you! You're so tall now, and I must say, that beard definitely does something for you, although I do miss seeing that dimple!"

"Mother, I apologise for not being able to get here in the last five years," he said, smiling, slightly embarrassed by her words.

"It doesn't matter, you're here now," she said, before stepping back and holding him at arms' length. She could clearly see the change in him; not only the physical changes, but also the mental ones; his air, the way he held himself and she knew in that instance, the boy she had raised had most definitely become a man, in all ways. She gently squeezed his arms, then released him and smiled warmly.

Her touch had allowed Morgan to feel the full force of her motherly love and also her lingering sorrow for the loss of her two baby sons, but the feelings she had for him warmed him beyond measure. Inver would always be remembered with affection, for it was the first place he had stayed where he had known he was welcomed; had felt safe, and he was also most grateful for that.

As far as he was concerned, Bronwyn and Richard were his parents. They had raised him as their own child; supported him, cared for him, but now he was a man. He looked around.

"No Colwyn?" he asked, although he could just feel something warm and loving touching the edges of his mind.

524

"Knowing her, she's probably watching from her balcony. She's been so excited, she's almost made herself ill, so I thought it best not to let her be here."

Morgan nodded, and let his eyes stray up the keep to where he knew Colwyn's rooms to be, and sure enough, there she was, with a huge grin on her face, and he saw her clasp her hands together in delight as he smiled and nodded at her.

Still smiling, he looked down at Bronwyn, graciously took her hand and escorted her up the steps, taking one last glance up to Colwyn's rooms and saw her suddenly give a start and glance guiltily behind her as if she had been caught doing something she ought not to have.

Once inside the keep, he raised Bronwyn's hand to his lips, kissed it and took his leave to go to his chambers.

His saddle bags had been unpacked by Ioan, and clothes hung neatly in the wardrobe. Hot water was ready for him in a basin so he could freshen up, and then relax for an hour or so, to recover from the ride.

Ioan had also poured him a goblet of wine and a plate with bread and meat was on the table, along with a carefully wrapped parcel. A present for Colwyn.

"Ioan, go and get a couple of hours sleep," Morgan told him as the steward started to assist his Lord out of his surcoat, mail and riding leathers. "I can manage."

"If you're sure, Your Grace, thank you." Ioan bowed respectfully and left the room.

Now stripped to the waist, Morgan quickly washed, ate some of the bread and meat and quenched his thirst with the wine. As he sat at the small table, he contemplated his surroundings, suddenly realising they were no longer suitable for a man of his age, or to his taste, and he made a mental note to have the rooms redecorated. He spied a chest that he knew contained his childhood toys, still sitting against one wall and smiled slightly as he tried to remember what was in there.

A battered old wooden sword, a small shield, and a beautifully carved knight astride a wooden horse came to mind. There had also been toys to test and train his dexterity and encourage his young mind. They had been happy days indeed, he thought, as he went through to his bedchamber and relaxed on the four-poster bed.

It was three hours later when he arrived at the antechamber behind the great hall. Near neighbours of Invermere were also present, including the aging Duke of Strathmere, Kenneth Dernley, father of young Giles; various earls from within the duchy, and Nigel McDowell, the Duke of Cottesmere, whose lands bordered Rossmere's northern boundary.

To say the air was frosty as Morgan faced the Duke, was putting it mildly. The two had never met in person before, and for some reason, Nigel perceived the youthful nobleman to be a threat. Morgan could not initially fathom out why, until Colwyn arrived on the scene.

During his five years of absence, she had grown several inches and was now on the brink of womanhood, although her body was still very immature. Her long chestnut hair was loosely tied back with a gold ribbon, and her simple cream dress fitted to perfection. The gold chained belt around her waist accentuated the beginnings of the birth of a young woman.

Morgan watched Nigel's eyes follow her, like a wolf stalking its prey, as she was presented to the King and Queen.

"My goodness!" Stuart exclaimed looking at her in surprise. "This is Colwyn?"

"Yes, my Liege," Richard replied.

"Colwyn, my dear girl, you're developing into a beautiful young woman."

Colwyn blushed at his compliment as she curtseyed, but her green eyes lit up with excitement.

"Your majesty is most kind," she whispered in awe, then kissed the sovereign hand.

Stuart smiled and assisted her to her feet.

"My dearest Colwyn," Alexandra said as the child curtseyed once more. "You are a true beauty. I can see you are going to break many a young man's heart when you are older." She leant forward and placed a kiss on her cheek, clearly showing the child was very much favoured by the Queen.

"Thank you, Your Majesty."

She moved along to Kenneth Dernley, who leant down to place a kiss on her cheek and at the same time, presented her with a wrapped package.

"For you, my dear," he said, his brown eyes smiling at her.

"Oh Duke Kenneth, you are most kind!"

"It's just a little something," he added as he straightened up.

"Whatever it is, I shall treasure it!"

She was presented to a number of Earls, and then, caught sight of Morgan. Eagerly she started to walk towards him but was intercepted by Nigel.

Morgan immediately noticed the change in her mood, and frowned in concern as to why the Duke of Cottesmere made her uneasy. It was so tangible, at least to him. He wondered why he was so acutely aware of it, and decided it was due to the affection they felt for each other. They were like brother and sister, so of course he would be more attuned to her feelings.

"My dear," Nigel began as she curtseyed, and he held her hand. "You are looking positively exquisite tonight." He seemed intent on holding her hand far longer than was necessary, immediately raising

Morgan's suspicions. He was aware of the rumours that the Duke of Cottesmere dabbled in the dark arts. Was he attempting to assert some kind of influence on the child?

However, before he could take any action, Colwyn jerked her hand free of the Cottesmere Duke and moved closer to her adopted brother.

"Colwyn." Morgan's voice seemed to caress her name.

"Duke Morgan," she replied very formally, curtseying once more as he took her hand and raised it to his lips.

"I hardly recognised you. How you've grown, and into such a beautiful young woman."

He released her hand then leant over and kissed her cheek.

She blushed furiously at his words and stammered an answer.

"My Lord is very gracious and kind," she managed to whisper. "You too have changed, matured and are most handsome."

Morgan rewarded her with one of his rare grins as he straightened up.

"I too, have brought you a present. I'm afraid it's not a toy though, it's something rather more practical."

He handed her a slightly larger package than Kenneth had done, that he had carefully kept hidden behind his back in his left hand and saw her eyes light up.

Gleefully, she looked around for somewhere to sit and open her packages. Morgan gestured to two chairs near the ornate fireplace and escorted her there.

"Would you mind if I sat with you?" he asked.

"Not at all Duke, I would be honoured."

So, they sat, and Morgan looked on indulgently as Colwyn opened Kenneth's present first. It was a small wooden jointed horse, that had been exquisitely carved. The quality of the workmanship was outstanding.

"May I?" Morgan asked.

Colwyn handed it to him without any hesitation, eager to open the present he had given her.

"This is an amazing piece of work. What will you do with it?"

"I'm going to paint it black," she replied without pausing. *Black, like your stallion*, she whispered in her mind. "What's your horse's name?"

"Banner. He's a young horse, and still learning," Morgan replied smiling, his eyes alight with mischief, as if he had heard her unspoken thoughts, but he was prevented from saying anything further, as she gasped in delight at the present he had given her, a box of the most delicate silk threads for embroidery, every colour of the rainbow.

"Oh... Oh Duke...they are beautiful! How did you know?"

"Your mother remarked that you had the gift for embroidery and needlework the last time I was here, so I thought, as I was passing through Applegarth on one of my journey's, I would purchase a selection of their finest threads for you. I take it you are pleased?"

"Oh, more than pleased! Thank you so much!" she carefully closed the lid of the box, placed it down by her feet, got up from her chair and gave him a hug and a kiss on the cheek. Morgan was almost overwhelmed by the intensity of the love that flowed like a gentle breeze, caressing him. "I shall use these for my best work."

Just then, her mother arrived. Colwyn reluctantly let go of the Duke, who swiftly rose to his feet, his manners impeccable as ever.

"Oh Mama, look what Duke Morgan has brought me! Applegarth silks! Aren't they beautiful? And Uncle Kenneth has brought me an exquisite wooden horse."

"Morgan, you shouldn't have gone to all that trouble to seek out a gift for Colwyn."

"'Twas no trouble. You always make me feel most welcome whenever I am here, so it was for this reason I did this, besides, I haven't seen my sister for five years, I think I owed her a gift of some kind. You have been like a family to me since I lost my parents. On every visit I receive love and affection from you. I felt it was the least I could do."

"Bless you. If I were to have a son, I would wish him to be exactly like you." She leant forward and stretched up to kiss his cheek. "You are the son I have not had." For a couple of seconds, her eyes brightened, then she recovered herself and smiled warmly at him.

Morgan blushed at the compliment. He was a Kadeau with magical powers. Friends and affection such as this were rare, and he treasured it beyond measure, but it saddened him that she had still not borne the son that Invermere so badly needed.

It was then announced that the banquet was ready. Morgan offered Colwyn his arm which she eagerly accepted, and they walked into the main hall to take their place at the head table. The King and Queen took centre stage, with Bronwyn next to the King, then Morgan and Colwyn on one side and Richard sat next to the Queen, with Kenneth and Nigel next to him. Other local dignitaries and their wives were seated at the tables below the main one.

There were generous quantities and varieties of food for the banquet and wine flowed freely. Even Colwyn was allowed to drink a little, interspersed with the purest spring water. She spoke to Morgan, whilst Bronwyn spoke in turn to both the King and Morgan.

The Duke asked Colwyn what she had been up to since he had last seen her.

"Papa has me sitting at court, to learn how the duchy operates," she replied seriously.

"He had me doing that too when I was young," Morgan said.

"I have also been out, meeting the people. Do you know, we have some very gifted women and children in our duchy. I am hoping to be able to help them."

"Oh, in what way, m'dear?" the King asked, eavesdropping on the conversation.

"Sire, I hope to be able to teach them our special embroidery and lace techniques, to help them earn a living."

"My, but that's an ambitious project for one so young," he replied, smiling kindly, looking thoughtfully at her. It was a shame she was a number of years older than the young prince, for he believed she had the makings of a fine wife and future Queen. In addition, he knew Alexandra was very fond of her as well; but by the time Prince Llewellyn was old enough to marry, Colwyn would be at least twenty, and the prince needed to marry a woman younger than himself. However, he would not dismiss the possibility entirely, yet.

"I want our people to flourish and prosper."

"That is a fine aspiration, Colwyn," Morgan said, amazed at the maturity she was exhibiting at her tender age.

"Thank you, Duke."

After everyone had eaten their fill at the banquet, entertainment followed. A jester amused the guests whilst the musicians moved to set up at the other end of the hall to provide music to dance to. The King invited Bronwyn to dance, whilst Richard escorted the Queen onto the floor. Colwyn looked on enviously as they moved around the floor to a farandole, tapping her foot to the beat of the music. Her mother had taught her to dance and she was eager to try it.

Morgan kept her company, not realising that she was desperate to dance herself and watched her as she followed everyone's movements around the hall. Then he suddenly became aware of her stiffening in fear. The feeling was so strong in his mind that it had almost been like receiving a slap round the face, and he looked up to see Duke Nigel McDowell approaching. He did not particularly like the man either, even though he had just met him for the first time this night, but he was curious to know what it was about him that made Colwyn react so. How McDowell could not sense her unease, he did not know, it was so tangible—or was it his Kadeau magic that made him far more sensitive to her feelings, because he cared about her?

If McDowell noticed, he made no comment, which implied there were underlying motives. The Duke was ambitious, Morgan did know that about him. Could it be he was looking to make a match with the young Lady Colwyn? Currently, as the only heir, she would be an exceedingly wealthy woman when her parents died, and a liaison between the two duchies would put Morgan in a rather dangerous situation. His eyes narrowed, as he realised this could be McDowell's ploy. The match would not be in Morgan's best interests, that much was certain, and not good for the kingdom either.

At that moment, Colwyn glanced up at him, her green eyes huge and, coming to an immediate decision, he smiled at her and asked quietly, "Colwyn, would you like to dance?"

"Oh yes!" she replied eagerly, her voice sounding relieved. She didn't even wait for him to assist her from her chair but stood up and literally forced her hand into his.

McDowell stopped abruptly and glared at Morgan for a few seconds, then continued to walk towards them.

"My dear," he said to Colwyn, ignoring Morgan completely. "I believe this is our dance."

With her hand safely within Morgan's she was no longer afraid and replied without hesitation. "You are mistaken, Duke. I promised this dance to the Duke of Rossmere. Perhaps later." She curtseyed politely and they walked away, leaving Nigel scowling after them. "I'm sorry Duke," she whispered to Morgan, making sure they were out of earshot of Nigel. "I know you don't really like dancing that much, and it was very kind of you to offer, but I believe Duke Nigel is watching. If we don't dance, then—"

"I understand perfectly," Morgan replied.

They joined a circle of dancers for a carola, and moved around the floor gracefully, also singing in a round. Colwyn was so pleased that her mother had taught her how to dance for the occasion, and Morgan was such a handsome partner, she glowed with the pleasure. They stayed on the floor for another dance; this time the Sarahbande, but towards the end of this one, Morgan noticed Nigel trying to casually make his way over.

"Colwyn, do you trust me?"

"Sir?" she questioned.

"Do you trust me?"

"With my life," she answered. "Why?"

"I take it you do not want McDowell near you, correct?"

He saw her expression of alarm, and smiled slightly, trying to offer reassurance.

"Very well, just follow my lead." With that, he swept her round in another direction, towards a small crowd of guests. Using them to hide their escape, he pulled Colwyn with him, out of the room and into the corridor.

Perfectly at home in the castle, he knew exactly where he was going, and moved swiftly along the corridor, causing Colwyn to have to make little running steps to keep up with him. He kept going at this pace until they had turned a corner, gone down another corridor, up a flight of stairs, and along to the library, which he knew would be deserted at this time.

The room was in total darkness as Morgan shut the door behind them. Colwyn felt him let go of her hand and chant something very quietly. Suddenly, there was a blue-white flame dancing on the palm of his right hand, that allowed them to find their way around the large room.

"Where do you think would be a good place to hide for a little while?" he asked her.

Colwyn didn't answer him immediately, she was fascinated by his open display of magic.

"May I?" she asked tentatively, holding out her hand.

Morgan smiled at her again. "If you like. Hold your palm out straight and flat, that's right." Carefully he transferred the flame across onto her hand. "Now you can lead the way."

"Oh, it's cold," she whispered in awe, staring mesmerised at the gently flickering flame. "Is it possible to teach me to do it?"

Morgan blinked. It was the last thing he'd expected her to ask.

"I don't know," he answered truthfully. "No one has ever asked me before, so I've never tried."

"Would you...would you try though, please?"

"Very well, if that is what you would like."

She smiled up at him and led the way across the huge room.

"There's a secret room over here. If Duke Nigel does perchance find his way here, he'll never find that room. Papa doesn't know that I know about it, but I don't think he'd be very cross. I'd have to know about it eventually, wouldn't I?"

Colwyn stopped at a huge section of shelves, and studied the titles on a row that was too tall for her to reach.

"See that big thick red book on the sixth shelf, the one entitled Tales from the Eastern Desert? If you pull it out, you should just be able to feel three small knots in the wood at the back, in a row? Using your three middle fingers, press the knots simultaneously and then push the middle knot again on its own, then put the book back."

No sooner had Morgan done this, when a panel to the left of the shelf sprung open. Using her left hand, Colwyn felt one of the stones that seemingly made up a solid wall next to the panel and suddenly, part of it slid back enough for them to creep through one at a time, closing behind them once again as Colwyn touched another stone inside the secret room.

Seeing some candles, Morgan used the flint lying near them to light them, and then turned to Colwyn.

"Hold your right hand thus," he instructed rotating it slowly, so it remained flat and palm down, and Colwyn's mouth dropped open as the flame migrated from her palm to the back of her hand. "Now make a circular movement like this, using your wrist..."

She obeyed his instructions and watched as the flame moved again so it was resting on the palm of her hand once more.

"Now, with your left hand, wipe it across the palm of your right."

She did as he instructed, and her blue-white flame vanished.

"That's the more flamboyant way of extinguishing it. The usual way is to just clench your fist." He looked around the room. "Come, sit over here, and let's begin your first lesson."

They sat next to one another on a small couch and Morgan began.

"The command to create the fire-light is *ignite lumine ignis*. Try repeating it a few times, so you get the pronunciation right."

"*Ignite lu-min-e ignis*," Colwyn said.

"That's almost correct, try again. *Ignite lumine ignis*."

She frowned, closed her eyes for a few moments as she silently mouthed the words and had another attempt.

"*Ignite lumine ignis*."

"Better. Again."

"*Ignite lumine ignis*."

"Excellent! Now that you have mastered the words of the spell, you now need to concentrate your mind. Focus it, think about what you are trying to do, and imagine the fire-light forming. Now, I guarantee you will not succeed the first few times. It may take you an hour or so, or even longer, so you mustn't be disheartened if you fail. This is something brand new, you've never done it before, and it takes a lot of time and patience. Magic can be very dangerous, so you must always be careful. Think of trying to empty your mind of everything except that fire-light. Come, try."

Colwyn went to speak straight away, but Morgan stopped her.

"No, don't speak it yet. Think about that flame, focus the image in your mind so that it appears as sharp as the edge of my sword. Once you have that image, then speak the words. As you speak them, on the last word, open your hand so the palm is flat."

Colwyn nodded and frowned in concentration, then tried.

"*Ignite lumine ignis.*"

Nothing happened. She fidgeted and tried again...and again...and again.

Morgan sensed her frustration building, and spoke softly, his deep voice instilling calm.

"Relax, calm...close your eyes and breathe deeply and slowly...feel the tension flow out of your body and see the flame in your mind... good...that's it...steady...now try again."

She did as she was told and for a fraction of a second there was the flash of the tiniest blue-white spark.

Colwyn squealed in delight and Morgan stared in surprise. He had not expected her to succeed at all, this evening.

"Calmly now," he urged, sensing her heightened emotions. "Remember what you did and try again."

She practiced doggedly for almost two hours and finally managed to conjure a tiny little flicker. Morgan was full of praise, but Colwyn was not impressed.

"It's not very bright, is it?" she said dolefully. "That isn't going to allow me to see where I'm going."

Morgan laughed kindly. "To have conjured it up at all is most impressive, Colwyn. You simply need to practice more; you are showing that you are beginning to focus your mind correctly. As you learn to do this more effectively, the flame will become stronger, larger and brighter. It's like everything, the more you practice, the better you become; like playing a musical instrument or learning to ride a horse. You're not an expert after the first lesson now, are you?"

Colwyn nodded in understanding. "No, no you're not." She frowned in concentration and quietly whispered the chant again. This time, her flame was a little larger and brighter. Her eyes lit up.

"See, you're getting better already. The key word is focus. Focus the mind on what you want to achieve. You can apply that principle to anything. Now, I know I don't need to say this, but I will anyway. Be careful where you do this. Very few people are tolerant of Kadeau magic."

"I understand you, Duke."

"Why so formal this evening? You always used to call me Morgan."

"Mama said I had to use the correct etiquette this evening, as the King and Queen were present."

"Oh, I see, but I don't think that refers to me; I'm your brother."

He watched her as she tried a few more times, then decided to ask her the question on his mind.

"Why don't you like Nigel McDowell?"

Her flame disappeared with a pop, and she looked up at him, suddenly feeling uneasy, but decided to answer his question without any pomp and circumstance.

"He's evil."

"Would you care to elaborate on that?"

"There's something about him. I don't trust him; he makes me feel uneasy and ill whenever he's near me. I can't explain it. He scares me too, and..." She swallowed, suddenly feeling tears welling in her eyes. "I know I'm of marriageable age now, and he's been visiting for years...I'm terrified that I might be forced to...marry him. I won't do it, I just won't! I'll... I'll run away, or I'll kill myself first!"

Morgan saw her bottom lip quiver and the tears in her eyes, and his heart went out to her. A woman had very little say in her future. Arranged marriages were the norm of the time and the horrors that sometimes brought did not bear thinking about.

"It...it's childish isn't it," she mumbled, but then the tears began to flow.

"Oh, my pet, I didn't mean to upset you with that question. It's just that I became acutely aware of his interest in you. We've had such a wonderful evening, and now I've gone and spoilt it for you. Please forgive me." Morgan held out his arms, and Colwyn collapsed into them.

"No, it's not your fault," she mumbled into his shoulder. "I—I didn't think anyone noticed how I felt about him."

"Have you spoken to mother about it?"

"I've told no one. I thought someone would notice, but...only you seem to have picked up on it, and I'd feel foolish telling Mama or Papa, they'd think I was being childish, and I don't want them to say I'm being petulant or anything."

Morgan sat and deliberated for a few moments.

"How about if I do some delving for you? Your mother considers me her son and your brother—one of the family—so let me take this opportunity to be an older brother to you and see what I can find out."

"Oh, thank you, Morgan, but you have always been like my older brother; I have fond memories of our time together in this castle; of the rides, even of you carrying me around, of the magic you performed to entertain me, singing to me, taking me on adventures, and you and Colin teaching me to swim."

"You remember all of that?" he questioned.

"Yes, all of it."

"That has warmed my heart, but now, I think perhaps it's time for you to go to bed. It's rather late, and there's a big day ahead and the day after, with the tournament and everything else that's going on. As King's Champion, I will have some fierce competition to overcome, and I shall need all the help I can get. This is my first contest since I gained the title and I would really like to successfully defend it, but I am up against a couple of knights who I have never faced before."

Colwyn studied him thoughtfully for a moment, then reached into one of the sleeves of her dress and pulled out a delicate handkerchief with her initials sewn into one corner, and a beautiful lace trim around the edge.

"Then take this favour sir, as a token of my support for you these coming days, and always."

Morgan accepted the gift and placed it carefully inside his jacket. "Thank you, my Lady. I will cherish and carry this with me always... along with the other one you sent to me via father." He kissed her hand, then helped her to her feet. "Come, I will escort you safely to your rooms."

They carefully retraced their steps and Morgan, true to his word, saw her safely to the care of her hand maiden, before returning to the great hall to inform her mother where she was.

"Thank you, Morgan. You have been so good to her this evening, I'm sure she's enjoyed your company very much, especially as you have treated her like an adult."

"Well, she is now of marriageable age, so by rights she is now an adult."

Bronwyn sighed heavily. "She may be considered an adult, but as yet, she is not a woman in the true sense of the word. Both Richard and I are planning to allow her to enjoy her childhood a while longer before we consider any marriage. Life is short enough as it is. I don't want her married off straight away, and with child...it's too dangerous for one so young."

For an instant, she saw a flash of pain cross his face, and realised what affect her words may have had on him.

"Oh Morgan, I'm sorry, that was insensitive of me, knowing what happened to—"

"No, don't apologise," he broke in hastily, and gave her a reassuring smile. "I believe Nigel McDowell is interested in approaching you regarding marriage. His interest has been very obvious this evening."

Bronwyn frowned and lowered her voice to a mere whisper. "He first approached us when Colwyn was but three years old," she confessed.

"What?!" Morgan was clearly shocked at this news. "Three!"

"Richard wasn't here when Nigel made his first visit, so I gave the Duke a polite refusal at the time, and intimated that marriage was not an option for several years, but he has visited a number of times. I don't think he would be right for her, or the Kingdom. I realise the possible danger of that liaison, as does my husband. Besides, although Colwyn has said nothing to us, I know she does not like the Duke. To be honest, I'm not that fond of him either, there is just something about him; something I do not trust. I would dearly love to see her marry someone who she cares deeply about, but we shall see. It could be the King already has plans for her."

"None that I am aware of, mother," Morgan replied. "As you say, there is no hurry."

"Morgan," Bronwyn placed a hand on his arm. "I know I have no right to ask but, you will watch over her, won't you? I know she is very fond of you."

"You have every right to ask that of me, and I will watch over her like an older brother. Remember, I vowed to protect her with my life the first time I saw her."

"Yes, you did. I remember. God bless you and keep you." She leant up and gently kissed his cheek.

"And how are you now, mother?" he asked. "Tell me the truth."

Her eyes grew a little brighter as she answered him. "I have... recovered, and I will admit I was in a very dark place for quite a while. I do not know why God has decided we should not have a son. But I have you."

"You must not give up. Promise me you will not give up."

"I don't think I could stand losing another baby. Each time it is harder."

"You are so much stronger than you think, mother. I will continue to be your son until you have one of your own. Have faith. I don't know why God is testing you, but He will see fit to grant your wish. He must, and I will pray every day."

Morgan leant over and kissed her cheek, then bowed deeply and took his leave, wanting to get a decent night's sleep before tomorrow's tournament began.

But sleep evaded him for a while, as his mind reviewed the conversation he had had with Bronwyn. Colwyn would be happier once he told her that her mother was aware of her feelings about McDowell, and that there were certainly no marriage plans in that direction or—for that matter—any other at present. What did worry him though, was the news that the Cottesmere Duke had been trying to win her hand for almost nine years! It appeared he was determined to try and make her his wife, and Morgan decided he was not going to allow that, no matter what the cost.

He had heard all about the Duke's attitude towards the House of Cantrell, and that he was highly ambitious. The nobleman would require careful watching going forward.

His mind then turned to the time he had spent with Colwyn in the hidden room. For her to have managed to conjure the fire-light at all, after only just a few hours was indeed a remarkable accomplishment, and he began to wonder more about her heritage. Was there Kadeau blood hidden somewhere in there? As far as he knew there wasn't, yet for her to have mastered that spell was an indication that maybe there was, somewhere in her past. Either that, or she had an exceptionally sharp and focused mind. He deliberated a while longer, but slowly he began to relax and finally fell into a deep, dreamless sleep.

CB ℬ CB ℬ

It had been a very long day for Colwyn, but sleep evaded her. Sarah had helped her undress and seen her safely to bed, but the youngster had not fallen asleep as expected.

"My Lady are you feeling unwell?" her maid asked her.

"No, Sarah. I'm fine. I've had an exciting time, I'm not really tired."

"You should be exhausted, you need to sleep, you have another long day tomorrow. Where's your handkerchief? I can't find it anywhere."

"I gave it to Morgan."

"You gave it to the Duke of Rossmere? What on earth for?"

"As a lady's favour. He is the King's Champion and mine, for the tournament. He said he would need all the help he could get, so I gave him a favour for good luck and encouragement."

"It was your best handkerchief!"

"I can make another one."

Sarah heaved a breath of what sounded like exasperation.

"It's only a handkerchief, Sarah. I don't see why you have to be so grumpy about it."

"I'm not 'grumpy', My Lady. You should not give favours away to anybody."

"He's not 'anybody', he's my brother! And if I want to give him a favour I will do so."

"Favours are usually reserved for those who have more of a... romantic interest, not for a sister to give to her brother."

"I don't care. He accepted it." She gave Sarah the benefit of a pout and jutted out her chin in pure defiance.

Sarah wisely held her tongue. A pout was sometimes a prelude to a tirade of some kind, and she knew the child was extremely tired, even if she was saying she wasn't.

"Come on, lie down and go to sleep," she said instead, and tucked her charge in for the night. "Goodnight, My Lady."

She leant over and blew out the candle that was sitting on the bedside table and left the room, shutting the door behind her.

Colwyn lay quietly for a while, listening for any movement in the outer room, but all was silent. She patiently let some more time go by, then sat up, and held her hand out palm up and concentrated.

"*Ignite lumine ignis*," she whispered, but nothing happened. She took a deep breath and tried again. "*Ignite lumine ignis*." Nothing. It wasn't working. Why wasn't it working?

Colwyn felt her control slipping and forced herself to relax. She cast her mind back to earlier in the evening, to remember what Morgan had told her. *Focus the mind, breathe deeply, close your eyes*, she thought to herself. *Concentrate, focus.* She kept this up for a couple of minutes, then opened her eyes and tried again.

"*Ignite lumine ignis.*" It was small, but there it was, her beautiful blue fire-light. She just managed to stop a squeal of delight as she watched it flickering rather feebly, but it was there, she'd done it, all on her own! She clenched her fist and tried again and succeeded straight away. It didn't seem to be any larger or brighter, but she was managing to do it. Colwyn repeated it another three times and succeeded on every attempt.

Suddenly feeling tired, she slowly rotated her hand, watching the flame as it moved from her palm to the back of her hand and once again to the palm, then extinguished it, and lay down.

Sleep came quickly, but she did dream of Morgan, and magic.

The following morning dawned bright and promised to be pleasantly warm. The castle was a hive of activity as the final, last minute preparations were finished off. The day of celebrations were to be formally opened after breakfast and events were to be both serious and for amusement. In addition to the formal tournament, which was to include swordsmanship, and skill with the bow and arrow, there was to be a demonstration by the young squires and pages to show how their proficiency was developing both in horsemanship and with weapons. The following day was the joust and to end the tournament there was going to be a pillow fight on horseback. The last man mounted would be declared the winner.

Colwyn had been awake over two hours before normal and her excitement was beginning to get the better of her. She had gulped down her breakfast and gone running off to see how everything was progressing. She also wanted to see Morgan before the events started, to wish him luck and tell him she would be supporting him to the bitter end.

She found him warming up in the practice ring. Seeing her approach, he stopped and went to the fence.

"Colwyn, you're up early," he said to her.

"I've been up over two hours, I'm so excited! I just wanted to see you before all the activities started, to wish you luck and tell you I will be supporting you all the way."

"Thank you, my pet." He pulled her handkerchief from under his sleeve. "See, I have your favour safely on me, for good luck as well."

She smiled a radiant smile, as he tucked it safely away again.

"Regarding our other conversation last night, about McDowell, I spoke to your mother, and you need not fear. She is aware you do not like him, and there are no plans to marry you off. Now, are you happy?"

"Oh yes! Thank you so much, Morgan."

He knelt as she ducked under the fence rail so she could give him a hug, and then boldly kissed his lips, which surprised and pleased him.

"I love you so much!" she said finally letting go of him. "Now I'd better get back, so I can watch you do battle." She was gone before he could say anything.

Morgan stood up and smiled to himself. He always received love and affection when he came to Invermere, and Colwyn, like her mother, thought the world of him. He turned round and spotted Nigel McDowell in the distance, staring at him and he suddenly felt the urge to upset the Duke as much as he could, during the tournament. It was an illogical feeling, and rather unknightly, but he just had to make sure that Nigel knew that he was the favoured one at Invermere, although he suspected Nigel might already be aware of that.

CB ∞ CB ∞

It was a well-known fact that Morgan had never been beaten in a sword fight since the age of fourteen, thus it was no surprise that he should reach the final of the swordplay. However, it was another fact that Nigel McDowell had also never been beaten since coming of age and had also reached the final. In addition, he was also eight years Bodine's senior and thus in theory, stronger and more experienced. The fight had drawn a large crowd, and as much as many feared Bodine, they liked the Duke of Cottesmere even less; his cruelty and selfish ambition were known throughout the Kingdom. Nigel resented the open show of warmth that the Coltranes bestowed upon the Kadeau Duke, so if there was an opportunity that he could defeat the young whippersnapper in front of them, he was going to grab it with open arms. This would be the first time the two would meet in any kind of battle.

Aware of the animosity that had developed in so short a time, everyone was eagerly looking forward to the forthcoming match and wagers on the outcome were flying around.

"So, Richard," the King began, "what do you wager on the outcome?"

"Strictly speaking, my Liege, McDowell's more experienced and has seen more action, so that speaks in his favour; however," Richard quickly continued seeing the King about to try and persuade him to wager something foolish, "Morgan is fitter, and more level-headed. It is a difficult decision."

"Father!" Colwyn chastised. "Morgan will win," she said confidently.

"And pray tell, young Colwyn, why this will be the outcome?" the King asked, an amused expression on his face.

"Because I want him to win."

The King laughed delightedly. "See, Richard, 'tis nothing to do with skill and experience, but what a woman wants!" He laughed again, clearly enjoying the day.

"Your Majesty," Colwyn said gravely. "Morgan is the best!"

He held out his arms to her. "Come, child, sit with me and let us see if you are right."

"Richard," Bronwyn whispered quietly to her husband, "do you think it wise that Colwyn watches this? It is likely to be a rather... heated fight, knowing how these two men feel towards each other."

"It is best she learns here of war; in play—rough though it might be—than to see the real thing first hand. Let her be."

A herald announced the arrival of the two opponents who walked into the arena and up to where the King and Queen's party were sitting. A great hush came over the audience as the two men bowed respectfully to their King, and then less amicably to one another. Each then made some final adjustments to their armour and it was at this time that Morgan made a great flourish of showing the fact that he possessed a lady's favour and bowed once again toward the royal entourage. The watching crowd murmured amongst themselves.

Curious as to who it could be, Bronwyn glanced along the line of ladies, then turned her head in the opposite direction, just in time to see her daughter's face light up with pure delight, incline her head slightly and give the most perfect of royal waves with her right hand.

"Methinks your daughter is growing up too fast," Richard murmured in his wife's general direction, making her smile. Whenever Colwyn did something 'unusual', she was always her mother's daughter, rather than her father's.

The King eyed Colwyn thoughtfully and contemplated a possible future for her.

And the whole show that Morgan put on had the desired effect on Nigel, who openly scowled at his opponent.

"Your Champion is playing with fire, Majesty," Richard stated quietly.

"We shall see." The King indicated with his right hand that he was ready for the final contest to begin.

The two dukes turned to face one another. The Kadeau Lord smiled amicably at his opponent, further fuelling the resentment.

"I shall wipe that smile off your face, Bodine, make no mistake," Nigel hissed.

"Sounds more to me like an old cockerel making a lot of noise to cover the fact he's no longer functioning as he should," Morgan retorted and smiled even more.

As the two men walked round in a large circle, sizing one another up, everyone was wondering who was going to land the first strike. Nigel attacked first, but Morgan lithely side-stepped and struck the first blow, as his sword made contact with his opponent's armour, knocking him sideward. The Duke parried and responded, the sword glancing off Morgan's shield. The swords continued to clash against each other, sparks flying, their movement almost a blur as they moved around the ring; the battle was fierce, for both men were very evenly matched. It looked like it was going to be decided by whichever one of them had the stamina to continue at such a pace for any length of time.

Colwyn was doing her utmost not to fidget too much as she sat on the King's lap watching the heated battle continue. It was the first time she had ever witnessed a real sword fight where the opponents seemed intent on inflicting as much damage on each other as they could. The crowd were gasping, cheering and making other sounds of approval at the skill of both swordsmen.

Morgan was still smiling, even though he was concentrating on how Nigel moved and handled his weapon and shield. He was learning a lot about his opponent who, it appeared, was not a particularly patient man when things were not going his way. Impatience usually led to mistakes, and this time was no exception, as he foolishly lunged at Morgan, who was effectively waiting for him to make such a move, and he countered with a heavy blow that sent the Cottesmere Duke flying past him to land on his face on the grass.

This did nothing to calm Nigel, especially when a loud cheer went up at his fall. Morgan gallantly allowed the Duke to regain his feet, and saw the fury appear on his face. Up on the royal dais, Colwyn clapped delightedly.

The Duke initiated a compound attack against Morgan, delivering a deluge of blows, driving him back, until he managed successive parries, and launched his own riposte. It became evident to the spectators that Nigel was losing both his patience and temper with the youthful Duke, who was still lithely moving around the enclosure, launching his own compound attack which drove Nigel back against the rail with nowhere to go.

Seeing that he was about to lose, Nigel resorted to some unknightly tactics; he lifted a mailed foot and kicked out at Morgan, catching him at the hip and sending him staggering backwards.

"Foul!" Colwyn shouted, for she knew all the tournament rules of engagement. "Foul, sir! Shame on you!"

The King glanced at her in amazement, wondering how she could possibly know of such things, but it immediately went out of his mind as the Duke of Cottesmere immediately followed up with a barrage of blows that Morgan parried from the ground.

Colwyn could not prevent a shriek as Nigel suddenly raised his sword to plunge it down into Morgan's chest. The cuirass was designed to stop the tip from piercing through his mail, but if brutal enough, could result in severe bruising or even a serious wound, despite the padded aketon underneath. Somehow, Morgan managed to use his shield to deflect it, and it caught his side instead. He grimaced as the blade sliced through one of the leather straps, punctured through the mail and the padded aketon underneath and Nigel, seeing he had wounded his opponent, tried to press on his attack, but the Rossmere Duke was far from finished and used his shield to knock his opponent off his feet.

With surprising agility, despite the wound he had received, Morgan gained his feet, knocked Nigel's shield from his hand, trod on the wrist of his sword arm, forcing him to let go of his weapon, and placed his own sword at his throat. The battle was over.

Forgetting all etiquette and manners, Colwyn leapt from the King's lap and stood up, clapping and cheering.

"Do you yield, McDowell?" Morgan asked. He was breathing heavily but looking pleased that he had scored a victory over his opponent to remain unbeaten in battle.

Nigel lay there, wincing at the amount of force Morgan was exerting on his wrist, and knew it was over. "I yield," he spat at the Kadeau Duke, and Morgan removed his foot. Nigel rubbed his wrist and looked at Morgan with hate in his eyes before gaining his feet.

Morgan nodded and walked away to stand directly below the dais where the King was now standing. Nigel went to stand next to him. They turned, removed their helms and saluted each other before turning, saluting the King, and sheathing their swords.

"Our champion of the sword; Morgan Bodine, Duke of Rossmere!" proclaimed King Stuart. Everyone cheered, and then the King motioned for them to ascend the dais to receive their rewards.

They both knelt in front of their King. Stuart handed Nigel a pouch of coins, then turned and handed the gold band to Colwyn and indicated for her to proceed. In awe and wonderment, she placed the gold band upon Morgan's head and another cheer went up. He looked up at her and she leant over and kissed his cheek. Gaining his feet, Morgan turned and acknowledged the crowd, then graciously bent over and kissed Colwyn's hand. He would now be able to rest, for the jousting was to take place the following day, which was just as well, as his side was feeling rather sore.

He was suddenly aware of Colwyn frowning at him, and he looked down at his right side. Suddenly suspicious, he placed his fingers on his surcoat, where Nigel's sword had penetrated, drew them back and saw the blood.

"Morgan!" Colwyn whispered.

"It's nothing; just a scratch," he assured her. "I will get my battle surgeon to check it. Do not worry."

"Make sure he does," the King said. "You have the jousting tomorrow. I expect my champion to win!"

"Yes, Sire." He bowed and indicated for Nigel to precede him down the steps of the dais, then went to find his battle surgeon.

Colwyn, concerned that her champion was hurt, curtsied to the King and Queen and ran after him, and Nigel's eyes narrowed as he watched them disappear from view.

Morgan went to his rooms and found Master Andrew reading a book he had borrowed from the library. He stood up as the Duke entered.

"Congratulations, Morgan. You won then," Andrew said, noting the gold band on his head.

"Yes."

"Your record continues. I assume you sent McDowell packing with his tail between his legs."

"Yes, but it's not over yet, there is the jousting tomorrow." Morgan dropped his gauntlets and helm onto the table, and removed the gold band and put it beside them, then looked around for his personal steward. "Where is Ioan?"

"I'm sorry, Morgan, I let him go and watch the activities. I wasn't expecting you to return so soon. Let me help you instead." Andrew unbuckled the sword belt and surcoat belt, and Morgan pulled the surcoat over his head, wincing slightly as he did so. It was as Andrew was undoing the buckles on the right side of the cuirass that he found the severed leather, and spied the blood. With a sense of urgency, he started to undo the other buckles, just as there was a knock on the door.

"Enter!" shouted Morgan and Colwyn came in. "Colwyn, you should not be here."

"You are my champion this weekend; I need to make sure you are all right." She walked up to him and started undoing the buckles on the left side of the cuirass.

Andrew looked at Bodine, who inclined his head, and they carried on. Andrew removed the cuirass and inspected the mail before lifting it over his head. "This will need repairing, Morgan," he said. The Duke did his best not to grimace as he lifted his right arm, so Andrew could pull the hauberk off.

Morgan looked down and saw the blood on his aketon. He undid the lacings and eased out of it, then out of his silk shirt. Now bare-chested, Andrew leant over and inspected the wound, which was still oozing blood. Colwyn stood quietly, looking on. As yet, she was still too young to appreciate the athletic build of her hero, or any sexual feeling of attraction. Morgan was broad-shouldered, with narrow hips; a slight dusting of hair on his chest. The skin was lightly bronzed and tight over the muscles. He had a small scar on his right arm from an old wound he had suffered in the past and another just below his right collarbone.

"Do you require a basin of water, Master Andrew?" Colwyn asked.

"Yes, Lady Colwyn, I do."

552

She immediately went to the dressing table and poured some water into a small basin and took it to Andrew, who had retrieved a pouch from his medical supplies and poured some powder from it into the water. Using a strip of cloth, again retrieved from his supplies, he dipped it in the bowl and wiped the wound clean. Morgan grimaced, for whatever was in the powder stung quite badly.

"This will stop any infection, Morgan," Andrew said as he then sprinkled another powder directly onto the wound to stop the bleeding.

Seeing that the wound wasn't too serious, Colwyn inspected the damage on the aketon and the surcoat. "I will get this cleaned and repaired in time for tomorrow, Morgan, if you will permit me."

"Colwyn, you don't need to do that."

"Yes, I do. I will return this by first thing in the morning. It's a good thing you bought me those silks." She also grabbed his shirt, turned on a heel and left.

Andrew watched her go, then returned his attention to treating the wound. "She loves you very much," he said to Morgan.

"Sisterly love," he replied.

"At the moment, yes, but that may change when she's older. Right, I want you to relax for a couple of hours; longer if you are able. It's stopped bleeding. I'll take your hauberk and cuirass to the blacksmith and get them repaired for tomorrow."

"Thank you, Andrew," Morgan replied, moving to the huge four-poster bed and lying down. He was feeling a little sore, so he decided to follow Andrew's advice and closed his eyes, breathing slowly and deeply, mulling over what Andrew had said about Colwyn.

Colwyn ran to her rooms to retrieve her needlework box.

"Colwyn, what are you doing here?" Sarah asked. "Shouldn't you be downstairs?"

"Sarah, would you try and get the blood out of this aketon, please, whilst I start work on the surcoat?"

Sarah looked at the coat of arms on it. The rampant guardant dragon clearly indicated that it belonged to the Duke of Rossmere.

"What are you doing with this?" she asked.

"I'm repairing it."

"You should be with the Duke and Duchess, my Lady."

"Morgan is my champion for this tournament, I must see that his attire is fit to wear. Now please, do as you are told." Colwyn sat at her little work table and inspected the surcoat. To her relief, she realised she could get away with sewing it, rather than darning, which would be a lot quicker, and set to work. The tear was only as wide as the sword that had done the damage and she completed the repair quickly. It was the same for his black silk shirt and that was also repaired by the time Sarah came back with the now clean aketon.

The aketon was a more difficult challenge, with four layers to repair, but she diligently worked on it, and after a couple of hours, it was done. She gave the repair a tug or two and was pleased that the stitching held. Satisfied with her work, she spot-cleaned the surcoat and the shirt and then took the items back to Morgan's rooms. She knocked quietly but there was no reply, so she carefully opened the door and entered. The day chamber was empty, so she assumed he was either out or in the bedchamber. Knowing he would need the items, she quietly entered his bedroom and saw him lying on the huge bed, apparently asleep.

Carefully, she laid the repaired items over a chair, then went to stand by the bed, and looked down at him. Something stirred within her; something new and strange that she didn't understand. Quietly, she reached for a blanket at the bottom of the bed and started to draw it up over him. She'd got as far as his hips when he suddenly awoke and, with lightning speed, he had retrieved a dagger from under his pillow and it stopped, mere millimetres from her throat.

Colwyn froze but made no sound. There was no fear in her eyes, just complete trust. "You have nothing to fear from me, Morgan," she said softly.

He gasped in shock at what he had nearly done, and slowly lowered the dagger. "Colwyn!" His voice shook as he surveyed the expression on her face. No one had ever looked at him the way she was looking at him now. "I – I could have killed you! W – what are you doing here?"

"No, you wouldn't, Morgan. You could never harm me. The damage to your aketon, surcoat and shirt was not as bad as I thought. I have repaired them." She dropped the blanket and indicated the chair the items were draped over. "I thought you looked cold, so I was just covering you with a blanket."

"Oh, my pet, I'm sorry, I'm just not used to all this affection." He put the dagger down and held his arms open.

Colwyn surrendered herself to him, wrapping her arms around him and hugging him tightly as her head nestled into his shoulder. "I could stay here forever," she whispered. "But I know I can't." She drew back slightly. "Will I see you at supper tonight, or are you dining here in your room?"

"You will see me tonight, Colwyn."

"In that case, I shall leave you to rest and recover. My champion has to win the jousting tomorrow." She looked down at his right side. "Does it hurt much?"

"No; a little sore. It's just a scratch."

"I wish I could make it better."

"Oh, Colwyn, your affection for me more than helps. Now, hadn't you better get back? I'm surprised no one has sent out a search party for you."

She giggled, then leant forward and kissed his lips. "I love you, Morgan Bodine," she whispered innocently, and then she was gone.

The Duke smiled and shook his head. It felt good to be loved.

Bronwyn decided to go in search of her daughter, and found her in her room. "And where have you been, young lady? I started to get worried."

"Mother, I had to take care of some repair work for my champion," Colwyn replied seriously.

"You didn't have to do that; one of the maids could have done it just as easily."

"But not as well," she replied. It was not a vain or boastful comment, but just a statement of fact, for Colwyn had a very rare talent in regard to anything associated with needlework.

"You are fond of Morgan, aren't you?" her mother asked.

"I love him with all of my heart," she answered seriously.

"And I am sure Morgan appreciates that greatly. He has not known a lot of love in his life. Now, are you changing for supper?"

"Yes, Mother."

"Very well; we shall see you downstairs shortly."

Sarah helped her young charge prepare for the evening and watched her skip out of her room.

In the King and Queen's chamber, Stuart was still thinking about Colwyn.

"Husband, what troubles you?" Alexandra asked.

"I was thinking about Colwyn. She would make a fine Queen for our son, but her age is against her."

"She will only be twenty when Llywelyn is ready to marry; that is still young enough to provide an heir; that is, if you think she would be right for him?"

"I think she would be, but we still have a few years, and, at the moment, she seems rather taken with Morgan Bodine."

"She is not right for him," Alexandra replied quickly; too quickly.

"Why do you still hate my Champion so much?" he asked her.

"He is Kadeau. That is reason enough."

"But the Cantrell family has always had Kadeau in their service and for protection. Morgan has more than proved his loyalty. There isn't a finer knight in the Kingdom. He is honourable; he excels in his duties, Llywelyn thinks the world of him, and so do I."

"I don't like him being near our son or this family, and I definitely do not like him being near Colwyn."

"Don't let her hear you say that; he is currently her hero, and she has given him a favour for this tournament."

"Yes, I saw that. I will speak to Bronwyn about having Colwyn at court so I can keep an eye on her, train her, and seek out a suitable husband, if it turns out not to be our son."

"Whomever is chosen, it needs to be for the good of the kingdom. Invermere and Rossmere would make an excellent match."

"I don't want to argue about it now. We are guests here. And, as you say, there is time."

Stuart kissed his wife and they went down to dine.

ణ ఐ ణ ఐ

The seating arrangements were the same as the previous night, and once again food was plenty, and wine flowed. Morgan was dancing with the Duchess after dinner and made polite conversation.

"Mother, Colwyn is truly gifted with regard to her needle skills," Morgan told her.

"She told me she had made the repairs to your attire herself. She would trust no one else with the job, because quite frankly, she is the best in the duchy even at her tender years."

"I can't even see where the repairs were made, they were so well done."

Bronwyn lowered her voice. "Morgan, you must tell me if she is making a nuisance of herself. She appears to have grown even more fond of you."

"Never a nuisance, Bronwyn. I love her very much, like my sister, and I believe she loves me like a brother."

Bronwyn considered his words for a few moments before whispering, "And what if that changes to another kind of love down the line?"

"That would be a few years from now; I guess things could change in that respect."

"Perhaps, but at the moment, she is fond of you, and I have no objections, Morgan, whatever happens. Now or going forward."

The Duke found himself colouring slightly.

"We would be honoured to have you in our family, one way or another."

"I – I don't know what to say."

"Then say nothing." She smiled at him.

Nigel, seeing Morgan was occupied, decided to approach Colwyn, who spotted him coming towards her, and she started looking for a way to escape. The King just happened to glance in her direction, and noticed her expression, as the Duke of Cottesmere approached.

"Colwyn, my dear," the King said. "I apologise, I believe this is our dance, is it not?"

"Yes, your Majesty, it is," she confirmed, amazed that her sovereign had come to her rescue.

Morgan had noticed the situation and breathed a sigh of relief as Stuart came to Colwyn's aid; but the King could not dance with her all evening. Sooner or later, Nigel was going to get his way and dance with the Duchess-in-Waiting.

In the end, Morgan was unable to save her, as the King had made the Queen dance with him. He could feel her dislike the entire dance, politely saying nothing, but Alexandra felt him stiffen as Nigel at last cornered Colwyn and she was left with no option or avenue of escape.

"You do not like Duke Nigel being near the Lady Colwyn?" the Queen asked him.

"My Queen, Colwyn is scared of the Duke, and I made a promise to Duchess Bronwyn that I would keep her daughter safe."

"Are you sure you do not have designs on her yourself?"

"Your Majesty, Colwyn is still a child, and I love her like my sister. The Coltranes have been so kind to me since I lost my parents. I now think of them as my family."

"She is of marriageable age, Duke."

"True, but she is still a child, and any marriage must be for the good of the kingdom."

The dance ended and Morgan escorted Alexandra back to her chair, bowing respectfully, before he turned and saw Colwyn still with Nigel and he frowned, concerned.

Colwyn had erected a stone wall in her mind and was not letting Nigel get close to her thoughts. She had disliked him for as long as she could remember and she had also heard rumours about him, that he was not actually a very nice person and that he liked to dabble in the black arts. Morgan had once told her about building barriers in her mind by imagining an impenetrable object, like a thick, solid wall or something similar, to guard against someone who might try to control her. She had begun to read about the Kadeau and their magic and even tried to follow some of the more simple spells. She was not about to let Nigel try anything like that on her.

"My dear," Nigel said conversationally. "You are again looking beautiful tonight."

Colwyn said nothing.

"I was thinking, perhaps when the tournament is over, you and I could get to know one another better. We have had so little time with each other."

"Why?" Colwyn asked rudely.

"If I didn't know better, I would suspect you have been avoiding me, which is not good, for I believe a man and a woman should get to know each other before they are wed."

It was no good. Shocked beyond belief, she stopped dancing at that instant and jerked her hands free of him.

"Know this Duke, I will never marry you!" she hissed quietly.

"You will do what your father tells you to do, and one day in the very near future, you will be mine," he whispered in reply, reaching for her.

"Just leave me alone!" she said, stepping back away from him and clasping her hands behind her, so Nigel couldn't grab them as he continued to advance towards her.

Suddenly, she reversed into an immovable object. Looking up and behind her, her eyes closed briefly in relief. It was Morgan. Without any preamble, he leant over and lifted her up into his arms, and she grabbed him round the neck, burying her head in his shoulder.

Even with all the finery of their clothing, he could feel her heart racing with fear, thudding against his chest. Morgan glared at Nigel, his grey eyes cold and menacing as he surveyed his adversary.

Nigel stepped forward. "Hang onto her whilst you can, Bodine. She will be mine," he whispered.

"Not whilst I have a breath in my body," Morgan replied quietly.

Nigel's eyes narrowed and he stepped closer. "Accidents happen quite often...in tournaments."

"Is that meant to be a threat?" Morgan asked, his grey eyes, starting to lose colour as the two men stood off, facing each other.

The Duke sneered and took a step closer. "Could be, Bodine, we'll see what happens in the joust tomorrow," he answered before turning and leaving the great hall.

Morgan took a deep breath and let it out slowly. "He's gone, my pet. I will avenge you tomorrow, in the joust," he said softly into her ear. He looked up to see Bronwyn's worried face, as she started towards them. Anxious to avoid a scene, he walked towards her, still carrying the child.

"Morgan, what's happened?" Bronwyn asked, worried.

The Duke shook his head, indicating this was not the place for a conversation. She nodded, immediately understanding and turned to the King and Queen.

"My daughter is over tired. Forgive us, Your Majesties as we put her to bed."

"Of course," Stuart said, but studied the interaction between Morgan and Colwyn carefully; he had witnessed the entire scene with Nigel from across the hall.

Curtseying and bowing, they made their exit, leaving Richard to look after their guests. Nothing was said on the journey to Colwyn's rooms, and she was very reluctant to let go of the Duke once they were there, until her mother reminded her that her champion had a jousting tournament tomorrow and needed to rest.

"Thank you, Morgan," Colwyn whispered, and kissed his cheek before he set her down on the ground.

"Do not worry, my pet. You will be safe, now."

"Sarah, please put my daughter to bed," Bronwyn instructed. "Goodnight, my darling." She bent down and kissed her daughter before exiting with Morgan. Outside, Bronwyn asked, "So what was all that about?"

Morgan sighed. "McDowell wants her for his wife."

"Oh, dear God! He didn't actually say that in front of her, did he?"

"Yes."

Bronwyn was horrified. "She must have been terrified. Oh Morgan, I'm so glad you were there. I had hoped he would have taken the hints by now." She saw him frown and continued. "Each time he has visited we have told him it is out of the question."

"And yet he is still trying. Obtaining Invermere would weaken Stuart's position substantially."

"I realise that. I believe Stuart would not allow it anyway because of the reason you just stated, but...McDowell is very ambitious. I also know Colwyn doesn't like him, and I'm not sure about him either. I will not allow her to marry him. Besides, it would put you in a rather dangerous position. Richard and I will need to think very carefully now about her future. We will keep her safe until she is older, and then we must think what we can do to stop McDowell getting his hands on her."

Morgan nodded. "You could send her to Ellesmere, and put her under the protection of the Queen," he suggested. "The King could arrange a marriage for her instead, but of course, that would mean her leaving home, and she loves it here. Plus, she has her own ambitions to help the people of Invermere."

Fleetingly, another thought popped into his head, but he immediately dismissed it. He was the King's Champion, and probably destined to eventually become General of the Armies. He needed to concentrate on that, and consequently, there was no time to divert to other activities. It would be unknightly to offer to step in as a prospective husband and slam the door shut on Nigel's wedding plans—as tempting as it was—but that could upset the Cottesmere nobleman further and perhaps lead to even more unpleasantness.

"Somehow, we will keep her safe," he finally added. "Now, if you will excuse me, mother, I need to get some rest for tomorrow. I will probably be up against McDowell again. I believe he is highly skilled at the joust."

"Of course, Morgan. But tell me, how are you? The wound?"

"Nothing much. I've had worse."

"Then we will see you tomorrow and cheer for you. But be careful. I really don't trust McDowell." She kissed his cheek and headed for her own rooms.

Morgan went to his own chambers, stripped off and made himself comfortable in his huge four poster bed. Sleep took a little while to claim him, as his mind was filled with thinking of ways to keep Colwyn safe from the clutches of McDowell.

In her own rooms, Bronwyn was deep in thought, when a knock at her door made her jump. Her maid, Dilys, opened it.

"It's His Grace, My Lady," she said.

Bronwyn nodded, and Dilys opened the door fully to allow him entry.

"Is everything all right?" Richard asked, approaching his wife.

"Yes, at least it is now."

"What happened?" He sat down next to her on the lounger she had in her day room.

Bronwyn thought carefully of how to tell him what had happened.

"You no doubt saw Nigel McDowell dancing with Colwyn this evening. Well..." she paused, then decided to be forthright. "He told Colwyn he was going to marry her."

It took a lot to rile the Duke, but Bronwyn could see he was angry. "Just like that? Without obtaining our approval? The audacity of the man!"

"Richard, I know you have the final say, but I'm telling you, he is not going to marry our daughter. It will be over my dead body before that ever happens!"

"It would be too dangerous a liaison. I don't think the King would approve it anyway."

"But you know how ambitious the Duke is. I've heard the whispers about the accident that killed his father and made him Duke of Cottesmere. You don't think they are true, do you?"

"Only McDowell can answer that one, and I don't believe he will be forthcoming with the answer. We will have to take steps to keep our daughter safe. She will go nowhere unaccompanied, both in the castle and outside."

Bronwyn wearily placed a hand on her forehead. "She isn't going to like that; you know what she's like."

"It's for her own safety. She must be made to understand."

"But I don't want to frighten her, and make her feel she is in danger, or that she is a prisoner in her own home, it isn't fair."

"Life isn't fair." Richard sat and pondered awhile. "Let us compromise then. Whilst McDowell is in the castle, she will be accompanied at all times...or at least an eye kept on her."

"That is more acceptable, thank you."

Richard leant forward and kissed her.

"I believe it will be a hard jousting tournament tomorrow. I saw our son and McDowell stand off against one another."

Bronwyn nodded and sighed with concern, but said nothing.

"The King wishes to see me before retiring. I will sleep in my own rooms tonight, so I do not disturb you. Goodnight, my love."

"Goodnight, husband."

℘ ℥ ℘ ℥

The following morning, after breakfast, everyone gathered at the jousting ring for the main event of the day. There was a lot of pageantry associated with the joust, with all the flags flying and tents just outside. It was a very colourful sight, and a gentle breeze accentuated this as the flags fluttered under its caress. The weather was good again, and the ground firm beneath the horses' feet.

Colwyn had wanted to go and wish Morgan luck, but the events of the previous evening had knocked her confidence, and she was subdued; unsure about wandering around her home on her own with Nigel present, so she had gone with her parents to the joust.

The King immediately noticed her change of mood and tried to cheer her up by again having her sit on his lap and ask her opinion of the opponents.

As expected, Morgan made it easily through the early rounds, and Colwyn started to relax again, however, when Nigel appeared, she was deathly silent. Stuart whispered softly in her ear.

"You have nothing to fear from McDowell; I will not allow him to harm you."

Colwyn smiled tentatively at him. "Thank you, Your Majesty," she said quietly, disappointed that the Duke managed to dispatch his opponent with ease and ride triumphantly out of the jousting arena so the next two opponents could enter.

"Now come, cheer; here is our champion," Stuart said, as Morgan again entered the jousting arena, and once again dispatched his opponent on the first run to reach the quarter final.

Morgan glanced up at the royal enclosure as he cantered out of the arena. He could see that Colwyn wasn't particularly happy. Whatever happened, he had to make sure Nigel hit the ground, to avenge her.

It took two lances to take down his next opponent in the quarter final, and another two to dispatch his opponent in the semi. Now it was the final and again, he was facing Nigel. The sword was Morgan's primary weapon of choice, but he had been practicing hard with the lance, which in all tournaments was the top award to win.

The Duke's young stallion, Banner, seemed to know they had reached the final, and was prancing with anticipation, making it difficult for Ioan to hand Morgan his lance. Bodine spoke to his spirited black steed, and the horse stood still long enough for him to take it from his steward.

The two opponents lined up at either end of the run, then kicked their horses into a canter. Lances were lined up and splintered as they hit each other's shields. A roar went up from the crowd. They cantered back past each other to pick up a replacement lance and lined up again. The flag went down, and they charged at each other again.

Up on the Dais, Colwyn was clutching the King's hand, willing Morgan to knock Nigel off his horse, but it was not to be. Nigel deliberately aimed for Morgan's right side, where he had injured him the day before. It did not work well as he wanted, and both riders sustained severe blows. Nigel was almost unseated but managed to hold on. Morgan was winded, despite the heavy padding of his aketon under the mail. They returned for the third lance.

"My Lord, are you all right?" Ioan asked Morgan as he took hold of the lance.

The Duke nodded, although he suspected the wound he had sustained the day before had started bleeding again.

At the other end of the run, Nigel had felt a rib crack under the last onslaught and was furious that Morgan had managed to inflict an injury on him.

Once again, they charged at each other. Morgan now thought he had seen a way through Nigel's defence, and this third run was to be the final confirmation. Both lances smashed against their shields and again, damage was inflicted on both sides. Morgan felt himself leaning forward, clutching his right side. He could probably manage a fourth lance, but after that, he wasn't sure he would be able to withstand any more. He grimaced beneath his helm as he took the fourth lance, and he was breathing heavily, but looking down the other end of the arena, he was pleased to see Nigel wasn't fairing much better.

Morgan's stallion picked up on his unease and started prancing again, jarring his injury. He squeezed his legs against the horse's flanks, and it leapt forward. He sighted his lance, and then at the last second, shifted it slightly to the left so it slid, scraping the side of the shield by the barest of measurements and struck Nigel's body. The force knocked the Cottesmere Duke from the saddle to hit the ground, but also travelled up Morgan's lance and through his arm, causing him to drop it. He collapsed forward on the saddle but managed not to fall.

Up on their vantage point, Colwyn at last cheered, but then the King heard her agonised, "Morgan!" as he collapsed forward in the saddle but managed to stay mounted.

His steward ran to the area below where the royal party were situated, ready to hold Banner when he reached the base of the steps to the dais. The Duke cantered back past Nigel, who was still on the floor, his steward at his side, and pulled up by Ioan, who grabbed the reins. Morgan dropped his shield on the ground and dismounted with a little difficulty. He pulled off his helm, dropped it and pushed the mail coif off his head. Wearily, he ascended the stairs towards his Liege.

Colwyn was standing once again, next to the King. Morgan bowed with some difficulty and straightened up again.

"Sire," he whispered.

"Our tournament champion!" Stuart proclaimed to everyone present. "Morgan Bodine, Duke of Rossmere!" Again, a large cheer ran out. "Colwyn, my dear, would you again do the honours?" He handed her a more ornate band than the one she had presented yesterday. Morgan knelt before her, and feeling immensely proud, she placed the band on his bowed head and again as he lifted it, kissed him. "Arise, champion," said Stuart.

Morgan winced as he got to his feet, but raised his hand and turned to the crowd, who cheered again. The King's Champion was unbeaten and had successfully defended his title to show why he held the position.

"Well done, Morgan," Stuart whispered. "Now go see your battle surgeon and get that injury seen to." He looked down at Colwyn. "My dear, accompany our champion."

Colwyn curtseyed and led the way down the dais to the arena. She glanced across to see that Nigel was just getting to his feet and was glad he'd been hurt, then paused to pat Bodine's stallion, who snorted at her. Ioan led the horse away; the Duke's shield was now hooked on the saddle, and the steward was carrying the helm. Morgan and Colwyn headed for the castle and his rooms.

Andrew was waiting for him. He had watched the proceedings and knew that Ioan would be seeing to the horse, so had returned to Morgan's rooms to help him out of his armour and examine his wounds.

With Colwyn's help, they removed the many layers that made up the armour and padding, until he was again, sitting shirtless on the bed. Colwyn fetched a basin of water for Andrew to start his ministrations.

The wound had indeed reopened, and was now accompanied by bruising, but apart from that, and some general aches and pains, Morgan appeared unharmed.

"Would you like me to arrange a bath for you, Morgan?" Colwyn asked him. "I can arrange it for a few hours' time, so you can rest a while, then get freshened up for the final banquet."

"Thank you, Colwyn, Morgan would appreciate that," Andrew answered for him.

"Very well, I will sort it out."

"Thank you, Colwyn," said Morgan, and he kissed her hand. He found it hard to believe that she was only coming up to twelve years of age; she acted far older, but then he remembered Bronwyn saying something about girls maturing much faster than boys.

"Okay Morgan, lie down, get some rest," Andrew ordered, and the Duke did as he was told, easing himself back against the pillows and mattress, relaxing with a heavy sigh.

"Thank you for avenging me," Colwyn whispered to him as Andrew busied himself tidying his tools and bandages away. "But I'm sorry you got hurt."

"It's nothing, my pet," Morgan replied softly. "I am the King's champion; injury is expected on occasion."

"Then I will leave you to rest," she said, and leant over and kissed him.

Morgan sighed and smiled. His eyes closed, his chest rose and fell slowly as he relaxed.

As she had promised, Colwyn arranged for a hot bath to be delivered to Morgan's rooms about two hours before the evening banquet. That done, she went in search of Sir John, and finally found him in the armoury, inspecting the weapons stored there, ensuring they were clean and in good order.

He looked up and smiled at her as she approached him.

"Good afternoon, Lady Colwyn."

"Good afternoon, Sir John," she replied reaching out to touch the hilt of a sword that he was about to return to its scabbard.

"So," he began conversationally, "what did you think of your first tournament?"

"It was very exciting! The atmosphere was...oh, I can't describe it!"

"I understand what you mean. Did you pay attention yesterday on how Duke Morgan performed in the sword contest?"

"Yes, I watched avidly."

"And so did I," said a voice from the doorway.

John and Colwyn looked up and saw Giles walking towards them.

"I understand what you meant now, Sir John," he said as he reached them. "About Duke Morgan. The final between Duke Nigel and him was most certainly worth watching."

"Yes. It was intense, fierce and partly entertaining. What did you learn?"

"Duke Nigel is short tempered," Colwyn said without hesitation.

"Very astute, Colwyn. Yes, he is very short tempered. A bad trait for a knight and especially a Duke."

"It made him impatient, and he made mistakes," Giles added.

John nodded. "Well spotted, Giles, you are correct."

"And he was unknightly," Colwyn added.

"Yes, that too. In tournaments, the rules must be obeyed. However, in battle, when you are fighting for your life, you will and must do everything you can think of to stay alive. You must remember to separate tournament from battle. Now, the banquet will be starting in an hour or so, isn't it about time you returned to your rooms to get ready?"

"Yes, Sir John. Thank you," Giles said. He turned to leave, then stopped when Colwyn didn't move. "Colwyn, aren't you coming?"

"In a minute, I just have a question for Sir John. You carry on."

Giles nodded and left. Colwyn turned back to face her teacher.

"So, my young Colwyn, what is it you wish to ask?"

"I won't ever be able to enter a tournament, will I?"

John took a deep breath and let it out slowly, as he shook his head.

"No, you won't. You are talented with the sword, and I have no doubt that you could in fact defeat a number of the pages, but it is not the done thing for a lady—or any woman for that matter—to even handle a sword let alone enter a tournament."

"It's not fair!"

"Life is often not fair, Colwyn, but that is the way things are."

"Can't the rules be changed?"

"Perhaps they will, but not in our lifetimes, and probably not for a long time to come. The rules pertaining to knighthood have stood for centuries. It is a man's duty to protect the innocent, the weak and women from harm, and from those with evil intent. The woman's duty is to be loyal and faithful to her husband, bear his children, care for him. In your case, unless your mother bears a son, you will have a duchy to rule, hence why you are being educated to enable you to do your duty."

Colwyn pouted. At that precise moment, she didn't care about ruling a duchy, she wanted to be a knight, but that was going to be denied to her, because of her sex.

"I'm sorry it's got to be like that, Colwyn. If you continue to progress as you are, know that I would be proud to have you battle beside me."

Colwyn's mouth dropped open, and her eyes grew wide at the compliment the Master-at-Arms had given her.

"Thank you, Sir John! You have no idea how much that means to me!" Impulsively, she threw her arms around his waist and hugged him. "I am so lucky to have you teaching me."

"Go on, off you go, or you'll get me into trouble for making you late to the banquet!"

She beamed at him, turned, and skipped away with a spring in her step, leaving John smiling after her.

 C$ \infty $ C$ \infty $

Chapter Thirty-Four

Everyone was seated for the celebratory banquet. Even Nigel was there, but he was moving very gingerly and carefully and had to ease himself down into his chair. Colwyn was delighted that he was hurt. Morgan arrived a little late, bowed to his King and Queen, kissed Bronwyn's hand and sat down next to Colwyn.

"You look much better now," Colwyn whispered to him.

"Thank you, my pet. The bath and rest has done me the world of good."

"What about your wound?"

"I'm a little sore, but it's fine."

"I'm glad. The tournament was very exciting. I'm so pleased you won it. I understand father has even won one in the past."

"Yes, but he won at least three or four. Unfortunately, it was me who ended his reign as tournament champion. He literally ordered me to do my best to defeat him, as he was not going to make it easy for me. It was the hardest thing I have ever had to do, battle against someone you love and admire."

"Oh, that must have been horrible for you!"

"It was, but he was so very proud of me, and at least we keep the title within the family."

"I wish I could have seen him in action today."

"As host, he does not enter. Perhaps he will enter the next one at Ellesmere, although he did say at his age, his tournament days are over."

"Oh, that's a shame, but he's not that old! I really would love to see him compete."

"I also had the pleasure of training with him when I was younger. In fact, he was the one who taught me one sword trick and gave me the incentive to be able to perform it with two swords at the same time."

"Really?"

"Yes, your father is a very good swordsman and jouster."

Colwyn sighed and changed the subject. "I see Duke Nigel seems to be in a lot of discomfort. Shame." There was no remorse or sincerity in her remark.

Morgan's lips twitched as he picked up the pleased tone within her voice. "That is not very gracious, Colwyn."

"He's not honourable, he deserved everything he got."

Morgan said nothing but was thinking the same thing.

"Are you staying at Inver long?"

"Another day or so, then I'm heading home to Belvoir."

"I would love to see Belvoir."

"Perhaps one day you will."

"If you're staying another couple of days..." she leant towards him and whispered in his ear. "...can we go swimming? I think I'm a little out of practice and need some tuition from you."

Morgan managed not to choke on his mouthful of wine. "I'm not sure it would be appropriate now that you are of marriageable age."

"But you're my brother. Why can't you take me?" She gave him the biggest sorrowful look in her repertoire, and he wavered as he saw the expression in her beautiful green eyes.

"All right," he conceded, and she smiled sweetly at him before tucking into her food.

As there had been the previous night, there was music and dancing, and Morgan had taken Colwyn onto the dance floor. That evening she even got to dance with her father, as well as the King, and Kenneth and she retired that night in a happy mood.

The following morning after breakfast, the King, Queen and their party left for Ellesmere. The Coltranes including Colwyn and Morgan, had seen them off. The Queen had even given the child a kiss on the cheek.

As they disappeared under the Barbican, Morgan turned to Colwyn and said, "The Queen favours you. That could be useful down the line."

"Why does she hate you so much?"

"You noticed?"

"It was very obvious. I can't see anyone hating you... apart from Nigel McDowell."

Morgan smiled slightly. "She hates me because I'm Kadeau."

"What has that got to do with anything? She's in the Cantrell House, what does she expect?"

"Her family were almost wiped out in the Reign of Terror."

"But that was hundreds of years ago! And you had no part in it!"

"For some the hatred is deeply ingrained." He paused and whispered, "Are you still wanting to go for that swim?"

Colwyn's eyes lit up. "Yes please," she whispered.

"Come on then. We'll get a picnic and make a day of it."

"Are we going on another adventure?" she asked, as they excused themselves.

"Where are you two going?" Richard called after them.

"Riding!" Colwyn shouted back. Very unlady-like she ran back to her chambers and changed into her riding leathers, then went down to the stable. Morgan was already there, waiting with the horses.

He gave her a leg up, mounted his own horse and they set off. "Beach or lake?" Morgan asked her.

"Lake," Colwyn replied.

"Okay, I know where we can go. It may take a couple of hours to get there."

They headed south for an hour and then turned east into the forest.

"There's a lake in the forest, nice and secluded so we can swim in peace."

"It sounds lovely."

After almost two hours had passed, they arrived at their destination. It was a clearing, and being summer, the sun was shining on the water and through the trees.

"Hopefully the water won't be too cold," Morgan said as they halted. He dismounted, then assisted Colwyn from the saddle.

They led their horses to the lake edge so they could have a drink, then looped their reins around some convenient branches before returning to the lake's shoreline.

"This is beautiful. I didn't know this was here."

"It's a pretty well hidden secret," Morgan replied as he surveyed the view before him. He took a deep breath, then stripped off his jacket and shirt, wincing as he forgot about his wound.

Colwyn looked at him. "Oh, I'm sorry, I've been very selfish. Are you okay to swim, Morgan. I don't want to cause you any more pain."

He smiled at her. "I've had to do more with worse," he said sitting down on a convenient rock and pulling his boots off. He paused. "What are you going to be wearing?" He was suddenly uneasy. Colwyn was almost twelve, almost legal marriageable age, and they were about to go swimming together, but on the other hand, he saw her as his sister, not as a prospective wife. Any feelings of love he held for her were purely family love, although his mind kept drifting back to the conversation he had had with Bronwyn the other day. He wasn't ready for a deeper involvement with a woman. He had too much responsibility elsewhere to devote to that kind of relationship.

"What I'm wearing mainly." She removed her jacket to reveal a sleeveless vest, then the skirt, to reveal a pair of breeches underneath. She sat on the rock Morgan had just vacated and pulled off her boots.

Morgan stared...*a woman in breeches*... then pulled himself together. "Ready?"

"Yes."

He held out his hand and looked down at her.

"You're so tall!" Colwyn said looking up at him as they walked into the water. "Oh, it's cold!"

He grinned at her, and it lit up his entire face.

"Can you remember what to do?" he asked.

"I think so."

"I'll support you until you're sure you're confident in what you're doing."

"Thank you, Morgan."

As it turned out, Colwyn hardly needed any support at all, and within a couple of minutes they were swimming. Morgan was impressed with her stamina and then looked at her arms and found them surprisingly muscled for a girl of any age. But he also realised she had always had a lot of energy that she had to burn off; that probably explained it. Never would he have guessed that she was training with the sword and learning to ride like a knight.

Then Colwyn splashed him and giggled, and made a break for the shoreline, with Morgan in hot pursuit so he could try and get his own back. With a longer reach, he finally caught her as they reached the shallows, grabbed her arm with one hand and splashed water back at her with the other making her squeal.

"Now we're even," Morgan laughed, and Colwyn stared at him. "What?" he asked.

"I love to hear you laugh," she said simply, and they left the water hand in hand.

Morgan walked to his horse and removed a blanket and his saddle bags. He spread the blanket out and invited Colwyn to sit on it, then sat himself and unpacked the saddlebags.

"Heavens!" Colwyn exclaimed. "Is there anything left to eat at the castle?"

Morgan laughed again. "You're a growing woman, and I have to maintain my strength," he replied.

They ate and drank in companionable silence, then lay side by side on the blanket and looked up at the sky, trying to identify patterns in the clouds that passed overhead. Eventually though, Morgan noticed the position of the sun and told her they needed to get ready to head back. They sat up and Colwyn turned to face him.

"Morgan, thank you for today. I've really enjoyed it," she said.

"As have I. I've been able to totally relax, so thank you for suggesting this."

They packed everything away, got dressed, then Morgan gave her a leg up back onto her horse. He went to move to his own, when her call stopped him, and he turned back. She leant over and kissed him. "I love you, Morgan Bodine," she said innocently.

He kissed her back. "And I love you, Colwyn Coltrane," he replied, his grey eyes twinkling, then he went to his horse, leapt into the saddle and they made their way back to the castle.

೮೫ ೮೨ ೮೫ ೮೨

Morgan left Inver the following morning, to hugs and kisses from Bronwyn and Colwyn, and a hug from Richard and decided to go via the farm of Elwyn and his family, who he hadn't seen for a few years. With him rode Master Andrew, Ioan, the Captain of the Guard, and twenty knights.

Elwyn looked up from planting a new field and saw the group of horsemen approaching. He frowned in concern until he spotted the golden dragon on the black surcoat, dropped the sack of seed and walked to the road to greet the riders.

Morgan reined up by his side.

"Your Grace," Elwyn bowed and straightened up. "It is good to see you."

"I could not return home without paying you a visit, Elwyn," Morgan replied. "How are you and your family?"

"We are well, thank you for asking, and yourself?"

"I am well." Morgan glanced over at the virgin ground. "You are expanding your cultivated land?"

"Yes, Your Grace. I need to rest a field; its yield has been dropping steadily over the past few years."

"Have you thought of allowing your animals to roam it? Duke Richard discovered allowing livestock and chickens to roam over it helps to improve the quality of the soil."

"Thank you, Your Grace. I have also been experimenting with different types of crops. That too is showing promise."

"The next time I am here, I would like to hear about your findings."

"I would be honoured. Please, may I offer you and your men some refreshment? My wife would be delighted to see you."

"We haven't been travelling that long, but one moment." He turned and issued orders to his Captain. The majority of the guard continued on their way, leaving Andrew, Ioan and two knights. Morgan turned to face Elwyn again. "We would be delighted." He held out his left arm. "Come."

Elwyn took the offered hand and leapt up behind him onto Morgan's horse. It was what he liked about the Duke. As a child he had shown friendship and support to Elwyn and his family. The farmer worked hard, and the Duke recognised good honest labour. There were not many members of the nobility who would offer a ride to a commoner. Morgan and perhaps the Duke of Invermere were the only two. Neither had any qualms about working with or talking to and helping the members of lower classes that had proved their worth.

Arriving at the farm cottage, Elwyn slid off Banner's back and called to his wife to bring refreshments for their guests.

Morgan, Andrew, and the guards dismounted as the door to the cottage opened and Gwenne appeared. Seeing who their guests were, she disappeared briefly then reappeared with her daughter, carrying goblets of mead.

"Your Grace," Gwenne said curtseying in front of the Duke, then offering him refreshment.

"Thank you, Gwenne," Morgan replied. "This is Aelwyn? She has grown considerably since I last saw her."

"As have you, Your Grace. You were but a boy on your last visit, now you are a grown man."

Morgan gave her one of his rare smiles and indicated her swelling abdomen.

"I see congratulations are in order. When are you due?"

"Three months to go, Your Grace, but I feel this one will be early."

"I hope the baby is delivered safely."

"Thank you, that means so very much to me."

"Elwyn tells me, on the whole, things are going well for you?"

"Yes. We have suffered from poorer crops, but no doubt Elwyn has already told you about his experiments?"

"Yes, he has. It sounds most interesting." He glanced at Gwenne's daughter. "Tell me, Aelwyn, how are you doing?"

"The Lady Colwyn has generously spent time teaching some of us lace making."

"Ah yes, Lady Colwyn was telling the King about it the other evening. He was most impressed." He glanced around. "I don't see Symon about."

"He is working in the farthest field, Your Grace," Gwenne replied. "He will be sorry to have missed you."

"I will make a detour when I leave here to give him my regards."

"Your Grace is most generous."

They finished their mead. Morgan kissed Gwenne and Aelwyn's hands making the younger woman blush.

"Thank you for the refreshments." He shook Elwyn's hand. "Wishing you the safe birth of your next child, good life and fortune." Then he turned and mounted Banner and led his tiny guard away and towards the other field where he knew Symon would be.

Elwyn's son was working hard walking behind an oxen ploughing a field, so initially didn't hear the horsemen approach until they were almost on top of him.

Startled, he straightened up and turned. For a second he frowned, and then recognition lit up his features.

"Your Grace! I almost didn't recognise you!"

"Good morning, Symon. I almost didn't recognise you either. It's only because your father told me where to find you, that I knew it was you!"

The boy laughed. "You've seen father already?"

"And your mother and sister. I also saw you will have a new sibling in a few months." Morgan dismounted to shake the boy's hand. "You are looking well."

"As are you, Your Grace... and if I may say so, much taller!"

Morgan chuckled. "And so are you. I just wanted to say hello. I am heading home to Belvoir."

"It has been good to see you. I wish you and your men a safe journey."

"Thank you. I wish your family every success with your farm. Take care."

Morgan remounted, gave Symon a final wave, and headed towards Rossmere and Belvoir, catching up with the rest of his guard a mile or so on.

They made good time, and three days later, they stopped briefly atop the hill that dropped to the fertile valley below. Morgan sat astride his horse, staring at Belvoir Castle, that lay upon the opposite hill. Although the castle was some distance away, he could see it in enough detail to study its layout and decided his retreat away from everyone at the beach was the better choice instead of the room in the tower. He gave some thought to the cave and decided he needed to hide it from view. He would consult the library for a suitable spell that could be maintained with little effort.

"Morgan?" Master Andrew jogged him from his reverie. "Is everything all right?"

"I was just thinking, I need to stay put in Rossmere for a bit of time. I was trying to work out how long I could get away with being here before the King summons me back to Ellesmere. I have neglected Rossmere for too long."

Andrew nodded. "The King did not give a date or length of time when we left Inver. Perhaps he too has realised your situation and

582

is granting you the required time. He will no doubt send word if he needs you."

Morgan smiled in agreement.

"Come on then, we're almost home!"

A few hours later they trotted through the main thoroughfare to the castle. People lining the street showed their respect as the Duke rode past, then finally he was at the keep and dismounted. He talked quietly to his horse and patted his neck and Banner nuzzled him. A page appeared and led the horse away to the stable once Morgan removed his saddlebags.

Edward waited on the top step. "Welcome home, Your Grace," he said bowing.

"Edward, good to see you. Has everything been all right whilst I've been away?"

"Everything has been fine, Your Grace. I have attended the council meetings as you instructed, and I believe I have acted in your best interests."

"You know I have every confidence in you."

"Your words make me feel very proud. Thank you. We can go through things tomorrow if that is agreeable. I assume you would like to bathe and relax this afternoon."

Morgan nodded.

"Do you wish to eat in your chambers?"

The Duke nodded again.

"Very well, I will arrange that for you."

"Thank you, Edward."

Morgan made his way to his chambers and dropped his saddlebags on the table. Ioan assisted him out of his armour and poured him a goblet of wine, which he accepted as he sank down on a chair, unconsciously placing a hand on his right side.

"Are you all right, Morgan?" Ioan asked observing as the Duke closed his eyes for a few seconds.

Morgan pulled himself together and smiled at his steward. "I'm fine, just tired."

"Is that wound giving you some trouble?"

"It just aches a bit. It's only been a couple of days; the bruises are coming out."

"As long as that's all it is. I'll arrange a bath for you, that will help ease it."

Morgan nodded. He was feeling tired. Tournaments always took their toll on him. It was a combination of stress, pressure and the physicality of the event. He planned to take it easy for a day or so, if he could.

The bath and hot water arrived. Ioan helped him undress and Morgan gratefully stepped into it and sat down.

"That wound looks angry," Ioan remarked as the Duke leant his head back against the back of the tub and closed his eyes. "Have you been doing something you shouldn't?"

The Duke didn't answer. Telling his steward he had been swimming with his sister and in a secluded lake, was not something he wished to divulge. Suddenly aware of a presence near him, he opened his eyes to find Ioan standing by the side of the tub with another large goblet of wine.

"Thank you, Ioan."

"If you will excuse me, Morgan, I will get you something to eat."

Morgan nodded again, took a large mouthful of wine, swirled it around in his mouth and swallowed it. He sighed heavily and winced, then closed his eyes again. The warmth of the water was exceedingly relaxing. Another sip of wine was taken then Ioan returned ten minutes later with a generous helping of food. He removed the goblet from Morgan's hand, then soaped and sponged his lord down.

Rinsed off, Morgan dipped completely under the water and came up again, then stood and stepped out of the tub. Ioan immediately towelled him dry, placed a thick dressing gown around him, and the Duke sat down at the table.

He was very quiet during the meal, which raised Ioan's concerns even more, little knowing that Morgan was wondering how he was going to continue dealing with his loneliness. He was surrounded by people and yet very much alone. Briefly, he remembered his encounter with Raven. To have a woman—a wife—in his life would ease the empty feeling, but he just wasn't ready to settle down yet, and he needed to feel comfortable with himself, his castle, and his roles.

Just as he finished, Andrew arrived.

"Andrew?" Morgan queried.

"I want to see that wound," he stated.

The Duke glared at Ioan who did not bat an eyelid. "Have you been telling tales on me?"

"I didn't like the look of that wound, so have asked for an expert opinion," Ioan replied defiantly, and Morgan was warmed that they cared so much for him.

"Come on Morgan, let's see it," Andrew insisted, and the Duke grudgingly shrugged out of the right sleeve of his dressing gown so the surgeon could take a closer look. "Mmm, that is looking a little angry." Andrew opened his bag of supplies and poured a powder into a small bowl of water that Ioan had placed on the table. Using some cloths, he bathed it, making the Duke flinch. "Anything else I should know that you haven't told me about?"

"No."

"In that case, I suggest a good night's sleep." He got up, went through to Morgan's bed chamber and turned down the covers. "Come on, Morgan. Remember, as your battle surgeon I have the last say!"

The Duke sighed, feeling like he was being ganged up on, but it also gave him a warm feeling that people did really care about him. He rose from his chair and did as he was told.

Happy that Morgan had obeyed him, Andrew pulled the bedding up over him.

"Sleep well, Morgan," he said as Ioan blew out the candles, and they left their master to sleep.

Ω ⅌ Ω ⅌

The following day Morgan attended his first council meeting since returning home. Edward had briefed him on the duchy's finances and matters on the agenda and he went in, prepared to do battle with his advisors if necessary.

On most items he agreed, or invited discussion, but there were two that became very heated.

"Your Grace, with regard to taxes for the forthcoming year, I think it advisable to raise them. This will result in a rise to the lower classes of one silver coin per year, and the wealthy by one gold coin, which will bring in additional revenue of—"

"I understand our income was up on the previous year and also previous to that. The financial report clearly shows the duchy's coffers are larger than they have ever been. We will not increase them this year."

"But Your Grace, the cost of—"

"I don't care! We can easily absorb not increasing taxes this year. Just because I've been absent these past years does not mean I haven't been taking note of what's been going on! My word is final. Taxes will stay the same." He slammed a fist on the table to emphasise the fact that he was in control, and glared at his council, his grey eyes steely. The air surrounding him seemed to almost crackle. "My duty is to the people, not to line your pockets and make you rich!"

Morgan saw a couple of his council colour with indignation, and the fact they had been found out. Edward did his utmost not to smile at seeing their discomfort. The majority of the council had thought the young Duke would be easy to control, he was only just a man and he had been absent for so long. They were wrong. He had received expert tuition from Richard, Rhisart and Stuart, and was not the ignorant young man they expected.

"I will hear no more arguments. The taxes stay the same. Final item on the agenda is yours, bishop."

Oliver Treherne stood up and took a deep breath. The young Duke was not going to be easy to manipulate at all. He was clearly his own man, but this was of importance. The duchy could not afford to be without a Duke should something happen to him.

"Your Grace, I wish to discuss a somewhat delicate matter."

At hearing those words, Morgan immediately felt a sense of déjà vu, of how a similar conversation had gone in Ellesmere between Stuart and his bishop. He hadn't been there, but Stuart had confided in him afterward. He swallowed and waited.

"Rossmere spent almost ten years without a recognised Duke until your investiture. The council, Master Justin and Master Edward, worked hard to keep order and look after the interests of the people and the duchy. Your position as King's champion and tournament champion means you are likely to be called to arms more often than dukes of other duchies.

"Your Grace, you need to marry as soon as possible and provide an heir to Rossmere."

Morgan fought with all his strength to keep from going red with embarrassment. He would have preferred to have had the discussion in private.

The bishop looked at him, waiting for a response. None was forthcoming.

"Your Grace?"

"I haven't given it any thought yet," he finally replied.

"I will draw up a possible list of suitable candidates."

"I'd sooner you didn't."

"But Your Grace, you need to take action sooner rather than later. There are a number of well born ladies that would make you a fine wife."

"If, or when I marry, I will choose my own bride. Someone I know who loves me for what I am. My choices are limited, I am Kadeau."

"If I may be so bold, Your Grace, I do know of one straight away who would be suitable and is close."

"Really?" The Duke was beginning to feel a little short tempered at others trying to run his life for him.

"The Lady Colwyn."

"She's my sister!"

"With respect, she is no such thing."

"She's too young."

"She will be of legal marriageable age next month, and in two years, be able to provide you with your heir."

"I don't love her in that way. I see her as my sister and that's all. If she can't provide a child for two years, then why do I have to marry her now?"

"To prevent another from claiming her."

Morgan immediately thought of the threat of Nigel McDowell. He stood up to be taller in height than his bishop and hopefully intimidate him.

"I'm not discussing this now, Oliver."

"You must. I will draw up a list of prospects."

"You make them sound like commodities."

"That's what they are."

"Enough! I refuse to discuss this now. This meeting is over! Edward, with me."

"Your Grace—"

"I said enough!" Morgan's grey eyes were losing colour as his anger rose. He kicked his chair back and strode out of the room, leaving his council gaping after him.

His strides back to his chambers were long and measured. Edward kept quiet as they walked, allowing the Duke to calm down.

"Your Grace," Edward finally dared to speak. "May I get you anything?"

Morgan shook his head as he kicked the door of his chambers open, causing it to swing back on its hinges and slam against the wall, before rebounding. Ioan practically jumped out of his skin at the noise and turned round. He noticed Edward was with him.

"Your Grace," he began, using the correct address. "Whatever's the matter?"

"They're trying to marry me off, Ioan! They want an heir. I'm not ready for that, and they suggested I marry my sister!"

"The lady Colwyn? Well, she does love you, Your Grace."

"Don't you start on me!"

"Never. I was just stating a fact."

Morgan closed his eyes and took a couple of deep breaths to calm himself down and reduce his heart rate.

"Are they always that annoying, Edward?"

"I'm afraid so, Your Grace."

"Then I am in awe of you and your father for having coped with them these last ten years."

"You flatter us, Your Grace. But I thank you for your kind words."

"I know I'm not supposed to ask this but...was I right to freeze taxes?"

"What you stated was correct, Your Grace. There is more than enough in the coffers, our grain stores will be full to bursting shortly. Short of some natural disaster, the duchy is safe and wealthy. Freezing the taxes will endure you to the hearts of your people."

"Then that's all I need to hear. We won't starve, we have coin should we need it. We are practically self-sufficient and the wine we produce brings in additional income. Thank you, Edward... would you join me in a glass of wine."

"Your Grace, I would be honoured but I am not an equal."

"Edward, I do not follow convention. Ioan, pour three glasses."

"At once, Your Grace."

They toasted one another and sat amicably around the table drinking their wine.

CR ℞ CR ℞

The year wore on, the crops were successfully harvested, the fields rested, and animals grazed on them to help replenish the goodness of the soil. The days grew shorter, and Christmas arrived once more.

It was at this time of year that Morgan felt the loneliness of not having someone to share the times spent in front of the large open fire, and he realised he was wallowing in self-pity. In an attempt to cure himself of the feeling, he challenged both Derec and Martyn to some hard sword practice.

If Derec had held any doubts about the Duke's ability with the sword, they were extinguished almost immediately as Morgan fought both of them at the same time and within a few minutes had disarmed them.

Derec apologised and asked if they could try again. They put up a better defence the second time, but the Duke still beat them, and their admiration for him went up a couple of notches.

January was bitter, the wind was icy, the temperatures well below freezing. The snow lay thick on the ground. Animals were brought inside to be fed and sheltered.

His bishop kept on reminding him about finding a wife and producing an heir, and Morgan wished the weather was better so he could hide from Oliver Traherne so he didn't have to listen to him go on and on about marriage and babies.

The Duke stood on the balcony outside his day chamber and studied the sky. It was grey and heavy with the threat of snow as far as the eye could see and looked to be settling in for the foreseeable future.

He sighed and returned to the warmth of the fire in the room, but he was restless. Games of tawlbwrdd with Ioan and Andrew didn't seem to alleviate the feeling either. It was as if he was waiting for something to happen.

A week or so later, the skies cleared, but the snow stayed on the ground due to the continuing cold temperatures.

Morgan found himself prowling the grounds and corridors of the castle to help pass the time. He'd had some practice sword sessions in the snow, but it was difficult when it was over a foot deep. Both he and his opponents had found themselves bogged down, or slipping and it was deemed just too dangerous, and he found himself wishing for spring, but that was still six to eight weeks away.

Then one evening, just after sunset, the peace and quiet was disrupted by Edward arriving breathless at his chambers.

"Your Grace! Your Grace!" He knocked on the door and opened it without waiting for permission.

"Edward, whatever's the matter?"

The steward attempted to recover his breath, as he pointed vaguely in a north-easterly direction. "The – the beacon!" he gasped. "The beacon is lit!"

Morgan stood up, his heart suddenly thudding in his chest. "The Ellesmere beacon?" he asked in a quiet voice.

"Yes, Your Grace."

The Duke swallowed and started towards the door. "Wh – what colour?"

"Red."

Edward saw Morgan's face go pale then he started running down the corridor and stairs to the entrance of the keep. The steward took a deep breath and started after him.

Morgan hadn't even bothered to grab a jacket to protect himself from the cold as he ran across the bailey to the north-east tower, up the stairs and out onto the battlements.

Two guards were looking off into the distance to a far hill but turned as Morgan approached. "Your Grace," one of them said, and pointed outwards across the valley.

Morgan's eyes followed the pointing finger, and on a distant hill, red flames were burning. His King was calling him to arms...

CB EO CB EO

Character Map

———•———

Aiden	Stuart's personal steward
Master Andrew	Battle surgeon to Morgan Bodine
William Aulean	Bishop of Inver
Eirian Bodine	Duchess of Rossmere, mother of Morgan. Kadeau
Morgan Bodine	Duke of Rossmere, a Kadeau with magical powers
Alexandra Cantrell	Queen of Devonmere, wife of Stuart, mother of Prince Llewellyn
Llewellyn Cantrell	Prince and heir to Devonmere, son of Stuart and Alexandra
Michael Cantrell	Prince of Devonmere and Duke of Connamere, brother to Stuart
Rhisart Eurion Cantrell	King of Devonmere
Stuart Cantrell	Prince, then King of Devonmere and Rhisart's first born, Husband of Alexandra, father of Prince Llewellyn,
Alys	Alexandra's maid
Bronwyn Coltrane	Duchess of Invermere, wife of Richard, mother of Colwyn
Colwyn Coltrane	Daughter of Richard and Bronwyn

Richard Coltrane	Duke of Invermere, husband of Bronwyn, father of Colwyn and one of the most trusted Dukes of Devonmere
Giles Dernley	Son of Kenneth Dernley, Duke of Strathmere
Kenneth Dernley	Duke of Strathmere, father of Giles
Dilys	Bronwyn's personal maid
James Douglas	Bishop of Ellesmere and King's Confessor. Also a Kadeau
Edward	High Steward to Morgan Bodine, responsible for the running of the Rossmere estate during the Duke's absence. Son of Justin
Justin	Father of Edward, retired steward of Rossmere.
Ioan	Personal steward to Morgan Bodine
Markus	Steward of Invermere
Lukas	Inver's weapon master
Sir John MacKenzie	Master of Arms for the Duchy of Invermere
Celwyn	Personal steward to Nigel McDowell
Alisdair McDowell	Former Duke of Cottesmere, father of Nigel McDowell
Nigel McDowell	Duke of Cottesmere, son of Alisdair McDowell
Colin McLeod	Cousin of Morgan Bodine, second son of Mereli and Rodric McLeod, former knight, now in the church and also a Kadeau.

Rodric McLeod	Duke of the High Meres, father of Colin, husband of Mereli
Mereli McLeod	Mother of Colin, Aunt to Morgan Bodine. Kadeau
Lady Nerys	A companion of Bronwyn
Arnell Prescott	Duke of the Eastern Marches, father of Owain
Owain Prescott	Squire, killed by Stuart. First son of Arnell
Taliesan Prescott	Second son of Arnell Prescott and the new Duke of the Eastern Marches
Sarah	Colwyn Coltrane's personal handmaiden
Master Stephen	Stuart Cantrell's Battle Surgeon
Osian Thomason	Master-of-the-Robes
Oliver Treherne	Bishop of Rossmere
Sir Trahaearn	King Rhisart's protector and champion.
Trystan	Richard's personal steward
Alwyn Ulrich	Father of Queen Alexandra
Iola Ulrich	Mother of Queen Alexandra
Kenzie Ulich	Sister of Queen Alexandra
Mistress Betrys	Inver mistress of lace
Lord Dafydd Hughes	General of the King's armies
Sir Derec	Trainer at Rossmere
Sir Martyn Welles	Captain of the Rossmere Guard
Eairdsidh Allbright	Duke of Stallesmere

Bibliography

Books which provided the source material for some of the knightly ceremonies:

- C. Mill, History of Chivalry (London, 1841)
- W.C. Mellor, A Knight's Life in the Days of Chivalry (London, 1924)
- Richard Barber, The Knight and Chivalry (Longmans, 1970)
- Julie Heller & Deirdre Headon, Knights (Bellow & Higton, 1982)

Information for the coronation was obtained from:

- The Royal Collection Trust
- Supplement to the London Gazette of Tuesday 26th September 1911.